He leaned closer, the length of him pressed up against her, the light stubble on his chin and jaw brushing against her neck until she ached for his touch. God help her if this made her wicked, but she could no longer deny the sensations that coursed through her whenever he was near—a wanton desire for his hands to caress her in places she rarely touched herself.

"May I kiss you now?" he asked, his words barely more than a breath of air against her flesh—flesh consumed with prickling heat.

"It's one of my requirements," she managed, attempting a touch of humor and hoping that she didn't sound too desperate in doing so.

"Only one?" His hand had found her face and his fingers were tickling her jawline, turning her head in his direction.

"One of many," she said, fearing that her galloping heart might escape from her chest.

"We'll have plenty of time to discuss the rest later." His breath caressed her cheek. "As for the one of kissing you—I'm only too happy to oblige."

By Sophie Barnes

Novels
THE SCANDAL IN KISSING AN HEIR
THE TROUBLE WITH BEING A DUKE
THE SECRET LIFE OF LADY LUCINDA
THERE'S SOMETHING ABOUT LADY MARY
LADY ALEXANDRA'S EXCELLENT ADVENTURE
HOW MISS RUTHERFORD GOT HER GROOVE BACK

Novellas
MISTLETOE MAGIC
(FROM *Five Golden Rings: A Christmas Collection*)

SOPHIE BARNES

THE SCANDAL IN KISSING AN HEIR

At the Kingsborough Ball

AVON

An Imprint of HarperCollinsPublishers

AVON BOOKS
An Imprint of HarperCollins*Publishers*
10 East 53rd Street
New York, New York 10022-5299

Copyright © 2014 by Sophie Barnes
Excerpt from *The Trouble with Being a Duke* copyright © 2013 by Sophie Barnes
ISBN 978-0-06-224517-5
www.avonromance.com

First Avon Books mass market printing: January 2014

Avon Trademark Reg. U.S. Pat. Off. and in Other Countries, Marca Registrada, Hecho en U.S.A.
HarperCollins® is a registered trademark of HarperCollins Publishers.

Printed in the U.S.A.

10 9 8 7 6 5 4 3 2 1

To my brother and sister with love.

Life itself is the most wonderful fairy tale of all.
HANS CHRISTIAN ANDERSEN

Acknowledgments

A book travels through the hands of so many people on its way to publication, and while I may be the one sitting at home, typing away on my keyboard, the efforts made by editors and publicists to make the work shine, deserve to be mentioned. I'd like to thank my wonderful editor, Erika Tsang, and her assistant, Chelsey Emmelhainz, for being so incredibly helpful and easy to talk to—working with both of you is an absolute pleasure!

Together with the rest of the Avon team, which includes (but is far from limited to) copyeditor Judy Myers, publicists Caroline Perny, Pam Spengler-Jaffee and Jessie Edwards, and senior director of marketing, Shawn Nicholls, they have offered guidance and support whenever it was needed. My sincerest thanks to all of you for being so wonderful!

Another person who must be acknowledged for his talent is artist Jon Paul, who has created the fabulous cover for this book, capturing not only the feel of the story but also the way in which I envisioned the characters looking—you've done such a beautiful job!

To my good friends, Monika and Vicky, who happily read through the first draft of my manuscript without the slightest coercion, offering opinions that have helped me improve upon the story—thank you so much. I owe you both a drink!

I would also like to thank Nancy Mayer for her assistance. Whenever I was faced with a question regarding the Regency era that I couldn't answer on my own, I turned to Nancy for advice. Her help has been invaluable.

My family and friends deserve my thanks as well, especially for reminding me to take a break occasionally, to step away from the computer and just unwind—I would be lost without you.

And to you, dear reader—thank you so much for taking the time to read this story. Your support is, as always, hugely appreciated!

THE
SCANDAL
IN KISSING AN HEIR

Chapter 1

Kingsborough Hall, Moxley, England
1817

Daniel Neville, heir to the Marquisate of Wolvington, removed himself to a corner of the Kingsborough ballroom—as good a place as any for a man who'd been labeled an outcast by Society.

Overhead, candles held by three large chandeliers spread their glow across the room, the jewels worn by countless women winking in response to the light. This was true opulence, and nobody did it better than the Kingsboroughs. Why, there was even a glass slipper sculpted from ice and a pumpkin carriage sitting outside on the lawn—a touch of fairy-tale splendor indicative of the theme that the dowager duchess had selected for her masquerade.

And what a masquerade. Never in his life had Daniel borne witness to so many feathers. They were everywhere—attached to gowns, on the edges of masks, and sprouting from women's hair.

The ball gowns were marvelous too. These were not the boring dresses generally on display at Almack's. Certainly, one could still tell the debutantes apart, due to their tepid choice of color, but they all had a bit of something extra, like crystal beads that sparkled when they moved.

It was refreshing to see, and yet as he stood there, watching the spectacle unfold, Daniel felt nothing but bland disinterest. It was only one hour since he'd arrived, but it felt more like four. God help him, but he'd never been so bored in his life. Perhaps he should have remained in London after all. At least there he had his friends to keep him company and could avoid the constant reminder of how unwelcome he was among the finer set. His aunt and uncle were in attendance of course, but as soon as they'd entered the ballroom, they'd been approached by Lady Deerford. Daniel had hastily slipped away in order to avoid the countess, who had a renowned tendency to talk the ear off anyone willing to listen. In hindsight, he was beginning to think that nodding his head in response to whatever she had to say would have been preferable to this self-imposed solitude. Recalling the glass of champagne in his hand, he took another sip of his drink and decided to request a brandy from one of the footmen at the first available opportunity. Stronger stuff would be required if he was to get through the rest of this evening. He watched as a group of ladies approached on their tour of the periphery. There were three of them, one being the Countess of Frompton. If Daniel wasn't mistaken, the two young ladies in her company were her granddaughters—typical debutantes dressed in gowns so pale it was hard to discern where the fabric ended and their skin began. It would do them both a great deal of good to get married, if for no other reason than to be able to add a touch of color to their attire.

As they came nearer, Lady Frompton glanced in Daniel's direction. Their eyes met briefly, then her ladyship quickly drew her granddaughters closer to her, circumventing Daniel in a wide arc that would have been insulting had it not been so expected. They weren't the first to avoid him that evening. Indeed, the three youngest Rockly sisters had beaten a hasty retreat a short while earlier when they'd realized who they'd been heading toward on their own tour of the ballroom. Daniel hadn't been surprised, for his reputation was so tarnished that he could probably ruin a lady by merely glancing in her direction. Why he'd bothered to attend the ball at all, when the chance of enjoying himself had been as distant a prospect as traipsing through the African jungle, was beyond him.

Well, not entirely.

He needed to find himself a wife, or so his uncle had informed him last week when he'd discovered that Daniel had hosted a most outrageous party at his bachelor lodgings—an event that had been sponsored indirectly by his uncle via Daniel's monthly allowance, where vingt-et-un had been played until most of the courtesans and gentlemen present had been divested of their clothing. What made the incident worse was the fact that Daniel had been so deep in his cups that night that he'd offered his mistress the diamond earrings his father had once bestowed upon his mother. They had been a treasured family heirloom but would now grace the lobes of Solange. "You're a bloody curse on this family!" Daniel's uncle, the Marquess of Wolvington, had said as soon as Daniel had entered his study the following day. The marquess had then delivered a long list of reasons as to why he'd thought this to be the case. "It's time you grew up and learned a thing or two about responsibility, or you'll end up running your inheritance into the ground after I'm gone. Heaven help me, I'd love nothing better than to disinherit you and allow Ralph to take up the reins, but—"

"My nephew?" Daniel had said, unable to help himself in light of the fact that his uncle would rather entrust his entire fortune to an infant.

"I doubt he'll do any worse than you." Daniel had winced in response to this retort, but he'd done his best to hide all signs of emotion as his uncle continued, "Your sister's a levelheaded woman, her husband too. I'm sure the two of them would be prepared to act wisely on Ralph's behalf, but since the law prevents such an outcome, I rather think it's beside the point.

"That said, your aunt and I have come to a mutual agreement—one which we hope will encourage you to get that head of yours on straight. You will cease your gaming immediately, or we will cut you off financially, which, to clarify, will mean that you will have to work for a living unless you wish to starve. Additionally, you will stop associating with loose women, engaging in haphazard carriage chases, or anything else that's likely to embarrass the name your father left you. And finally, you will get yourself engaged within a month and married by the end of the Season."

Daniel had stared back at his uncle in horror. The older gentleman, however, had looked alarmingly smug and satisfied with his new plan. Daniel had turned to his aunt, whose presence had only served to increase

Daniel's humiliation tenfold. Although she was not his blood relative, she had always been kind toward Daniel, had treated him like the son she'd never been blessed with, and had often stood up for him against his uncle, who'd been more stern and restrictive. "He cannot be serious," he'd said, hoping to incur a bit of sympathy from her.

She'd glanced up at him, eyes crinkling at the corners as she'd offered him a sad little smile. "I'm afraid so, love, and I have to say that I am in full agreement. You cannot continue down this path, Daniel—it will be detrimental if you do. Please try to understand that we're only looking out for your best interests, as well as those of the family at large." Her eyes had been filled with disappointment.

Of course he'd understood, but he'd still been furious with both of them.

A wife—ha! Raising his glass to his lips, Daniel took another sip. As if finding one here was likely to happen when no self-respecting parents or guardians would allow their daughters and wards within a ten-foot radius of him.

No, Daniel was there because it had been Kingsborough who'd issued the invitation. They'd moved in the same circles once, and Daniel had always enjoyed the duke's company immensely. Things were different now though. The duke had reformed, abandoning his rakehell ways in favor of supporting his family. There was much to be admired in the strength of character Kingsborough had shown, and Daniel had wanted to offer his friend some respect for everything he'd been through—the difficulty he must have endured in dealing with his father's demise. But with so many people in attendance, Kingsborough had only been able to speak with Daniel briefly, as there were many others who craved his attention.

Daniel fleetingly considered asking one of the widows to dance, but he decided against it. No sense in wasting time on fruitless pursuits, since none of them had any inclination to remarry. They'd gained their independence and had every intention of holding on to it. The only thing he could hope for was to enjoy the comfort of their beds later, but that would hardly hasten his progress to the altar, nor would it improve his aunt and uncle's opinion of him if they happened to find out. Knowing them, they'd probably decide he'd gone too far in thwarting their wishes and cut him off before the month was up—an unwelcome prospect, to say the least.

Across the floor, he finally spotted someone who would appreciate his presence. He and Casper Goodard often gambled together, and Daniel decided to go and greet him. With wife hunting being a futile endeavor here, sharing a bit of friendly banter over a game of cards would be a welcome distraction.

Squaring his shoulders, Daniel started to head in Goodard's direction when a flutter of red met the corner of his eye. Glancing toward it, he took a sharp breath . . . and froze.

Who on earth is that?

Next to the terrace doors, partially concealed by a pillar and an oversized arrangement of daffodils, stood a woman unlike any other he'd ever seen before. Her hair was black, and from the looks of it, exceptionally long, for it wasn't cut in the style that was fashionable but piled high on her head in an intricate coif. And her skin . . . it was not the milky white tone that made most English women appear a touch too pale for his liking. On the contrary, it looked bronzed— as if she'd been basking in the afternoon sun. It took a moment for Daniel to come to his senses and realize that he was not only staring openly at her but gaping as well. Quickly snapping his mouth shut, he cursed himself for being such a fool—it was just hair, after all.

And yet he suddenly had the most bizarre and un-controllable urge to unpin it and run his fingers through it. Of course, it didn't hurt that the woman promised to be a tantalizing beauty if the fullness of her lips was anything to go by. Unfortunately, the upper half of her face was concealed by a mask, but if he could only get close enough, he ought to at least be able to see the color of her eyes.

He began going over all the ladies he'd ever been in-troduced to, attempting to recall someone who shared her attributes, but it was to no avail. Clearly, he'd never encountered this woman before, and he found the mys-tery most intriguing.

Moving closer, he watched as she tilted her chin in profile, her jawline fine and delicate beneath her high cheekbones. A lock of hair falling softly against the sweep of her neckline had come to rest against the bare skin of her right shoulder, and the unexpected urge he felt to brush it aside and place a kiss there in its stead was startling. Daniel hesitated briefly. Women didn't affect him, and whatever was said to the contrary was untrue, for the charm and soulful eyes he chose to dis-play were no more than tools he applied in his endless pursuit of pleasure. He was methodical in his seduction. If he placed a kiss against a lady's shoulder, it would be for a reason, not because he couldn't stop himself. The fact that he'd felt a helpless need to do so now, however brief it had been, disturbed him.

Whoever she was, she couldn't possibly be an innocent, dressed as she was in scarlet silk. He wondered if she might be somebody's mistress, or if not, then perhaps a widow he hadn't yet met—one who might be willing to remarry? As unlikely as that was, he could always hope.

Knowing that the only way to find out would be to talk to her, he decided to do the unthinkable—ignore etiquette and address her without being formally introduced. After all, it wasn't as if his reputation was likely to suffer further damage at this point, and considering her gown, he thought it unlikely that hers would either. Dressed in such a bold color, the lady could hardly be a saint.

One thing was for certain, however—he needed a wife, and he needed one fast. If her reputation did suffer a little from his talking to her, then so be it. Perhaps he'd marry her and tell all the gossipmongers to go hang. The corner of his mouth lifted at the very idea of it. What a satisfying outcome that would be. Hands clasped behind his back, he stepped up beside her and quietly whispered, "Would you care to dance?"

Rebecca flinched, startled out of her reverie by a deep, masculine voice brushing across her skin. Turning her head, she caught her breath, her body responding instinctively as it flooded with heat from the top of her head all the way down to the tips of her toes. The man who stood beside her was nothing short of magnificent—imposing even, with his black satin mask that matched his all-black evening attire.

His jawline was square and angular, his nose perfectly straight, and the brown eyes that stared down at her from behind the slits of his mask sent a shiver racing down her spine—there was more intensity and determination there than Rebecca had ever seen before in her life. He wanted something from her, no doubt about that, and as nervous as that made her, it also spoke to her adventurous streak and filled her with excitement. "Good evening," she said quietly, returning his salutation with a smile.

He studied her for a moment, and then he smiled as well, the corners of his mouth dimpling as he did so. Oh, he was a charmer, this one. "I hope you will forgive me, considering we haven't been formally introduced, but I saw you standing here from across the way and found myself quite unable to place you. Naturally, I had no choice but to make your acquaintance. I am Mr. Neville at your service, and you are . . . ?"

Rebecca knew her mouth was scrunching together in an attempt to keep a straight face. Oh, how she'd love to tell him exactly who she was. The knowledge would undoubtedly shock him, but unfortunately the risk of discovery was far too great for her to divulge her true identity.

Rebecca gazed up at the gentleman before her. "This is a masquerade, Mr. Neville, is it not?" she asked, deciding to keep his company a little while longer. How pleasant it was to be in the presence of a young and handsome gentleman for a change, rather than suffer the attentions of men who coughed, croaked and hobbled their way through what remained of their lives, as was the case with the suitors her aunt and uncle kept pressing upon her.

"It is," Mr. Neville said, dragging out the last word with a touch of wariness.

"Then part of the amusement comes from the mystery of not always knowing the identity of the person with whom you're speaking. Wouldn't you agree?"

She watched as Mr. Neville's eyes brightened and his smile turned to one of mischief. "Tell me honestly," he said, ignoring her question, "are you married?"

"Certainly not," she said, attempting to sound as affronted as possible, which in turn made him laugh. Surrendering, she allowed the smile that threatened to take control of her lips. "If I were, I would have ignored you completely and rudely walked away."

"Is that so?"

"Quite."

"Well, then I suppose I should inquire if you have any brothers that I ought to live in fear of."

She grinned this time and shook her head with amusement. "You are incorrigible."

"I've been called much worse, I assure you."

"I do not doubt it for a second." And it was the truth, though she had no intention of sharing any of the adjectives that were presently coursing through her own mind, like *magnificent* and *delicious*. Her cheeks grew instantly hot and she cringed inwardly, praying he wouldn't notice her blush. Heaven forbid if either word ever crossed her lips—the embarrassment of it would likely be impossible to survive, particularly since her mind had now decided to turn those two words into one singular descriptive, namely *magnificently delicious*. Her cheeks grew hotter still, though she hadn't thought such a thing possible.

"Would you care for some air? You're looking a bit flushed."

Oh dear.

She'd rather hoped he wouldn't have been able to tell. Looking over her shoulder, she considered the escape the French doors offered. She wouldn't mind the cooler outdoors right now, not only to cure her overheated re-action to Mr. Neville but also to avoid for just a little while longer the task she'd set herself. Looking the way she did, how on earth was she to make a good impres-sion on any of the young gentlemen present? She wasn't sure, though she knew she'd have to figure it out before the evening ended and she lost her chance altogether.

Her eyes met Mr. Neville's, and the promise of trouble in them only compounded her instinct to dis-miss him as a possible candidate. But instinct could be wrong, couldn't it? So far, he was the only person she'd spoken to, the only man who'd asked her to dance. Granted, hiding behind a pillar probably hadn't helped her much in that regard. Still, despite her better judg-ment, she couldn't help but acknowledge that when Mr. Neville looked at her in that particular way, she lost all interest in the other gentlemen present. Perhaps she ought to consider him after all.

"It's very kind of you to offer," she said as she looked him squarely in the eye, "but I must consider my repu-tation. Why, you look precisely like the sort of man who'd happily kiss me in some secluded corner without a second thought for the consequences."

Mr. Neville's mouth quite literally dropped open. She knew her words were bold and inappropriate and that she probably ought to have been mortified by what she'd just said. But she wasn't. Mr. Neville's reaction was entirely too satisfying to allow for any measure of regret. Folding her hands neatly in front of her, she stared back at him instead, challenging him to respond while doing her best to maintain a serious demeanor.

"I . . . er . . . assure you that I would do no such thing," he blustered, glancing sideways as if to assure himself that nobody else had heard what she'd just said.

It was all too much, and Rebecca quickly covered her mouth with one hand in a hopeless attempt to contain the laughter that bubbled forth. "My apologies, but I was merely having a bit of sport at your expense. I hope you'll forgive me—and my rather peculiar sense of humor."

He leaned closer to her then—so close in fact that she could smell him, the rich scent of sandalwood enveloping her senses until she found herself leaning toward him. She stopped herself and pulled back.

"Of course . . . *Nuit*." His eyes twinkled. "I must call you something, and considering the color of your hair, I cannot help but be reminded of the night sky. I hope you don't mind."

"Not at all," she said, attempting a nonchalant sound to her voice, though her heart had picked up its pace as he'd said it, the endearment feeling like a gentle caress of her soul.

Who was this man? Could she really have been so fortunate to have stumbled upon the man of her dreams? A man who might potentially agree to marry her once she confessed to him the true nature of her situation? She dismissed the hope, for it was far too naïve and unrealistic. Besides, Mr. Neville's suave demeanor screamed rake and scoundrel rather than incurable romantic, which was what she would need. In fact, he was probably precisely the sort of man she should try to avoid, although . . . she made an attempt to look beyond the debonair smile and the lure of his eyes. Could he be genuine? Surely, if he really was a rake, he wouldn't have been so shocked by her suggestion that he might try to compromise her. Would he? She wasn't sure and decided to give him the benefit of the doubt instead.

The edge of her lips curled upward into a smile. "How about a refreshment," she suggested. "A glass of champagne, perhaps? And then I believe I'd like to take you up on that offer to dance."

"Yes, of course," Mr. Neville said as he glanced sideways, undoubtedly trying to locate the nearest footman. There was none close by at present. "If you will please wait here, I'll be right back."

Rebecca followed him with her eyes as he walked away, his confident stride reflecting his purpose. She was not unaware of the looks of reproach he received from those he passed, and she couldn't help but wonder if her instincts about him had been correct after all. Was she wasting her time on a scoundrel? She hoped not, for she'd quite enjoyed their conversation. It had been comfortable and unpretentious, spiced with a sense of humor.

As he vanished from sight, she gave her attention to the rest of the guests. One gentleman, she noticed, was making his way toward a cluster of young ladies with quick determination. She watched him, wondering which of the women had caught his interest. But right before he reached them, another gentleman cut in front of him and offered his hand to one of them—a lovely brunette dressed in a dusty pink gown. Placing her hand upon his arm, the pair walked off without as much as acknowledging the presence of the first gentleman. Rebecca wondered if they'd even seen him. Perhaps not, she decided, except that the second gentleman suddenly looked back, grinning with victory at the first gentleman.

What cheek!

She was just about to turn her attention elsewhere when a man's voice said, "I don't believe I've ever had the pleasure of making your acquaintance."

Turning her head, she was forced to look up until her eyes settled upon a handsome face, but where there was something playful about Mr. Neville's features, this man looked almost menacing—as though he was not the sort who was used to having his wishes denied. "I really wouldn't know," Rebecca told him, feigning boredom as she did her best to still her quaking nerves. Whoever he was, he was huge—the sort of man who could easily fling her over his shoulder and carry her off without anyone being able to stop him. "Perhaps if you told me your name . . ."

He smirked. "Lord Starkly at your service. And you are?"

She offered him a tight smile in return. She was not about to play the same coy game with this man as she'd done with Mr. Neville. That would only lead to trouble. But she could hardly give her real name either, so she said, "Lady Nuit."

Lord Starkly frowned. "I don't believe I—"

"This is a masquerade, my lord, is it not?" She heard the impatience in her voice but didn't bother to change it. "Let's just say that I'd rather not give away my real name for personal reasons."

"Yes, of course," Lord Starkly said, his features relaxing a little. The predatory glimmer returned to his eyes. "I understand completely why a woman such as yourself would prefer to remain incognito, though I—"

"A woman such as myself?" Rebecca asked, unable to keep the blunt tone of indignation from seeping into her voice. She shouldn't have been shocked, considering her gown, but she didn't seem to be able to stop herself.

"Come now, *Lady Nuit.* There's no need for you to keep up your charade for my benefit. I mean, what other reason would a woman possibly have for engaging in conversation with Mr. Neville unless she was already a fallen angel? Not to mention that your attire is rather indicative of your . . . ah . . . experience in certain areas." He paused, leaned closer and lowered his voice to a whisper. "I trust that you are his mistress or perhaps hoping to become so, which is why I decided to hurry over here and proposition you myself."

Rebecca could only stare at him, agog. Who was he to so blatantly insult a woman as if she was nothing more than bothersome dirt tainting his boots? She so desperately wanted to hit him that she could barely contain her enthusiasm to do so, her fingers already curling into a tight fist at her side. And what was it he'd said about Mr. Neville? That keeping his company was what had led him to believe that she was a doxy in the first place? Disappointment washed over her. She should have known. Mr. Neville had only his own interests in mind as far as she went, and they would not include marriage. He might have more charm than Lord Starkly, but when it came to it, they were cut from the same cloth—libertines through and through. Neither man would do. Rebecca needed the permanence and security of marriage, not to a relic but to a man of her own choosing, if she was to escape the future her aunt and uncle had in mind for her, and for that, she would have to look elsewhere. Deciding she'd had enough of Lord Starkly's presence and hoping to be gone before Mr. Neville returned, she resolved to walk away and find someone else entirely.

With a swift "If you'll please excuse me," she spun on her heel, only to barrel straight into Mr. Neville, who'd just come up behind her with two champagne flutes in hand, the bubbly liquid spilling onto both of them in the process.

Chapter 2

There were few people in the world Daniel disliked, but Nigel Coulter, the fourth Earl of Starkly, was definitely one of them. Seeing the raven-haired beauty Daniel had playfully named Nuit talking to the fellow he detested, ignited something dangerous within Daniel—something possessive that he had no right or reason to feel. He approached the two of them, coming up behind Lady Nuit just as she turned into him, causing him to spill the champagne he'd been carrying.

"Forgive me," she gasped.

"No need, my lady," he said, trying not to follow the direction in which the liquid was going as it ran down her chest. He offered her his handkerchief and returned his attention to the other man. "Lord Starkly," he ground out, his eyes on the smug face of the earl, who was shamelessly perusing Lady Nuit's figure. It took little imagination to know what was going through his sordid mind, and the thought of it made Daniel want to slam his fist right into the blighter's arrogant smile.

He stopped himself, wary of drawing unwanted attention. It wouldn't benefit Lady Nuit if everyone present became aware of the fact that she was keeping company with two of England's foremost scoundrels. There was little comfort to be had in knowing that he was a much better man than the earl, for Daniel was well aware that Society made no distinction between the two of them regarding their reputations. On the contrary, the earl had always been more discreet, whereas Daniel, in his youthful stupidity, had flaunted his conquests and bragged about his escapades to anyone willing to listen.

"Ah, Neville," Starkly said, his gaze meeting Daniel's. "So good of you to join us."

"I hadn't thought you'd be here . . . imagined Kingsborough would have better taste regarding his guests."

"The same could be said of you," Starkly drawled. "After all, it's a well-known fact that you're not accepted into polite Society. In fact, I expect this invitation is the only one you'll receive this year."

Daniel felt his whole body tense as he fought for a calm composure. His situation was not a secret, but he still doubted that it was one Lady Nuit was aware of, for there had been no recognition in her eyes when he'd introduced himself to her. He feared now that if Starkly said anything further, she'd want nothing to do with him—a thought he did not relish in the least, because as far as marriage prospects went, Lady Nuit was his only option so far. He'd rather hoped to make a good impression on her.

Frustrated, he glared back at Starkly with distaste. "And what of you? From what I hear, your membership was revoked from Brooks's last week when you were found cheating at cards." The barb struck, judging from Starkly's rigid expression.

"Take care, Neville." Starkly's eyes narrowed with menace. "Considering your uncle's good health, it will be decades before you outrank me. Until then, I suggest you address me in the manner that is my due."

"Go rot," was all Daniel could say to that as he turned away with every intention of removing himself and Lady Nuit from Starkly's presence, only to find that she was no longer standing next to him.

In fact, the lady had completely vanished.

Hell and damnation.

"Where did she go?" he asked as he looked around the room. What he really wanted to know was how much of the conversation she'd heard before taking her leave.

Starkly laughed. "It would appear that she's slipped through your fingers." Leaning closer to Daniel, he lowered his voice to a whisper. "And since it's just become clear to me that you and the lady are not attached, I do believe I'll double my efforts to get her into my bed. Care to wager on my success?"

Forcing back a scathing remark, Daniel waited for Starkly to leave before downing the contents of both champagne flutes. He then abandoned the glasses on a footman's tray and went in search of his quarry, ignoring the disapproving glances that followed in his wake. One would think he'd committed murder the way everyone was treating him. God, how he hated the hypocrisy of the *ton*—as if most of the men present didn't engage in illicit affairs while their wives turned a blind eye. He'd done far less. For one thing, he wasn't married, and for another, he'd never seduced someone who was. Nor had he ever taken a woman's innocence. He smiled at that thought. No, there was nothing innocent at all about the women he'd taken to his bed. He'd just been too . . . blatant about it, he supposed. It didn't help that he had a penchant for scandalous wagers as well. He ought to be proud of himself for not accepting Starkly's, but instead he just felt irritable. Where the bloody hell was she?

Skirting the perimeter of the room, Rebecca's gaze eventually settled upon a young gentleman who was offering three wallflowers a great deal of attention. He said something to which they laughed, and then he bowed, said something else and waited while they all hesitated until one by one the three women shook their heads and took a retreating step backward. Had they just turned him down? It seemed unbelievable. And yet the gentleman bowed again, placing a kiss upon each of their hands before making a graceful retreat. This was the sort of man Rebecca was looking for—someone thoughtful and selfless.

"I knew that gown would suit you."

Turning, Rebecca was not at all surprised to find Lady Trapleigh at her side. She was dressed in a gown of purple lace, her shoulders provocatively bare. Ordinarily, the widow would not be considered an appropriate friend for an innocent, but aside from Rebecca's maid, Laura, Lady Trapleigh had been Rebecca's only confidante during her two-year confinement at Roselyn Castle—the only person who had bothered to visit a woman who'd been declared mad by the attending physician.

It was also she who had given Rebecca a gown to wear for this evening's event. When Laura had first shown it to her, Rebecca had laughed. She should have known that turning to Lady Trapleigh for help would have had such a shocking result. The lady was notorious for her conquests—it was no secret that she kept many lovers, for she spoke of them openly and in much the same way that other women might speak of their bonnets.

From what little she'd shared with Rebecca, it was clear that Lady Trapleigh's marriage had been an unhappy one. Her husband had been fifty years her senior, so when she'd heard of Rebecca's situation, she'd immediately offered her sympathy, and the two had formed an acquaintance. She'd been the only person, aside from her maid, in whom Rebecca had confided her plan to escape marrying a man old enough to be her grandfather. Rebecca had confided in Lady Trapleigh not because they'd been particularly close, but rather because the challenge ahead had seemed so overwhelming that Rebecca had needed the encouragement she'd known Lady Trapleigh would give her.

Rebecca had not been disappointed in that regard, for the widow had not only voiced her admiration but had also promised to help in whatever way she could.

"I cannot tell you how grateful I am to you for your assistance in loaning me this gown," Rebecca said. "Thank you."

Lady Trapleigh's features remained quite serious. "I am more than happy to help you escape the fate that was forced on me. There's no need for you to thank me, Lady Rebecca." Fanning her face with a fluffy black ostrich plume fan, Lady Trapleigh nodded toward the spot where Mr. Neville and Lord Starkly were still standing. "I couldn't help but notice that you were keeping company with two of England's foremost rakes," she said.

"I was about to come save you but couldn't decide if you'd even want me to. You looked quite taken with Mr. Neville in particular."

Good grief!

Surely her appreciation for the man's good looks had not been so clear. Rebecca shrugged, feigning indifference. "I've no idea what you mean."

At this, Lady Trapleigh laughed. "Don't play innocent with me, my dear." She paused. "I don't blame you—the man can be hard to resist. As a potential husband, however, I should caution you." She lowered her voice to a whisper. "Mr. Neville is renowned for having a penchant for the outrageous and has hosted several scandalous soirees at his bachelor lodgings—the most recent of which, I've been told, resulted in vast amounts of nudity."

Rebecca gasped. It was a rare occasion when something shocked her, but the thought of a party where the guests appeared in a state of undress did. A hot flush rose in her cheeks at the very idea of Mr. Neville *en deshabille*. She did her best to force the vision away, as persistent as it was, and made a stoic effort to listen to what Lady Trapleigh was saying.

"They've been in the family for generations and were supposed to go to his future wife."

Rebecca blinked. "I beg your pardon?" she said. "I fear you lost me for a moment. What item are you speaking of?"

"Why, the diamond earrings that Mr. Neville is reported to have given his mistress. Either the man is a fool or he's hopelessly in love with the woman—in which case he'll never give her up even if he does one day marry."

Rebecca sighed. The lady spoke the truth. "Thank you for telling me this. It is clear that I cannot afford to waste my time on him."

Lady Trapleigh shook her head. "No, considering what you want for yourself, it would probably only lead to unhappiness, as unfortunate as that is." She turned her gaze away from the two gentlemen with a look of disinterest. "May I offer you a bit of advice?"

Rebecca nodded. "By all means."

"You see that gentleman over there—the blonde one who's been speaking to the wallflowers? He's a viscount—Brekenbridge is his name—and from what I've been told, he's currently looking for a wife. Eagerly so, I might add. He's a good lad, not the sort prone to visiting gambling hells or entertaining courtesans. He'll be faithful to you, of that I have no doubt. Unless of course you favor dark-haired gentlemen, in which case you may wish to consider Lord Carvingdale over there—the one dancing with the lady in the green gown."

Rebecca followed Lady Trapleigh's line of vision and quickly spotted the gentleman in question. "And he's available?" Rebecca asked as she eyed his dance partner.

"He is, and also on the market for a wife, though I believe he does have a tendency to gamble."

Not an ideal match then, Rebecca decided, not to mention the fact that she was quite a bit taller than him and had always imagined looking up to her future husband rather than down. Apparently, if height was what she wanted, she'd have to aim for either Brekenbridge or Mr. Neville, who was both tall and dark haired. Except he was a rake, she reminded herself, and not to be trusted. "I believe I shall set my cap for the viscount then," she said, speaking in a hushed tone that only Lady Trapleigh could hear.

The widow nodded. "A good choice," she said as if Rebecca had just picked out a fabric for a new gown rather than the man she was to marry. "I think you will be happy with him."

Biding her time, Rebecca waited until the gentleman in question had excused himself from the wallflowers and started toward the refreshment table before heading after him. He wasn't as handsome as Mr. Neville, nor was he quite as tall or as broad shouldered, but his features were pleasant enough, and he obviously had a good heart. Stepping up beside him, Rebecca did precisely what Mr. Neville had done earlier—she tossed aside the rules of propriety and spoke to him without introduction. "I hope you'll forgive me for approaching you like this, but I couldn't help but be impressed by the kindness you showed toward the ladies with whom you just offered to dance."

"They are just as deserving of my attention as everyone else here," he said as he turned to face her. Confusion registered upon his face as he gazed back into her eyes from behind a silver mask. "I don't believe we've met—Viscount Brekenbridge at your service."

"It's a pleasure to make your acquaintance, my lord. You may call me Lady Nuit." Tilting her head, she offered him a bashful smile. He didn't appear to take any notice of the way in which she was dressed, or if he did, he was so discreet about his observation that it didn't show upon his face. His eyes were warm and friendly instead, for which she was thankful. "Well, I just thought you ought to be commended for your efforts. However, it appears that the first dance is about to commence. I really mustn't keep you from your partner."

"I don't see why not, since the ladies you just mentioned denied my request. I believe they were too shy in the end."

Attempting a look of complete befuddlement, Rebecca shook her head. "What a shame."

"Perhaps you would do me the honor of partnering with me?" Brekenbridge asked abruptly, hope brimming in his eyes while his hands worked nervously at his sides. "If you're available, that is."

"Certainly," Rebecca said, pleased by Brekenbridge's enthusiasm. It seemed Lady Trapleigh was correct in her assessment, for his eagerness was only too apparent. He would probably propose soon if she voiced an interest, though he did not strike her as the passionate sort, the way Mr. Neville had. Heavens but he'd looked quite ready to rip Starkly's head right off his neck when she'd last seen him. No, Lord Brekenbridge seemed very proper and civil by comparison— the sort of man who was looking to do the responsible thing and saw no reason for delay when it came to seeking a wife. He would suit her perfectly.

Allowing herself a satisfied smile, which Brekenbridge happily returned, he offered her his arm and started leading her toward the dance floor.

"You move with remarkable grace, my lady," Brekenbridge said mere moments later as he and Rebecca made their way along the line of couples in a longways country dance.

"The same can be said of you, my lord," Rebecca replied. She broadened her smile as she gazed up at him from beneath her lashes. His hold on her tightened just enough to strengthen her hope in him.

"You are too kind," he murmured, giving her hand a little squeeze before the dance forced them apart once more. As they stood facing each other while other couples danced between them, Rebecca met Brenken-bridge's gaze and found a resolve there that mirrored her own. Perhaps escaping Roselyn Castle wouldn't be as difficult as she'd first expected.

"I hope you don't think me presumptuous," Brek-enbridge said when next he stepped toward her, "but I must ask if you're spoken for. You see, I . . . well, the thing of it is—"

"No, my lord, I am not," Rebecca said, rushing to his aid.

Relief flooded the viscount's features. "Well then, perhaps you would be so good as to introduce me to your father later. I assume he's in attendance this eve-ning?" he asked. "I would be very pleased to make his acquaintance—your mother's too of course."

With her hand upon his, Rebecca followed his lead as they turned about in the middle of the dance floor, crisscrossing between other couples as they did so. "I live with my aunt and uncle, my lord. You see, my par-ents passed away some years ago."

A pained expression settled in Brekenbridge's eyes. "My apologies, Lady Nuit . . ."

"It's quite all right," she said, hoping to calm his dis-tress. "As I said, it was not recent."

They parted ways again, and as they stood apart, she realized she wouldn't be able to lie to him as easily as she had to Mr. Neville and Lord Starkly—not if he was to court her. For that, he'd have to know where she lived. She steeled herself, a bit wary of revealing her true identity to someone. She had little choice but to trust her instinct though, and instinct told her that he was not the sort of man who would abandon her once he knew the truth.

"Are your intentions toward me . . ." she began, speaking in a hushed tone when they approached each other once more, her gown swishing about her legs as they twirled around. Now was not the time to lose one's nerve. "That is to say . . . I was wondering if you were inquiring about my parents because you were interested in calling on me."

"Rest assured, Lady Nuit, I am most keen to further our acquaintance, if that is what you also desire."

She gave a little nod, took a deep, fortifying breath and said, "In that case, there is something that I must tell you. You see—" She was given no chance to make her confession, however, as the music faded and the dance came to an end. Having bowed and curtsied, Rebecca was just about to suggest they take a turn about the room so they could continue their conversation when Mr. Neville stepped in front of them, blocking their way. "Brekenbridge," he said, though his eyes remained on Rebecca. "Always a pleasure."

"Likewise," Brekenbridge said politely.

Mr. Neville finally turned his gaze on Brekenbridge. "If you don't mind, I do believe the lady has promised me the next dance."

An endless string of curses streamed through Rebecca's mind at that moment. Why, the arrogant nerve of the man! Here she was, trying her best to secure a match for herself with a real gentleman, and this . . . this libertine had the gall to try and stake his claim with a lie. The rudeness of it was infuriating. If only Brekenbridge would think of an excuse—something (anything at all) that might prevent her from having to leave his side and dance with Mr. Neville. But of course that was unthinkable. Brekenbridge was far too well mannered to oppose any man who'd claimed a dance. "Of course," he said as he disengaged his arm from Rebecca's. Turning to face her, he offered her another bow. "Perhaps we can talk later, my lady? There is a great deal I'd like to discuss with you." Brekenbridge's eyes held hers, offering hope. His meaning was clear.

Rebecca smiled at him and nodded. "I will look forward to it, my lord." And then the moment was over and she was being led away toward the dance floor by Mr. Neville, acutely (and annoyingly) aware of the firm, masculine confidence he exuded. She would not allow her body to respond to his, to how sturdy he felt at her side, the tantalizing scent of him—sandalwood again—and the heat that entered her hand at the point of contact. Heavens! She felt well and truly flushed.

No, she would keep her mind focused and think of what Brekenbridge had promised with his gaze. She could be happy with him, of that she was certain. And yet, when Mr. Neville swept her into his arms, to a waltz, no less, she feared she might be doomed. Oh, she'd found him charming and attractive before, but with his hand resting against her waist she was finding it alarmingly difficult to form a coherent thought.

"The viscount seemed very taken with you," Mr. Neville said as he spun her in a wide circle. "I wouldn't be surprised if he's wording his proposal as we speak."

One can only hope.

"It was badly done of you to interfere like that," she

said, deciding to give him a set down and hoping that being stern with him would stop her from wondering what it might be like to kiss him. Turning her head away from him, she determined to watch the other dancers. She would *not* look at Mr. Neville's lips. No, only disaster lay in that direction.

"I take it you desire his advances then?" There was an edge of flint to his tone as his hold on her tightened.

"He is a fine gentleman, and from what I've seen, he's also kind. I believe he will treat me well. A lady could do far worse." She turned her head back toward him, daring herself to meet his gaze in a pointed look. Thank heavens she was as good an actress as she was or she would probably have burst into flames in response to the look he was giving her in return. There was nothing polite about it. Indeed, it was a possessive look with the promise of wicked, forbidden pleasures—the sort of look that Rebecca imagined to be reserved for widows and the demimonde. It certainly wasn't the way a respectable gentleman ought to be looking at an innocent young lady, and to Rebecca's horror, she found herself responding to it in a most unwelcome way, feeling things in places that weren't at all proper. She cursed herself for looking at him. It had been a mistake.

"How well do you know him?" Mr. Neville asked.

"Well enough," she replied, only too eager to end this topic of discussion.

Mr. Neville held quiet a moment, then said, "You've only just met him, haven't you?"

"No, of course not. I mean, to consider marriage from someone I've only shared one dance with—why, that would be ridiculous."

"Is that so? Then pray tell, what is his name?"

Rebecca glanced up just enough to see the corner of his mouth edge upward into a smile—a cheeky smile.

"Well, that's easy enough. It's Brekenbridge."

A chuckle escaped Mr. Neville's lips. "Nice try, Lady Nuit, but I was referring to his Christian name. If you've known him long enough to consider marrying him, then surely you must have discovered what it is."

Ugh! He had her there. Not one to give up so easily, she spoke the first name that came to mind. "Daniel."

Mr. Neville's eyebrows snapped together, and for a split second he looked at her rather queerly. He then smiled. "A lady to my liking—one who enjoys a good gamble even when the chance of winning is close to impossible." Lowering his head, he whispered close to her ear, "His name is Thomas Brinkly."

"Very well," she said, shaking off the shivers that had run down her spine as he'd spoken, "so we still have much to learn about each other, but that doesn't mean we won't suit. On the contrary, it promises to be a typical Society courtship, followed by a typical Society wedding."

Mr. Neville raised an eyebrow. "And yet you don't strike me as a typical Society lady. Quite the opposite."

The music drew to a close, preventing Rebecca from telling him that he had no business passing judgment. She'd never considered herself the sort of woman who would marry for any reason other than love, which made what she now planned on doing so much more ironic. But then again, this was about winning her freedom, limited as it might be as the wife of a peer.

"Come, walk with me," Mr. Neville said once they'd bowed and curtsied to each other.

From the corner of her eye, Rebecca could see Lord

Brekenbridge trying to make his way toward them through the crowd. She ought to pull away from Mr. Neville and go to him, yet when Mr. Neville urged her along, she found herself moving forward alongside him until cool air greeted them and they stepped out onto the terrace. "I shouldn't be here with you," she said, not because they were alone, for they were not the only ones looking to escape the heat of the ballroom, and not because she was afraid he might try to compromise her in some way, but because she didn't trust herself to be alone with him. Brekenbridge offered security, while Mr. Neville offered scandal. She would have to be a fool . . . hell she was already a fool, for if Brekenbridge saw them together, her efforts with him would be for naught.

"I merely want a moment of your time," Mr. Neville said as he steered her toward the terrace steps. "You see, I find it curious that you're so eager to marry that you'd throw yourself away without the slightest hesitation on a man like Brekenbridge."

"Who's a perfect gentleman, if I may remind you," Rebecca said.

"True, but he's also a veritable bore—you'll get very little excitement from him."

"Perhaps I don't care for excitement. Perhaps I'd like a quiet life at home, caring for my husband and children, having friends over for tea, doing charity work and such."

"Sounds positively thrilling," Mr. Neville muttered.

"What? Many ladies take great pleasure in such things. Who are you to diminish it?"

"I think the better question, my lady," he said as he stopped in his tracks and turned to face her, "is not so much who *I* am, but rather who *you* are."

Rebecca sucked in a breath as her whole body went rigid.

"Ah, I see I struck a nerve."

"You don't know the first thing about me." She had the uncanny feeling that Mr. Neville had just pulled the string that would unravel all of her secrets.

"I believe I know you better than you know Brekenbridge. For one thing, you do want excitement in your life, Lady Nuit—the desperate need for marriage that has you plotting, along with the ambiguity about you, your desire for anonymity, they attest to it. This is an adventure for you, isn't it? I wonder how many of those you've had in the past, and more importantly, will you be willing to give them up in the future?"

They resumed walking. He had a point, to be sure, but he was making it without knowing all the facts. Yes, her life with Brekenbridge might be a bit more placid than what she would have wished for, but it would surely be better than marrying an aging cripple. She winced at the very idea of it.

They started down the stairs leading to the lawn below. "Let's take a stroll in the garden," he said. "The fewer people who see us together, the better—for your sake."

She eyed him dubiously. "Have you any idea of how that sounds?"

"What do you mean?" he asked, turning his head and meeting her gaze with a frown.

"It sounds as though you'd rather keep to dark corners and the cover of trees and bushes, all the while hoping to have me believe that it's for my *own* benefit." She gave him a look that she hoped would underline her innuendo.

If she wasn't mistaken, his eyes widened a little behind his mask. "Point taken," he said with a wry smile, "though I can assure you that doing so would benefit both of us equally."

The way her stomach twisted itself into a tight knot told her that he was no longer speaking of protecting her from ruin but quite possibly the opposite. She sucked in a breath and tried to ignore the sturdy feel of his arm beneath her gloved hand and how elegantly he guided her down toward the path below.

"Tell me, *Nuit,* what's the most outrageous thing you've ever done?"

As much as she would have liked to blame her gown for causing her to lose her footing as he spoke those words, she simply couldn't. Thankfully, he caught her before she had the chance to fall, the only problem (aside from the obvious embarrassment the situation offered) being that he couldn't possibly ignore her reaction. To her annoyance, he even chuckled. "So you have done something outrageous then? And to think that I was only fishing." The smile he gave her was a conspiratorial one filled with the promise that he would keep whatever secrets she might be willing to share with him. "Tell me something shocking, Nuit—I dare you."

I dare you.

Rebecca had never in her life backed down from a dare. A stubborn trait that had landed her in trouble plenty of times as a child. She considered her options carefully before admitting, "I wasn't invited here this evening. In fact, I snuck in through the garden."

"Really?" Though he was looking straight ahead, preventing her from seeing his expression clearly, his voice held a note of mirth to it. "And how exactly did you manage that? I would have thought that there were hedges and fences around the perimeter."

"Oh, there are, but it's not impossible to climb over them."

At this he turned to give her a head-to-toe perusal, as if to verify that she was indeed dressed in a ball gown. Eventually he burst out laughing. "Heaven above, but you're something, Nuit. I almost hope that Brekenbridge proposes just so I can enjoy watching him try to manage you. What on earth are you thinking going after someone like him? It will never work."

"Oh, and I suppose you're about to tell me that I should marry you instead?" she asked, knowing full well that the most she was likely to receive from him was a tryst out here in the garden, rake that he was.

"And why not?" he asked, surprising her beyond all possible measure. "I'm beginning to think you'd make an excellent wife and with that in mind, I do believe I'll try my luck before Brekenbridge gets the chance. Will you marry me, Lady Nuit?"

"You can't be serious, Mr. Neville. Men like you don't marry."

"Why on earth not?"

"Because you enjoy your carefree existence too much—the gambling and outrageous parties, which I hear you are quite an expert at hosting—and because you hold your mistress in such high esteem that you offered her a pair of earrings which, rumor has it, were meant for your future wife. No woman in her right mind would attach herself to someone so careless and indiscreet. Besides, from what little I've been told, men like you are notorious for getting themselves into scrapes. For all I know, you've depleted your funds and now hope to get your hands on my dowry so you can settle whatever debts you may have."

"Good God, woman! Must you paint such a dastardly picture of me? It threatens to ruin my image."

Rebecca smiled. "I rather think it underlines it quite nicely."

When he laughed, there was a genuine ring to it that made her wonder if perhaps she'd been too harsh in her dismissal of him. She knew he was a rake and not at all the sort of man with whom she should have been strolling alone in the garden, especially not since she suspected that his reasons for seeking her company in the first place had probably been less than honorable. Why else would a man of his caliber speak to a lady dressed as she was in a scarlet gown? He probably thought her a widow, or worse . . . a courtesan with whom he could spend a night of unconditional pleasure.

And yet he'd just offered her marriage. Rebecca shook her head at *that* conundrum. Surely he had an agenda in which he hoped she'd play a part. Whatever it was, she couldn't possibly accept. She wasn't going to delude herself into thinking that marrying any man hastily would lead to love, but she certainly didn't want to share her husband, whoever he might be, with a horde of other women.

Nevertheless, she could not deny that she enjoyed his company. There was just something about him that made him easy for her to be around. It was as if she could truly be herself when she was with him, something she hadn't had the chance to be for so long, not even in Laura's or Lady Trapleigh's company. It felt wonderful . . . liberating.

Glancing up at him as they passed another torch, she marveled at the way in which the light and shadow played across his face. What a handsome devil he was. Dangerous too, since her heart was once again beating a little bit faster. Intent on returning to their previous conversation, she said, "I believe it's your turn to tell *me* something outrageous."

Her playful nature was captivating. With a smile, Daniel glanced down at her. She was looking right at him, all serious expectancy, but with a gleam in her eyes that betrayed her. She was having just as much fun with this as he was. "Very well." He paused to consider his options. As far as outrageous exploits went, he could probably outdo the most daring and the most debauched, but there was a limit to what he would share with any lady, no matter who she might be. And then, of course, there was also her opinion of him to consider. He was still furious with his uncle, but unless he wanted to lose his allowance, he had no choice. So far, Lady Nuit appeared to be his best chance, if for no other reason than the fact that she was at least willing to speak to him.

"I did on one occasion pretend to be the fiancé of a certain Miss Brighton," he said, recalling one of his more successful endeavors.

"Surely you jest." Lady Nuit's voice sounded just as doubtful as Miss Brighton's had when he'd first told her of his plan.

He shook his head. "You see, Miss Brighton and my sister went to finishing school together. They became close friends and have kept in touch ever since. When my sister discovered that Miss Brighton's parents were eager for her to marry, she invited her to London for the

Season, hoping that this would improve her chances of making a good match."

"That was very good of your sister," Lady Nuit said.

"I suppose it was," Daniel agreed, "and being the married woman that she now is, she was able to act as chaperone for Miss Brighton. You see, my sister's husband is the Earl of Chilton and—"

"Your sister's a countess?" Lady Nuit asked with unabashed surprise.

"Well yes, she is, and as such, she's well enough connected to—"

"But you're *Mr.* Neville, which means that she was not a titled lady before she married, correct?"

Daniel nodded. Lady Nuit was obviously having a difficult time understanding how a mere miss had ended up marrying an earl. Her confusion was easy to understand, since it was rare for any member of the *ton* to marry someone without pedigree. "It's quite simple really," he explained. "My aunt and uncle are the Marquess and Marchioness of Wolvington, and my sister was one of the most coveted ladies on the marriage mart the year she made her debut."

"Oh . . . well that explains it," Lady Nuit said. She looked up at Daniel as if waiting for something. When he said nothing further, she said, "So then what happened?"

"I beg your pardon?" In the dim light of the garden, Daniel couldn't tell what color her eyes might be. They looked dark, so he supposed they had to be brown, but he couldn't be sure. What he could see was that they were filled with warmth and happiness.

"Miss Brighton. What happened to her?"

"Well, I believe Miss Brighton's parents were hoping

my sister's good fortune would rub off, but unfortunately nobody paid the poor woman any mind."

"So you offered to escort her home as the fiancé her parents had hoped for?"

Daniel shrugged. "They had no way of knowing we weren't really engaged, so yes, I did. We spent a lovely week there together before I returned to London on some fictitious business."

Looking away, she quietly asked, "And are you still fictitiously engaged to her?"

"Oh no. I actually took ill and died a few weeks later."

Lady Nuit gasped, eyes wide with shock. "How dreadful for poor Miss Brighton."

"She got what she wanted—an engagement to an earl and the reprieve that a year of mourning would give her."

"You played the part of an earl?"

"Well yes. I wanted Miss Brighton's parents to be thoroughly impressed with the good catch she'd made." He waggled his eyebrows, eliciting a peel of laughter from Lady Nuit.

"Goodness me, Mr. Neville." Her eyes were warm and . . . understanding? Curious, that. "You're quite the schemer, aren't you?"

My dear, you have no idea.

"Not really. I was just trying to be helpful." This was true, for he'd genuinely liked Miss Brighton—kind and gentle as she was. Seeing the desperation on her face at the prospect of returning home empty-handed had prompted him to concoct yet another harebrained exploit.

"And I admire you for it," Lady Nuit said as they turned onto another graveled path, which would take them past some flowerbeds and to the opposite side of the lawn.

"You do?" Daniel coughed, hoping to mask the surprise in his voice.

"Why, of course. You acted very selflessly."

He considered that as they continued along the path, realizing that he couldn't recall when someone had last said anything positive about him. It felt strange somehow—undeserving almost. Especially since the only reason he was keeping Lady Nuit's company at all was that he needed her help. Well, there was also the fact that he genuinely liked her. She was different from other women—freer somehow—as if she wanted to embrace life and live it to its fullest. In that regard, he had to admit that they were very similar, and it was this that also convinced him that they would get on very well with each other once they were married. He smiled brightly. "You see, I'm not so bad after all."

Grinning, she shook her head with amusement. "Perhaps not the worst rake there is, but still a rake, nonetheless." She lowered her voice to a conspiratorial whisper. "Not that I would presume to know anything about your lifestyle, Mr. Neville, but I can only assume that it must be rather costly to be a rake. I mean, the women—"

"Lady Nuit, this is hardly an appropriate topic for conversation."

"No, I suppose not," she relented. A sly smile captured her lips. "Then again, I fail to believe there's anything appropriate about you." Her voice was light and teasing—delightful in every way.

"Perhaps not, but I have every intention of changing that."

"*What*? Surely you're not planning to reform?"

"Surely *you're* not imagining that I would be contemplating marriage if I weren't. I'm not that great a scoundrel you know—I just like to have fun once in a while."

She eyed him for a second. "Perhaps," she said. "But then again, we both know that you weren't being serious."

"I wasn't?"

"Well, of course not—you're a rake!"

"Yes, I believe we've established that much already." Trying to keep his irritation at bay, he sighed heavily. "You won't even give me a chance, will you?"

"To what? Court me or seduce me?" Without waiting for him to answer, she continued. "I'm not saying that people can't change, Mr. Neville. I just don't think they do so without good reason—especially not from one day to the next. There's something you're not telling me. After all, you know nothing about me. In fact, we've only just met." She shook her head with a sigh. "Forgive me, but it's just very difficult for me to understand why you would want to marry me."

"Look around you, Lady Nuit. I'm shunned by everyone. Finding a wife will be a chore, and I must find one eventually." Looking down at her, he was once again aware of how comfortable he felt in her company. He could never have had this sort of conversation with any other lady—it would have been preposterous to even consider it. "I will be Marquess of Wolvington one day, and as such, I will need an heir."

The blush that crept into Lady Nuit's cheeks was beyond charming. There was no denying that he affected her, not when she blushed so easily in his presence. This at least was reassuring.

They'd reached the far side of the lawn. It was dimmer here with trees lining one side of the path—the perfect place to steal a kiss. Ordinarily, he would have grasped the opportunity with open arms, but the fact that she probably expected him to do just that gave him pause. He had one chance to get this right, and while he was certain that she would be putty in his arms and that they'd both take pleasure in the moment, instinct warned him against acting rashly, for it would only prove him to be precisely the irresponsible cad she suspected him of being. No, better to find out where she lived and woo her properly. After all, he was competing with a bloody viscount. If he wanted to win her hand, he'd have to get her to like him enough to make her doubt her decision to accept Brekenbridge once he offered—which he would, no doubt about that.

Daniel almost laughed. How the hell was he supposed to survive this ordeal unscathed when just walking along like this, her hand tucked in the crook of his arm, was enough to heat his blood? Damned if he knew, but at least there was comfort to be had in knowing that if he succeeded, he'd be engaged to her within three weeks, and then he'd be able to spend the rest of his life kissing her. "Come," he said as he guided her onto the lawn, the April grass springy beneath their feet. "Let's liven things up a bit, shall we?"

"What on earth do you mean?" Her eyes had grown large with merriment, her features brightening just as a burst of light exploded in the sky.

"Walking is for the old and ailing. Let's dance instead beneath the fireworks." And before she could protest, he unhooked her hand from his elbow and spun her into his arms, the momentum carrying them both forward in the direction of the pumpkin carriage while Lady Nuit squealed with laughter.

"May I call on you tomorrow?" he asked, taking advantage of the lighter mood that had descended over them. "I've enjoyed your company this evening."

For a split second, her features turned serious, but then she smiled at him and nodded. "You can always try, I suppose, but I must warn you, my aunt and uncle are not the easiest people to get along with. They may not even admit you."

Daniel wouldn't be so easily discouraged. He could charm even the worst of dragons—had done so on more than one occasion. "I will need to know where you live if I am to pay a social visit," he said. "Your real name would be helpful too."

Her smile widened and turned to a grin of pure and utter delight, as if she was enjoying a private joke. "My real name, Mr. Neville, is Lady Rebecca, and I live at Roselyn Castle—in the tower room, to be precise."

Lady Rebecca from Roselyn Castle? Surely not. She was supposed to be completely cracked in the head—a perfect candidate for Bedlam, from what he'd heard. Yet there was nothing crazy about the woman whose company he'd been keeping this evening. Instead, she was fun and lively and easy to talk to, not to mention of perfectly sound mind. He smiled down at her. The minx. She'd almost had him duped, but he should have known from her inability to keep a straight face that she'd only been jesting with him. Well, he wouldn't be so easily brushed aside. "Nice try," he said, "but—"

A loud crack sounded, the lady in his arms went limp with no more than a low utterance, and whatever Daniel had been about to say trailed off into the night.

Time ground to a halt, and everything else around him fell away. In that instant, Daniel Neville was conscious of only two things: himself, and the lady in his arms. And as he stood there, suspended in that split second of a moment, feeling more helpless than ever before, he knew that if she died here tonight—if she drew her last breath as he held her against him—his life would be over too.

Stay with me. Please, for the love of God, stay with me.

Chapter 3

The next hour happened in a daze. Shortly after Lady Nuit was shot, Daniel's host, the Duke of Kingsborough, came to his aid. He had been standing close by with his family, watching the fireworks display, and Daniel was now thankful for the assistance that he offered. "Get her on the ground," Kingsborough said to Daniel as he hastily removed his jacket for Lady Nuit to lie on.

Daniel quickly followed the duke's instructions without hesitation, cradling Lady Nuit's head in his hands while the duke undid his cravat, bundled it into a tight wad and shoved it toward Daniel. "Put this on her wound, add some pressure and try to stop the bleeding."

An ache rose in Daniel's throat as he snatched the fabric from the duke and pushed it down against the raw flesh of Lady Nuit's left shoulder, the white piece of linen turning crimson as her blood seeped out of her. Daniel blinked against his blurry vision and pushed down harder, eliciting a faint groan from the lady herself.

Kingsborough turned to his brother, who'd also arrived on the scene along with two other gentlemen, one of whom Daniel recognized as Lord Roxberry. "Winston, I'm leaving you in charge here while I try to find out what the devil happened." Rising, the duke then hurried off in the direction of the terrace.

With quaking fingers, Daniel eased Lady Nuit's mask away from her face, hoping that would make it easier for her to breathe.

"We should probably get her inside," Lord Winston said. "The wound will need cleaning, and I'm sure she'll be more comfortable too."

"I couldn't agree more," came a soft-spoken female voice. Looking up, Daniel saw that it was the dowager duchess who'd spoken, her mouth set in a firm line of determination. "And since we've no way of knowing how serious the lady's injury is, I suggest we hurry."

Fresh panic descended over Daniel. His whole body was trembling with it. Dear God, she couldn't die so easily. The injustice of it was overwhelming. No, he had to save her. She *had* to live.

Scooping her up in his arms, he ignored the fear that clutched at his heart. Only clearheaded resolve would help her. As he held her close, her head resting against his right arm, he quickly strode toward the stairs leading up to the terrace. There was no need for him to look over his shoulder to know that Lord Winston and the duchess were following in his wake, their faces grave with concern.

Stepping onto the terrace, Daniel headed toward the French doors leading into the ballroom. He'd almost made it when a plump, elderly woman stepped forward, blocking his path. "What is the meaning of this?" she asked, eyes razor sharp as she looked from Lady Nuit's face to Daniel's and back again. A stout gentleman stood beside her with a deep frown upon his forehead.

"The lady has been shot. Please move out of my way," Daniel said, his tone rough with the frustration of being delayed.

"Show me," the lady demanded.

Who the devil was this rude and thoughtless person?

"Why don't you join us inside?" the duchess suggested. Daniel quietly admired her calm. If it had been up to him, he'd have tossed the impertinent lady aside and been on his way. Did she not understand the urgency?

Eyes meeting Daniel's in a hard glare, the lady nodded and stepped back, allowing him entry. Anger flaring as he strode across the ballroom floor, he looked forward to giving the woman a proper set down. How dare she put Lady Nuit's life at further risk by detaining them?

Climbing the steps leading up to the foyer, Daniel was met by Kingsborough, who was looking a bit out of sorts, suggesting that he'd had little success in locating the shooter.

"This way," he said as he led Daniel down a corridor and into a parlor that had been furnished in various shades of green. "You can set her down over there, Neville. I've sent for a doctor, but in the meantime . . ." He hesitated a moment. "Is she alive?"

Daniel felt his throat tighten as he placed Lady Nuit on one of the silk sofas. Unable to speak, he just nodded.

"It appears so," Winston said.

The dowager duchess, who'd followed Daniel over to the sofa, gently urged him out of the way. She then began pulling Lady Nuit's sleeve down over her shoulder. "The least we can do is try to clean this," she explained. "Would you please give me some brandy and another cravat? This one's soaked through."

Eager to assist, Daniel hastily undid his cravat while Kingsborough poured a measure of brandy into a glass and placed it on the table next to where the duchess knelt. He then held out his hand toward Daniel, who dropped the long piece of linen into it. The duke handed it to his mother, who dipped the length of fabric into the glass and pressed it against Lady Nuit's open wound. "I thought she was—" the duke said, sounding confused.

"Quite," the plump lady snapped, cutting him off. "Apparently she pulled the wool over all of our eyes."

For a moment it looked as if the duke might argue the point, but then his features softened as he addressed both the plump lady and her husband. "Unfortunately, I have no idea who did this. It appears the culprit fled the premises before I could apprehend him, but I have sent for the constable, so hopefully the matter will soon be resolved. In the meantime, I take full responsibility for the incident and hope that you will accept my sincerest apologies."

The couple gave a curt nod and the duke turned to everyone else, saying, "I ought to go explain the situation to our guests, but I'll be back soon. Can you manage until I return?"

"We'll be fine," the duchess assured him, upon which he exited the room.

Daniel stood rooted to the floor, his gaze moving first to Lady Nuit's shoulder, the wound there flashing angrily in and out of view as the duchess dabbed away at it, and then to the bitter expressions of the lady and gentleman, whom he did not recognize. The only reason he could think of to explain why they'd questioned him, and why the duchess had suggested they follow, was that they were Lady Nuit's parents or related to her in some other way. But if that was the case, then why would they have been invited to the ball without her? It didn't make any sense . . . unless, of course, what she'd told him was true. He considered the plump lady's words with a frown.

Intent on finding answers, he stepped toward the couple and bowed. "Allow me to introduce myself," he said, aware of the sharp scrutiny that befell him the instant he did so. "I am Mr. Neville." Attempting a slight smile, he waited warily for any sign of recognition his name might bring. None, as far as he could tell. They were just as unaware of his identity as he was of theirs.

"Lord Grifton," the stout man responded. "And this is my wife, Lady Grifton."

"A pleasure to make your acquaintance," Daniel said, aiming for the most polite tone he could manage.

Lady Grifton, who looked on the verge of an apoplectic fit, narrowed her eyes on him like a hawk zeroing in on its prey. "I can't say that I share your sentiment," she said. "Had it not been for you, she probably wouldn't have gotten herself shot."

Daniel wasn't sure how she'd drawn that conclusion. "We were just dancing," he explained, determined not to be cowed by her. "I don't see how—"

"Then it is *entirely* your fault, Mr. Neville. You, sir, clearly led her into the line of fire," Lady Grifton hissed. She turned to her husband. "I cannot wait to have a few choice words with her when she comes to."

Daniel took a deep, steadying breath. The insinuation that Lady Nuit—correction, Lady Rebecca—had been shot because of him made him sick.

"An explanation is most certainly in order," Lord Grifton agreed.

"Right." Lady Grifton crossed her arms and raised her chin, her expression scornful. "And as soon as she's recovered, she's marrying one of those suitors. Why, it's clear as day what she's been playing at these past two years. Well, the game's up. She'll do her duty if I have to drag her to the altar myself!"

The dowager duchess raised her head, eyes wide with alarm. "Lady Grifton, I understand that you must be stunned to find Lady Rebecca here. I have to admit that it is unexpected. But please try to calm down. She needs rest and medical attention. In fact, she's welcome to remain here until she recovers if that would be—"

"Thank you, Your Grace, that's very generous of you, but it's also completely out of the question," Lady Grifton said. "We're taking her back to Roselyn Castle with us as soon as the doctor has seen to her. She can get the same amount of rest there as she can here, and I can assure you that now that I'm aware of her scheming ways, I'll be keeping a closer eye on her. The next time she gets into this sort of mischief, her husband will be the one to deal with it."

Daniel gaped at her. He couldn't believe the venom with which Lady Grifton spoke of her ward. "How can you say that?" he asked, his voice low as he fought for control. "She could have died tonight. She still might."

Lady Grifton stepped toward him, looking not the least bit intimidated by his greater size. Staring up at him, she smiled. "I take it you're smitten with her?

Well, I suggest you get that fancy out of your head, sir." Her eyes swept over him with distaste. "She is a lady of breeding. I would be a fool to waste her on an untitled gentleman when an earl and a duke are showing great interest in her."

"If I may," Lord Winston said. "I think—"

"Quite right," Daniel clipped, sensing that it wouldn't matter one whit to this woman that he was next in line to the Marquisate of Wolvington. At present, he was untitled, and that was apparently all that the arrogant woman cared about.

He considered her words. Lady Grifton had spoken of Lady Rebecca as scheming. Daniel quietly recalled reading about Lady Rebecca's riding accident two years earlier. She'd taken a severe blow to the head, the papers had said, and had since been declared mad. It wasn't as if everyone talked about her though—at least not anymore—but everyone knew *of* her, although Daniel had to admit that he probably knew less than most. His interest in the drama surrounding Roselyn Castle had never been great, so he'd never really given it much thought.

Was it possible that Lady Rebecca's entire illness had been nothing but a front? And if so, then how did the shooter fit into the scenario? He couldn't imagine anyone wanting to harm Lady Rebecca, but on the other hand, he had to acknowledge that he knew very little about her. Perhaps she'd done something far more terrible than feign insanity—something that had resulted in someone wishing her dead.

Daniel tossed the idea aside with a shake of his head. It was ludicrous to imagine such a thing when instinct told him that she would make him an excellent match.

He decided then and there that he would still try to win Lady Rebecca's hand, and, being the reckless man that he was, Daniel was not about to walk away from the challenge that doing so would pose. On the contrary, he looked forward to it with great anticipation, because if there was one thing he was certain of, it was that she would rather marry him than whoever the Griftons had in mind, and now that he knew where to find her, all he had to do was think of a way in which to gain access to her.

Really, how hard could it possibly be?

Chapter 4

Heaven help her, she was in pain. While the doctor had assured her aunt and uncle that she would survive, having a lead ball extracted and getting stitched up afterward had still hurt like blazes.

"Did you at least enjoy yourself last night, my lady?" Laura asked. The maid was sitting at Rebecca's bedside, eyes filled with concern.

Rebecca took a deep breath and exhaled it. "Yes," she said, her eyes closing at the memory of it. She could still see Mr. Neville's handsome face as he smiled back at her. "It was spectacular."

"Well, I suppose that's something," Laura said. She shook her head. "I never should have agreed to let you go. Lord, you could have been killed!"

"It would still have been worth it," Rebecca muttered, too low for Laura to hear. After returning home, she'd been locked inside her room with a promise from her aunt that the next time she ventured outside, it would be to entertain Lord Topperly and the Duke of Grover.

"You *will* marry one of them," her aunt had said.

"Naturally, we will decide which of them will suit you best. After everything you've put us through—embarrassing us by showing up at the ball the way you did—I daresay we're looking forward to being rid of you!"

"All I wanted was the chance to find a husband of my own choosing," Rebecca had said. "Why won't you let me do that? Have you no desire to see me happy?"

"Happy? By God, you're as spoiled as your mother was—always making demands. It's *her* fault my brother's dead, and yet I took you in after they both perished in that fire, even though you're just as unlikeable as she was. You ought to be grateful that I'm even capable of finding a man who's interested in you, given that unfortunate coloring of yours. Why, you look as if you haven't bathed in a year, and yet I have worked a miracle, finding not one but two titled gentlemen willing to be your husband—old ones, even, whom you'll soon outlive. If you're smart about it, you'll hurry up and give the one you marry a son as soon as possible to secure your own position. Now get to bed—the sooner you recover, the sooner we can get the matter settled."

Her aunt had then left, locking the door behind her and leaving Rebecca to wonder exactly how long it would take before her aunt and uncle deemed her fit enough to meet with her suitors. No more than a week, she imagined.

With little comfort to be had in light of what her future probably held for her, Rebecca had been overjoyed to discover that Laura had managed to convince the Griftons that she'd played no part in Rebecca's escapade. The cunning maid had actually told the Griftons that Rebecca, being of the sound mind that she was, must have switched the laudanum-laced tea that Laura was supposed to serve to pacify Rebecca when she was at her worst with Laura's untainted cup. She'd apologized profusely to them for not keeping a better eye on Rebecca, going so far as to claim that Rebecca obviously didn't know what was best for her and that it was obvious that the Griftons were only trying to do what was in Rebecca's best interest. They'd swallowed the fib without further question.

"I don't suppose there's any chance that a handsome young gentleman might call on you soon?" Laura asked. "I'd hate to see you married to either of the men that the earl and countess have selected for you. *Why* they refuse to find someone who's closer to you in age and whom you might actually stand a chance of happiness with, I cannot imagine."

Rebecca groaned, her shoulder aching as she turned a little so she could better see Laura. "They probably don't want to bother with the hassle of going to the City and dragging me from one ballroom to the next when there are already two gentlemen willing to take me off their hands here, and with no extra expense—you know how fickle they are."

Laura nodded. "That's true, though I still have this niggling suspicion that there's more to it than that. They're too insistent." Her brow creased as she shook her head. "There's something odd about the whole situation if you ask me."

The thought had occurred to Rebecca before, though she'd yet to discover if there was any merit to it. "I don't know," she said. "I've no reason to believe that they just want to be rid of me."

"Perhaps," Laura agreed, though she was looking

doubtful. On a deep breath, she suddenly smiled. "So, *is* there a young gentleman, my lady? Did you meet someone last night from whom you might expect a visit . . . or perhaps a proposal?"

A slow smile captured Rebecca's lips as she thought of the troublemaking rake. "There is one whose company I particularly enjoyed."

A squeal of excitement escaped Laura. She quickly clapped a hand over her mouth, eyes wide with curiosity. Removing her hand slowly, she spoke in a whisper, as if there had been others present who might overhear. "Who is he?"

"Well . . ." Rebecca dragged out the word for dramatic effect. "His name is Mr. Neville, and he is the heir to the Marquisate of Wolvington."

Laura's eyebrows shot up. "He must be a handsome devil—charming too, I'd imagine."

"Why do you say that?" Rebecca asked curiously.

"Because of the way you speak his name, my lady." When Rebecca frowned, Laura imitated the dreamy way in which she'd spoken. She chuckled as she got up from her chair and went to fetch Rebecca a cup of tea. Looking over her shoulder, she gave her mistress a knowing smile. "I believe you're quite smitten."

Rebecca couldn't lie. "I must confess that I cannot stop thinking about him, although I fear marrying him is completely out of the question—he won't suit."

"And why is that?" Laura asked, returning to Rebecca's bedside and handing her the warm cup.

"Because he's a rake who will never be able to offer me the happy family life I'm seeking. You would be shocked to hear of some of the things he's done, but even if I chose to accept his faults, I doubt that Aunt and Uncle would approve—not when there's an earl and a duke in the running."

"But if he's an heir—"

"You know as well as I that they won't care about that. All they'll see is a man who's presently untitled and accompanied by a poor reputation." She shook her head, feeling terribly sad that her relatives were so shallow, but they were not the only ones, as evidenced by the scowls of disapproval Mr. Neville had received from almost everyone the night before. She took a sip of her tea before sinking back against her pillow and closing her eyes. "What am I saying? I'm talking as if I expect him to call on me, which he will be unlikely to do now that he knows who I am. I'm a charlatan, Laura, and not even a very pretty one at that, which makes Mr. Neville's interest in me so much more suspicious. No, I'll probably end up with Topperly or . . ." She scrunched her nose. "Grover."

Opening her eyes, she found Laura watching her. "How many times must I tell you that you're beautiful before you believe me?"

Rebecca forced a smile. "My skin tone is darker than everyone else's and I have black hair. Don't think I've forgotten the way other girls mocked me when I was a child. They used to call me *gypsy,* and I wouldn't be surprised if some of them still do."

"If that is the case, then they've no idea what a gypsy looks like. You have your mother's Spanish blood in you, that's all. It's nothing to be ashamed of, my lady. If anything, you should embrace how different you are from everyone else. I wouldn't be the least bit surprised if this is what drew Mr. Neville to you in the first place. Besides, even if he is a rake, as you say, there's always the possibility that he might reform," Laura said. "The duke did."

Rebecca sighed. "Yes, I suppose that's true, but he also had good reason to do so. There's a lot of responsibility resting on his shoulders. Mr. Neville, however—"

"Has no responsibility? You just said that he's the heir to the Wolvington title. Surely he will need a wife and an heir of his own one day."

"I'm sure he will," Rebecca agreed. In fact, Mr. Neville had pointed out the exact same thing. But just because he gave her his name did not mean that he would give her his loyalty . . . his fidelity. She handed her now empty teacup back to Laura and settled back against her pillow with a yawn. "Forgive me, Laura, but I'm suddenly very tired. I think I'll try to get some rest."

"You do that, my lady, and I'll go and cut some of those daffodils I promised you."

"Thank you," Rebecca sighed, her eyes closing to the sound of Laura shuffling about the room. The door opened and closed, silence settled over her, and she slowly drifted off to sleep, her last thought being of Mr. Neville's smile as he twirled her in his arms, dancing.

Chapter 5

"Why, Lady Rebecca," the Earl of Topperly was saying loudly as his light blue eyes slid over her figure with great appreciation, "you look exquisite today."

One day of rest: that was all her aunt and uncle had afforded her before insisting that she ready herself for meeting her suitors. "It's not as if you were shot in the leg," her aunt had said as she'd picked out a gown for her to wear. "You can easily take a walk with them in the garden."

So here she was, parading about between the flower-beds with a relic on one arm and a fossil on the other. "Thank you, my lord, you're most kind."

"And may I say," the Duke of Grover told her, his eyes gleaming as he dropped his gaze to her bosom and leaned closer to her ear, "that you look riper than ever before. Wouldn't you agree, Topperly?"

"Hmm? I beg your pardon, Your Grace?" the earl asked. He was partly deaf and rarely heard what anyone was saying unless they spoke loudly enough.

"I was merely remarking on how lovely Lady Rebecca's hair is," Grover shouted back. "Such a bold color against her unblemished skin. I find it quite striking."

"Oh yes, yes indeed," Topperly agreed.

"Now, I know a decision has yet to be made," Grover added, his voice once again soft so that Topperly wouldn't hear, "but I thought you'd be pleased to know that I'm just as functional as any young buck and with a very healthy appetite. You won't be disappointed in that regard."

Oh dear Lord, she was going to be sick.

"Let's pick some daffodils," Rebecca said. It was the first thing that came to mind as a possible means of distraction. If only they would soon leave. Didn't people their age require a midday nap? Disengaging herself from their arms, she crouched down and began collecting the flowers while both men watched. She didn't mind Topperly's presence so much. He came across as a harmless gentleman who merely sought a bit of company in his old age as well as someone who'd be capable of looking after him. His reasoning behind seeking a young wife made sense, but that didn't make Rebecca any more eager to accept him as her husband. Perhaps she was being selfish, she reflected, but she couldn't help it; she was too spirited and adventurous to be the least bit tempted by the idea of nursing an old man in his dotage, no matter how much money he'd leave to her once he departed this earth. Looking over her shoulder, she smiled up at him, silently wishing him many more years of good health.

Grover, on the other hand . . . She turned her attention back to her task when she caught a disturbing leer upon his lips. The things he said to her and the way in which his eyes were forever inappropriately fixed upon her person made her skin crawl.

"I hope you took my meaning seriously before, Lady Rebecca," Grover said as he bent down to pluck a daffodil from the flowerbed, his forearm brushing against the side of Rebecca's breast as he did so. "I mean to beget at least one son off of you before I die. I hope you're fit for the challenge."

Swallowing the sharp rejoinder that threatened to escape her, she smiled tightly. "I shall do my best to be a dutiful wife to whomever I marry." Rising, she then offered him a large bouquet of daffodils. "Would you please carry these for me?" She might have to suffer his company and his rude behavior, but at least she'd just thought of a way to discourage his touch—for now.

"Would you care for some tea?" she asked when they arrived back inside and a maid relieved Grover of the daffodils he carried.

"Perhaps I can offer both gentlemen a brandy in my study instead," Rebecca's uncle said as he stepped out into the hallway and gestured for the earl and the duke to follow him. "We have some business to discuss."

"Yes, of course," Grover said. "A brandy would be most welcome."

"Indeed it would," Topperly agreed.

Both men turned to Rebecca, bowed to her and excused themselves, the door to her uncle's study closing behind them.

Expelling a sigh of relief over not having to entertain the pair any further, Rebecca turned toward her aunt, who'd entered from the parlor. "I suppose you will escort me back upstairs now?"

"Don't be impertinent," her aunt snapped. "That Neville fellow arrived while you were in the garden, and against my better judgment I granted him entry.

He brought flowers, as you can see—a lovely bouquet that I believe will look splendid on that little round table in my bedroom." For an instant, her eyes took on a dreamy look, but then they sharpened and narrowed, and she took a step closer to Rebecca. "Apparently he wishes to see you, to ensure that you have recovered after the shooting."

In spite of her aunt's harsh words, Rebecca's heart soared. Mr. Neville had come to call on her, just as she'd hoped he would. What a blessing it was that her aunt had not turned him away. Eager to see him, she stepped toward the door. Her aunt held her back, a firm hand staying Rebecca's progress. "Before you get too excited, I thought you ought to know that your uncle and I are leaning toward the duke. He will make a very prestigious match for you, you know." Lady Grifton's mouth tilted in a smug smile, her eyes filled with venom. "As for Mr. Neville, I expect you to send him on his way for good."

"Why must you be so cruel?" Rebecca's voice was low and angry. "Have you no care for what my wishes might be?"

"That's enough!" Tightening her grip, her aunt leaned closer. "When will you learn that when it comes to marriage, your *feelings* are of no concern? This is business—that's all. Now get in there and entertain the man so we can be rid of him again."

Steadying herself with a deep breath, Rebecca opened the door and stepped inside the parlor, her heart skipping a beat at the sight of Mr. Neville smiling back at her as she entered. "Good afternoon. What a pleasure it is to see you again." No truer words had ever been spoken.

"You're even more radiant than I remember," he said, taking her hand in his and bowing over it. He placed a gentle kiss upon her knuckles, his lips lingering just a fraction longer than what was considered proper.

A cough from the open doorway had him straightening himself again. Turning slightly, Rebecca looked over her shoulder to find her aunt watching them with a critical eye. "You've fifteen minutes before my niece must return to her chambers to ready herself for another caller, who's expected to arrive shortly, and if you think to steal a kiss in that time, Mr. Neville, I suggest you think again. This door will remain wide open." With a stiff nod to underline her statement, Lady Grifton then turned about and marched off. Heat flared in Rebecca's cheeks as she watched her aunt disappear from view. Fifteen minutes was not a lot of time. Her aunt had lied about there being another caller, of course—yet another reminder of the future that lay ahead, one that would not include Mr. Neville. Attempting to calm her nerves and put her feelings of desperation aside, Rebecca turned back toward Mr. Neville and gestured toward the love seat. "Please, won't you sit down?"

Setting his hat and gloves on a vacant chair, Mr. Neville followed her advice.

Rebecca clasped her hands together in front of her and went to sit next to him. "I suppose an explanation is in order," she said, not daring to meet his eyes.

"If you like," he told her quietly, "though I would first like to inquire about your health. How are you feeling?" His voice was gentle and soothing as he spoke.

"Sore," Rebecca admitted, "but at least I'm able to move about. Plus, I'll live, which I suppose is something."

"You gave me quite the fright, you know. One minute we were dancing, and the next . . ." The words trailed off with a hint of despair. "Any idea why someone might want to kill you?"

Rebecca jerked her head toward him. "You think it was deliberate?" Of course it had been. She just hadn't wanted to think about it.

Mr. Neville nodded. "I'm just not sure if you're the person they were aiming at. That's why I asked."

Allowing her mind to return to the evening of the ball, Rebecca thought of the other people who'd been close by at the time she'd been shot. She recalled seeing the Duke of Kingsborough and his mother, but the rest were a blur—probably because she was not acquainted with them. "As far as I know, I have no enemies and can think of no one who would wish me dead." Pasting a bright smile on her face she said, "Thank you for your concern, Mr. Neville, but there's really no need for it. As you can see, I'm absolutely fine."

A slight crease appeared upon his forehead. "When we first met, you led me to believe that your situation was somewhat desperate." He raised his hand to stop the protest that she was about to make. "Why else would you have gone to the lengths you did to attend the ball? Why the eagerness to catch a husband?" He regarded her pensively before speaking again. "When you told me that you were Lady Rebecca of Roselyn Castle, I didn't believe you. How could I, when Lady Rebecca was supposed to be mad and you were anything but? Whatever reason you might have had for such duplicity can only have been born out of sheer desperation. Having met your guardians, I suspect that they have something to do with it. Am I right?"

There was little point in denying the obvious, so Rebecca quietly nodded. "They want me to marry either the Earl of Topperly or the Duke of Grover."

"Bloody hell! I mean . . . forgive me, my lady, I should not have spoken like that in your presence."

"It's quite all right, Mr. Neville. My sensibilities are not so easily offended, and besides, I share your sentiment."

"But they must be at least fifty years your senior. Why would your aunt and uncle demand something like that of you when there are plenty of eligible young bachelors available?"

Rebecca shrugged. "Topperly is an old friend of my uncle's, and Grover is a duke. Marrying me off to either of them would certainly be a feather in their caps. Aside from that, I can't be sure. My maid and I were just discussing the matter recently and decided that it might be because they want to avoid the trouble and," she dropped her gaze, "the expense of giving me a proper Season, since there are already two eager suitors available."

"You have no other relatives whom you can turn to for help? Whoever inherited your father's title, for instance?"

"My father's title went to one of his cousins," Rebecca said softly, recalling the serious gentleman she'd seen only once when she was a child. After her parents had died, she'd been long gone from Scarsdale Manor before he'd arrived to claim his inheritance. "The new Earl of Scarsdale has no responsibility toward me, Mr. Neville. He's not my guardian, and yet it was he who provided me with my dowry when my aunt and uncle begged him to help. I thought it quite generous of him, really."

"I'm happy to hear that you've been shown some measure of kindness."

Rebecca allowed a smile. Mr. Neville's aggravation on her account was endearing. "Thank you." She looked at him with a steady gaze. "There's no need for you to pity me, you know. In fact, I would prefer that you don't. Going to the ball was a risk I was willing to take—quite possibly my only chance at securing a match on my own terms. And while getting caught wasn't part of my plan, I've no regrets."

The corner of his mouth edged upward. "Aside from getting shot."

Her smile broadened. "Yes. Aside from that." She paused. "I've been cowering away behind these ancient walls for two years, Mr. Neville. Time is passing me by, and before I know it, not even a doddering old man will want me."

"Pfft . . . nonsense," he said with a shake of his head.

Rebecca gave him a frank stare. "I'm not a debutante any longer. I'm three and twenty years of age and growing older every day."

Mr. Neville blinked. "You don't look it. In fact, if I may say so, I think you're absolutely stunning."

She felt her cheeks grow warm in response to his compliment. "Thank you for your kindness," she said, attempting a pleasant smile. If only he meant it, but she knew her own appearance all too well to think him sincere. Mr. Neville was trying to flatter her—quite possibly with his own motives in mind.

He regarded her pensively for a moment before saying, "I sympathize with you, Lady Rebecca. Your situation is far from a pleasant one. For what it's worth, I have to say that I admire your courage—and your creativity. It can't have been easy for you."

Relief washed over her. His acceptance of her in spite of what she'd done was invaluable, like a balm upon her tortured soul. "So," he continued, "you had a compelling reason to go to the ball in search of a husband—someone who can help you avoid marrying the men your aunt and uncle are favoring."

"All I wanted was a chance to make a better match for myself."

"An understandable desire," he said. He hesitated briefly before continuing. "Unfortunately, you aunt is not very fond of me, and frankly, I cannot blame her. Apparently she's inquired about me since meeting me the other evening and has discovered that I have very little to recommend myself at present."

"I see," Rebecca said. For the past two years she'd managed to keep her spirits high, yet in the space of only two days, she'd found all hope of a happy future dashed. It was hopeless to think she might end up married to a man as handsome as Mr. Neville. What reason would he possibly have to suffer the trouble of going up against her aunt and uncle? It would be a pointless endeavor for him to embark on, and given what he'd just said, he'd realized that marrying her would not be easy. Indeed, it would be impossible. In all likelihood, this would be the last time she'd ever see him.

A warm hand settled over hers, and Rebecca's head turned toward Mr. Neville. There was kindness to be found in the depths of his eyes, but there was also undeniable pity. How she longed for the heated gazes he'd given her the night of the ball.

"You mustn't lose hope," he told her as he gently squeezed her hand. "I'm sure there's a way out of this for you."

Pulling her hand away from his, she pasted a happy smile upon her face and rose to her feet, while he did the same. She would not allow anyone to know the depths of her longings or the pain in her heart—not when her fate was all but sealed. She would remain brave and stoic even though she felt helpless. "Perhaps there is, Mr. Neville, but not today. Now, I must ready myself as my aunt has requested and bid you a good day. Thank you so much for calling on me. It was most kind."

"It was the least I could do," he said. He paused a moment before saying, "Your aunt does not approve of me, but I have every intention of pressing my suit with your uncle."

Rebecca froze as the implication of his statement sank in, her heart thumping wildly at the very idea of it. He was going to try to marry her. There was only one question marring the happiness that filled her. *Why?* "Your determination in that regard makes me even more curious about your motive. And please don't tell me that no other woman will have you, for it is not a good enough reason."

"I . . . I can honestly tell you that I genuinely like you, Lady Rebecca. I think we would suit quite well."

His sheepishness attested to his unwillingness to tell her the entire truth. Certainly this was part of it, but it was not the driving force behind his decision. For whatever reason, Mr. Neville *had* to marry. He'd probably decided that she would make a fine candidate—a woman so desperate that she'd likely marry anyone just to escape her aunt and uncle's care. Now that Mr. Neville knew who her suitors were, he was probably more confident than ever that she would agree to become his wife if her uncle gave his approval. He wasn't wrong in that regard, but Rebecca wished that there was more to it than that—that he wanted her passionately. She sighed, giving herself a mental kick. She was too romantic by half if she imagined that she would ever be able to inspire such strong feelings in a rake.

But did it really matter? She couldn't deny the degree with which he drew her and how much she longed to be held by him, kissed by him. . . . Surely if they married, she would have at least that much. He was frowning at her, she noticed, and she became instantly aware that it was taking her too long to respond. Oh bother. "Speak to my uncle," she said. "And if he gives you his blessing, then I will agree to marry you."

A smile spread its way across his lips. Reaching for her hand, he raised it to his lips and kissed it, his eyes meeting hers as he did so. The effect made her stomach flutter, while an undeniable heat spread its way across her skin. If only she affected him the same way.

"Then by all means, wish me luck," he said.

She did, without hesitation and with all her heart.

Ten minutes later, Rebecca was still standing in the hallway when the door to her uncle's office opened and Mr. Neville stepped out, his face completely inscrutable. "Lady Rebecca," he said, smiling stiffly. "There is some business that I must attend to in London. I will return in two days with the hope of resolving everything then." Bowing, his eyes met hers. "Fret not, though. I believe everything will work out the way you had hoped."

And then he was gone, leaving Rebecca speechless.

"How did it go?" Laura asked when Rebecca returned to her room. Taking Rebecca's bonnet from her, the maid began boxing it away in the wardrobe.

"Topperly was harmless as always, while Grover was his usual, charming self," she said, her voice turning bitter at the mention of the duke. Tugging at the fingers of her gloves, she went to look out the window.

"And?" her maid inquired. "I sense there's something more."

Turning, Rebecca met Laura's gaze and immediately smiled. "Mr. Neville came to call on me as well."

"Did he now?"

Rebecca nodded. "Yes. In fact, he has asked Uncle for his blessing."

"And?" Laura asked, her hands clasped together at her chest and hope brimming in her eyes.

Perching herself on the windowsill, Rebecca returned her attention to the garden below.

"I've no idea. When he left, Mr. Neville mentioned something about some business that needed attending to first, though he did reassure me that everything would work out to my advantage." She met Laura's gaze. "What do you suppose it means?"

Laura shrugged. "I can't begin to imagine. Men's stuff, I suppose."

Rebecca frowned. "Perhaps you're right," she said. She was suddenly terribly worried that Mr. Neville would not succeed in his efforts and that her uncle would turn him away the next time he called. It was an outcome she ought to expect, yet she found herself praying that it would not be so—that she might be allowed some measure of happiness in her life. "It's just . . . I have a strong feeling that Aunt and Uncle are hoping to gain something from my marriage, though I've yet to determine what exactly. Aunt has made it clear to me that she wants me to marry the duke and that Mr. Neville will never do, so I fear that whatever

Mr. Neville's agreement may be with my uncle, it will come to naught."

"You mustn't distress yourself so much until there is cause to do so. It is clear that Mr. Neville is determined to win your hand. Why not give him a chance to prove himself without doubting his capabilities? Trust him, my lady. I'm sure he'll find a way to make you his. Come, why don't you work a bit on your watercolors? They always seem to lift your spirits whenever you're feeling out of sorts."

"You are by far the best maid a lady could wish for, Laura."

"Thank you, my lady." Walking over to the table, she poured a cup of tea and brought it over to Rebecca. "Two days isn't so long. He'll be back soon enough, and then everything will be resolved."

The thought of seeing Mr. Neville again filled Rebecca's mind, and she allowed a smile to surface as a warm feeling of anticipation settled over her. She looked forward to his next visit and to discovering what on earth he could possibly have done to change her uncle's mind.

Chapter 6

Thirteen thousand pounds. It was an outrageous sum of money by any standard, but Lord Grifton had shown no sign of remorse when he'd mentioned it to Daniel. He had simply spoken the number with a careless abandon as if it had been his due. And Daniel had accepted the challenge. He spurred his horse onward, determined to make it to London before it was too late in the day. How the hell he was going to obtain so much money when his own coffers were practically depleted he couldn't say. But he knew that he had to at least try, because if he was certain of anything at all, it was that he desperately wanted to make Lady Rebecca his.

Christ! The very thought of her having to share a bed with Topperly or Grover turned his stomach. When they'd walked in the garden at Kingsborough Hall, there had been a spark in her eyes, but that had significantly dwindled between then and today, as if she'd now resigned herself to her fate. Somehow he had to find the means to save her. Never in his life had he seen a woman more beautiful than she. He longed to run his fingers along her smooth skin, skin that looked tanned and healthy rather than pale and sickly, as was customary among the *ton*. And her hair! Lord, he couldn't ignore his constant urge to pull it free of its fastenings and watch it cascade over her shoulders . . . sleek as rich black satin.

But when he'd complimented her on her looks, she'd looked apprehensive. She'd made an attempt to cover it with a smile, but he'd seen the doubt in the depths of her eyes. For whatever reason, Lady Rebecca had no idea that Mother Nature had blessed her with an abundance of beauty. Her dark brown eyes framed by thick black lashes, high cheekbones, a delicate jawline and full lips that reminded him of rose petals should have been the envy of every woman. And then there was her figure. Daniel winced at the sudden discomfort that overtook him at just thinking about the fullness of her breasts, her slim waistline and the curve of her hips. But none of this would have been enough to inspire the sort of lust he felt for her had it not been for the clever rejoinders and wit that she'd shared with him at the ball. Since then, he'd been unable to get her out of his mind, the most alluring thoughts of her driving him mad with need.

Daniel was not so dishonest that he would lie to himself about his intentions regarding Lady Rebecca. As far as potential wives went, she was sure to make a good companion, but that said, there was absolutely no doubt that he meant to seduce her. To do so, however, he would have to convince her of how lovely she really was, because while she put on a confident front, Daniel sensed a great deal of uncertainty beneath the surface. He wondered what might have caused it and decided that her aunt and uncle were probably to blame—if not entirely, then at least in part. Daniel cursed the pair of them for trying to break a woman who should have been given the chance to shine like a star.

After spending much of the following day discussing the issue with his uncle, Daniel was forced to acknowledge that he'd get no help from that quarter. Burying his pride, he called on a few friends, hoping that one of them might be able to assist, but just as he'd thought, none of them was in possession of that kind of money.

It was early evening when Daniel eventually made his way over to his sister's residency on Berkeley Square and hurried up the steps of Chilton House.

"You look as though you've just raced across the English countryside," his sister said as she greeted him in the parlor. "But then I don't suppose I ought to be surprised. You always were a wild one."

"It's good to see you too, Audrey," Daniel said as he went to kiss her on the cheek. "Please forgive the late hour. I hope I'm not disturbing you or the rest of the family."

"Not at all, Daniel. Michael has yet to return from White's, and Ralph is in the nursery with his nanny. So you see, I am free to discuss whatever's on your mind, and besides, it's been far too long since I last saw you." Once she was seated, he placed himself in an armchair across from her. Pouring them each a cup of tea, she said, "To what do I owe the pleasure?"

"I don't suppose you've heard of Uncle's latest request?"

When she shook her head, he began relating everything that had happened over the past two weeks. She didn't interrupt him once, though her eyes did reflect both surprise and interest at certain parts of the story.

"He's given you quite the challenge," she said after taking a moment to digest it all. "And given your less than stellar reputation, I'm not sure how on earth you plan to fulfill his wishes. Then again, I suppose it was to be expected with you being the heir—you have to come up to scratch at some point." She spoke matter-of-factly and without sounding the least bit judgmental, for which Daniel was grateful.

"Yes, but to give me only a month is unreasonable, don't you think?"

At this she nodded. "Although I have to say that Lady Rebecca sounds like a lovely woman and just the sort who'd make you an excellent wife."

"I couldn't agree with you more," he said, "which is part of the reason why I'm here."

Audrey smiled. "I knew it wasn't merely because you missed me."

They'd never been very close, their lack of shared interests building rarely overlapping paths. Where Daniel had gotten into scrapes, his arm broken twice and his leg once, Audrey had always been the obedient daughter who'd sat quietly in a corner doing needlework, reading poetry or working on her watercolors. She played the pianoforte and the violin as well as any well-bred young lady ought to, and her manners were impeccable.

Daniel, on the other hand, had always been a bit rough around the edges—not that he didn't know how to behave, for he could be just as suave and elegant as the rest of them, perhaps more so when he set his mind to it. But when the chance to race or gamble or, heaven forbid, accept a dare to swim naked in the Serpentine after nightfall had presented itself, he'd always found it hard to resist.

And then of course there had been the women. He was young though and refused to apologize for his appetite in that department, particularly when he hadn't deflowered anyone and the women themselves had practically begged him to take them to bed. Yes, he'd flirted with a few young innocents, but it had only been for show, a bit of a kick in the shin for the *ton* that he so despised. When would they learn that they weren't in the least bit superior when it came to morality, gossiping about each other the way they did, committing adultery behind closed doors, snubbing anyone who didn't dress with just the right amount of flair or wore a color that had said *adieu* to fashion the previous week?

Never would be the answer to that question.

"The Griftons will only allow me to marry her if I am able to pay them thirteen thousand pounds."

At this, Audrey leaned back in her chair, her eyes fixed on Daniel. She took a deep breath, then exhaled it. "That is a rather exorbitant amount."

"I know. Naturally, I would never even think to ask you if I knew that I would be able to seek help elsewhere, but there is none other than you and Uncle who might be able to lend me such a large sum. I went to Uncle first, hoping that he would assist, since I'm trying to do as he asked, but he refused. He wants me to find a way to resolve the issue on my own, even if that means abandoning all hope of marrying Lady Rebecca, which I cannot."

"She has clearly affected you greatly," Audrey said, her words softly spoken and pensive.

"More than you can possibly know. Indeed, I cannot think of anything but her."

"And this eagerness of yours to make her your bride, is it for her benefit as much as it is yours?"

"Of course it is," Daniel said. "She'll be free from the Griftons and from having to marry Topperly or Grover."

"What I am asking, Daniel, is whether you have her best interests at heart and are doing this partly because you wish to rescue her, or if your only motivation is to maintain your allowance."

"I . . ." Daniel began. "I don't enjoy seeing her distressed and ill-treated. While it will not be a love match, her happiness is important to me, and I believe that I will make her happier than either Topperly or Grover."

Audrey nodded but said nothing further. Instead, she rose to her feet and walked across to her escritoire, took a seat, placed a piece of paper in front of her and dipped her quill in the ink pot. "Michael will never give you such a large sum," she said as she began to write. "He thinks you too untrustworthy, given your spending habits."

Daniel's heart fell. He liked his brother-in-law well enough and even admired the ease with which he seemed to run his estates. His sister had done well by marrying him, for he was the sort of man who took care of his finances, nurtured them and watched his investments profit.

After scribbling a few more lines, Audrey put her quill aside, folded the piece of paper neatly, then closed it with a seal depicting a bird in flight. She turned in her seat and offered the missive to Daniel. "But I will."

Dumbfounded by her generosity, Daniel slowly picked the paper from her hand.

"In my letter," she said, "I have assured the Griftons

that if they allow Lady Rebecca to marry you, I will supply them with the funds that they require."

Daniel stared at her. "I had no idea you were so independently wealthy."

She tilted her head. "Part of it is from my dowry, which was substantial. When Michael and I married, he and Uncle drew up a settlement that was entirely to my benefit. I was given full access to all of my funds and was granted additional pin money from Michael. Since I'm not a frivolous spender, I've set most of that aside with the intention of saving it for the future."

Daniel frowned. "Surely it is not necessary for you to be so careful."

Audrey chuckled lightly. "It is no secret that women are at a disadvantage in our day and age, forever under the foot of one man or other. Should Michael and I ever be blessed with a daughter, I would like to leave her with something that belongs to nobody but her—to do with as she pleases. Which is why you must promise that you will repay this loan to me one day."

Daniel stared down at the folded piece of paper. He swallowed hard, his chest tightening with the understanding of the sacrifice his sister was making on his behalf, and the extraordinary level of trust she was placing in him. "I will not fail you," he said. "You have my word on it."

Chapter 7

"Would you care for a game of cards, my lady?" Laura asked two days later.

Rebecca shrugged. She'd been feeling miserable all day. Not just from her shoulder wound, which still pained her, but from the hopelessness she felt at the thought of what awaited her. Mr. Neville still hadn't returned, and Rebecca had begun losing hope that he would.

Laura, who was making a clear effort to be more positive, had told her that he could have been delayed by any number of things. But even if he did return, who was to say that her aunt and uncle wouldn't turn him away? They might do it just to spite her. She certainly wouldn't put it past them—especially not her aunt. She could well imagine her taking perverse pleasure in seeing Rebecca married off to an old relic. It was disheartening.

"How about a play?" Laura continued. "We could reenact *Twelfth Night*. I know how much you love that piece."

Rebecca forced a smile. "True. It always makes me

laugh." She paused as she met Laura's hopeful expression, then nodded. "Very well, *Twelfth Night* it is."

They had just started on act five, scene one, with Laura saying, "Be quiet, people. Wherefore throng you hither?" when a soft tapping sound came from the window. Both women turned to stare. "Did you hear that, my lady?" Laura asked.

"It's probably just a bird," Rebecca said, eager to get on with the play. They were getting to her favorite part. "To fetch my poor distracted husband hence," she continued. "Let us —"

Tap, tap, tap.

"Whatever it is, it's really quite distracting," Rebecca said, hands folded in her lap as she stared toward the window. Since it was late evening and dark outside, it was impossible for her to discern the source of the noise from her current position, especially with oil lanterns and a fire lighting her room.

"I'll just have a look, shall I?" Laura said as she walked across to the window and looked out. She must have been unable to see anything, for she leaned closer, so close that her face was almost pressed up against the glass. There was a beat, and then she suddenly pulled back with a shriek.

Intrigued, Rebecca sat up a bit straighter. "What is it, Laura? What did you see?"

Laura turned toward her, ashen-faced. "Do you believe in ghosts, my lady?" she asked, her voice shaky.

Rebecca frowned. "Of course not, Laura." Determined to investigate, she rose and tightened the sash of her dressing gown. "What is it with you? Ghosts indeed."

"Well, then perhaps you'd care to explain how a man might be levitating outside your window."

"A man *what*?" Skeptical but unwilling to dismiss Laura's claim, considering how shaken she looked, Rebecca approached the window. She was certain that there had to be a logical explanation for this, but if there wasn't and it was indeed a ghost, then she had every intention of seeing it for herself.

"Do be careful, my lady," Laura warned as Rebecca went closer.

It wasn't until she was all the way to the window and blocking some of the light from the room with her body that Rebecca finally caught a glimpse of a blurry face. She flinched a little but quickly regained her composure and continued her approach until the face sharpened around a pair of familiar eyes. Lord help her if it wasn't Mr. Neville. How he'd gotten up there she dared not imagine, but her heart made a funny little leap at finding him returned. He had not forgotten about her after all.

Feeling almost giddy with the pleasure of her discovery, she undid the latch and opened the window just enough for her to pop her head outside. "Good evening, Mr. Neville," she said, amazed by how nonchalant her voice sounded—as if his standing there perched on one of the last rungs of a rickety ladder had been the most natural thing in the world. "How are you doing?"

"Quite well," he said, smiling up at her. "As you can see, I'm having a bit of an adventure."

"Oh, is that what this is?" A bit of choked-back laughter from below drew her attention to two men holding the ladder steady. "And I see that you've brought friends with you."

"Mr. Shaw and his son Gerard," Mr. Neville said as

he let go of the ladder with one hand and waved toward the men below.

"Pleased to meet you," Rebecca called down to them.

"Shh!" Mr. Neville quieted her. "It took a lot of effort for me to accomplish this feat. I'd rather not ruin it so soon by being found out."

"Is that so?" Rebecca asked. She finally allowed herself a smile—one of pure mischief. "And what exactly would you expect me to do upon discovering a dangerous intruder at my window?"

"Dangerous, eh?" One of Mr. Neville's eyebrows shot up.

"Terrifying," Rebecca said, her face once again serious to underscore the sarcasm.

"I don't suppose a cup of tea is likely?"

The absurdity of Mr. Neville standing there on that ladder in the cold, looking up at her imploringly as he asked to be invited for tea, made it impossible for Rebecca to keep a straight face. Grinning back at him, she shook her head with resignation. "What about Mr. Shaw and his son? What will they do while they wait for you?"

The look on Mr. Neville's face suggested that this was a part of the plan he hadn't considered. Turning slightly, he looked down at their upturned faces. "I don't suppose I could convince you to come back and fetch me in an hour?" he asked.

"Add a couple of shillings and we'll be happy to," Mr. Shaw told him.

Mr. Neville looked back at Rebecca. "Move aside, please, my lady. I'm coming in."

Given his size, Rebecca had to admit that she was

quite impressed with how nimbly Mr. Neville entered her room through the window, landing on his feet with the stealth of a cat.

"My lady, this is highly irregular," Laura said from somewhere behind Rebecca's right shoulder. "I realize that you mean to marry him, but to invite a gentleman into your bedchamber . . . it's scandalous, not to mention the punishment that will likely befall us all if your aunt and uncle find out."

Rebecca turned toward her maid with a smile. "But they won't find out, Laura. Besides, this is hardly any worse than you suggesting that I drugged you so I could escape your care and attend the ball. Yes, it may be unconventional, it's true, but you're here to protect my virtue."

It took a moment, but Laura eventually nodded. She had good reason to react the way she did, Rebecca realized, for not only was she not acquainted with Mr. Neville but, as she'd correctly said, having a gentleman of any kind visit an unmarried lady in her bedchamber was unseemly, and a rake was far worse, regardless of whether or not a chaperone was present. Of course, Rebecca's circumstances were a bit more unusual than most, and Laura knew that. Rebecca was well aware that Laura would do whatever she could to protect her, but she also knew that Laura wanted her to be happy. "It's all right," Rebecca told her. "But now that the gentleman is here and with no means of leaving until his companions return with the ladder, perhaps I ought to introduce you. Laura, this is Mr. Neville." Turning to her guest, Rebecca added, "Mr. Neville, I'd like for you to meet my màid, Laura. Had it not been for her, you and I would never have met."

With warmth in his eyes and an inviting smile, Mr. Neville stepped toward Laura. He reached for her hand, bowed over it and placed a kiss upon her knuckles. Straightening, he said, "It is a great pleasure to make your acquaintance, Laura."

Rebecca hid a grin. She'd never seen her maid turn so red before. Of course, she couldn't blame her for it. Mr. Neville was a striking man indeed. Swallowing hard as she fought to ignore the flutter in her stomach, Rebecca turned away from him and headed toward a small table with two chairs. This was ridiculous. She'd always considered herself the reasonable sort, but lately she'd been getting all flustered whenever Mr. Neville was near. Looking for a distraction, she started busying herself with the tea. "Was the front door too obvious a choice for you?" she asked, desperate for the stability a bit of light conversation might offer.

He didn't answer her immediately but came to stand beside her instead—a little closer than what most would consider appropriate. With a reprimanding cough from Laura, he distanced himself a little.

Rebecca pressed her lips together to stop from laughing as she pushed one newly filled cup across the table before pouring the next. "I must admit that I'd begun to think you'd never return, yet here you are, stealing through my window in the dark."

"That is because there is something I must tell you," he said.

Rebecca tilted her face toward him, her hand still resting on the teacup. "Why do I get the feeling that things did not go as you had planned in London?"

"Because your instinct isn't wrong—as unfortunate as that is."

Pushing her cup slowly across the table, Rebecca lowered herself onto one of the empty seats, while Mr. Neville did the same. She took a sip of her tea. "I'm sorry," she said, even though *sorry* didn't come close to describing the way she presently felt. "I don't know what you were hoping to achieve by going to Town, but I do hope you will tell me your reason for doing so."

Crossing his arms, Mr. Neville rested them on the table and leaned toward her. "I know I allowed you to believe that all would be well when we last spoke . . . but now . . ." He shook his head and sat back against his chair. "It isn't going to be as simple as I had hoped."

Rebecca blinked—once, twice and then again. "I don't . . ." she managed.

"I paid a visit to your uncle this afternoon," Mr. Neville said, his eyes never leaving Rebecca's. "It appears the Duke of Grover is quite determined to have you."

"But when you were last here, you said you believed that everything would work out," Rebecca said. She was doing her best to remain calm even though her heart was now fluttering wildly in her chest. "What's changed?" The fear of knowing was there, creeping along her every nerve as it made her tremble. She wasn't used to being afraid of anything, usually avoiding the state altogether by taking matters into her own hands, yet it had just become alarmingly clear that the hope of happiness she'd dared allow herself was being torn to pieces. "Tell me," she said, bracing herself for the worst. As reluctant as she was to hear the truth, she needed to know precisely why her uncle had turned down Mr. Neville's suit.

With his jaw set in a firm line and his eyes boring into hers, Mr. Neville said, "They are, in effect, auctioning you off to the highest bidder."

"I'm sorry—what?" Surely her ears deceived her. Not even her aunt and uncle could be that callous.

"The Griftons," Mr. Neville said, "are eager to get as much out of your marriage as they possibly can. They know that Topperly and Grover are both quite desperate to have you, so they're biding their time, I believe, until they've achieved the highest possible sum in your stead." He leaned forward a little. "When I met with your uncle last, he explained that Topperly has offered him ten thousand pounds and Grover twelve thousand in exchange for your hand. Additionally, they are both willing to fund the renovations Roselyn Castle requires."

Rebecca gasped, astonished by the amounts and the audacity.

"When I went to London, it was to procure the necessary funds required to ensure your hand. Doing so took a little time, and in the end my efforts were to no avail; Grover increased his offer to fifteen thousand this morning." Mr. Neville clenched his jaw. He looked truly vexed. "I'm sorry, my lady, but I cannot compete with that, not without my uncle's assistance, and he has refused to get involved."

In spite of everything, Rebecca couldn't help but smile. Here was a man with no obligation toward her whatsoever, who had done as much as he possibly could to try and save her. "Thank you," she said. "You have done more for me than most would have done had they been in your shoes. You are a true friend, and I will never forget your kindness."

Reaching across the table, Mr. Neville placed his hand upon hers—a startling gesture, since neither of them was wearing gloves. The spark that lit in her chest was instantaneous, bursting outward in hot little embers that raced across her skin until she felt herself trembling. Instinct told her to pull away, yet she couldn't seem to move, his gaze holding hers with deep intensity. "Come to Gretna Green with me," he whispered. "Let me save you from this nightmare."

It was tempting, especially when he looked at her in such a beseeching way—as if she was the most incredible woman he'd ever set eyes upon, as if he would love and cherish her forever . . . as if she stood apart from all the other women he'd ever been with. This, of course, was fantasy, and a distant voice warned her of it. He was not the sort of man who would ever be happy with one single woman, no matter what he might say, and though he'd been nothing but pleasant toward her, she feared he might be employing his skill with her right now in an attempt to manipulate her. She could not trust him, but she was still curious. "Why are you really so eager to marry me, Mr. Neville? I do not accept that it is merely because no other virtuous woman will go near you, for that is not a proper reason. It doesn't explain your haste."

He released her hand and leaned back against his chair, leaving her with an unpleasant feeling of neglect. "To be perfectly honest, my aunt and uncle request that I abandon my rakish ways, all gambling included, and get myself married. It seems they believe that a wife would make me more responsible."

Rebecca stared back at him for a second. Realizing that he was indeed being quite serious, she started to laugh—the sort of laugh that made the stomach hurt and tears well in the eyes. He watched her with a look of befuddlement that only made her laugh even more. When she eventually got herself under some measure of control, she managed, "And you decided that I should be the one to help you accomplish that? A woman who has pretended to be mad for two years in order to avoid marriage? One who climbs hedges dressed in an evening gown so she can attend a ball uninvited? Forgive me, Mr. Neville, but surely you can see how unlikely that would be." Pressing her lips together, she forced back her mirth.

"I suppose you have a point there," he admitted. "But as I've told you before, finding a wife isn't so easy for me. Nobody wants to associate with me, let alone allow their daughter to bear my name." He shook his head, a few stray locks brushing his forehead. "In hindsight, I should have behaved better in my younger years, but regrettably, I can't undo all of that now."

There was so much remorse in the way he said it that Rebecca felt her heart swell for him. "I know that you're not as bad as they say. What you did for Miss Brighton, for instance, and the way you refrained from attempting anything untoward with me at the ball when you had the opportunity to do so confirms that. It's also possible that you think yourself capable of putting your rakehell ways behind you. I just don't believe that your attempt to do so will last."

"You doubt my resolve. Why?" He sounded hurt. "If Kingsborough could do it, then why wouldn't you think me capable?"

"Because he has incentive," she said, trying to be honest in spite of how guilty she felt as she looked back into his wounded eyes. "His entire family depends on him doing what is right, of him behaving properly. What incentive do you have other than that your aunt and uncle wish it?"

Mr. Neville clenched his jaw. His eyes grew dark, and when he spoke again, there was deep resentment in his voice. "Because they'll cut me off without a penny if I don't come up to scratch."

Rebecca's jaw dropped. Finally, it all made sense. She sank back against her seat. "Just as I feared, you were going to use me to your own advantage."

"As if it's any worse than what you've been contemplating—marriage to a man of your own choosing so you can escape the suitors your aunt and uncle have in mind for you."

"Of course it's worse," she said, both stunned and disappointed at discovering that he hadn't been sincere in his pursuit of her, although deep inside she'd known he would never have considered her an option if he'd had a choice. "I am not attempting to marry for material gain, Mr. Neville, but to avoid a life that I would not be able to bear living. Money will be of no consequence to me if I am unhappily wed and forced to suffer the marriage bed with a man old enough to be my grandfather." She caught herself, realizing that her voice had risen in frustration. Taking a deep breath, she attempted to speak calmly. "But by marrying you instead . . ." Dear Lord, she dared not contemplate the heartache that marrying Mr. Neville might bring. With the effect that he was having on her this early on, she feared it would only be a matter of time before she fell in love with him, a man whom she doubted would ever accept the affections of only one woman. Eventually he would stray, and once he did, it would break her heart. "You will have accomplished the task set for you by your aunt and uncle, while I will have exchanged one predicament for another."

"How so?"

Was he serious?

"Because the only reason you wish to marry me is for financial gain."

"And the only reason you wish to marry me is so you do not have to marry Topperly or Grover," Mr. Neville insisted. "You may wish to pretend that one reason is more noble than the other, but I disagree."

She would not argue with him, for in a sense he had a point. Furthermore, he did not have the advantage of knowing her heart's desire or the pain she was currently feeling at being equated with a bag of gold. She'd allowed herself to imagine that he looked at her with appreciation and some measure of desire, but all it had been was greed—not for her but for the allowance that she would secure for him if they married. Worst of all was the fact that she still wanted him as desperately as a woman lost in a desert longed for water.

Feigning indifference, she said, "I will elope with you on one condition," she said.

His eyes widened with expectancy; they were dark, so dark she felt sure she'd be able to stare into their depths indefinitely without growing tired. She licked her lips as she pondered her decision and then finally said, "You must convince me that I will never look back on doing so with regret. You are young and healthy, Mr. Neville, so I have every reason to believe that our marriage will be a lengthy one—one I won't escape anytime soon should I accept your offer." She paused for a moment, unwilling to give away too much of her concerns, as she feared doing so would suggest deeper feelings than she was willing to admit. But she had to know if he cared enough about her to at least try to have a marriage based on trust and loyalty, so she said, "Can you assure me that we will be happy together?"

He looked perplexed. "You are asking me to promise you the impossible when I have no inkling of what the future may hold for us."

"No," she said, all seriousness. "I am asking you to stop being Mr. Neville the rake in favor of just being yourself. I believe I've glimpsed that man a few times already, and I have decided that I rather enjoy his company. So if you can bring him to the surface more, then I believe our marriage will stand a chance."

He frowned. "I'm not sure I understand. Being a rake and being myself are one and the same thing."

"Are you certain about that?" she asked. She had little evidence to the contrary other than that he'd confessed to embellishing the truth where his past exploits were concerned. But then of course there was the extent to which he'd gone in order to marry her. Yes, he stood to gain from their union, but instinct told her that he'd done it just as much to save her. Squaring him with a steady gaze, she added, "I realize that I have few choices available to me, Mr. Neville, but be that as it may, I have always hoped to marry a man who would remain faithful to me. To be sure, I have no reason to expect such loyalty from you . . . indeed, I imagine the task may prove difficult, but I would like to know that the risk I'd be taking in accepting your offer—the risk of discovery as we make our escape would be worth it and that you'll at least try."

Silence settled upon them for what seemed like an eternity. Their eyes locked unflinchingly on each other, but Mr. Neville was the first to look away. Pushing back from the table, he stood up. "Thank you for the tea, my lady. You've given me a great deal to think about." He looked at her for a long moment before saying, "I will call on you again tomorrow if that is agreeable with you."

Rebecca nodded, a slight smile tugging at her lips. She didn't betray any of the overwhelming feelings that were building inside her as she rose from her own chair and walked across to the window with him, then simply said, "Yes, I would like that."

Chapter 8

I will elope with you on one condition.

The words resonated inside Daniel's head as he lay in bed later that night, picturing Lady Rebecca in his mind's eye. What a lovely creature she was, and not the least bit shy about speaking her mind. She'd told him honestly about the reservations she had about becoming his wife, but she'd also shown awareness for his true nature—a gentler, more considerate side that he kept hidden from most behind his roguish façade.

When his mother had cuckolded his father and fled to America, the devastation her selfish wrongdoing had wrought had awarded Daniel with a front-row seat to the more negative aspects of love. The day after she'd left, his father had enlisted in the army without further thought for his son and had been killed in action shortly thereafter.

That was what love had done to Daniel. It had destroyed his family and taken away both of his parents. He'd have been a fool to fall victim to it, so he'd resolved to live a life of reckless abandon instead, enjoying life's pleasures without emotional attachment, choosing to live from one day to the next on the allowance that his aunt and uncle had provided for him.

He didn't want to lose that comfortable lifestyle. If he could only convince Lady Rebecca to marry him, then he was sure they could live happily together. She'd made it clear that she wanted a respectable marriage with a husband who would remain loyal to her. She'd also made it clear that she didn't think Daniel capable of being that man, but she was wrong about that. Lady Rebecca was exactly the sort of woman who would be able to hold his interest. She was smart and funny, engaging to talk to . . . exceedingly beautiful. If there was any woman of whom he wouldn't tire, then it was her. He would not be able to offer her love, since that would mean letting down his guard and becoming vulnerable, but he would be able to make her smile. And with time, he'd prove himself worthy of her by doing precisely what she didn't think him capable of—staying faithful to her, and her alone.

Happy with his plan, Daniel climbed the rungs of the ladder as it bowed to his weight the following evening. Reaching the window, he tapped three times and waited. From within, he could see a blurry figure moving through a yellow glow of light toward him. A click sounded, the window opened and Lady Rebecca's smiling face came into view. God, she was beautiful.

"Right on time," she said as he climbed over the windowsill.

"Like thieves, we rakes are well aware of the importance of punctuality. As much as a second too late or too early could lead to unpleasant consequences."

Seeing Laura, he nodded his head in her direction. "Good evening."

"And like thieves, rakes take great pleasure in stealing that which does not belong to them," the maid said, her eyes locking with his in a silent acknowledgement of the danger he posed to her mistress.

So she hadn't warmed to him yet. Ah well. She would come around sooner or later, but for now, he decided to shock her instead. Without looking away, he told her seriously, "I can assure you, Laura, that when it comes to me, the lady takes equal pleasure in giving me what I desire."

Laura's jaw dropped. "You . . . you . . . cad!" she stammered, her hands waving about in a mad gesture, as if she hoped to somehow shoo him from the room.

Rebecca, on the other hand, was giggling wildly. "You mustn't tease her like that, Mr. Neville. It's terribly inconsiderate of you."

Whoever said anything about teasing?

"My apologies," he said with a slight bow in Laura's direction. "I meant no harm—truly. You have my word that I will be on my best behavior, but what you said led to the possibility of a rejoinder too tempting to be ignored. Can you forgive me?"

Eyes moving from Lady Rebecca to him and back again, Laura looked undecided. She eventually nodded, much to his relief, and took her seat in the corner, where, picking up her needlework, she looked positively oblivious to anything going on around her. Daniel knew better though. He'd pressed his luck with the joke and would not risk jeopardizing his chance of enjoying Lady Rebecca's company any further. No; he must behave as the perfect gentleman even if he was tempted to do otherwise, and Lord help him if he wasn't tempted.

How he longed to run his hands along the edge of Lady Rebecca's shoulders, to plant a row of kisses across the back of her neck as he eased the sleeves of her gown down over her arms, exposing her breasts. He could well imagine how they would feel in the palms of his hands, had considered it repeatedly since making her acquaintance . . . thoughts that led to restless nights of aching need and unfulfilled pleasure.

Clenching his hands, he made a stoic attempt to ignore the stirring desire that threatened. He could not allow it to show—would not embarrass himself or her in that way. So he followed her quickly to the table and chairs instead and promptly sat, removing all evidence from view. Belatedly, he recognized his mistake. A gentleman did not take his seat before a lady. Unfortunately, he'd been left with little choice. He moved with the intention to get back up, but before he could manage it, she'd thankfully taken her seat as well.

"My apologies," he said. "That was ill mannered of me."

Saying nothing to the contrary, she simply began pouring the tea. "Think nothing of it." Her voice was sweet like music when she finally spoke, with that trace of humor that always made her tone so delightfully light. He loved listening to her speak. "In case you haven't noticed, I'm not much of a stickler when it comes to propriety or etiquette, though your apology is much appreciated." The left corner of her mouth drew up as it always did when she was speaking her mind with mischief.

"Then you will not mind if I dance on the table or swing from the rafters?" he asked, goading her.

"Not in the least, Mr. Neville. On the contrary, I would probably join you."

He laughed at the image that presented and shook his head with wonderment. "Lady Rebecca. Of all the women I've ever known, you are by far the most charming and memorable."

She'd been taking a sip of her tea as he'd said it and now lowered her cup slowly to the table while her eyes remained locked with his. It was impossible for him to look away, not that he wanted to do so in the least, for it was almost as if she was mesmerized by something—something that made him wonder what exactly she might be seeing. The good in him, he hoped. For he *was* good, deep down beneath the façade he'd erected to ward off pain and heartache. Yes, he'd lived a tainted life, always trying to escape the fate that had been his father's. If he could just enjoy himself and have some fun without getting close to anyone, then he could keep himself and his heart safe from harm.

But there was something about this woman, an openness and freedom of spirit that made him want to leap blindly into marriage with her, knowing full well what the risks would be. And the risks would be massive, for he liked her well enough already, enjoyed her company more than that of anyone else he'd ever met before, and knew they could easily be friends . . . lovers . . . and with time . . . so much more. The notion was not without danger, yet if he married as he had to, then he couldn't envision himself with anyone else. Only Lady Rebecca would do.

"Thank you," she said, her voice a little breathless and a great deal surprised.

Recalling her reaction when he'd told her she was stunning, he suspected that praising her for her looks would lead him nowhere. Judging from her present response, however, he deduced that she appreciated being admired for how distinctive she was. Perhaps she was self-conscious about it? He decided to broach the issue gently. "I've noticed many women over the years, Lady Rebecca, but the truth of it is that most of them bore me."

"Do go on, Mr. Neville," she said, leaning forward a little as she cradled her teacup between her hands.

Pleased to have gotten her attention, Daniel said, "They are all the same in every conceivable way, most of them without a thought of their own."

Lady Rebecca scrunched her nose. "That is not very flattering."

"It wasn't meant to be." He smiled conspiratorially at her. "You see, what oftentimes occurs is that one of these women, whether she be a debutante or older, becomes so immensely popular that everyone else starts to mirror the way she is dressed, how she sets her hair, the places she enjoys frequenting, along with the things she says. They are like sheep, if you must know, and not the least bit unique.

"You, on the other hand . . ." Reaching across the table, he took her hand in his, just as he'd done the previous evening, only this time, he brushed the pad of his thumb against it and was rewarded as an undeniable spark ignited in her eyes. "You are so different in every way, from your looks to your daring personality, and I simply cannot help but be fascinated by it."

A flush crept over her skin, and he heard her breath catch. Her hand trembled ever so slightly and she slowly lowered her lashes, her gaze fixed somewhere on the table. "There are those who would disagree," she said.

"There always are, and if you ask me, they can all go hang."

She laughed at that, but not wholeheartedly. Something—some niggling insecurity, no doubt—was holding her back, reminding him that this was a subject with which she wasn't comfortable. "I must confess that I've always wished I looked like all the other women so I wouldn't stand apart as much as I do."

A deep sigh escaped Daniel. He'd suspected as much, but having her confirm it and know that a woman of her great beauty would ever doubt herself to such a degree made his heart ache. "I can think of no greater pity than for you to look like all the rest when you are as perfect as you are. You may think that I am saying this to flatter you, but that is not the case. I am saying it because it is the truth—at least in my eyes."

He squeezed her hand a little and was touched to find her eyes glistening as she stared back at him from across the table. "Thank you," she said.

They sat like that for another moment until the silence between them grew heavy, at which point Daniel pulled his hand away from hers, leaving him bereft. It was not a pleasant feeling in the least, and one he quickly hoped to disband by finding something else to talk about. She beat him to it, however, asking plainly, "How does a man go about becoming a rake anyway?"

Having just taken a sip of his tea, Daniel almost choked. "Excuse me?"

"I mean, is it something he decides to become from one day to the next the way other men might choose a profession, or is it something that happens gradually?"

Why, the little minx. If she wasn't giving him the most mischievous smile at the moment, then he wasn't sure what was happening. Clearly she'd returned to her bold and adventurous self.

Daniel decided not to point out how irregular such a question was when posed by a young lady, since that would only be stating the obvious, so he said instead, "I believe every man's situation is different, but I can tell you that in my case, it was a night of heavy drinking that led me down that path. That and a bleak mood."

She nodded thoughtfully, as if this made perfect sense to her. "I imagine such a state would prompt anyone to seek comfort in some way or other, and I suppose that seeking the company of women is as good a way as any. It's certainly better for your health than excessive eating. That is of course unless you happen to catch the French disease the way my cousin Vincent apparently did. He eventually died from it, you know." She narrowed her eyes and then posed the most damning question of all. "You don't have the French disease by any chance? Do you, Mr. Neville?"

Daniel gaped at her. Of all the brazen things to ask a man. "No," he finally managed. "No, I do not."

"You're quite sure?" she pressed, her face perfectly serious. "From what I understand, it can sneak up on you—catch you by surprise."

"How on earth would you know that?" He just couldn't help but ask. The conversation was far too peculiar for him not to.

"Well, when it became clear that Vincent had taken a turn for the worse, my mother took me aside one day and explained what had happened to him. I was only thirteen years of age at the time and had not imagined that a man and a woman would do more than hold hands with one another or perhaps steal an occasional kiss. As you can imagine, my mother's talk put fear in my young mind—the very idea that getting too close to a man could actually result in death was indeed quite frightening."

Daniel blinked. He could not believe that they were having this discussion. "And er . . . does the idea of being . . . close with a man still terrify you?"

"Not as long as I have every confidence that the man in question is a gentleman, for you see, Lady Trapleigh has informed me that if he is, he will have taken certain measures to prevent catching the disease." She frowned, her nose scrunching quite adorably as she did so. She then said, "Though I can't begin to imagine what such measures might entail. I believe I should have asked her to be more specific when we spoke on the subject."

Bloody hell.

"I think perhaps she was trying to spare your sensibilities," Daniel said.

"Perhaps you're right." She took a sip of her tea and leaned back in her seat. When she met his gaze again, there was great intensity to be found in her eyes. "You are not exactly a gentleman, Mr. Neville, for you are considered a rake, and yet you have behaved very gentlemanly toward me, for which I am grateful. When thinking logically about the matter, I must deduce that you are a man of great experience, and as such, you must have taken precautions to ensure that you would not risk your health while entertaining your paramours. Am I correct?"

Daniel nodded numbly. This visit was by far the

most unusual one he'd ever enjoyed. The topic, not to mention the implication of everything she was saying, was completely outrageous, and yet he liked her better for it. There was something to be said for being honest and direct, for speaking one's mind, something that most people were too cowardly to do. Not Lady Rebecca though. She had more courage than any other woman he'd known, and it was intoxicating.

"Well then," she said. "If I do decide to take you up on your offer of elopement, I'll have nothing to worry about."

Daniel couldn't help himself. Reaching out, he cupped her chin with his hand and ran his fingers gently back and forth against the smooth skin there, marveling at the way her breath hitched in response and the rosy hue that appeared upon her cheeks. "On the contrary," he murmured, "you have every reason to look forward to it with great anticipation, for I promise you that it will be marvelous."

Her blush deepened, and he removed his hand and rose.

She followed him to the window and watched as he climbed back out. Pausing on the ladder, he met her gaze. "I have enjoyed your company immensely this evening, my lady." And he meant every word of it. "I shall return again tomorrow at the same hour."

Rebecca waited until he was on the ground, hoping that he might look back at her one last time, but he didn't—he just turned his back and walked away, fading into the darkness until there was no trace of him left.

"You like him a great deal, my lady. I can see it in your eyes."

Startled from her reverie, Rebecca spun around to find Laura standing close. Denying it would be pointless, since Laura had already guessed the truth, so Rebecca nodded and said, "I must admit that I do—so much it frightens me."

"Is that why you tried to shock him?" Laura asked, her round cheeks dimpling as she spoke.

"You heard that, did you?" Rebecca took a deep breath and walked across to her bed, the mattress sagging as she flopped down onto it. Covering her face with the palms of her hands, she groaned, "Why didn't you stop me? I can't believe I said all those things to him. The man must think me completely addled, not to mention inappropriately forward, but once I got started I couldn't seem to stop."

"Hush now. I don't believe Mr. Neville's so easy to scare off. If anything, I think he quite enjoyed himself—his face seemed to radiate with enthusiasm. And the way he was looking at you the entire time he was here . . . why, I do believe it would be a chore for anyone to try and change his mind about marrying you. The only thing that remains to be seen is whether or not you'll accept and elope with him."

Lowering her hands, Rebecca said, "You know that I will, Laura. The alternative would be unthinkable."

Chapter 9

When Daniel returned to Roselyn Castle the following evening, it was with renewed determination. Tonight he would make another effort at convincing her to place her trust in him. He knew that she had reasons to be apprehensive, not only because of his past but also because of what would probably happen to her should they get caught before they were married. The Griftons were not forgiving people and would likely punish her severely for thwarting their wishes yet again. It was imperative that he prevent such an outcome, not only because of his own pride but also because of a deep need to make her happy. He couldn't say precisely when he'd started to care so much about her well-being. In all likelihood, he'd fallen for her the moment they'd met, drawn to her company by her spark. But the emotions that now shot through him at the thought of her in the arms of any other man were intense—a need to both protect and possess that had developed gradually since the night of the ball. Since then, his longing for her had not diminished but grown, until he found himself tossing and turning at night, restless with thoughts of loving her the way she deserved to be loved.

Tapping gently on the window, he waited impatiently for it to open, but when it finally did, it was Laura who greeted him rather than the lady herself—surely not a good sign. "May I come in?" he asked.

Laura nodded. "I think she could do with a bit of cheering up."

Daniel paused a moment, wary of the state in which he would find the otherwise vibrant Lady Rebecca. He would do anything to make her smile again, and without further hesitation, he quickly swung himself through the window and signaled for Mr. Shaw and his son to fall back.

He then looked around the room in search of the lady in question, except she was nowhere to be found. Puzzled, he turned to Laura, who nodded toward a massive wardrobe. "She sits in there from time to time when she wants to be alone with her thoughts." He moved toward it, but Laura stayed him with her hand and said, "You ought to know that things have progressed. His Grace, the Duke of Grover, has gained the right to marry her."

Fresh rage swept through Daniel. "Not if I can help it," he muttered. He then stepped toward the piece of furniture that Lady Rebecca had retreated to and knocked gently on the door. When no answer came, he slowly eased it open.

It was dark inside but not overly full of clothes, making it easier for him to spot the slight figure of Lady Rebecca as she huddled against one corner. Crouching down, Daniel silently pushed a box aside and eased himself into the narrow space beside her. He then pulled on the door until it remained just slightly ajar and the light within had been diminished to a murky blackness.

"It's good to see you again," she said, her voice dismal when compared with the happiness it usually contained. "Has Laura told you the news?"

Daniel's greatest desire in that instant was to restore her characteristic joy and laughter. He hated seeing her like this, but he could not blame her; she had good reason to feel miserable. "I want to help you," he said, preparing to fight for her. "Will you allow me to do so?"

A beat of silence followed, and then she said, "I fear it may be too late. My aunt and uncle have already accepted the Duke of Grover as my future husband. The lawyers will be stopping by the day after tomorrow to handle the settlement, and then we're off to London to announce the engagement. It is all settled."

Fumbling about, he found her arm and followed the length of it with his fingers until he reached her hand. Wrapping his fingers around it, he gave it a gentle squeeze that he hoped would reassure her of his friendship and his willingness to assist her in any way possible. She didn't pull away, but he heard a sharp intake of breath the moment he touched her. Was that a good or a bad thing? he wondered. It was difficult to tell.

"It is not too late until you speak your vows," he said as his thumb brushed back and forth against her soft skin. He heard her swallow, her breathing grow a little deeper, and he couldn't help but smile. He'd been aware of the effect he had on her a few times before, but he had buried his own urges because he'd wanted her to think well of him. This was still the case, of course, especially if he was going to convince her to come with him, but it also supplied him with the confidence he needed to press his case. "Elope with me to Scotland. I'll marry you, and your aunt and uncle won't ever be able to hurt you like this again. You'll be under my protection."

Mr. Neville's willingness to risk scandal on her account touched her heart, and whatever qualms she'd previously had about accepting him were long gone now that she'd become affianced to the Duke of Grover—a man fifty-five years her senior who'd alluded to some most explicit bedroom activities that had made her stomach churn.

On the other hand, considering what she knew about Mr. Neville, she still wasn't entirely sure she could trust him, particularly when it came to her dowry. All of it would become his property if a settlement wasn't drawn up, and it wouldn't be, not if they eloped. In fact, he would be able to disappear with her five thousand pounds the moment they were wed—a possibility that ought not to be dismissed, considering that he was marrying her for money to begin with.

All prospects considered, however, it was a chance she was willing to take, because if he *did* stand by her, she sensed that their marriage would be a happy one, filled with friendship, laughter and . . . passion, if the effect she had on him equaled the one he had on her. Even now, as he barely touched her, she could feel a flush creeping across her skin and her breasts beginning to tighten. With the very surreal feeling that she was leaping blindly into an abyss, Rebecca whispered, "I will accept your offer, Mr. Neville, if you will grant me a favor."

"Anything—just name it."

"That Laura is allowed to come with us. I won't leave her behind."

"Yes, of course," he said, his voice low and thick in

the darkness. Dear Lord, she didn't have to see him to know that the heat radiating from his eyes would probably burn her to cinders. "You've made me extremely happy, my lady, and I will endeavor not to disappoint. The last thing I want is for you to regret your decision."

He leaned closer, the length of him pressed up against her, the light stubble on his chin and jaw brushing against her neck until she ached for his touch. God help her if this made her wicked, but she could no longer deny the sensations that coursed through her whenever he was near—a wanton desire for his hands to caress her in places she rarely touched herself.

"May I kiss you now?" he asked, his words barely more than a breath of air against her flesh—flesh consumed with prickling heat.

"It's one of my requirements," she managed, attempting a touch of humor and hoping that she didn't sound too desperate in doing so.

"Only one?" His hand had found her face and his fingers were tickling her jawline, turning her head in his direction.

"One of many," she said, fearing that her galloping heart might escape from her chest.

"We'll have plenty of time to discuss the rest later." His breath caressed her cheek. "As for the one of kissing you—I'm only too happy to oblige."

And then he did, his lips touching the corner of her own so gently that she scarcely felt it at all. But then he adjusted himself, his mouth finding hers with greater pressure. It felt good, though not as cataclysmic as she'd expected, given the way her body responded. Somehow, she'd imagined the kiss would increase her pleasure and this need she felt to crawl all over him with complete abandon, but it didn't really. It was both puzzling and distressing.

"Why so tense?" he asked, pulling back just enough so he could speak.

Tense?

Rebecca forced her awareness back to her own body and realized that yes, she was. The reason for it came a second later. This man was a rake. He'd kissed count-less women and had probably bedded an equal amount, while she had no experience at all. This was her first kiss and she was worried she'd disappoint, though she'd probably done so already. Why else would he have commented? "I'm sorry," she muttered. "I know I lack the experience of—"

"Shh . . . not another word, Becky. May I call you Becky?"

She'd never had a pet name before, and the fact that he'd just given her one warmed her heart. "I like it," she said.

"Good. Then you must call me Daniel from now on. Agreed?" She did, and he pulled her closer. "Now, let's try that kiss again, shall we? Just relax and let me guide you."

This time, she felt his tongue first as he brushed it against her lower lip, eliciting a helpless groan from her throat. His teeth came next, tugging gently at the plump flesh while his tongue pressed forward. Her mouth opened of its own accord, and he was there, ready to accept the invitation she offered.

This was what she'd wanted. Though she'd lacked the experience, her body had sensed that something had been missing. Daniel gave it to her now, stroke for stroke as his tongue slid over hers, teaching and directing as the pleasure of his kiss awakened other parts of her. She felt her nipples tighten against the fabric of her bodice and could think of nothing more wonderful than for him to touch her there. How sinful that would be—a notion that swiftly sent a wave of heat straight down between her thighs. She gasped, and Daniel pulled away, leaving her bereft.

"You learn quickly," he rasped, "and I look forward to teaching you more, but if we don't stop now, then I fear I may not be able to."

The implication of his words sank in, and no matter how much she wished he'd act on his rakish impulses, she knew that he was right.

"I will return for you and Laura tomorrow evening," he said.

"Thank you," she said, happy that he'd mentioned her maid as well.

When they emerged from the wardrobe, they found Laura diligently mending some garment or other. "Have you come to an agreement?" she asked, setting her work aside and coming to place a blanket across Rebecca's shoulders.

In the close confinement of the wardrobe, Rebecca had been unaware of the chill that filled the rest of the room. "Yes, Laura. We leave tomorrow. Mr. Neville has graciously offered to take me to Scotland, where we shall be married."

The relief that flooded Laura's features was beyond touching. "Thank you, sir," she said as her eyes brimmed with tears. "I kept hoping you'd save her, and now you have. You're a good man."

Rebecca smiled, happy that the two most important people in her life were going to get along just fine.

Chapter 10

Things did *not* go according to plan.

When Rebecca awoke the next morning, she finished her toilette and started working on her watercolors while she waited for breakfast to arrive. Now was not the time to pack; she would do so later in the day when her aunt and uncle napped and she was unlikely to be disturbed by either of them. But when her aunt arrived instead of Wendy, who usually brought her breakfast, Rebecca set down her paintbrush and gave the woman her full attention. Something wasn't right.

"I've brought you some sustenance," her aunt said haughtily. Either she believed she was doing Rebecca a huge favor by feeding her, or she believed that having to climb all the stairs to get there had been a great inconvenience. Both were likely the case.

"Thank you," Rebecca said. She looked warily at Laura, who'd risen as soon as Lady Grifton had arrived. She'd bobbed the expected curtsy and now appeared to be very much on edge.

Setting the tray on the table, Lady Grifton turned her usual scornful glare on Rebecca. "Frankly, I don't know why any man would want you with that black hair and dark complexion, but then again, I doubt His Grace has any interest in what's fashionable as long as you're willing to tend to his needs." Lady Grifton laughed. "Don't think I haven't noticed the way he looks at you—I've no doubt you'll be spending a lot of time confined to your bedchamber once he takes you off our hands."

Rebecca chose not to respond to her aunt's inappropriate innuendo with the scathing retort that sat on the tip of her tongue, for she knew that Lady Grifton's sole intent was to provoke her temper. Unwilling to give her the power to do so, Rebecca told her calmly, "I'm sure you're right, Aunt, and I can assure you that I have no intention of shirking my wifely duties." Though she'd every intention of fulfilling them with Daniel rather than with Grover. "However, I do think it would be wise of you to remember that once I say my vows, I will be Duchess of Grover, a position that far outranks your own."

Fury drew her aunt's lips into a tight line. "Don't get ahead of yourself, you impertinent girl. You're still in our care, and as long as that is the case, you will do as we say." Her features softened into a smirk. "Your eagerness for your new title is fortunate, though, since His Grace has just suggested we forgo the formalities of a lengthy engagement and the crying of banns."

A cold shiver ran down Rebecca's spine, but she managed to feign a look of genuine interest. "What do you mean?"

"I suppose he's quite keen for you to be his." The nonchalance of Lady Grifton's tone was far from comforting as she continued, "He has gone to London, intent on meeting with the archbishop and acquiring a special license."

"Oh?" Rebecca silently thanked God for her ability to keep her voice steady. She would not appear weak in front of her aunt by allowing her despair to show.

"He has asked that we join him later today." Lady Grifton's gaze met Rebecca's with cold menace. "We depart for London in an hour, so I suggest you start packing."

"But what about the settlement?" Surely there had to be a way to delay this. If she left now, she'd lose all hope of marrying Daniel instead.

"We are to meet His Grace at Grover House for precisely that purpose. Once that is done, it's off to the altar with you." Her aunt sashayed across to the door, where her pudgy hand found the handle. "Do I detect a bit of trepidation?" She grinned mockingly as she opened the door. "Your acting skills aren't what they used to be, Rebecca. I can see right through that stoic façade of yours."

The door closed and Rebecca realized for the first time that her whole body was trembling. Lord help her, she'd never been so livid.

"I'm so sorry," Laura said from the other corner of the room.

"They will not win," Rebecca muttered, her mind already working on seeking a means of escape. "I'll find a way to stop this, no matter what."

"But if we're to go to London today and His Grace is procuring a special license, then I'm sure he means to marry you tomorrow at the latest," Laura said.

"You're probably right." Getting up, Rebecca started to pace about the room. If she could only delay the duke's plans enough to find a solution. She considered her options, and as she did, an idea began to take shape. If she could pull it off, then this would be yet another impressive scheme. Her adventurous spirit soared, and she turned to Laura with a smile. "I believe I have a plan."

Seated on a lovely settee of light blue silk, Rebecca waited patiently for her intended to make his appearance. He'd been ensconced in his study for the past hour with her uncle and two lawyers, finalizing the financial aspects of the marriage—the settlement and the transfer of fifteen thousand pounds from Grover's bank account to her uncle's. From what Rebecca understood, the costs involved with the rehabilitation of Roselyn Castle would be charged directly to Grover. There was no doubt that her aunt and uncle had made a coup, though Rebecca was convinced that Grover was equally pleased with his end of the bargain, for there had been no end to the lascivious smiles he'd given her.

Rebecca squirmed on the inside just thinking about it, but on the outside she managed to remain calm as her mind busied itself with her plans of escape.

"And it's teeming with servants," Rebecca's aunt said. Since arriving at the duke's residency she'd been prattling on about how good His Grace had been to rent a splendid town house for them to live in during their stay in London.

The door opened and Grover stepped into the parlor, followed closely by Rebecca's uncle. The duke smiled at Rebecca, eyes gleaming with unabashed greed. "Everything has been settled and we can finally focus on the wedding."

"What splendid news." Rebecca was pleased with how happy she sounded. She met his gaze. "Perhaps we could have a moment alone together, Your Grace? With everything that's been happening, we've hardly had a chance to talk to each other."

"Of course, my dear." His voice was silky as he turned to Rebecca's aunt and uncle. "If you'll please excuse us."

"But we—" Rebecca's aunt began, suspicion flickering in the gray depths of her eyes as she glared at Rebecca. Clearly she didn't trust her and was unwilling to accommodate her request.

"The door will remain ajar," Grover said, cutting her off. He then swept his hand toward the exit. "If you please."

"Very well," Rebecca's aunt conceded as she straightened her back and stood up. "If that is what you wish, I see no reason to object."

Rebecca waited for them to leave before turning her attention on her fiancé. "Will you come and sit with me?" she asked, patting the empty seat beside her.

Grover beamed. "With great pleasure." The emphasis he placed on the word *pleasure* would have given anyone with less resolve cause to reconsider, but Rebecca was determined to do what she must, more so now than ever before. Time was running out.

Placing her hand over Grover's, she turned to him with a pleading gaze. "Your Grace, I understand your eagerness for haste in regards to our marriage, but I was rather hoping that I might convince you to offer me a boon."

A frown appeared upon his brow, but then he lowered his gaze to the rise and fall of her bosom and all signs of concern were immediately erased. Raising her hand to his lips, he pressed a moist kiss against each knuckle while Rebecca did her best to remain still. She could not allow her distaste for the man to show. "I suppose it is the least I can do for you," he murmured, "considering what you will be offering me later."

She shuddered to think of it and sincerely hoped that it would never come to that.

"I was hoping that you would consider hosting an engagement ball, Your Grace."

Grover leaned back, his frown returning. "I see no need for that, my lady, though you are more than welcome to host as many balls and soirees as you desire once you are duchess."

"That is most generous of you, but don't you think it would be wise to quench any suspicions that the *ton* may have regarding our marriage? Would it not be best to assure them that I am marrying you because I wish to and because the union is beneficial to us both?"

"My dear, I may be old, but I am not a fool. We both know that you would likely have preferred a young buck if given a choice."

"Perhaps," she conceded, "but I also appreciate the value of experience . . . and to be perfectly honest, money. I believe that Your Grace has both in ample supply." Lowering her lashes, she delivered a shy smile.

"Unquestionably," Grover replied. He licked his lips, leaned closer to her and said, "If it weren't for your aunt and uncle, I'd be happy to give you a little demonstration right now. Even more reason to hasten things along if you ask me."

Rebecca forced back the urge to leap from her seat and run screaming out of the room. "Your Grace," she said, her face feeling hot. "You really mustn't say such things. It's highly inappropriate."

Grover chuckled. He ran his leathery index finger along the length of her arm. "What a pleasure it is to see that I can so easily affect you," he said, mistaking her mortification with something else entirely. "You're so pretty when you're all flushed and excited."

Yuck!

"Well, your words are quite . . . ahem . . . suggestive. However," she said, determined to move on quickly before he attempted to kiss her or, God forbid, worse, "I do believe that showing a mutual desire to marry will be to our advantage—especially if we are to marry by special license. Once the *ton* sees that we have come to an understanding with each other, they will have no reason to spread rumors."

"You think that I care if they say that I married a fortune hunter? I'm a duke, for heaven's sake. They can say what they please."

This was not going as well as she'd hoped. "I care, Your Grace. I'm young and not nearly as good at dealing with such things. I'm afraid that if you marry me like this and without giving the *ton* a chance to at least see me beforehand, they'll make the worst assumptions about me. Please try to understand that I am relying on you to help me." She squeezed his hand a little. "All I want is for us to be happy."

Grover sighed. "I can see how troubled you are by all of this, so if having a ball to stop the gossips' tongues from wagging will ease your concerns and allow you to focus your energy on me instead, then I suppose I can accommodate your wish."

"You are most kind, Your Grace."

"Don't thank me yet. You have two days in which to make the necessary arrangements, after which I want to see you in church. Is that understood?"

"Perfectly. I will get to work on the invitations without further delay."

Grover's lips drew up to show a set of yellow, uneven teeth. "And I will do my best to keep my longing for you at bay."

Fearing any further contact with the man, Rebecca slipped out from beneath his heated gaze, stepped toward the door and dropped into a deep curtsy. "You flatter me, Your Grace, and I thank you for it. But if there is to be a ball this Friday, then I have much to attend to." She offered him her most benign smile and began to heap on the compliments; the benefits of flattery were not to be dismissed. "To be frank, I wasn't very pleased when my aunt and uncle decided to choose my husband on my behalf, but I have since come to realize that they were wise in doing so. You have shown yourself to be magnanimous, and I have every confidence that you will make a most excellent husband." Pausing for emphasis, she then added, "It will be an honor to be the mother of your children."

Later that night, after writing over a hundred invitations that would be mailed out in the morning, Rebecca considered her conversation with Grover. The lies she'd told him didn't sit well with her, yet she didn't regret what she was about to do. In spite of what she'd said, Grover was just as selfish and lowly in character as her aunt and uncle. He'd practically bought her, for heaven's sake, and his disgusting insinuations regarding what he required her for were abhorrent.

Closing her eyes, she thought of Daniel and dearly

hoped that he found her note and would still be willing to help. With their last conversation in mind, she believed that he would, for he'd seemed sincere in his promise, and the kiss they'd shared . . . well, that had been quite something. Warming at the memory of it and hopeful that he would come and save her, Rebecca finally drifted off to sleep.

Chapter 11

Having asked a footman for a glass of brandy in favor of the champagne that everyone else was drinking, Daniel looked out over the crowd of people who had thronged together at Grover House and decided that he was positively sick of attending balls. Every inhabitant of Mayfair, it seemed, was in attendance, no doubt curious about the woman who would soon become Duchess of Grover.

The footman returned with the brandy, and Daniel took a long sip. Having arrived late, he'd yet to catch a glimpse of Rebecca, who was probably somewhere deep within the crush. If only he'd asked her to run away with him as soon as she'd agreed to do so, they could have been married by now, but he'd wanted to give her time to prepare, certain that there were things she wished to take with her. How was he to know that Grover would make a change of plans? At least Rebecca had left a note, though he'd almost missed it in the darkness, wedged as it had been between the window and its ledge. And then Laura had arrived at the small apartment he rented on Hill Street. Without crossing the threshold, she'd handed him an invitation for this evening, along with yet another note detailing Rebecca's plan in the hope that he would still be willing to help. Of course he was, not just because he needed a wife but because he'd begun to realize that he was completely mad for this lively woman who'd decided to take her future into her own hands.

"We meet again, Neville."

There was no need for Daniel to turn his head to recognize that voice. Starkly. "What a coincidence."

"No such thing," Starkly said. "I say, is that a brandy?"

Daniel didn't bother answering that question with words but took another sip.

"I'd kill for one of those instead of all this bubbly stuff that everyone else is so fond of." Stopping a passing footman, Starkly made his request. He then turned his attention back to Daniel. "So . . . come to wallow in a bit of self-pity, have you?"

"You must be in your cups, Starkly. You're making no sense."

"Ha! As if Grover isn't about to marry *Lady Nuit,* otherwise known as the lovely Lady Rebecca that you were chasing after at the Kingsborough Ball. At least I can find comfort in knowing I wasn't the only one who lost her to that weathered old toad."

"As if you ever stood a chance," Daniel muttered.

"No, I suppose not," Starkly said, his voice taking on a bitterness that Daniel had never heard from him before. "It's difficult to compete with any man who's as rich as Croesus.

"Especially," Starkly continued, "when he promises to depart this earth at any given moment and leave everything to her."

"She's not mercenary, if that's what you're implying," Daniel said, not bothering to glance in Starkly's direction.

Starkly chuckled. "No, I suppose not." His voice was heavy with sarcasm. He patted Daniel on the shoulder. "Never mind, though. There are plenty of other ladies present this evening. I'll see if one of them might be willing to take a walk with me in the garden."

Once he'd gone, Daniel pulled out his fob watch. Twenty minutes to ten. He still had a bit of time to spare but decided to stay put. The last thing he needed right now was to get stuck in that crowd. Downing the remainder of his drink, he stepped back out into the hallway instead and began heading toward the back of the house.

"Well, well, well," a smooth voice said. "What a pleasure it is to find you here."

Stopping in his tracks, Daniel peered into the murky darkness of an alcove to find Lady Vernon seductively reclining on a window seat. She was one of the more notorious widows, known for her sexual appetites, which were so ravenous that even Daniel had found her exhausting at times. There was something predatory about her this evening that quickly put him on edge. He could not afford this sort of distraction right now and certainly didn't wish for Rebecca to find him in her company.

"Thank you, my lady, but I have a pressing matter to attend to. If you'll excuse me."

"Surely it can wait five minutes," she said, stopping him again with her words. "After all, it's not as if it will take much longer than that for us to do what I have in mind."

"In case you are not aware, we are in the Duke of Grover's home." He had to get away from her, and the faster the better.

Lady Vernon chuckled. "As if such an inconvenience has stopped either of us before." Rising, she sauntered toward him, her hips swaying gently beneath the folds of her gown. "May I remind you of the pleasure we once shared behind a Chinese screen at the Thakerry Ball? Or how about at the opera when we—"

"That's quite enough," Daniel told her as he glanced around. "Someone might hear you."

When he looked back at her, he saw that she'd stepped closer. She leaned toward him, so close that their lips almost touched. Daniel tried to step away, but the lady latched onto his arm. "Have you abandoned your rakish tendencies completely then?" she asked. "I confess that I did hear a rumor, but I failed to believe it." One of her hands came up to caress his cheek.

"Don't," he ground out.

"Are you sure I can't entice you? We used to have such fun together, if you recall."

Do I ever?

Now was not the time to contemplate his past liaisons. He had to get rid of her before Rebecca found him in her company. "Meet me outside in the garden in half an hour and I'll show you that I have not forgotten how to please you."

In a swift move that Daniel had not anticipated, Lady Vernon's lips met his, hard and demanding. He'd never felt anything but lust for the woman, but even that was no longer the case. Instead, she left him cold and with a feeling of disgust not only for her but for himself as well. There was only one lady who could stir his blood these days, and to his horror, he found her glaring back at him as Lady Vernon sashayed away. "I can explain," he whispered when Rebecca was close enough to hear.

"Later." The clipped word was like a bucket of ice water dumped on his head. The last time he'd seen Rebecca, he'd kissed her. It had been magnificent, and now this. He longed to tell her that Lady Vernon meant nothing to him and that *she* had kissed him, not the other way around. But Rebecca was right—they had to hurry if they were to accomplish their goal. An explanation would have to wait until later.

Side by side, they continued toward the servants' stairs, where they found Laura waiting. "The staff is busy this evening, so as long as you move quickly, I doubt that any of them will raise an eyebrow," Laura said as she handed Rebecca a brown woolen cloak and then held out a satchel for Daniel to carry. "I've packed a few necessities—clothes in particular—along with your watercolors and the other items we discussed. As agreed, I will remain behind in case further distraction will be required. That is of course unless your ladyship has changed her mind and would rather I accompany you." Laura's expression was stern. Had she perhaps noticed her mistress's displeasure with Daniel? He suspected that she must have, and he found himself holding his breath while he waited for Rebecca to answer. She was hesitating, a clear indication that her trust in him had just been diminished. By how much, he dared not even guess.

"No," Rebecca finally said as she wrapped the cloak around her shoulders and pulled the hood over her head. "We cannot change the plan. It's far too risky."

"Very well then." Laura met Daniel's gaze with flint

in her eyes. "Just promise me that you'll take good care of her."

"I'll guard her with my life," he told her.

Laura didn't smile but nodded quickly before hurrying away. Daniel pulled open the stairwell door and ushered Rebecca inside, where they almost collided with a footman who was carrying a tray of canapés up from the kitchen. "Watch where you're going," he said, recovering from a near stumble. With his attention riveted upon the tray and its contents, he paid no heed to who the people were who had almost made him fall and just continued past them, muttering an oath. Daniel breathed a sigh of relief.

Below stairs, everything was in upheaval. If Daniel hadn't known better, he would have suspected that a war was going on, with servants forming troops and carrying out orders issued to them by a very pompous-looking man and a woman who came close to Lady Grifton in austerity. These were undoubtedly the first and second in command, otherwise known as the butler and the housekeeper.

Looking about in search of the exit, Daniel gave Rebecca's hand a hard tug. The last thing he needed now was to be questioned by either of these two people. But of course, that was too much to ask for, and when he turned back around, he found the butler staring down his nose at him. "I believe you must have gone astray," he said. "This is the kitchen."

"I am well aware of that," Daniel replied with an edge of arrogance to match. "Perhaps you'd care to tell us how to get out of here."

"May I suggest going back the way you came? The ball is, after all, upstairs."

Daniel raised an eyebrow. Did the man think him an idiot, or was he just particularly fond of stating the obvious? Time to make his excuses. "Right you are. However, I am hoping to leave here in the company of this lady." He lowered his voice to a whisper and leaned toward the butler. "She has just now agreed to become my mistress, you see, and since her reputation is of the more questionable variety, I thought it best if we tried to leave without causing a stir. However, if you think it would be better for me to drag her through the ballroom instead, then—"

"Down that corridor and to your left," the butler said, looking slightly flustered.

With no intention of lingering for another second, Daniel pulled Rebecca after him at a brisk pace, arriving quickly in the street behind Grover House, where a groomsman awaited with a phaeton.

"Wouldn't a landau have been better suited?" Rebecca asked a short while later as they drove past Regent's Park and out of London.

Daniel whipped the reins, urging the horses into a gallop. "This is faster." His pride stopped him from admitting that it was also the only carriage he owned. "It's a Roberts, just so you know."

"I'm guessing that's a good thing?"

"It's a very good thing in this case, since they manufacture the best carriages in England. I'm surprised you don't know them—they're based in Moxley."

"A town that I've seen very little of," she said, reminding him of everything she'd had to endure under the guardianship of her aunt and uncle. If an opportunity for him to right his wrongs had ever presented itself, then this was it.

"No matter. The point is that I've raced many opponents in this vehicle without losing once. I've every confidence that we'll make it to Scotland without impediment from either the Griftons or from Grover."

Their conversation died and Daniel gave his attention to the horses. He could tell that Rebecca was piqued with him, for there was a tenseness about her posture, forcing him to wonder if she might be regretting her decision to run away with him. That notion made it even more important that he clarify the situation she'd witnessed between himself and Lady Vernon, but now was not the time for such a serious discussion, no matter how much he hated the uncomfortable silence that had descended upon them.

It was midnight before Daniel dared to stop for a break, but he'd exhausted the horses by pushing them past the twenty-mile limit and had no choice but to change them. "Do you think they'll catch up with us?" Rebecca asked as he handed her down from the carriage at one of the many posting inns along the North Road.

"I doubt it." There was no question as to who *they* referred to. If the duke was in pursuit, the Griftons would be with him. "It would have taken at least ten minutes before your absence became known, and even then the duke would not have been able to leave his guests immediately without causing a stir. The phaeton's also faster than whatever vehicle he chooses—a landau, I suspect—affording us at least a good half hour's advantage."

Rebecca nodded and said no more while a groom exchanged the horses for fresh ones. "Would you like me to add some more oil to your lanterns?" he asked Daniel.

"Please do," Daniel told him. Pulling out a couple of coins, he paid the man and handed Rebecca back up.

"Do you plan to continue straight through the night?" Rebecca asked an hour later. As annoyed as she was with what Daniel had done, the silence between them bothered her. She wasn't used to being quiet for such long stretches of time, least of all when she wasn't alone, but seeing him kiss that woman had brought to life a jealousy that irked her in every conceivable way. She didn't want to be jealous, because that would mean that she'd started to have deeper feelings for this man—feelings that bordered on the possessive. She had to try and tamp them down, because the last thing she needed was to fall in love with a man who in spite of his promises and good intentions was very much the rake he'd always been. What a fool she'd been. When he'd told her how much he appreciated her for being different, she'd allowed herself to believe that there could be something more between them—that he had begun developing a tendre for her just as she had for him. But the woman he'd been kissing was everything Rebecca was not—blonde, with a pale complexion. She probably had blue eyes as well, though Rebecca had not had a chance to notice.

She sighed. Nothing had changed, except that he now needed a wife just as much as she needed a husband. But if he couldn't say no to another woman mere minutes before eloping with her, then how was he going to be faithful for the duration of their marriage? Regret surfaced briefly, but Rebecca forced it back. The alternative was inconceivable. At least where Daniel was concerned, he was young and fun. She was also confident that he would treat her kindly, but she would do well to remember that theirs was a practical agreement, nothing more, and once they were married, she would do her best to accept him for who he was, provided that he didn't bring his paramours home with him. Perhaps she would take a lover as well . . . or maybe two or three?

"Are you woolgathering?" Daniel's voice jerked her back to awareness.

"I beg your pardon?"

His eyes never strayed from the road as the phaeton continued onward. "You asked me a question which I've long since answered, but you haven't replied to mine."

"Oh. I'm so sorry. I suppose my thoughts must have been elsewhere. What did you say?"

"I was merely wondering if you were tired, because if you are, then you're welcome to lean your head against my shoulder and try to get some sleep."

Sleep?

She'd just left her fiancé to elope with a rake and was presently traveling north at breakneck speed, and Daniel thought she might be capable of sleep? "I'm fine," she said, "but if you're growing weary of driving, then I'd be more than happy to relieve you."

Daniel laughed. "I'm sure you would, but a phaeton is not so easy to manage. Have you ever driven one before?"

"No, but I'm a quick study. How hard can it be?"

"Even in daylight many have been known to lose control of the vehicle. Given the speed at which we're traveling, toppling over would be life threatening. I'd rather not risk it, but perhaps on the way back you can have a go. Is that acceptable?"

It was better than what she'd expected, and the fact that he was willing to at least let her try improved her mood dramatically. "Thank you, Daniel. I would like that very much."

He chuckled. "Yes, I know. Don't think I've forgotten your adventurous inclination. I just hope I'll be able to keep you out of trouble once we're married."

She knew he was joking, yet she couldn't resist saying, "That's rich, coming from a renowned rake." Her tone sounded far too snide for her own liking.

"Having second thoughts?"

All humor had abandoned his voice, and Rebecca found herself in one of those situations where she dearly wanted to apologize and make things right between them but couldn't seem to stop herself from lashing out. He'd hurt her, and the acknowledgement of it fueled her resentment of him. "No," she said. "My options are limited and you are the better choice, no matter your flaws."

"I see. Because if you'd rather go back, then all you have to do is say the word and I'll turn these horses around." He sounded angry, but what reason would he possibly have for that? "After everything I've done for you, the least I'd expect is a little bit of gratitude, not for you to make insinuations about my character."

Well, that was probably a pretty good reason.

"My apologies," she said. No sense in arguing when she'd already decided to accept him for who he was. "You're absolutely right, and believe me, I'm very grateful to you for coming to my rescue the way you did. It was most gallant of you."

"No need for you to overdo it," he said, his tone softening until she was certain he had to be smiling.

"I only speak the truth."

"Well, if that is the case, then it's time for me to be honest too. I know you saw me with Lady Vernon, and I—"

"Oh, is that her name? Well, it's no matter. You really needn't explain yourself. Of course, I can't deny that I was momentarily surprised, but on second thought I see no reason why I should be. You've led quite a colorful life before me, and considering our unique circumstances, it would be unreasonable for me to expect that to change. After all, it's not as if either of us is in love with the other, though I do hope we can be friends."

"I, er—"

"Just be honest with me and treat me with respect, and I'm sure we'll have a splendid time together."

"You're missing the point, Rebecca."

"Am I? Because as far as I could tell you were quite busy kissing Lady Vernon mere minutes before eloping with me, and that's discounting the kiss that you and I shared just three days ago, so no, I don't think I'm missing the point at all. You're the sort of man who wants to enjoy whatever pleasures come your way, and however much you'd like to convince both of us of the contrary, the fact remains that you don't possess the sort of willpower required to avoid temptation. Don't worry though; I'm perfectly fine with it as long as you keep your liaisons discreet and away from me." She nudged him playfully in the side, hoping the gesture would convince him of her sincerity—a sincerity she wasn't remotely close to feeling. The very idea of him frolicking in another woman's arms made her stomach churn, but if that was what he intended to do, then she might as well accept it rather than waste her time pining for the fidelity of a man who would never give himself to her alone.

Unwilling to discuss the matter any further, she did as he'd suggested earlier and snuggled up against him, her head coming to rest against a firm shoulder. "I think you were right before. I am tired. It's been a long day. Mind if I get some rest?"

"It's what I suggested," he said. He spoke slowly and thoughtfully.

Rebecca closed her eyes and willed herself to sleep. She longed for a brief escape from it all, especially since Daniel was probably already contemplating his good fortune in finding a woman who would not only marry him but also allow him to go on as he'd done before. An ache settled in the pit of her stomach at the very idea, but she would not humiliate herself by begging him to go against his true nature. What right did she even have to do so? They were doing each other a favor, and they would make the most of it as friends. Anything more than that was pure fantasy.

Chapter 12

What the bloody hell was going on? Pacing the upstairs hallway of the inn where they'd arrived a half hour earlier, Daniel contemplated every word they'd spoken to each other during their journey. He was beyond tense, not only from the close proximity he'd shared with Rebecca in the phaeton for the past four hours, her soft scent teasing him as she'd slept peacefully at his side, but from pure, uncomplicated lust for her. He couldn't recall ever wanting to bed a woman as much as he wanted to bed her, but then she'd started prattling on about how accepting she was of his lifestyle and that she wouldn't expect him to change on her account. His nerves had been frayed by the end of it. Had she really encouraged him to take mistresses as long as he didn't bring them home with him?

Good God!

Everything from that point on had happened in a daze, for which his state of exhaustion was probably also to blame. When they'd reached Huntington, he'd decided to stop for the night. If Grover and the Griftons were in pursuit, he doubted that they would be traveling without rest, when Daniel, who was so much younger than all of them, was in dire need of sleep. As long as they got an early start, he was confident they could maintain their lead.

However, he had yet to find the comfort of his bed after agreeing with Rebecca's request that he allow her to ready herself while he waited outside in the hallway. She'd wanted separate rooms, but since the inn was small and had been filled to capacity, this had not been possible, and Daniel was grateful for it. He wanted her company, regardless of the strange discussion they'd had with each other earlier in the evening. He still couldn't come to grips with how frank she'd been about her expectations for their marriage. There was no doubt in his mind that her opinion of him had been altered after seeing him with Lady Vernon, and while he knew that he was to blame for that, he couldn't help but feel frustrated by her blunt dismissal of him.

When will she be ready?

He'd given her ample time to disrobe and climb into bed, and he decided to give the door a light knock. "Enter," he heard her call from within, so he did, finding the room in complete darkness—so much so that he could barely make out the shape of the bed. He edged his way forward, closing and locking the door behind him. Continuing his progress toward the bed, he began removing his clothes; first his jacket and then his cravat and shirt, which he tossed on a chair that stood against the wall.

Reaching the bed, he sat down on the edge so he could pull off his boots, all the while aware of Rebecca's huddled form. She hadn't spoken a word since he'd entered the room, and as far as he could tell, her back was turned toward him in a stubborn gesture to avoid having to interact. Daniel muttered an oath beneath his breath as he gave his boot a hard tug. His annoyance at how pear-shaped everything had gone was beginning to tax his nerves. Pulling off the other boot, he enjoyed the thud that it made as it hit the floor.

Rising, he started unfastening his breeches and pulling them down over his hips until he was clad only in his drawers. Eyes settling on the lump Rebecca created on the other side of the bed, he fleetingly wondered how she'd respond if he took them off and climbed into bed completely naked. He couldn't help but smile with mischief, but he decided that doing so would probably not be the best way to earn her forgiveness. So, pulling the covers aside, he sank down onto the mattress and, with a deep sigh, luxuriated in the comfort that the bed and the pillow offered.

Christ, it was good to lie down and close his eyes. He shifted a little and reached down to adjust the fabric of his drawers, which were gathering uncomfortably around his hips. It was no use, so he turned onto his side, but in doing so he uncovered his back. He turned back again and gave his undergarment another tug.

"Would you please stop moving," Rebecca said. Her voice was hushed and with a distinct trace of irritation to it.

Daniel stilled on a sigh and stretched out his legs. "I'm sorry," he whispered back, "but I'm not used to sleeping like this."

There was a beat and then the inevitable question: "What do you mean?"

A wide smile spread its way across Daniel's face. "I never sleep in any of my attire but always completely and utterly nude." It sounded as if she sucked in a breath. His smile broadened. "Wearing even so much as my unmentionables is causing me severe discomfort, though I am more than happy to oblige for your sake. Considering that you wanted separate rooms, I thought you'd disapprove of discovering me in such a . . . bare state. Am I correct?"

"Y-yes. I mean . . . of course," she muttered, and then, "thank you."

Really, he ought to be commended for his ability to suppress a grin in response to her befuddlement. It was most amusing. "You are welcome," he murmured. There was a moment's silence before he added, "Sleep well."

"You too," she whispered back.

Thankfully, his tiredness trumped his discomfort, and it didn't take too long before Daniel slipped off to sleep, his dreams filled with the woman he was planning to marry, and of what their first night together *could* have been like had she not seen him kissing Lady Vernon. Naturally, he awoke to a state of complete and utter discomfort, though this time it had nothing to do with his clothing. Turning his head, he almost came nose to nose with Rebecca. She was so beautiful with her long black lashes fanned out against her bronzed skin. His gaze slipped to her lips, luscious lips that had felt so perfect when he'd last kissed her.

He wanted to kiss her again right now, but he stopped himself, unsure of how she'd react, considering how strained everything had been between them last night. Tomorrow he would marry her. If he wanted to kiss her, then why shouldn't he? *Because she doesn't want you to,* an annoying voice told him. With a sigh,

Daniel rolled over and got out of bed, retrieving his garments and dressing with the briskness of a man who desperately needed to remove himself from temptation if he was to avoid succumbing to it.

He needed air. Lots and lots of cool morning air to dampen his ardor. Shrugging into his jacket, he did up the buttons and headed for the door, placing as much distance between himself and Rebecca as the small room allowed. Dear God, the covers had slipped lower on her and he could see . . . his mouth went dry and he tried to swallow. A gentleman would look away, but Daniel was no gentleman, or at least his eyes were not in the least bit noble, for they remained quite determinedly fixed on the gentle rise and fall of her bosom. Was she aware that the soft outline of each breast was visible beneath her nightgown? Probably not, for it appeared to be chaste in design, but with the morning light streaming through the window even the dark center of each breast was revealed. Daniel blinked.

Lord help me.

"Rebecca," he said, hoping to wake her. She shifted a little and the covers slid sideways, offering Daniel a first-rate view of one of her long legs, half bare since her nightgown had crawled all the way up past her knees. "Rebecca," he repeated, louder this time, and was afforded a groan. "It's time to wake up so we can be on our way."

Her eyes opened and she met his gaze, surprise registering upon her face. "You're already fully dressed."

"Yes. I'll leave so you can do the same. If you hurry, we may have time for some breakfast before we depart." And then he opened the door and fled without another backward glance.

"**W**hat a perfect day to get married," Rebecca said, surprising him with her cheerfulness as they drove along beneath a clear blue sky.

"I couldn't agree more," Daniel said. She seemed her usual self this morning and he was happy for it, since an unhappy demeanor didn't suit her in the least. Perhaps everything would be all right between them after all. He hoped so, though he couldn't forget what she'd said in regards to their marriage or how distant and standoffish she'd been toward him since leaving London.

Watching the horses toss their manes, he considered addressing the issue but decided against it. She'd mistaken what she'd seen at the ball for something more than what it really was. He'd thought her upset about it, but then she'd voiced her support, and he'd been left with the impression that what he'd taken to be annoyance had been nothing more than the emotional turmoil of having to adapt to a different situation altogether. She'd made her opinion clear: he was nothing more than a rake who was rescuing a damsel in distress, not only for her benefit but for his as well, and while she appreciated him for doing so, he ought not delude himself that he would ever amount to anything more in her eyes.

But what if he proved her wrong? After making her acquaintance, he had no desire for the company of any other women. Surely he would be able to convince her of that if he set his mind to it. But was that even something she would want? When she'd spoken, she'd sounded so insistent on the whole marriage of convenience idea that he'd felt whatever hope he'd started to have of sharing something more with her begin to dwindle. Surely she wouldn't have suggested such a thing if she'd developed feelings for him that went beyond those of friendship.

What was he thinking? Of course she wouldn't have. They'd barely known each other a week, and he certainly wasn't in love with her either, although he definitely liked her a lot—more than any other woman he'd ever met, and that made him want to do right by her. It bothered him that she was so willing to let him stray. Perhaps with time they would form a closer bond and this would change, but until then, he would try to put a bit more effort into romancing her. After all, he'd barely had a chance to do so.

A thought struck him: they still had their wedding night ahead of them. The corner of his lips edged upward. Poor Becky, she had no idea of what she was getting herself into by marrying a rake.

"How long until we arrive?" she asked once they'd passed through Penrith.

"Another hour, I'd imagine."

"Then don't you think it's time we got to know each other a bit better?"

Daniel glanced toward her. "What do you have in mind?"

"Well, I suppose most couples have the fortune of engaging in a lengthy courtship before either of them agrees to the permanence of marriage, but since we've been tossed together somewhat abruptly, we haven't really had much opportunity to do so. All we have are a few brief conversations. So what I propose is that we start asking each other questions, anything at all that we want to know. The only rule is that the person being asked must answer with complete honesty. I think it will strengthen our bond and improve our regard for each other."

Or diminish it.

"Very well," Daniel said, eager for the easy, care-free banter that he'd gotten used to enjoying with her. "Would you like to go first?"

"Certainly." She bit her lip for a second before asking, "What's the naughtiest thing you ever did as a child?"

He glanced sideways at her for a moment, then returned his attention to the road ahead and said, "I think I'd have to say pouring a bucket of water over my grandmamma."

Rebecca gasped. "Surely you didn't."

"On the contrary, I got her quite wet."

She couldn't help herself from laughing. "What on earth would have possessed you?"

Daniel chuckled as he whipped the horses onward. "My parents and I had gone to visit Grandmamma and Grandpapa for a couple of weeks at their country estate one year. It was summer, and as we were sitting outside one day, Grandmamma began complaining about the heat. Papa suggested that she ought to go for a swim in the lake in order to cool off, but she dismissed the idea, saying that she was too old for that sort of thing."

"So you decided to see to her comfort by soaking her through?"

"In a manner of speaking, yes. I was only five years old at the time, and while Grandmamma and Grandpapa took it rather well, my parents didn't find it the least bit amusing and promptly sent me to my room."

"Oh dear."

Daniel shrugged. "It's all right. They felt bad about it the next day and instructed the cook to prepare my favorite sweet—crêpes with raspberry marmalade."

"Sounds delicious," Rebecca said. "Now it's your turn. Ask me anything you like."

"Are you musically inclined?" Most ladies of breeding sang or played an instrument. He was curious if the same could be said of Rebecca.

"Not particularly, though I do like to whistle."

"Whistle?"

"Precisely." And then, to prove her point, she puckered her lips and did just that.

Daniel almost lost control of the horses. "That was er . . . hmm."

Rebecca laughed. "It's quite all right, you know. I'm well aware that I cannot carry a tune, hence the reason I don't play an instrument. The music teacher I had as a child eventually deemed me impossible to work with. What can I say? I suppose I lack the ear for it."

There was something so endearing about the way she said it, not to mention her unabashed performance, that Daniel felt his heart swell a little more for her. He loved that she didn't feel embarrassed whistling in front of him even though she knew well enough that her tune was false.

"How about you?" she asked. "Are you fond of the arts?"

"I don't paint or write and I'm not very musical either, though I do like to sing when I'm alone."

"Really?" Her eyes widened with interest. "How about a demonstration?"

Not the least bit self-conscious but feeling rather

cheeky instead, Daniel started belting out one of his favorite tunes, while Rebecca squealed with laughter. "She tells me with claret she cannot agree, and she thinks of a hogshead when e'er she sees me!"

Ten minutes later Rebecca had picked up the words and joined him with equal gusto, though she sounded like a dying cat as she hollered, "For I smell like a beast and therefore must I, resolve to forsake her or claret deny."

Their questioning quite forgotten due to the song, they continued like this until they rolled into Gretna Green, the camaraderie between them restored to what it had been the night of the Kingsborough Ball. Daniel was thankful for it. He hadn't enjoyed the seriousness and the quiet pensiveness that had settled over them after leaving London and was pleased to have finally overcome it. Rebecca was once again her vibrant self—the woman whose carefree nature had first sparked his interest.

"This will do," he said, pulling the phaeton over at a modest-looking establishment and helping Rebecca down.

Allowing a groom to handle the horses, Daniel escorted Rebecca inside, where they were greeted by a large man who stood behind the bar in the taproom, his arms resting on a counter as he chatted with a couple of customers seated across from him.

"We're here to be married!" Daniel announced without as much as a "how do you do." His spirits were much too high to consider formality.

All eyes turned to him and Rebecca. There was a beat of silence, then the large man said, "Well, you've come to the right place then. Follow me."

Leading them through a back door and out into an open courtyard, the large man, who stood roughly a head over Daniel, pointed toward a wall from behind which could be heard a loud clanging sound. "Smithy's right over there. He'll see to the formalities, and once you're done, I'll be happy to let you a room for the night."

"Thank you, sir." Daniel stuck out his hand. "You've been most helpful. Are you by any chance the innkeeper?"

"Yes," the man responded. He accepted Daniel's hand and gave it a hard shake.

"Then perhaps you'd also be good enough to prepare some food for us? We're both quite famished."

The innkeeper gave them a few options, from which they chose a meat and potato stew, requesting a pitcher of red wine to go with it.

"Ready?" Daniel asked as soon as the innkeeper had gone back inside. Daniel offered Rebecca his arm, which she accepted with a smile.

"Ready as I'll ever be," she said, upon which they started toward a new chapter in each of their lives as they strolled over to see the blacksmith.

"That was surprisingly painless," Daniel said as they sat across from each other twenty minutes later enjoying the first bites of their supper.

Rebecca looked up from her stew, her eyes filled with merriment. "You do realize that the leg-shackle is a metaphor, right?"

Daniel attempted a serious expression. "Really? Who would have thought?" Reaching for the pitcher of wine, Daniel filled both of their glasses. "A toast," he said, "to you, our friendship and the future ahead."

"And to you as well, my husband," Rebecca said, her radiant smile not leaving her face for an instant while she took a sip of her wine.

Daniel stared at her. He really had been fortunate to find her, and now she would be his forever, to have and to hold . . . to wed and to bed. He chuckled, admonishing himself for his wayward thoughts.

"What's so funny?" she asked, her eyes pinning him with an impishness he'd come to adore.

"Nothing really. I'm just really happy right now and grateful that you would have me."

A tiny frown creased her forehead. "Well, my options were limited and—"

"Don't ruin it," he said. He reached for her hand, noticing how still she grew as they made contact. His heart began to race with the expectation of what would happen next. "Becky . . . whatever our circumstances were, I want you to know that I'm grateful for the way things turned out. In all likelihood it would have taken me years yet to get married if my uncle hadn't forced me to do so now, and I have to say that while jumping into matrimony with you may have been rash, I think we're quite well suited. We can be good together you and I, don't you think?"

She'd been studying him as he'd spoken, but now she nodded. "Yes, I do. We share a similar sense of humor at least—I'm sure our life together will be filled with laughter."

"An essential element to a happy union if you ask me."

"I couldn't agree more."

"Shall we take the pitcher upstairs with us?" Daniel asked once their meal was over. He knew that she had to be feeling a little apprehensive about the prospect of what was to come, and he hoped that the wine would help ease her concerns. She said nothing but nodded instead, allowing him to lead the way. "It's not much, I suppose," he said as they stood inside the small room the innkeeper had given them. There was barely enough space for anything other than the bed, which seemed exceptionally large—so much so that it practically taunted them.

"I suppose we should try to get some rest," Rebecca said, her eyes fixed on the dwarfing piece of furniture.

Rest?

He reached out his hand to pull her into his arms, but she stepped inside the room, her back turned toward him as she started circumventing the bed, oblivious of his intentions. Apparently this was going to be harder than he'd expected.

Closing the door behind him and turning the lock, Daniel watched as Rebecca went to the window and looked out. Her hair was set in a neat coiffure that she'd somehow managed to arrange on her own, though a few loose tendrils had come undone since this morning and were now snaking their way between her shoulder blades. As on the night of the ball, he longed to unpin the entire mass and watch it cascade over her shoulders, to run his fingers through its softness while he kissed the sweep of that long and delicate neck.

Blood roared through his veins at the thought of it, of what she would taste like and how she would respond. If the kiss they'd shared in her wardrobe was any indication, she would eagerly return his sensual ministrations. With her back still turned, he shrugged out of his jacket and began undoing his cravat. "Anything out there catch your interest?" he asked.

She looked over her shoulder at him and shrugged. "Nothing much." Her eyes narrowed and she turned to face him. "Surely you're not planning on getting completely undressed."

Daniel grinned. "Why? Would you like to have that honor?"

She rolled her eyes and plopped down on the bed, lying down with her arms crossed over her belly and looking completely uninviting. Daniel's fingers paused on a cuff link. "Is something the matter?" he asked.

Her eyes met his, and he knew instinctively that she was not as eager for them to consummate their marriage as he was. Hell and damnation! He'd thought she felt as much desire for him as he did for her. Could he have been wrong?

"Look, it's not that I don't like you, Daniel, because I find your company to be delightfully entertaining," she said, smiling as usual. "But we've already established that you'd like to continue seeking the company of whatever woman strikes your fancy."

Daniel frowned. "I don't believe I—"

"I've no intention of demanding that you don't see other women, Daniel. The last thing I want is for you to grow to resent me. Besides, it's not as if I ever expected you to be faithful, but seeing it firsthand . . . well, I suppose I can admit that my pride was momentarily wounded."

Aha! So she *had* been jealous. This was a good sign.

"But as you can see, I've now recovered and am prepared to accept you for who you are."

"And who exactly would that be?" he asked, wary of the way she'd said it—as if he was some sort of rare specimen she'd happened to stumble upon.

"Why, a rake of course. A man who takes his pleasure with whatever woman he desires." Her eyes gleamed with curiosity as she rose up on one elbow. "Is it true that you usually set them up in a house of their own? Do you still have such a house?"

Good God!

Was he really having this conversation with his wife?

She gazed at him knowingly as she said, "Forget I asked, for I can see that you do."

Of course he did. Between speaking with his uncle and attending the Kingsborough Ball, he'd barely had enough time to send his mistress packing, let alone rid himself of the apartment he'd rented for her to live in. He nodded his response, but not without noticing a brief flicker of pain in Rebecca's eyes. Perhaps she wasn't as indifferent as she wanted to let on. Deciding to play along, Daniel sat on the edge of the bed and began pulling off his boots. "And what of you? What will you do while I'm out entertaining all these women?"

Her voice was decidedly terser when she spoke again. "I suppose I'll have Laura for company, although I imagine that in time I'll probably take a lover as well."

Daniel stiffened. This was a turn in the conversation that he hadn't anticipated. "You're mad," he muttered, not the least bit pleased about the thought of Rebecca in the arms of another man.

"No, Daniel, I'm not," she said as if they'd been discussing something as mundane as the weather, "but I am the adventurous sort, in case you hadn't noticed, and I will not sit at home playing the dutiful wife while you go out and have all the fun. If that was what you wanted, then you should have married someone else."

Daniel clenched his jaw. He felt a strong headache coming on. "What if I told you that I have no interest in any other women, but that you're the only woman I want?"

Rebecca took a deep breath, held it for a moment and then expelled the air with a deep sigh. "Daniel, I've known you for a mere week, and while you did go to great effort to save me, you did so not for my benefit alone but for yours as well. I will admit that I did dream of us running away together, falling madly in love and living happily ever after, but it's just a fantasy, as proven by the fact that as soon as another offer presented itself, you took it."

"Lady Vernon means nothing to me, Becky."

"And that's supposed to console me? That you would so easily share a kiss with another woman—one who means *nothing* to you?"

Damn it all, but this conversation was not going well.

"You know, it's my own fault really," Rebecca continued quietly as she stared up at the ceiling. "Lady Trapleigh warned me that—"

Daniel grimaced. "She's hardly the sort of woman you ought to place your trust in."

Rebecca turned her head to look at him. "Why? Because she's your female counterpart?"

Touché.

Rebecca's gaze returned to the ceiling. "She helped me when I needed it. The red gown I wore to the ball was hers."

"Of course it was." Who else would have given a scarlet gown to an unmarried lady?

"I'm sorry, Daniel, but you've given me reason to believe that you'll eventually be tempted into another woman's bed. If it is to be an inevitability, then I'd rather accept it than pretend it won't happen. I like you, and I want us to get along, but please try to understand that as long as you're likely to stray, you and I cannot be more than friends, and our bedroom activities will serve two purposes alone—the consummation of this marriage and the production of an heir. Once both have been achieved, it will probably be best if we limit any intimacy between us."

Bloody hell!

Daniel stared back at her. He was horrified, not just by her words—words that took a hatchet to their blooming relationship—but at himself for the mistake he'd made in not being more insistent in pushing Lady Vernon away. It was a mistake that had cost him Rebecca's trust. The question now was, What could he say to get them back on the right path—one where his wife wasn't so bloody intent on their living beneath the same roof as friends while they each went off to entertain their lovers? Of everything he'd seen and heard over the years, this was by far the most outrageous. Feeling as if he was losing control, he decided to change his tactics. He had to assert himself before he lost her forever. "Forgive me, Becky, but I'm your husband now, and I will not be denied a proper marriage."

She sat up with a start and glared back at him. Perhaps he'd overdone it a touch?

"Will you force yourself on me then?"

"No, of course not," he said. He'd never forced himself on anyone and was not about to start doing so now.

"I may have turned to you for help when I needed it, Daniel, but I am not some simpering Society miss who's going to let anyone tell her what to do, and I will certainly not allow you to take such liberties with me when . . ."

"When what?" he asked, his curiosity piqued.

"Nothing," she muttered. "Forget I said anything."

Well, now he was *really* curious. He decided not to press her though, since he already had a fair assumption of what had led to this argument in the first place. She'd said she liked him and that she'd imagined something more for them than just friendship. Seeing him with Lady Vernon, however, had put a damper on things, and she now refused to get too close, most likely because she wanted to protect herself from the pain of losing him to another woman . . . or other women. Her defenses were up, and rather than risk getting hurt she'd suggested the harebrained notion of a highly unconventional marriage. He wouldn't allow it of course. Instead, he would prove her wrong about him. He would do whatever was required of him to earn her trust so they could be truly happy together—a feat that would probably prove more difficult than he anticipated.

Recalling their best moments together, he decided to strategize. After all the times he'd gambled at cards, this was one game that he had no intention of losing. He decided to make his first move and stretched out on the bed beside her. "You're probably right about our marriage and how we ought to proceed in order to make the best of it," he said.

There was a long pause.

"You agree with me then?" She didn't sound convinced.

"Upon further consideration, I think you make a valid argument." Was she grinding her teeth together? He hid a smile. "In fact, I quite admire your honesty. I hope we can always be this forthright with each other."

"I'm not partial to deceit amidst friends," she said.

Turning onto his side, he watched her face . . . so beautiful. Instinct urged him to brush his fingers against her cheek, to lean over and kiss her. But he wouldn't. He'd seduced many women over the years and was now embarking on the greatest challenge of all—his own wife. "Me neither. So, how about if we continue with the game we started on our drive up here?"

She turned her head to meet his gaze, and he could see the interest lurching in the depths of her dark eyes. Filled with reassurance, he offered her an encouraging smile and said, "Go on, ask me a question."

Chapter 13

Feeling much like a piece of driftwood in a turbulent sea, Rebecca looked at the man lying next to her. He was her husband now and held more power over her than any other. It wasn't as if she hadn't considered this before, yet it had suddenly become so much more real now that they were tucked away in this bedroom together behind a locked door.

Apprehension swept over her as she studied his handsome face. What a fool she'd been to think that a kiss from him would mean as much to him as it had to her. She hadn't even realized just how much it had meant until now, when he'd finally agreed to accept her proposal. What on earth had she been thinking to say such a thing to him, pushing him away like that when all she wanted was to hug him close against her? The feelings that sprang to life within her though, like blossoms unfolding beneath the sun, were frightening. It was unlike anything she'd ever felt before, and she had no idea how to handle it. If only there was someone she could turn to for guidance, but there wasn't. Somehow she would have to figure this out on her own, and for now, the only thing she could think of was to guard her own heart.

Moving onto her side so she faced him completely, she asked softly, "What exactly happened to your parents?" His smile slipped, and she almost regretted the question, but it was an important one, one she felt she ought to know the answer to.

"Well," he began, "I suppose my mother woke up one morning and decided that she loved someone else more than she loved me and my father—an American plantation owner, from what little my uncle has told me. I believe he was visiting London on business, they met at a musicale, and three weeks later she was gone. I was eight years old at the time."

"She didn't even say good-bye to you?" It was one thing that his mother had left the man she'd married, but Rebecca couldn't imagine what sort of woman would abandon her child like that.

Daniel shrugged. He was clearly trying to look unaffected, but Rebecca sensed that the wound from his mother's betrayal still ran deep. "There was a brief note for me with the words *Forgive me* on it."

No mention of love?

"And your father?" Rebecca asked hesitantly.

"The moment she was gone, he enlisted in the army and was quickly killed. My uncle became my guardian."

An image of Daniel dealing with so much loss and pain at such a young age filled her mind. No wonder he'd eventually sought comfort wherever he'd been able to find it, both at the gaming tables and in the arms of women.

"What about *your* parents?" he asked.

"They perished in a fire five years ago." The taste of smoke was there again, as real as it had been the night Laura had woken her and led her outside to safety. "I don't know how it started, but I'm guessing that my mother must have fallen asleep with a candle still burning. When Papa went to save her, he got trapped."

"I'm so sorry," Daniel whispered. "I recall hearing about it, now that you mention it. My apologies for bringing it up." He reached for her hand and just held it in his own.

"It's all right," she said before adding, "I went to live with the parish vicar and his wife until my aunt and uncle eventually arrived, claiming that they were my guardians."

"Your parents named them?" Daniel asked, sounding surprised.

Rebecca nodded. "The will had been drawn up years earlier, when they were the only ones capable of taking on such a task. Papa was never very close with his sister, since she was ten years his senior, but she was his closest relative. I don't think he realized what sort of woman she'd become. He probably didn't imagine that she would treat any of his children any different than she would her own."

"She has children?" Daniel asked, his voice rife with disbelief.

Rebecca nodded. "Perhaps you've heard of them— Viscountess Ficklesby and Lady Gerald Paisley."

"I don't believe I've ever met Lady Gerald or the viscountess, but I do know who Lord Ficklesby is. Can't say I'm surprised to learn that he's the Griftons' son-in-law."

"No, I suppose not," she said, recalling a man with

a pointy nose and fat lips that always looked wet. "He's quite distasteful, wouldn't you agree?"

"Slimy, I'd say, if such a word can be used to describe a person."

Rebecca grinned. "I think it suits him perfectly. You know, I've always thought that there was something vulgar about him and that he wasn't a man to be trusted."

"Your intuition isn't far wrong." Daniel frowned, his hesitation suggesting that he knew something but wasn't sure if he should share it with her.

"What is it?" Rebecca asked.

"I spotted him a few times at one of the gambling hells on Piccadilly, always with a drab on his lap. The management asked him to leave one time because they thought his behavior too off-putting for the other guests." Daniel shook his head. "Forgive me. I really shouldn't be discussing such things with you."

"Why ever not?" Rebecca asked.

"It's hardly an appropriate topic for a lady, even if you are now married." There was a hint of a smile on his lips as he said it.

"Consider it a lesson then in the understanding of those peculiar creatures called men," Rebecca said, delighting in the way that Daniel's face lit with amusement, the corners of his eyes crinkling as he laughed. She gave his shoulder a playful nudge. "If you're not going to teach me, I can't imagine who will."

"You're going off on a tangent," he said with a touch of mischief. "We're supposed to be asking questions about each other, remember?"

"Very well." She took a moment to think of what to ask and eventually said, "Have you ever fought a duel?"

To her surprise, he nodded. "Once," he said. "It was a silly misunderstanding where the other gentleman had become convinced that I was having an affair with his wife."

"And were you?" she asked, unable to help herself.

"No," he said softly, "and you should also know that I've never taken an innocent to my bed."

As their eyes met, Rebecca felt that same heat that was growing all too familiar whenever he was near, pooling in her belly, where it threatened to fan out to the rest of her body. In that simple sentence, spoken with such care, Daniel had given Rebecca a silent promise. She was sure of it, and she found herself filled with the unbidden certainty that he would never abuse the trust she placed in him. His words told her that whatever his reputation, he would never take her by force, and that when she gave herself to him, it would not be something that he would take lightly but a gift that he would cherish.

The realization startled her, and she found herself grasping for something to say, some lighthearted rejoinder that would take her safely back to shallower waters. "I'm sure that's not what the rest of the world thinks, or they wouldn't have cast you in such a villainous role— the greatest rake that ever lived." The last part was said in a pompous tone that earned her a chuckle.

"Let's just say that in my younger years I was very fond of bragging about my many exploits. It's possible I may have elaborated a touch in the process."

Rebecca wasn't surprised. His confession was in perfect accord with the sort of man who would choose to climb a ladder for a secret rendezvous, propose to a lady he'd only just met and then steal said lady from under the nose of her fiancé. Perhaps his sins were fewer than the *ton* would like to believe, but he was still spurred on by a wild streak, perhaps even a secret fondness for the outrageous, considering how unashamed he seemed about it all. It took courage to stand against Society in pursuit of your own desires, and to do so as boldly as Daniel had done was something that spoke to Rebecca's own resolve. She studied the beautiful planes of his face as she reflected on how drastically her life had changed since her parents had died. She knew all too well what it was like to want something more out of life than what was being offered, but rather than bow to her aunt and uncle's demands, she'd opposed them in spite of the risk of doing so. It was unlikely that anyone would ever understand or accept her actions, yet Daniel did.

"How did you avoid losing yourself these past two years?" Daniel asked, bringing Rebecca's attention back to him. "I mean, to put on an act for so long cannot have been easy."

"It wasn't," she said, his question guiding her helplessly back to the tower of Roselyn Castle and the table where she'd sat hunched over for hours on end while she'd mumbled her gibberish, ensuring that her voice carried beyond her sanctuary, confirming to those who might have been skeptical that Lady Rebecca had suffered severely from her fall. "I was lucky that the Griftons allowed Laura to remain by my side, though I'm sure that they did so only to avoid the trouble of figuring out how else to care for me. Had it not been for Laura's company though—a normal conversation here and there amidst the pretense—I might have succumbed to the madness for good."

"I can't imagine being imprisoned like that," Daniel said softly, "even if it was a prison of your own making."

Rebecca shrugged. "I suppose I make it sound quite somber, but there were fun moments too, like finding new ways in which to shock my aunt whenever she came to check on me." She smiled at the memory. "You should have seen her face when she arrived once to find me facedown on top of the bookcase flapping my arms as if I was flying, or when I chose to put my gown on backward," Rebecca grinned. "I'm sure she thought my head had been twisted all the way around on my neck."

Daniel laughed as Rebecca imitated her aunt's horrified expression. "You have quite an impressive imagination, Becky." His face grew serious, and he reached his hand toward her, his fingertips gliding across the soft rise of her cheek. Rebecca held her breath while the heat in her belly rose toward her breasts. Her heart fluttered with rapid beats, and her skin felt feverish. "You're the most incredible woman I've ever known," he muttered, the words leaving his lips with deep admiration.

Powerless against the lure of his touch, Rebecca leaned into it, her eyelids gently lowering until darkness settled upon her, enhancing the feel of his thumb as it roamed along her jawline to her chin. He paused, and Rebecca could feel his eyes upon her. She briefly wondered what he might be thinking, but then she felt him stir, sensed him rising up across from her until the warm caress of his breath washed over her. His fingers fanned out, cupping her face more firmly, and she felt his lips brush against hers. Her chest shuddered in response, reminding her of how much she wanted this, how she'd longed for it since he'd last kissed her in her wardrobe. Rebecca considered pushing him away. She hated how easily she responded to him, fearful of what it would lead to and dreading the truth that lurked beneath the surface—that she was falling fast for a man who would never be satisfied with her alone. It was a difficult thought to contemplate though, especially when he made her feel so mushy inside, her defenses crumbling like chalk beneath a booted foot. As he pulled her toward him, the pressure of his lips increasing, Rebecca had trouble recalling why she should stop herself from surrendering to him, and when she felt his tongue requesting entrance, she no longer had the will to resist.

Eager to experience the pleasure she'd known only once before, Rebecca parted her lips and gave him what he sought. He didn't hesitate, dragging her body toward him until her chest was flush against his, the beat of his heart keeping pace with her own. This time, however, she knew what to do, her tongue gliding forward to greet his, and she thrilled at the low rumble that escaped his throat upon contact. Her arms slid up along the firm outline of his arms, his shirtsleeves bunching ever so slightly at her touch, and a sudden yearning to pull the fabric away and to feel the heat of the skin that lived beneath it overtook her.

Rebecca gasped as other thoughts assaulted her languorous mind, wicked thoughts brought to life by her own burning flesh. She wanted to feel his touch all over, craved it even, and wondered what that said about her own character. She ought to pull away and distance herself from him, to stop this before they ventured beyond the point of no return. There was only one problem with that; lost to Daniel's ministrations, Rebecca hadn't noticed as his expert hands had crept around to her back and loosened the buttons of her gown—not until her bodice and chemise slipped lower and cool air whispered across her breasts.

She didn't dare look at him, so she kept her eyes tightly shut while his hungry mouth continued its descent, his destination clear and utterly scandalous. Incapable of heeding her voice of reason and finding herself growing desperate with anticipation, Rebecca shut away the little voice that warned of what would happen if she continued down this path and gave herself up to the pleasure her husband evoked instead, but when he reached her breasts he pulled away, increasing Rebecca's sense of neediness tenfold. She arched toward him and was rewarded with the moist flick of his tongue against one of her nipples, the groan that escaped her throat assuring him of her thirst for more. To her relief, Daniel acceded, his mouth closing over one breast while his hands dragged her gown lower to pool around her waist, but it was still not enough to satisfy the hunger that had taken hold of her.

Unwilling to just sit there and take the pleasure Daniel offered, Rebecca brought her arms around his neck, her fingers keenly burying themselves in the thickness of his dark brown hair. Hugging him against her while he diligently laved and nibbled, the sensitivity of each breast rose until the slightest touch sent sparks of pleasure shooting straight between her thighs. The pulsing ache that settled there was growing too strong and urgent to ignore. It evoked the most scandalous thought of wanting to be touched there by him, and as Rebecca allowed the thought to manifest, her breathing grew heavier. Was this normal? She couldn't help but wonder if he would be repelled by her if she asked him to place his able fingers where she wanted them the most, but even she, as outspoken as she might be, couldn't possibly manage such a bold request. When Daniel's mouth returned to hers, his arms hugging her close, Rebecca sent her hands drifting over his back.

"God, you're beautiful!" Daniel's words broke through the silence that had settled over them. He still couldn't believe that this wonderful creature in his arms was his. The thought of marrying her had never been an unpleasant one, quite the opposite, and yet the more they spoke and the better acquainted they became with each other, the more certain he was that marrying Rebecca was the best thing he'd ever done.

She was so different from any other woman he'd ever encountered, her resolve to thwart those who'd wished her ill by playing the part of a madwoman a feat he couldn't help but admire. To have done so had taken great courage and strength, and rather than turn bitter and vengeful, she'd kept her spirits high. Daniel loved how easily she laughed, the way she joked without reserve and spoke her mind without wavering.

But when she'd spoken of the two years she'd spent trapped in the tower of Roselyn Castle, Daniel had felt his heart break for her. She'd forced a smile or two, pretending she'd remained unaffected by the confinement, but evidence of her struggle had been there in her eyes and in the gentle crease of her brow.

Unable to help himself and wishing to offer comfort, Daniel had done what came naturally to him and had reached out to her. She'd been ever so soft beneath his touch, and when her eyes had drifted shut, he'd taken a moment to study her face—the dark lashes that fanned out against her rosy cheeks, the delicate nose sitting proudly above a pair of full lips that reminded him of rose petals. Powerless against the temptation they offered, Daniel had leaned forward and kissed them, his stomach tightening with fear that she would reject him.

She hadn't though, and pure masculine elation had swept through him, yet he was not about to fall victim to arrogance. He knew that she had reservations, for which he could not blame her, but because of that, he would have to be careful. If he managed to seduce her, as was his intent, then the last thing he wanted was for her to look back on it with regret. So he'd taken things slow, allowing her time to adjust or to pull away if she so desired, except it had become increasingly obvious that what she desired was something else entirely.

Now, as he felt her hands pulling at his shirt, freeing it from his breeches so they could venture beneath, his yearning for her—to possess her in the most elemental way possible—set his blood ablaze. It was with tremendous restraint that he held back, reining in the lust that urged him to toss her on her back and ravage her, and allowed her the chance to explore him instead.

Meanwhile, he had every intention of guiding her toward unparalleled bliss. Delighting in how proficient she'd become in her kisses, he met her tongue stroke for stroke while his curious hands roamed across the parts of her body that were bare to his touch.

"Will you take off your shirt?" she asked, her words sounding shy and so different from her usual confident way of being.

Daniel absently wondered how long she'd been trying to voice her question. He wouldn't deny her for a second, however, and, leaning back, he went to work on the buttons.

Lifting his gaze, he was met with the fullness of her breasts as they jutted toward him, sending a shock of scorching heat straight to his groin. He was hard already. Hell, when was he not when she was near? But the way she looked, with her naked torso emerging from the crumpled silk of her gown, the pink flush that shimmered upon her skin and the slight parting of her lips as she waited for him to make the next move, was turning his determination to do the right thing into undeniable torture.

Shrugging out of his shirt, Daniel wound his arms around Rebecca and eased them both down onto the bed, rolling over until she was lying on her back with him on top of her. Gazing down at her, he saw the expectant look upon her face. This was his area of expertise, yet he found himself worried that he would somehow disappoint her. It was of the utmost importance that he didn't. He wanted to give her pleasure beyond her wildest imaginings.

Running his hand along the curve of her waist, he lowered his lips to her ear and quietly whispered, "I'm going to remove your gown now, Becky, and once that's done, I'll finally be able to give you the proper attention that you deserve."

A tortured sigh was her only response, one that suggested that she'd likely expire from want if he didn't follow through on his promise. He smiled to himself with devilish glee as he tugged on the bunched fabric and proceeded to slide it down over her slender legs, her chemise resisting only a little as he nudged it over her hips, discarding both garments at the foot of the bed. Only her stockings remained, so he went to work on them next, rolling each one down until her toes wiggled free. "Open your eyes," he murmured as he lifted a leg so he could place a tender kiss against the arch of one foot. "Look at me."

It took a moment before she complied, and even then she only opened her eyes a fraction and with great hesitation, as if she feared the sight that was there to greet her. Nuzzling her calf, Daniel met her gaze. "Don't be shy," he said. "I love it when you're brazen."

She licked her lips, her teeth denting the plump flesh. "It's just that I . . . I feel so very naked."

Daniel grinned, and to his relief she smiled in return, though there was still a measure of uncertainty to it. "Perhaps that's because you *are* naked," he said, allowing his fingers to glide along the length of her leg. She gasped when he reached her bottom, and then again when he circled around to trace the edge of her inner thigh. "I like you best like this though."

She was looking directly at him now, her eyes widening as she followed the movement of his hands, her breath growing raspy as she realized his intent. Easing her legs slowly apart, Daniel knelt between them, opening her up to his perusal. God, how he wanted her!

Heart throbbing in his chest, he took a moment to admire his efforts. With one leg on either side of him, Rebecca had been spread completely wide, a hint of moisture beckoning from between her tender flesh—an invitation for him to bury himself in her depths. Raising his gaze, he followed the sweep of her pelvis up over her belly button until he reached her breasts and finally her face. Her eyes appeared glazed. "Would you like me to touch you?" he asked, his voice a coaxing whisper.

Rebecca nodded. "Yes."

Daniel reached for her left breast and gave it a gentle squeeze. "Here?" he asked.

She shook her head with obvious frustration, bringing out in full force the cheeky devil within him. "How about here?" he asked as he gave his attention to her other breast.

"No, not there," she said, restlessly wriggling her bottom as if to draw his attention toward her pelvis.

Daniel allowed both hands to trail down the length of her abdomen, stopping at her hips, where he proceeded to massage her. Was she holding her breath? He was starting to pity the state of torment she was in and decided to meet her need. "Then perhaps here," he said as he brushed his fingers along the seam of Rebecca's womanhood.

"Yes," she sighed, her hips rising in response to his touch while she threw her head backward, eyes closed with a look of complete and utter satisfaction capturing her features.

Daniel stroked her again, parting the slick folds of her flesh so his expert fingers could seek the pleasure point hidden beneath. He rubbed it gently with his thumb, pleased with the groan that she made as she pushed herself against his touch, her every move increasing his own want until he feared he might go blind from the carnal need that she stirred in him. He'd always prided himself on his restraint and ability to remain in complete control, but this woman was making it nearly impossible for him to do so.

Desperate for more closeness, he paused in his ministrations so he could finish undressing. With a few quick movements that spoke of his urgent desire, he tugged off his breeches and climbed back onto the bed.

"Tell me what you're thinking," he said as he lowered his head and kissed her inner thigh, ending the caress with a light nibble.

"I'm thinking that this is wonderful," she murmured, "and that I must be incredibly wicked to like it as much as I do."

"Hmm . . . and it gets so much better," he promised.

"Really?" She sounded incredulous, so he decided to show her just how much better it could be as he sank down between her outstretched limbs and licked the place where his thumb had been just moments earlier.

"Oh dear God," she panted. He loved her openness, how unashamed she was of letting him know that she liked what he was doing. He fleetingly wondered if he might one day convince her to pleasure him in a similar way. He pushed the thought aside, his restraint already dangling from a fragile thread, and with one more lick, he rose so he could look her in the eye as he pushed one finger inside her.

Her lips parted on a gasp and he was there in an instant, kissing her wildly as he added another finger. "You like that, don't you?" he asked, taking immeasurable gratification in her whispered yes. He wanted to be there with her though when her pleasure peaked, so he pulled away, unable to stop a smile when she whimpered at the loss of him. "I've been told that the first time can hurt for a woman, but I'll do my best to make it good for you. I promise," he said as he settled himself between her thighs, his hand caressing the side of her face.

"If what you've done so far is any indication of what is to come," she said, gazing up at him with needy hunger brimming in her eyes, "then I give you my full approval."

"I'll try to go slow," he said as he found her entrance, braced himself on his elbows and started easing himself inside. They both sighed with contentment at exactly the same time, leading to a shared burst of laughter immediately after. It quickly faded when Daniel reached between them and started to stroke her again, her hips rising, accepting more of him until he reached the proof of her innocence. Crushing his mouth over hers, he pushed forward, burying himself deep within her welcoming warmth, her gasp of surprise swallowed by their kiss.

With a supreme effort born from the determination to cause her as little discomfort as possible, Daniel stilled and waited for Rebecca to recover. He took the time to savor the wonderful feeling of being inside her as he bit back the instinct to thrust again. But when she finally moved beneath him, he pulled out a little, then pushed himself carefully back inside while his thumb remained devoted to bringing her pleasure. "How do you feel?" he asked, concerned that the pain she must have felt when he'd taken her innocence might have lingered.

She gazed up at him from beneath the sweep of her lashes and smiled a seductive smile that any temptress should have envied the ability to deliver. "Wonderful," she sighed as she pulled him down for a long kiss. "And completely . . . oh God, Daniel!"

"That's it, my sweet, just relax." He licked the lobe of her ear and added a bit more pressure to his thumb, his own rhythm steady as he moved in and out of her. "Come for me, Becky, let yourself go."

On a near scream of ecstasy, Rebecca's muscles contracted around him, pulling him along with her on the wave of euphoria that claimed them both, until a climax more forceful than any Daniel had ever experienced before overcame him. He gasped, as if coming up for air after an underwater swim, then kissed Rebecca thoroughly to assure her of his gratitude before rolling off her and pulling her up against his side, her head cradled against his arm. A satisfied smile spread its way across his face as he delighted in what their coupling had just confirmed—that just as he'd thought, they would get on very well together indeed.

Chapter 14

They returned to London three days later and headed straight to Bedford Square. The three-story town house had remained uninhabited since his father's death, but now that Daniel was married, it would be his. The brown brick façade had been unaltered in all the years that had come and gone since he'd last set foot inside, linking him to a past that invariably led to unhappy memories of abandonment. Pulling up in front, Daniel gazed up at the third-floor window furthest to the right. Beyond it lay the room that had once been his nursery, a room in which his mother had read stories and his father had battled toy soldiers with him. It was also the room in which he'd eventually found his mother's note: *Forgive me*—two words that had brought his young life crashing down around him.

Burying the pain that threatened to surface, Daniel leapt down from his perch on the phaeton and reached up for Rebecca. What good would it do to revisit the past? He was better off pushing such memories and wishful thoughts of what could have been aside. But when Rebecca took the arm he offered her and they started up the front steps, Daniel couldn't help but feel the sad eyes of his younger self gazing down at him from the nursery window.

With a deliberate effort, he focused his mind on the present, relishing the feel of Rebecca's arm linked with his own as he led her up the front steps. Hopefully the sparse staff his uncle had kept on at the house had received the message he'd sent them informing them of his and Rebecca's imminent arrival.

"Hawkins," Daniel said when a young man his own age opened the door after the second knock. He was breathing a little harder than usual. "Where's Mr. Tenant? I would have expected him to be the first to greet us."

Hawkins looked perplexed. Avoiding an explanation, he gave his attention to Rebecca and offered her a bow. "Lady Rebecca Neville, what a pleasure it is to make your acquaintance. Welcome to Avern House."

Daniel frowned but decided not to question his valet any further. He turned to his wife instead and made the necessary introduction. "Perhaps you'd be good enough to see to it that the phaeton is brought around to the mews," he then said to Hawkins. "And if refreshments are available, we'd both be most appreciative."

"Not a problem, sir," Hawkins said. "I'll see to it right away."

"Shall I give you the grand tour?" Daniel asked Rebecca once Hawkins left their presence.

"I can think of nothing better," she said, beaming up at him with her beautiful smile.

Daniel could think of lots of better things for them to do, but he chose to keep those thoughts to himself.

Instead, he guided Rebecca toward the parlor and through to the music room, then onward to the study, where he was once again assaulted by the past, a vision of his father sitting at the cherrywood desk flooding him with an overwhelming sense of loss. He would have to refurnish to escape such memories, and as he hurried Rebecca along to the library and, finally, the dining room, he made a mental note to do so.

"This is perfect," Rebecca said, trailing her fingers along the edge of the dining room table as she walked across to a bay window.

Daniel followed her and looked out. The garden that met his gaze was modest but well kept, with a flagstone terrace and a patch of grass surrounded by flowerbeds brimming with daffodils and hyacinths.

The touch of Rebecca's hand curling around his own made him turn his head toward her. "I believe we're going to be very happy here," she said, the sparkle in her eyes enhanced by the rosy blush in her cheeks.

"I'm sure we will," he said, hoping she was right. The absence of staff troubled him. He would have to ask Hawkins later, but he didn't want to ruin the moment for Rebecca. After everything she'd been through, he was pleased with how happy she seemed to finally have a place of her own, free from the overbearing clutches of her aunt and uncle. He gave her hand a little tug. "Come along. I'll show you the upstairs."

Arriving at the top of the stairs, they stepped off the landing and into a neat salon with windows facing the street on one side and doors leading off to two different rooms on the other. There was a plush sofa facing two armchairs with a table between them; it was a cozy spot where Daniel's mother had sometimes entertained her closest friends and family and where both his parents had taken their Sunday breakfast. Daniel opened the first door on his left, revealing a moderately sized bedroom with a bed draped in creamy silks, the coverlet embroidered in gold thread.

"There's a small dressing room over there," he said, watching as Rebecca walked over to take a closer look.

"I love it," she said, her voice filled with delight. "It's so beautiful and elegant."

Daniel nodded. He considered joining her in the room and locking the door behind him so they could become better acquainted with the bed, but he decided to wait. There were other pressing matters to attend to, like calling on his aunt and uncle. With no way of knowing how they would greet him and his wife, Daniel had decided that it would be best if he handled the first visit alone. He would do so as soon as he'd spoken to Hawkins and satisfied his aching stomach. Lord help him he was hungry!

Moving on, he showed Rebecca another bedroom, which was quite a bit larger than the first. "For guests," he lied.

Standing at his side, Rebecca said nothing, saving Daniel from having to explain that he'd rather walk barefooted through hell than spend one night in the room that had once belonged to his parents. Unlike so many other members of the *ton*, they had not kept separate bedchambers, and Daniel had always imagined that he and his wife would share a similar intimacy. From what he knew of Rebecca so far, he suspected that she would be amenable to the idea.

"How very practical that is," Rebecca said, confirming his thoughts. "Honestly, I've never understood why a husband and wife should have separate rooms. I'm relieved to know that we'll be spending more time together."

Closing the door again, he quietly wondered if she'd become aware of the demons that haunted him with every step he took. "I'll show you the third floor later," he said when Hawkins arrived to inform him that the phaeton had been safely parked and that Cook was preparing a small meal that a maid would bring up shortly.

A cook *and* a maid? Daniel couldn't help but be relieved. He'd begun to imagine that poor Hawkins might have taken on the duties of all the servants Avern House required, for he'd seen no one else since his arrival.

"And what is your name?" Rebecca asked when a sprightly young girl arrived carrying a tray that to Daniel's eye looked rather inviting. Was that freshly baked bread?

"My name's Molly, my lady," she said, her voice warm and her smile completely unabashed—not at all the sort of maid that Daniel was used to his aunt and uncle employing. They were a far more somber lot, trained to avoid meeting the gaze of their superiors. Molly, however, just stood there beaming, as if they'd all been jolly good friends.

Daniel felt himself smile in response and decided that he liked the girl. Rebecca must have too, judging from the way she offered to help Molly lay out the plates, teacups and saucers while Hawkins watched with quiet surprise. Daniel had known his valet for years, and though Hawkins wasn't exactly conservative (he and Daniel would never have gotten along if

he had been), he did look as if he was feeling a bit uncomfortable with his new mistress leaping to the aid
of a maid, when most ladies would have sat silently
and watched until the maid was done. Thankfully Rebecca was not so prim, Daniel mused, unable to stop
himself from smiling as she and Molly chatted about
this and that.

"She'll get on famously with Laura once we bring
her over," Rebecca said a short while later when both
Molly and Hawkins had departed, allowing Rebecca
and Daniel to enjoy the ham, cheese and bread that
Cook had sent up.

"I'll send a messenger over to Grover House as soon
as we've finished eating. I imagine she'll be either there
or with the Griftons."

Rebecca nodded. "I expect my aunt and uncle will
call on us as soon as they are made aware of our return,"
she said with a touch of dread. "Now *that's* a visit that
I'm not particularly looking forward to."

"You mustn't worry. You're married to me now,
Becky. They no longer have the power to bend you to
their will, so really, why does it matter what they say?"

"You're right," she said with a thoughtful nod. "It
doesn't." Taking a sip of her tea, she looked at Daniel.
"What else shall we do for the rest of the day? I'd love
to see the park if it's not too far. I haven't been there
since I was a child, but I remember it being quite impressive."

"While such an outing does sound tempting, we will
have to delay until tomorrow. Right now I have to have
a word with Hawkins—see if there are any pressing
matters that need my immediate attention—and then I
will pay a call on my aunt and uncle."

"Oh, I'd love to join you," Rebecca said, looking terribly excited. "May I?"

Hating to disappoint, Daniel didn't enjoy telling her that it would be best if he went to see them on his own. "You mustn't forget that our wedding was quite hasty and unexpected. Considering we eloped and left a duke standing at his own engagement ball without his fiancée, it may take a while for them to adjust. When they're ready, they will invite us both over for tea so they can make your acquaintance."

Rebecca frowned. "That sounds awfully formal, Daniel."

"Yes, well, my aunt and uncle are the formal sort, you know." An issue he'd had enough difficulty dealing with over the years, since it meant he'd always been at odds with them.

Leaving Rebecca to explore the upstairs, Daniel went in search of Hawkins. He eventually found him in the courtyard next to the kitchen, pumping water for Cook. The valet paused at his task when he spotted Daniel.

"Have we no footmen to handle such things?" Daniel asked, knowing that the answer would likely be no.

"As you may have noticed, sir, the household staff is somewhat depleted. There are only the three of us."

Daniel stepped closer and crossed his arms. "I don't suppose that's because my aunt and uncle were unaware that I would be returning with a bride and in need of a fully functional home?"

"No," he said with great reluctance.

"Are you able to explain why there are no more servants then? Mr. Tenant, the butler, remained at this address even after my parents were gone. I'm surprised he's not here."

Hawkins took a deep breath. "I received a missive from Lord Wolvington's secretary two days ago requesting that I leave the gentleman lodgings where you have been residing and come here instead. Cook was already busy in the kitchen when I arrived. I believe your mother initially hired her, whereas Molly . . . well, from what I gather, she didn't suit the Wolvington household." Hawkins met Daniel's gaze seriously. "You needn't concern yourself though—we may be few, but we've all decided to make this work as best we can. We won't be leaving you."

"Thank you," Daniel said, touched by the man's loyalty. "And since you're prepared to do so much for me, the least I can do is help you with that water. Here . . . I'll carry it down to Cook while you fill the next bucket."

As soon as they were done, Daniel and Hawkins climbed back upstairs, where Hawkins abandoned his role as footman in favor of his much-preferred position as valet, offering Daniel a clean set of clothes that he'd brought with him from the apartment. With his cravat tied to perfection and his entire person so immaculate that neither his aunt nor his uncle would possibly find fault with his appearance, Daniel said good-bye to Rebecca and stepped out into the street, where a hackney awaited, yet another service for which he had Hawkins to thank.

Settling back against the squabs, Daniel waited for the horses to take off at a trot, then set his mind to preparing for the interview ahead. Whatever game his uncle was playing at, Daniel would not allow him to drag Rebecca into it, and he had every intention of telling him so.

"**I**'ve a good mind to throttle you," Lord Wolvington said when Daniel was shown into his study and the butler had exited, closing the door behind him.

Daniel grimaced. "And here I was thinking that you would congratulate me."

"Congratulate you?" His uncle looked as if he was having a bout of indigestion. "Whatever for?"

Daniel frowned. Had his uncle grown forgetful in his old age? "I did what you asked of me," he said. "I got married—and to a lovely woman, I might add."

"What I asked for . . ." his uncle sputtered. "Are you mad, boy? I did not ask you to steal a duke's fiancée or to elope with an earl's ward!" He slammed his fist onto his desk. The action made his quill bounce, while ink flew from the inkwell and spattered across the polished surface. "Have you any idea of the scandal you've caused? The Duke of Grover has been made a laughingstock of London. He's absolutely furious, and rightfully so."

Daniel blinked. He'd known there would likely be hell to pay, but he'd put off worrying about it in favor of just enjoying Rebecca's company. "Will he be wanting a duel?" he asked.

"He did, but I managed to talk him out of that notion. The last thing we need right now is for you to kill the man." Daniel's uncle shook his head. "Honestly, Daniel, what were you thinking?"

"Well, for one thing I wanted to please you," Daniel confessed, "and since Rebecca was the only woman I met who was willing to even speak to me, she seemed like the obvious choice."

"Didn't she tell you that she was engaged?"

"She wasn't when we met." Daniel then told his uncle everything—how Rebecca had feigned madness for two years to escape marriage, the way the Griftons had encouraged Grover and Topperly to bid for her, and how Daniel had offered her a means of escape. "They're despicable people," Daniel said at the end of it all.

"And I suppose you think yourself the hero in all of this?" his uncle said. He didn't wait for an answer, saying instead, "I never cared for any of these people, you know, but that doesn't excuse what you did. What I wanted for you, Daniel, was for you to find a way to clear your name of scandal, not tarnish it even further. I'm sorry, but I don't see how I can help you with this situation without affecting your aunt or your sister's family. The gossips are already having a splendid time with this. They're ready to rip you to shreds."

"And here I thought I was doing not only the right thing but the noble and just thing as well," Daniel muttered. He slumped down on one of the seats across from his uncle. "Instead I just gave them the scoundrel they expected, but then again, it's a part I've played for so long it would probably be difficult for me to be anything else. I was a fool to think otherwise."

"Devil take it, Daniel, you're a perfectly good man at heart, but you have to stop acting like this." Wolvington leaned back in his chair and stared at his nephew. "I know it's been tough on you since your mother left and your father died—I miss him too, you know—but you can't keep using their actions to excuse your own."

"That's not what this is about," Daniel ground out. He'd no desire to talk about his parents right now.

"Is that so?"

Daniel stared back at his relative as he thought about the lifestyle he'd grown so accustomed to, the company he'd kept and his taste for adventure—how he hated being alone with his own thoughts. An overwhelming sense of clarity descended upon him, and he suddenly saw his life for what it was. Good God, he'd behaved like an ungrateful scamp, heedless of those around him. Swallowing hard, he tried not to think of what a burden he must have been for his aunt and uncle. They had been stricken by grief as well, yet they had set it aside in order to offer him comfort. In return, they'd gotten a rebellious youth who'd acted out in the most selfish way possible, bringing scandal upon their name. It was a miracle they hadn't offered him an ultimatum before now.

"Forgive me," he muttered, because really, what else was there to say? The revelation had startled him, and yet he felt freer somehow because of it. He took a deep breath and thought of Rebecca. "Whatever mistakes I made in the past, I must consider the future now. I have a wife to care for, and I've no intention of letting her down."

"I'm pleased to hear it," his uncle grumbled, "but that doesn't make me any more able to assist. I'm afraid you're on your own."

Daniel tensed. "What do you mean?"

"That by getting yourself married the way you did, you've left me with no choice but to distance myself from you socially. The only reason you're getting the house is because it was your father's. You've every right to it, but as far as servants are concerned, you'll have to hire your own. Cook, as you know, was hired by your mother, so she may stay."

"What about Molly?" Daniel asked. He felt numb.

"After I sacked her, I suggested that you might want her in your employ."

"And Mr. Tenant? He was always there when I was a boy."

"He left when he discovered that I would no longer be paying his wages," Wolvington said. "I don't believe he had much faith in you in that regard."

"Are you cutting me off completely then?" Daniel asked, dreading the answer that would come.

"There's a hundred pounds in the safe behind the painting in your study. Here's the key to it." The marquess slid a silver key across the table to Daniel. "I'm sorry, but I cannot support your actions, Daniel. I hope you understand."

Daniel stared blankly at him.

Wolvington sighed. His eyes met Daniel's. "I'm glad to see that you didn't just marry her for your own sake, though but that you actually seem to care about her. I wish you the best, Daniel, truly I do, but the dust needs to settle before you and I can be seen associating with each other, and that's going to take time."

With a nod, Daniel rose and prepared to leave. His uncle had made himself clear.

"You are aware that since she eloped with you and there is no settlement, your wife's dowry belongs to you," Lord Wolvington said, stopping Daniel in his tracks. "You are free to do with it as you please."

"No." Daniel shook his head with complete resolve. "I won't touch her money. I'd rather work for a living if I must."

Wolvington nodded, and Daniel saw in his eyes something that he'd never seen before—admiration.

"Well then. It looks as though you know what to do." Rising, he reached across the table, offering Daniel his outstretched hand. "Best of luck to you."

In a daze, Daniel accepted the peace offering from his uncle. He couldn't be angry with him for cutting him off. Daniel had lost his head over a woman and had acted rashly. Even if his uncle agreed with his actions, he couldn't support them and had no choice but to leave him to fend for himself.

Dear God, Daniel thought as he walked back to Avern House. He dreaded what was to come, knowing that he would no longer be the only one shunned by Society. Rebecca would be too now, and he realized that while he might have saved her from one hellish nightmare, he'd very likely dragged her into another. The *ton* was an unforgiving lot who would rather feed on the faults of others than draw attention to their own.

Even now as he walked he was not unaware of how empty the pavement was, noting that every person who came toward him crossed the street as soon as they became aware of who he was. He wanted to yell at them all for taking the side of the Griftons and Grover. *They* were the villains in this; it was *they* who should have been ostracized, not him and Rebecca. And what the hell was he going to say to Rebecca anyway? "Sorry, love, but we're facing imminent poverty. Thank you for marrying me though." He laughed bitterly.

She would tell him to use her dowry of course. In fact, knowing her, she'd probably demand it. A smile touched the corner of his lips for a brief second before flittering off in the breeze. He'd meant what he'd told his uncle—he wouldn't use her money, which meant that he wouldn't be able to tell her about the financial straits they were now in. Taking a job was one solution, except he lacked the skills for the sort of position that would earn him the income he'd require.

A hundred pounds was all the money he had right now, and somehow he would have to make it last. There was only one way he could think of to make that happen, and he only hoped that if he went down that road, neither his uncle nor Rebecca would ever find out.

What was he thinking? He couldn't risk gambling away what little money he had, no matter how good a player he was—not when he had a wife and servants who depended on him. A thought struck him. He didn't have to gamble away *all* the money. What if he chose to risk only twenty pounds at the tables? He could then invest another thirty pounds in some profitable enterprise. But in what? Daniel had no idea which companies prospered and which didn't, but Audrey's husband, the Earl of Chilton, did. In fact, Daniel knew that he was very good at it. Perhaps he would be willing to advise Daniel on how to spend his thirty pounds? Meanwhile, he would still have another fifty set aside in case he failed to prosper from either of these ventures.

Decision made, Daniel arrived home, hoping to enjoy Rebecca's delightful company for the rest of the day, when a high-pitched squawk reached his ears. It seemed to have come from the parlor.

With no sign of Hawkins around, Daniel went to the door and opened it, discovering two matronly dragons, as well as Lady Grifton, all of them looking stern-faced at Rebecca, who was staring back at them wide-eyed and openmouthed. "Good afternoon, ladies," Daniel said jovially. Three sets of glaring eyes turned on him, but he was indifferent to their vehemence and merely smiled. "What a delightful surprise."

"I assure you that we take little delight in coming here," Lady Grifton said.

"Are you sure about that?" Daniel asked, his smile slipping as his words grew angry. "Seems to me you've all come to take a good look at the new Mrs. Neville, perhaps even give her a piece of your mind."

"Why, I—" Lady Grifton said, looking aghast.

"May I remind you," Daniel continued, not caring the least for what the countess might have wished to say, "that you are in her home. Why, she's even shown you the courtesy of inviting you to stay for tea."

"After everything that my husband and I have done for her," Lady Grifton sneered while her friends nodded their heads with sisterly compassion, "not to mention forcing us to traipse all over creation in search of you after you so scandalously ran off with her, the least she can do is apologize for her actions. A public announcement to this effect would certainly go a long way in appeasing the damage the two of you have done."

"If that is all, then I would advise you to take your leave now. After all, you wouldn't want anyone to see you in our company, now, would you?"

A look of concern flashed in the eyes of the three ladies. "Quite right," Lady Grifton finally said, getting up and turning her back on Rebecca. "But I warn you, Mr. Neville—this matter is far from over. Mark my word."

And with that ominous promise, Lady Grifton and her two friends paraded past him, taking their hatred with them as they exited his home. Daniel turned to Rebecca. "I'm sorry you had to endure that. Had I known your aunt would call while I was away, I would have postponed my visit with my uncle so I could have been here with you."

"It's all right," Rebecca said. "You needn't worry about me. I'm fine." Getting up, she came toward him. "I'm far more interested in learning how your meeting with your uncle went. Will he forgive us for running away together?"

"He understands why we did it," Daniel said, not exactly answering her question but hoping to ease her concerns, "but unfortunately our little adventure has caused quite a stir, as evidenced by your aunt's instant visit. My uncle has requested that we distance ourselves from them for a time."

Rebecca's eyes widened. "They will not support our decision?"

"They cannot," Daniel said, adding hastily, "fear not, though. It's only temporary. As soon as the gossip dies down everything will return to normal."

"But if we tell everyone the truth, Daniel—how poorly my aunt and uncle have treated me and that Grover practically bought me from them, then surely—"

"Arranged marriages are not uncommon among the *ton,* and neither are settlements. I daresay there won't be many who'll be sympathetic to our cause regardless of how unpleasant your aunt and uncle may be. Besides, your uncle is an earl," Daniel told her gently as he took her hands in his. "You were under his guardianship, and all anyone will see is a young woman who was fortunate enough to win the attention of a duke only to publicly humiliate him by running off with a rake."

She nodded, her expression unusually serious.

"Well, at least we have a place to live, although I would have thought we'd have more servants."

"My uncle only supplied us with the bare minimum, since he thought we might like to hire the rest of our staff ourselves." As he said it, Daniel wondered how many lies he would end up telling in order to protect Rebecca from the truth.

Rebecca's features relaxed, and she even managed a bit of a smile. "How thoughtful of him," she said. "I shall start interviewing maids and footmen as soon as possible then. Molly and Hawkins are in desperate need of assistance."

Daniel stopped himself from protesting. It was enough that he had to worry about paying the salaries that would come with extra staff. He wouldn't bother Rebecca with all of that. "It's growing late," he said, "and we've had a rather long day. Let us have an early supper and then a bath before bed. I believe we could both use one after our journey."

"I'd love nothing more, but I don't want to send Hawkins running up and down the stairs with buckets of water either. It just isn't fair. I can manage with a washbasin and a sponge for now."

"You're kind, Becky, do you know that? Which is why I shall ensure that you have the bath you so desire."

"But—" she protested.

"I will help Hawkins carry the water," Daniel said, "as long as you will accept taking your bath here in the parlor. Does that sound reasonable?"

"I don't want the servants to think me spoiled or demanding," Rebecca said.

"Don't worry. I'll tell them that I insisted on it." And then he pulled her into his embrace and placed his mouth over hers in a hungry kiss that stole her breath. Releasing her with the satisfaction that he'd managed to daze her, he stepped away and went to the door. "I'll ask Molly to start a fire in the hearth so you don't catch a chill, and for Hawkins to bring the tub."

"And what should I do?" Rebecca asked. "I hope you don't expect me to just sit here and look pretty while you do all the work?"

Daniel grinned. "You may accompany me downstairs, then to the kitchen if you like. It's time you met Cook."

Chapter 15

The sounds and smells that greeted Rebecca were not entirely unfamiliar. When her parents had been alive, she'd been forbidden from venturing below stairs for two reasons: first, because proper ladies never entered the servants' domain, and second, because her parents hadn't wanted her to get in anyone's way. But, being the lively child that she'd been, such rules hadn't been enough to stop her, and she'd many a time snuck into the kitchen to steal a freshly baked bun or two. Later, at Roselyn Castle, she'd entered the kitchen only once. After accidentally knocking over a bucket of water, the cook had yelled at her to get out, and her aunt had later punished her by sending her to bed without supper— the first warning of the sort of treatment she would come to expect from her relative.

Hesitant about what awaited her in the kitchen of Avern House, Rebecca allowed Daniel to lead the way. The rich aroma of meat mingling with spices drifted toward her, teasing her senses. When she finally entered the room itself, heat coming from a massive oven in the corner embraced her. She stepped forward and glanced around, taking in the vast array of copper pots that hung suspended under the ceiling alongside bunches of dried herbs. A middle-aged woman dressed all in black and with a rather shapely figure came into view. Rebecca stared as the woman grabbed a spoon and poured some liquid, which Rebecca suspected might have been wine, into one of the pots on the stove. Somehow she'd drawn the conclusion that all cooks were of the more plump variety, as had been the case both during her childhood and at Roselyn Castle. Clearly she had been mistaken and was only grateful that the woman she was now looking at was past her prime and unlikely to catch her husband's interest.

Rebecca shook the thought away. What was she thinking? That Daniel would actually try to seduce the help? Even she knew that he was better than that, yet the thought had entered her mind without restraint, reminding her that she still worried about his ability to remain faithful to her, more so now that she'd actually given herself to him. The trouble was that she feared it wasn't just her body he'd conquered on their wedding night but her heart as well.

"Rebecca," Daniel said, taking her by the hand and leading her forward. "May I introduce you to Madame Renarde? A fine cook if I may say so."

Of course she would be French, Rebecca mused. She smiled at the woman, who was also quite pretty, save for a slight burn mark on her left cheek. "I hope you don't mind me intruding on your domain," Rebecca said, "but I was curious to see the rest of the house. I am Lady Rebecca Neville."

Madame Renarde smiled, her hand still stirring the simmering liquid in the pot. Whatever it was, it smelled heavenly. "It is a pleasure to make your acquaintance, my lady." Her voice sang with lyrical French undertones. "I hope you will forgive me for not coming upstairs to greet you earlier upon your arrival as is customary," Madame Renarde continued, "but as you can see, there is a lot of work to be done."

"I'd be happy to help," Rebecca blurted without thinking. Madame Renarde's raised eyebrows and a stunned silence from Molly, Daniel and Hawkins, who'd been discussing the procedure of tending to Rebecca's bath later, were indicative of a mutual surprise. Rebecca turned, hands on hips, and looked at Daniel. "I see no reason why I cannot lend a hand here when you are prepared to act as footman."

Her husband stared back at her, but then the corner of his mouth twitched, giving way to a broad smile. "I believe we've both proven ourselves unsuitable for traditional conventions. This is your home as well as it is mine. You may do as you please, my dear."

Her heart swelling with infinite joy, Rebecca grabbed an apron from a hook behind the door and proceeded to follow whatever instructions Madame Renarde and Molly gave her, fetching dishes, chopping herbs, grinding pepper and crushing garlic.

"It's a good thing you're having a bath later," Daniel whispered as he strode past the spot where Rebecca was working. "You're starting to smell like quite the meal yourself." Heat rose to her cheeks as he said it, his words suggesting that he wouldn't mind partaking in the delicacies she had to offer. It was a wonder that she didn't burst into flames at the very idea of it.

"Thank you so much for helping us," Madame Renarde said when the only task that remained was carrying the food upstairs. "I don't believe any other lady would have done the same."

"You're very welcome," Rebecca said, "and since I'm going up anyway, I can easily take something along if you like."

"There's a dumbwaiter right over there, Rebecca," Daniel said. Having returned to the kitchen after helping Hawkins with the tub, he'd stepped up beside Rebecca and was now pointing to a square-shaped hole in the wall. "It will bring the food directly to the dining room."

Marveling at the ingenious bit of engineering, Rebecca allowed Daniel to escort her back upstairs while Molly followed behind them. "I know you're eager to see it at work," Daniel said, leading Rebecca past the dining room table and toward a small square-shaped door located in the wall at the far end of the room. Grabbing the brass handle on the bottom of it, Daniel pushed the door up, revealing a shaft inside the wall. Rebecca stared, impressed by the convenience this simple idea offered. She'd always been used to large estates, where the food was tepid at best by the time it traveled the long distance from the kitchen to the dining room.

Reaching for a chord that hung beside the dumbwaiter, Daniel gave it a slight pull. There was a brief moment of silence, and then a whirring sound as ropes yanked the elevator containing Daniel's and Rebecca's dinner upward. "Let's take our seats now," Daniel said as soon as Rebecca caught sight of a tray with three covered dishes on it, "and allow Molly here to do her job." When they were alone again and their plates had been filled with succulent chicken breasts, as well as potato slices fried in butter and herbs and covered in a light but piquant red wine sauce, Daniel said, "I really appreciate everything you did this evening. It was well done of you, Becky, and I know that the servants will respect you more for it. Just don't forget that they must feel useful as well. You have to give them the chance to serve you."

"I'm sorry," she said. "I'm just not very used to that concept, I suppose. After arriving at Roselyn Castle, Laura quickly became more than just my maid. She became my only friend, and rather than just sit about being bored out of my wits, I often helped her with her chores."

"And I believe that you're a better person because of it," Daniel said with a look of understanding in his eyes. "All I'm saying is that you should take care not to make any of them feel as if they're superfluous. They take pride in their work."

Rebecca stared back at him as he stabbed a piece of chicken with his fork and put it in his mouth, his features dissolving with pleasure as he began to chew. What a conundrum he was— an heir to a marquisate and renowned rakehell who seemed to understand his servants better than he did his peers, and who'd been willing to rescue her when any other sensible man would have run in the opposite direction. He'd had his own reasons, to be sure, she reminded herself, yet she couldn't help but feel that he would have done it anyway, even if he'd had nothing to gain except her hand.

Rebecca was distracted from her thoughts when she noticed that Molly had appeared in the dining room doorway. She had a somewhat apologetic look upon her face. "I'm sorry for disturbing your dinner," she said, "but I thought you might like to know that your lady's maid has just arrived, my lady."

"That is excellent news," Daniel said, looking equally pleased.

"Would you be so kind as to ask her if she's hungry, Molly?" Rebecca asked. "And if so, please ensure that she gets a proper meal, after which she may come and see me in the . . ." Rebecca considered her options. The parlor was being readied for her bath, so that wouldn't be a very good place to talk.

"You may ask her to join us in the library when she's ready," Daniel suggested.

"Very good, sir," Molly said, bobbing a curtsy and disappearing out of sight.

"Isn't it customary for gentlemen to retire to their study alone after supper?" Rebecca asked with a bit of a twist to her lips.

Taking a sip of his wine, Daniel eyed her with amusement. "And enjoy my after-dinner drink in complete solitude? Sounds perfectly dull, if you ask me."

"I suppose it does," Rebecca agreed, happy that he was openly seeking her company.

"Besides, I'm not the conventional sort," he continued, "and I'm also rather eager to discover if my wife is as talented at cards as she is at playing charades."

Rebecca could feel her cheeks grow warm beneath his gaze. "And what about Laura?" Rebecca asked. "I'm sure she'll be up shortly."

"And I am confident that we can manage at least one game of vingt-et-un before she graces us with her presence," Daniel said. He set his napkin aside and walked over to Rebecca, who'd risen as well, and offered her his arm.

On second thought, Rebecca believed he was probably right, especially if Laura would be partaking of the same delicious meal that Rebecca and Daniel had just enjoyed, for it was not the sort of food one rushed through for any reason. As it turned out, Rebecca managed to beat Daniel twice at the game he'd just taught her before anyone came to disturb them. She took a sip of the claret he'd poured for her when they'd started playing.

"I don't suppose you'd care to try my brandy?" Daniel asked with a hint of devilish mischief.

"Are you trying to cloud my judgment by getting me foxed?" Rebecca asked, feigning outrage.

He placed his hand over his heart and looked well and truly shocked. "I would never!" A firm knock sounded at the door. Daniel looked suddenly distraught. "And just when I was winning," he said as he tossed his cards on the table and said, "enter!"

The door opened just in time to stop Rebecca from rolling her eyes at Daniel. *Win indeed.* It was little wonder that his uncle had insisted he stop gambling. If he could lose so easily to her, she dared not contemplate how much money he'd lost to more experienced players. Giggling at the silliness of it all, she leapt up, almost knocking over her claret in her excitement to get to Laura. "It's so good to see you again," she said, taking her maid's hands in her own. The gesture was much too familiar to be shared between an employer and an employee, but Rebecca didn't care—not when Laura had been so kind and loyal toward her.

"It is certainly a relief to see you as well," Laura said with a bright smile pulling at her cheeks. She looked toward Daniel. "Good evening, sir, and thank you for sending for me. May I congratulate you on your marriage?"

"You certainly may," Daniel said. Having risen, he offered Laura a respectful bow. Rebecca understood him. Had it not been for Laura, the two of them might not have managed to escape Grover's ball and she might very well have been duchess now instead. He turned his attention on Rebecca. "I will leave the two of you to talk while I see to it that the tub gets filled. I'll call you when your bath is ready, Becky."

"You're happy," Laura said as soon as she and Rebecca were alone. "I can see it on your face and in your eyes."

Rebecca smiled. She seemed to be doing a lot of that lately—especially whenever Daniel was around. "I am, Laura—very happy indeed."

"I'm glad to hear it," Laura said as Rebecca gestured toward the chair that Daniel had just vacated, then resumed her own. "His Grace was livid, you know, the Griftons too, though they managed to explain away your absence from the ball by telling everyone you'd taken ill and retired for the evening."

"It must have been a very difficult situation for you," Rebecca said, regretting everything she'd put her trusty maid through recently—the lies she'd asked Laura to tell on her behalf.

Laura shrugged, the corner of her mouth edging upward to form a slight smile. "It was worth it, my lady. The Griftons were suspicious of my involvement even though they couldn't prove anything. I kept expecting them to sack me, but instead they just cut my wages and demoted me to scullery maid."

"Oh dear heavens—they're perfectly beastly! I'm so sorry, Laura!"

"There's nothing for you to be sorry for," Laura told her gently. "But I will admit that I was relieved to receive a summons from your husband. I'm here now, so you mustn't distress yourself about the past, though I would like you to know that I'd gladly do it all again if I had to."

"Oh, Laura! You truly are a gem, do you know that?" Rebecca could almost cry at the thought of what this dear woman had suffered by staying on in the Grifton household.

Laura blushed. "You're too kind, my lady." Straightening her back, she took a deep breath. "Now, I do believe that I have duties to attend to. Your husband mentioned a bath, and it has come to my notice that the staff here is quite sparse. I ought to help the others."

Rebecca chuckled. "If you insist, though you're free to get an early night's rest if you'd rather do that. You can start work tomorrow."

"No time better than the present," Laura said, rising to her feet and bobbing a curtsy, "and I wouldn't want the others to think me lazy. Besides, you'll need someone to attend to you, and there's nobody better suited for that than I, since I've done it many times before."

Rebecca bit back another chuckle as she followed Laura to the door. She suspected that Daniel had hoped to attend to her and wondered how he would go about saying that to Laura. Keen for a bit of fun, Rebecca decided that she wouldn't be the one to broach the issue— much better to let them work that out together. For now, however, she had no intention of doing as Daniel had asked and waiting for him to call her. If everyone else was struggling to prepare her bath, then she was going to do her part instead of just sitting about like some pampered princess. She said as much when Daniel met her in the parlor doorway. He'd discarded his jacket and cravat and had rolled up his shirtsleeves, the very portrait of an able man as he stood there with an empty bucket in his hand. There was something so elemental about it that spoke to Rebecca's feminine side, heating her insides until they felt like mush. "Too many cooks spoil the broth," he told her lightly as he held her gaze.

"How fortunate then that I am not a picky eater. I shall help Molly fetch some towels and some soap."

Half an hour later, the tub was finally full, with steam rising off the surface of the water and heating the air with moisture that left the windows looking foggy. A screen had been erected in an attempt to contain the heat in the vicinity of the bath to diminish the risk of Rebecca's catching a chill, the fire burning in the grate on the other side of the tub keeping the air balmy.

"Thank you," Daniel said, addressing Molly and Laura, who stood ready to offer Rebecca further assistance. "That will be all for the rest of the evening."

Both maids looked momentarily perplexed by this announcement.

"Thank you, sir, but I do believe our mistress will be in need of further assistance," Laura said, finding her tongue and sounding as if she suspected Daniel must have overlooked this matter. "It will be difficult for her to manage on her own."

"Thank you, Laura," Daniel said, a slight frown the only indication of any discomfort on his part. "I am well aware of that, which is why I shall be happy to take on that particular responsibility myself."

There was a second of hushed silence and then the sound of shuffling feet as both Laura and Molly hurried toward the door, bobbing hasty curtsies as they went, the implication of Daniel's words turning both their cheeks scarlet. Daniel grinned at Rebecca as the door closed and he turned the key in the lock. "I do believe they think I'm up to no good."

"And are you?" Rebecca asked daringly. She felt a sudden prickle of warmth against the back of her arms. Daniel's eyes grew hot, and Rebecca found herself holding her breath as he came toward her with slow, deliberate steps.

"I must admit that I've been looking forward to picking up where we left off at that last inn we stayed at." Bending his head, he kissed the side of her neck. "Seems like an eternity ago."

"And yet it was only yesterday," Rebecca gasped, her hands grasping at his shoulders while a buzz of energy shot straight to her core. What a fool she'd been to think that she would be able to limit their coupling, that she would be able to deny him once she got with child when she so desperately needed him.

He didn't respond but began undressing her instead, his slow progress building a tension within her that made her yearn for his touch. But as she'd come to expect, he didn't touch her where she wanted him to the most, his hands teasing along her flesh, coming close to those aching parts of her that craved his attention without quite doing so.

"You're so unbelievably beautiful," he whispered against the back of her neck, and she believed him—so much so that it almost brought tears to her eyes. What this wonderful man had done for her in only a few days was nothing short of miraculous. She had hated the way she looked for so long, her dark attributes a constant reminder of the way other girls had teased her as a child. Those taunts had scarred her, preventing her from forming close friendships with others, but since she'd met Daniel, he'd gradually made her realize that there was nothing wrong with being different—that being unique was a trait to be preferred. Lately, he had shown her with his heated gazes, caresses and words of sincerity that to him, she was the most stunning woman in the world, and that was all that mattered.

He slid her silk chemise up over her bottom, bunching it around her waist before slowly dragging it over her head, the soft fabric grazing against her sensitized nipples as he did so, hardening them into two tight peaks. Still holding her flimsy garment in his hand, he ran it along the length of her front while he licked the lobe of her ear.

Rebecca sighed with expectant pleasure, trembling a little when his hand swept over her pelvis. Perhaps she should just forget about the bath and beg him to carry her upstairs to bed instead.

"Delightfully responsive too," he murmured as he swept her into his arms and carried her toward the tub, the warm water lapping at her skin as he lowered her into it.

Leaning back, Rebecca closed her eyes and tried to relax. She'd grown accustomed to being naked with her husband, but knowing that he was aware of what she desired still made her shy on occasion. This was especially true now, for while he remained dressed, her body had been put on display, the evidence of her want visible in the pebbling of her nipples. God, how she craved his touch. She expelled a deep breath, felt her heart drum restlessly in her chest, and then she felt him—a gentle caress of fingertips trailing down her arm, a kiss against her cheek as his day-old stubble scraped her skin, and the slippery lather of soap across her shoulder.

Helpless against his attention, Rebecca arched upward, a gasp escaping her throat as she shed the warm water in favor of the cooler air. A hand rubbed her breast, tweaking the nipple there before moving on to the other side. "I must clean you well," Daniel murmured against her ear while liquid heat flooded her from head to toe. "Now, if you'll please raise one leg so I may attend to it."

She did as he asked, despairing when his hands stopped their ascent at her knees. "Stand up please so I can wash the rest of you." Opening her eyes, she complied, shivering a little as cool air brushed against her skin once more. Standing perfectly still, she watched as Daniel ran the soap up over her thighs and around to her bottom, then up the length of her back. Setting the soap aside, he then used his hands to produce a thick lather. Not once did he make an attempt to quench the need that had grown to the point of bursting within her. Instead, he asked her to sit back down so the soap could be washed off. Truly, the man was most vexing.

"Here, let me help you dress," he said, holding up a silk dressing gown for her to slip into after drying her off with a towel. "Why don't you go upstairs and slip into bed? I'll just take a quick bath myself before joining you." He kissed her deeply and then added, "I suspect you're eager to receive the reward that I plan on giving you for allowing me to bathe you."

Eager? Desperate was more like it.

Pressing his lips against hers once more, Daniel hugged her against him, kissing her until she felt herself grow giddy. He then carefully released her and smiled with scandalous intent. "Go on, Becky," he said with a nod toward the door. "I won't be long."

Startled awake, Rebecca sat up abruptly and stared through the murky darkness of her bedroom, realizing with a groan that she must have fallen asleep while waiting for Daniel, exhausted after the long day she'd had. Relaxing a little, she looked down, expecting to find him asleep beside her only to discover that his side of the bed was empty. Disappointment gripped her with startling force. She'd longed for him earlier but had denied them both their pleasure by succumbing to sleep, and now that she wanted nothing more than to snuggle up close to him, he wasn't there.

This of course presented another question. If he wasn't in bed with her, then where on earth was he? In his study perhaps? Rebecca considered going downstairs to check. If he was having difficulty sleeping, he might welcome her company. She pushed the coverlet aside just as the door opened and Daniel appeared, his body silhouetted in the doorway for a brief moment before he closed it behind him.

"Couldn't sleep?" Rebecca asked, her voice a little slurry.

He paused, then tossed his jacket on a nearby chair and started undoing his cravat. "No. After finding you so peacefully asleep earlier, I must have dozed off myself for a couple of hours before waking up again. I went downstairs to read for a bit so I wouldn't disturb you."

With a nod, Rebecca slumped back down on her pillow. "Which book did you pick? Anything of interest?"

"*Gulliver's Travels*," he said as he scuffled about.

Rebecca sighed dreamily. "That's a good one." She rolled onto her side just as Daniel slipped beneath the covers, his arm snaking its way around her waist and dragging her closer until her head was resting on his shoulder. He dropped a kiss against her brow, and she snuggled closer, peacefully content as sleep once again claimed her.

Chapter 16

When Daniel awoke the following day, he found Rebecca gone from the bedroom. Looking across at the clock on the dresser, he wasn't surprised—it was almost two in the afternoon. After discovering Rebecca asleep the previous evening, he'd gotten dressed and headed out, hiring a hackney to take him to Piccadilly. It had been close to three in the morning before he'd returned home, but at least he'd doubled his money at the gaming tables.

Stretching, he allowed himself a smile of contentment. Rebecca must think him a terrible card player after he'd let her win yesterday. He wanted her to get a taste for the game though, and he knew that there was nothing more discouraging than constantly losing. Truth was that in spite of his uncle's complaints, he was one of the best gamblers he knew of. His biggest problem had been his love of spending—parties, the phaeton, courtesans and jewels required to keep his mistresses exclusively to himself. It all seemed so ridiculous now in hindsight, but he'd been a reckless fool back then without a care for the future.

Things were different now. He had a wife to care for and employees in need of wages. Last night's winnings would help with that, his only regret being the secretiveness of it all and the lie he'd told Rebecca about reading *Gulliver's Travels*. He couldn't tell her what he'd been doing though—not if he wanted to manage without her help. And he did. For the first time in his life, Daniel Neville, heir to the Marquisate of Wolvington, wanted to prove himself capable of standing on his own two feet. Receiving help wasn't an option.

Swinging his legs out of bed, he got up and padded across to the washbasin, where he picked up a sponge and proceeded to clean the most necessary areas. He then added a touch of cologne and went to select a clean shirt from the dresser—no need to bother Hawkins, who had other tasks to see to. As he buttoned the shirt, his gaze went to last night's cravat, which was hanging across an armrest where it had landed after he'd tossed it aside. A good thing Rebecca hadn't noticed, or she might have wondered why he'd bothered to put it back on if all he'd been doing had been reading quietly in the library—the reason why he hadn't tried to rouse her with caresses. He made a mental note to discard his waistcoat, jacket and cravat before returning to the bedroom the next time he ventured out.

"Where's my wife?" he asked Molly as soon as he was seated at the dining room table and had summoned the cheerful maid to bring him a pot of coffee.

"She went out with Laura for a stroll in the park," she said as she poured the steaming hot liquid into his cup. "The weather's beautiful, and she seemed quite eager to take a look around Town. Would you care for some breakfast or lunch, sir? Madame Renarde made an excellent chicken pie earlier, or if you prefer, there's toast with the usual toppings . . . eggs too, should that meet your fancy."

"Thank you, Molly—perhaps a bit of that pie you mentioned. I'll retire to the library once I'm done eating. Perhaps you'd be good enough to ensure that my wife comes to see me there when she returns. I'd like to speak with her."

"Very good, sir," Molly said, bobbing once too many times as she retreated from the room.

Daniel grinned and took a sip of his coffee. He liked the rambunctious maid and found her most amusing, though he had to agree with his uncle's dismissal of her; she wasn't suited to the Wolvington household at all.

After finishing his food, Daniel penned a quick missive to Lord Chilton requesting a meeting and asked Hawkins to deliver it. He needed to speak to his brother-in-law as soon as possible so he could become more respectable, making money from investments rather than from gambling, a vital part of the plan he'd made to turn his life around.

It was almost three thirty before a quiet knock at the library door announced Rebecca's arrival. Keen to see her, Daniel hurried across the floor and opened the door with a smile, his pleasure at seeing her almost overshadowed by how stunning she looked, with her bright smile and flushed cheeks, her hair swept up in an intricate coiffure. "You look radiant," he said, taking her hand and leading her across to a chair. She took her seat and he bent to place a kiss against her cheek before going back to close the door. "Did you enjoy your walk?"

"Oh yes," she said, eyes glowing with delight. "It was marvelous, really—so many people dressed in the most exquisite clothes, either on horseback, in carriages or just strolling about. I even saw a group of people picnicking, though I must admit I thought it a bit nippy for that. Oh, and there were boats on the Serpentine too—again, something I'd prefer to try when the weather gets a bit warmer."

Daniel grinned. "I'm glad you had fun," he said, "but then again, you're generally quite cheerful by nature. I have a feeling you delight in most things, and frankly, I must admit that it's one of the things that I . . ." He stopped himself from saying *love about you*. It was just a turn of phrase of course, but he suddenly worried that she might get the wrong idea. God forbid if she actually thought him in love with her. He wasn't, of course. Men like him did not fall prey to Cupid's arrow so easily, but that didn't mean that he couldn't like her and respect her.

In Scotland, she'd prattled on about him keeping mistresses while she took a lover, but he'd suspected that she'd made the suggestion not because it was the sort of marriage she wanted but because she was convinced it was all she could expect. He wanted to give her more, especially since they suited each other so well that he saw no reason to bother with other women. But he couldn't allow her to think him smitten either, so instead he said, "admire about you."

She looked at him quizzically, but when she didn't comment, he decided to proceed with the matter at hand. "Actually, there was something specific I wished to discuss with you— namely, the matter of your pin money."

"Daniel, that's really not necessary," she said, her features not nearly as lively as when she'd first entered the room. "I have my dowry, which is more than sufficient. Unless of course you're saying that it now belongs to you, which technically it does, and that you're considering how much of it I should have access to each month."

"That's . . ." Daniel shook his head. "No, I've no designs on your dowry, Becky."

"Then there's no need for me to burden you with pin money when no such agreement was ever made." She leaned forward in her seat. "Ours is a marriage of convenience—one meant to help both of us. I'd hate for you to think that I expect more than freedom from you, so if you agree, I'll handle my own expenses, though I do thank you for wanting to offer me more."

It took every ounce of willpower not to gape at her. Not burden him . . . a marriage of convenience . . . she wanted freedom. Her words resonated in his head, darkening his mood. He forced himself to relax, and he managed a smile that he hoped looked sincere. "Look, regardless of the circumstances surrounding our marriage, I still like you, Becky, and now that you're my wife, I care about your well-being and wish to ensure that you're properly cared for. However, if you feel more comfortable spending your own money, then of course you're welcome to do so. Just know that I don't consider you a burden in any way. In fact, I genuinely enjoy your company and doubt I would have gotten along this well with someone else."

"I'm happy to hear it," she said, her smile returning. "As far as I am concerned, marrying you was one of the best decisions I ever made—I'm certain of it."

Daniel felt his whole body sag with relief. When the devil had this woman's happiness become so important to him? *When you held her limp body in your arms,* a tiny voice called from the back of his mind. He considered that and knew it was true. Since she'd been shot, he'd felt an innate responsibility to protect her. It was yet another reason why he wouldn't humiliate her by taking a mistress, and though he'd told her as much already, he wanted to make it clear. "When we were in Scotland, you spoke at great length about your expectations in regard to our marriage." He paused as he studied her but found it impossible to discern her emotions. "I want you to know that I meant what I said when I told you that I have no interest in any other women."

She hesitated briefly, then nodded. "As I've mentioned before, I want us to be honest with each other, for I believe that the best relationships are built on trust, and I want to be able to trust you, Daniel. I realize that I expect you to stray based on your history and reputation, but I also think that you deserve the chance to prove yourself. You say that Lady Vernon approached you, that she kissed you and that you have no intention of accepting anything more from her." She paused, her gaze intense, as if gauging his reaction. "I will trust you in this, Daniel, because I want more than anything for our marriage to be a pleasant one, and for our . . . friendship to last."

"I want the same, Becky," he said, and as he did so, he wondered once again if he should tell her about the gambling now and just be done with it. She had a right to know. In fact he owed it to her, but he also didn't want her to worry, and he certainly didn't want her help. This was something he had to handle on his own, so he decided to wait a while. Once his investments began to grow and sustain themselves, he would stop the gambling and confide in her the truth. She'd probably be shocked at first, but once that dissipated, he was sure she'd be proud.

By the time ten o'clock rolled around that evening, Daniel could scarcely wait to get out the door. He'd received a response from the Earl of Chilton in the afternoon, inviting Daniel to meet with the earl at his home the following day, but until then, Daniel intended to try and make some more money at the gaming tables. What harm was there really, when he was applying discipline and only intended to risk the money he'd already won?

"You look tired," he told Rebecca when they retired after dinner and yet another game of cards at which he hadn't been quite so lenient with her as he'd been the previous evening. She'd looked at him suspiciously, but he'd just grinned, shrugged a little and blamed his win on a stroke of good luck, though he was pretty sure she'd seen straight through him.

"Not as tired as yesterday," she said as she presented him with her back, allowing him the pleasure of unfastening the long row of buttons belonging to her gown, "and since I denied both of us our pleasure then, I've every intention of doubling my efforts right now."

Her suggestion, spoken in a sultry tone with a hint of shyness, sent a bolt of heat straight to Daniel's groin. Dear God, how he longed to bury himself in her warmth. Besides, it was probably best if he arrived at the gaming tables later, when the other players had filled themselves with drink and had lost a bit of reserve. He also didn't want to give rise to suspicion, and of course he wanted to give his wife the pleasure she deserved. Allowing her to slip away from him, he watched as she walked toward the bed, hips swaying with every step.

Looking over her shoulder at him, she slid her hands down the length of her sides until she reached the hem of her chemise. She then started pulling the flimsy garment slowly up over her luscious curves, her hands caressing her body as she did so.

Daniel forced himself to remain still, sensing that she was enjoying the opportunity to lure and entice him as much as he was enjoying the show. She tossed the chemise aside and crawled onto the bed, where she settled back against the pillows and began to run one hand up over her breasts while the other trailed down along the length of her thigh. Dear Lord, she wouldn't, would she? Daniel knew he'd ceased breathing and that his heart would likely stop at any second, yet the only thing he seemed capable of doing was staring at his wife as he hoped she might . . .

Licking her lips as she stared straight back at him, Rebecca allowed her legs to fall open, and as she gently caressed the plump flesh of her breast, her other hand found her core—at which point Daniel finally gasped for air. Heaven above if he hadn't married the greatest seductress of all time. Never before had he feared that he might expire from desire, yet as he stood there now, watching his wife give herself pleasure, he felt dangerously close to doing precisely that and quickly went to work on his breeches.

"Do I tempt you?" she asked when he came toward her completely naked.

"Do you really need to ask?" he watched as her gaze settled on the hard length of him. He heard her suck in a breath. It wasn't the first time she'd been afforded a good look at him, and it pleased Daniel to see that she was admiring him just as much as she had the first time. He lowered his gaze to the juncture between her thighs. "Would you like me to assist you with that?"

"I can think of nothing better," she said, removing her hand and allowing him access.

"You're impossible for me to resist," he said as he climbed up onto the bed and kneeled between her legs, his blood heating as he feasted his eyes on her every curve. "Do you know that?"

"I believe the evidence is far too great to be ignored," she said smoothly.

"And do you approve?" he asked, enjoying the naughty banter between them as he reached out and gently stroked the flesh of her womanhood.

"Oh yes," she sighed, "very much so."

Holding her gaze, he slipped a finger inside her, loving the groan of pleasure that escaped her lips as he did so and the way in which her hands found her breasts again as he started to move in and out of her, adding another finger to increase the fullness. It wasn't until he felt her muscles starting to tense that he drew away, determined to join with her completely before she took her pleasure. Christ, it was a miracle that he hadn't spent himself already from just looking at her spread out the way she was before him. He wanted her desperately, but this time, he was hoping to try something new.

"Do you trust me?" he asked as he lifted her leg to place a kiss against her calf.

"More than I've ever trusted anyone," she murmured, her eyes still glazed with want as she reached for him, most likely determined to pull him down on top of her.

But he had other plans. "Then roll over onto your stomach and get up onto your knees."

Confusion flickered across her lovely face, and it was all Daniel could do to hope that she would not deny him. "Forgive me, but I'm not sure that I understand your intent."

"Then please allow me to show you," he said. "I promise you that I won't hurt you in any way, and if you don't enjoy it, we'll stop, but I have every confidence that this is something that you're going to like a great deal."

A second passed and then she nodded, doing what he asked without further hesitation. "Here, lean forward onto this pillow," he told her as he gently nudged her shoulder blades down until her perfectly rounded bottom was the only part of her sticking up in the air. Daniel could feel his heart knocking furiously against his chest as he took in the tantalizing sight she portrayed, and he leaned forward to lick her where his fingers had been only moments earlier, tasting her in the most intimate way possible.

"Please . . ." she murmured, her voice filled with desperation.

He had to have her right now, this instant, and he knew that her need was as great as his own. Straightening himself, he moved up behind her until he felt himself pressed against her wetness, the tip of him already nudging its way between her slick folds. "I'm going to make this good for you," he promised, his breath heavy with lust as he gripped her hips and started pushing himself inside her, burying himself to the hilt.

He pulled out slightly and then thrust himself back inside, a little harder this time.

"Oh my God," Rebecca gasped.

"Tell me you like it," was all he could manage as he settled into a practiced rhythm, the first tingles already starting to climb his legs.

"Yes," she almost screamed as she moved with him, her fingers clawing at the sheets.

"I knew you would," he grunted as he pushed back inside her. "And this is only the beginning, Becky—I have a long list of wicked things I plan to do with you."

"Tell me," she demanded.

Daniel could scarcely breathe. How the bloody hell was he going to prevent himself from coming before her when she fueled his pleasure the way she did? "I plan to take you in front of a mirror," he said, his voice raspy as he fought for restraint. "In a carriage too, one day, and perhaps even in the park up against a tree." Slipping his hand in front of her, he found her pleasure spot and rubbed it gently.

"Oh God," she gasped as she met his thrusts.

The breath upon her lips was labored, a wanton sound that spurred his own lust beyond measure. "The theater is a place I've fantasized about as well," he said. "Just think of what my fingers can do for you if we have our own private box. I daresay nobody will be the wiser."

"Daniel!"

He felt her muscles begin to contract, signaling the start of her orgasm, and a moment later he felt her quiver around him, her burst of pleasure so overwhelming that it drove him over the edge a mere second later. On a groan, he reveled in the trembling heat that pulsed through him, leaving him not only sated but completely spent as well.

Easing out of Rebecca, he planted a row of tender kisses along the length of her spine before collapsing next to her on the bed. Bloody hell if the sex he'd had with her since their wedding wasn't the best he'd ever had in his life! Not once had a mistress, courtesan, actress or opera singer stirred his blood the way she did, and after a moment of contemplation, the reason for this became clear: Rebecca was more open than the rest, and she not only wanted him but she also had no qualms about expressing that want, which in turn excited him beyond measure.

Raising his head, he pressed a kiss against her lips. "Thank you," he said. "That was marvelous."

She chuckled. "If it was half as good for you as it was for me, then you're probably right."

Good Lord, he was a fortunate man!

Hugging her against him, Daniel waited until her breathing grew steady with the onset of sleep. He waited another five minutes before easing out from underneath the arm she'd flung across his chest, then he rose to his feet. Ten minutes later, after turning out the oil lamp on the dresser, he went back downstairs, grabbed his hat and gloves, and left through the front door.

"**I**'ve missed you," a silky voice whispered at Daniel's left shoulder as he picked up the cards the dealer had dealt him from the table.

He didn't need to turn to look at the woman who'd spoken to know that it was one of his former mistresses.

"I can't say I'm surprised to find you here, Solange. It's as good a place as any for you to find a new protector, I suppose—unless of course you already have one."

She didn't respond immediately, and it took little imagination for Daniel to know that she'd bristled at his words. He placed his bet and heard her voice again—closer this time, as her breath brushed against his cheek. "I have none yet, which is why I've come to inquire if you might have reconsidered. We used to have fun together, you and I. Remember?"

In light of his recent marriage and the bond he was currently forming with Rebecca, he'd much rather forget. Following the other players' leads, he asked the dealer for another card. "I told you when last we spoke that I intended to marry, and so I have. Consequently, I have put my rakish ways behind me and am currently attempting to live up to my uncle's expectations."

He felt her arm curl its way around his neck in an embrace far too intimate for his liking. "Poor *chéri*," she murmured as the first card was put into play. "Your uncle has asked you to do the impossible." Spreading her fingers, she allowed her hand to trail across his chest. "Men like you never change. You have needs, Daniel, and when you discover that your wife is incapable of satisfying them all, I shall be here waiting."

He caught her wrist before she managed to slip away and turned to look at her, shocked by his lack of attraction for the woman who'd once been his chosen bedmate. His eyes settled on the diamond earrings that dripped from her lobes. What an idiot he'd been to give them to her, drunk or not. "Don't," he said, with a savageness that startled them both. "I've moved on, Solange, and I suggest you do the same."

"*Putin!*" she hissed, her face contorting into something that Daniel suddenly despised. Spinning away from him, her fuchsia-colored gown twirling about her legs, she stormed off, while Daniel excused himself to his fellow players for causing a scene. He won the game a second later with a pair of tens and happily pocketed his first winnings of the evening. Another five games and he'd doubled his money again. He was now twenty pounds richer than he'd been when he'd arrived. Deciding that he'd had enough and that he'd better return home before Rebecca found him missing, he got up and began making his way toward the exit when Lord Starkly stepped in his way.

"Back at the tables, I see," Starkly said as he took Daniel by the arm and began leading him off toward the bar, "and doing quite well, from what I hear."

"Leave me be," Daniel muttered, attempting to free himself from the earl's grasp.

"I just want a word with you, that's all," Starkly muttered, the low timbre of his voice piquing Daniel's interest.

"Two brandies," Starkly told the bartender as he tossed some coins on the counter and turned to Daniel. "I understand you're a married man now, Neville. Word has it that you stole Lady Rebecca from under Grover's nose. My felicitations to you and your lovely wife. I must admit, I'm rather jealous myself."

"And so you should be," Daniel said. He was well aware that Starkly had shared an interest in Rebecca at the Kingsborough Ball. Starkly eyed him with deep contemplation for a moment before saying, "Well, I thought you should know that I'm not the only one. All things considered, it's no wonder the old bastard wants revenge—your wife is beautiful, Neville. Grover's never going to find a woman to match her attributes again."

Daniel frowned. "What exactly do you mean by revenge? From what I understand, the duke has admitted defeat and has withdrawn from Society."

Starkly chuckled. "You don't honestly believe that a man like Grover, a duke, mind you, would allow an untitled rakehell such as yourself to elope with his fiancée and not want retribution? His honor demands it, for Christ sake. You'll be lucky if he doesn't kill you for it—that's what I would do."

Bloody hell!

When Daniel's uncle had told him that he'd convinced Grover not to duel, Daniel had thought the matter settled. He'd never once considered that the duke might resort to more devious methods, though he should have, considering the sum the duke had offered the Griftons in exchange for Rebecca. Daniel cursed himself. He was a fool to have thought that Grover would leave him in peace. "Why are you telling me this?" he asked. "Why not let Grover do his worst and rejoice in my demise? You and I have never liked each other—I see no reason why you'd want to help me now."

"Let's just say that I have my own demons to live with and that I will take whatever chances I get to redeem myself. Besides, I don't think London would be as much fun without you."

"Hmph!" It was a vague reason, but probably the best one Daniel was likely to get from the earl, he realized. "In that case, thank you. I shall take your warning under advisement and strive to be more careful."

"I would suggest you avoid walking after dark. Take a hackney instead. Here, I'll walk you out, just in case."

Chapter 17

Rebecca stared down at her husband's sleeping figure as the morning light illuminated his skin. He'd told her only yesterday that he had no intention of taking a mistress, but more importantly, he'd promised Rebecca that he would not lie to her. And yet he had, without the slightest hesitation. When he'd left their bedroom last night, the sound of the door closing had woken her. Finding Daniel gone, she'd risen, put on her dressing gown and followed him out, intent on asking him if he wanted her company. But rather than go to the library, he'd exited the front door. The truth had struck her with startling force as the blurry memory of him returning to their bedroom on the previous evening had filled her mind. He hadn't been reading in the library, as he'd claimed, but had gone out instead. Why else would he have gotten fully dressed after taking his bath?

The betrayal hurt. Not because she'd expected him to be faithful to her but because she'd wanted to believe him when he'd told her that he had no interest in other women anymore. Of course it was possible that he'd simply been to visit one of his clubs, but if that was the case, why would he have lied? She'd stupidly ignored her earlier misgivings because of what his promise had meant—that he cared for her and that she meant more to him than any of the other women who'd come before. She should have known better though and listened to her instinct instead of allowing her pride to cloud her judgment. The man was a charmer, and he had done what he did best, seducing her into his bed with exceptional skill until she'd been willing to give him everything, including her heart.

Anger spread like ivy within her until she felt she might suffocate from it. She wasn't sure which part of his deception was worse—that he'd deliberately lied to her or that he thought himself capable of getting away with it. No, the worst of it was that like the idiot she was, she'd allowed herself to fall in love with him, and she knew herself well enough to know that she'd passed the point of no return—she'd given herself completely to a renowned scoundrel.

Feeling just about as stiff as a tin soldier, Rebecca took a calming breath and tried to convince her body to relax. She'd always hated conflict and generally chose to try and avoid it, but this was a situation that demanded confrontation. The last thing she wanted was a marriage filled with deceptions and people sneaking about in the middle of the night. And since a tiny part of her still clung to the hope that she was wrong in her assumption and that Daniel had had a legitimate reason for his dishonesty—though she couldn't fathom what that might be—she intended to find out the truth, to preserve her own sanity if for nothing else.

Determined not to wait another instant, and not being in the most loving mood at the moment, Rebecca leaned forward and snapped her fingers together right next to Daniel's ear. He groaned and swatted her away with his hand, so she did it again, and this time, he opened his eyes just enough to peek out from beneath his lashes. "Unless there's a fire that you wish to warn me about, do you think perhaps you could just let me sleep?" He closed his eyes again and yawned.

Annoyed by his calm composure, Rebecca went to the dresser, yanked open a drawer and pulled out a clean shirt, her hands crumpling the fabric as she flung it on the bed. She found a pair of breeches for him next, which quickly landed on top of the shirt. "There's something that I would like to discuss with you, Daniel." *Now,* she wanted to say, because really, she just couldn't wait any longer to find out what it was he was hiding. She needed to know, no matter what the truth turned out to be.

"Can't it wait until later?" he asked, his voice still slurry from sleep, and then he reached out his arm and tried to grab hold of her. Rebecca did a quick sidestep, avoiding his touch completely. Daniel frowned. "Come on, Becky, why don't you climb back into bed?"

"Because I need to have a word with you." The last thing she wanted right now was for him to start kissing and touching her, for in spite of her temper, she didn't trust herself not to melt in his arms. "So get dressed and meet me in the parlor in half an hour." Turning her back on him, she went to the door and exited the room.

By the time Daniel finally appeared in the parlor as she'd requested, Rebecca had gone over every possible scenario in her mind once again. She'd also spent a lot of time considering what she would say to him, until she'd been quite satisfied with the little speech she'd rehearsed in her head. But the instant her eyes met his, she knew that would never do and that she would have to get straight to the point if she wished to state her case, for the disarming smile upon his face and the sparkle in his eyes was enough to make her want to forgive and forget everything else.

Doing so however—ignoring what he'd done and going on as they had before—was not something she could live with in the long run, so the instant the door was closed behind him she bluntly said, "Where were you last night?"

She watched as the smile fell from his face and his eyes filled with a mixture of concern and dismay. "I—"

"And don't you dare tell me that you were reading *Gulliver's Travels* in the library, for I know that you weren't. You didn't do so the day before that either, did you? I was too tired to realize it at the time, but last night when I saw you leave the house, I remembered how odd it had been that you would have gotten formally dressed after taking your bath and finding me asleep if all you'd been doing was reading a book in the comfort of your own home." She tried to keep her voice steady, since the last thing she wanted to sound like was a railing shrew, but the task was proving difficult.

"You saw me leave?" he muttered, his voice sounding unusually detached.

Rebecca nodded, took a deep breath to rein in her emotions and quietly said, "I would like an explanation, please." *Well done, Rebecca,* she congratulated herself. She actually sounded quite sensible and magnanimous.

Daniel stared at her while the clock on the mantelpiece ticked away three seconds. Eventually he said, "I went gambling."

Rebecca blinked. "Are you serious?"

He nodded, sincerity marring his features, and she realized with undeniable surprise that he'd told her the truth. "What on earth were you thinking? Your uncle made it clear to you that you must refrain from such things if you wish to keep your monthly allowance. What if he finds out? Heaven above, he'll cut you off. He'll cut *us* off, and that's without considering what a poor player you are. I hope your game of choice was something other than vingt-et-un."

Rebecca's mind was churning with the implications of what he'd just told her. *Gambling.* Did that mean that he hadn't been with a mistress or some other woman? She knew that gambling hells were not the sort of place a proper lady would ever set her feet in, and she was now wondering if it wasn't precisely the sort of place where loose women went in search of protectors. What if he was telling her only half the truth?

"About that," Daniel said, halting Rebecca's line of thought, "my uncle has already withdrawn all financial support."

Rebecca's jaw dropped. "He's cut us off," she muttered as she stared back at her husband. "Why wouldn't you tell me this, Daniel? Don't you think I have a right to know?"

"I wanted to protect you, Becky, and—"

"Why?" she asked, dumbfounded that he had lied to her not only about where he'd been at night but also about the state of their finances. He'd offered her pin money, for heaven's sake! "So I could live in a fantasy while the world crumbled around me? So I could go on living in comfort, oblivious of the truth until waking up one day and discovering my life in ruins? Why would you do that to me, Daniel, when all I ever asked of you was honesty?"

"Because I wanted to prove myself capable of taking care of my family on my own," he said, his voice rising with steely determination. "Because I didn't want to accept handouts from anyone, least of all from you."

"Handouts? My dowry belongs to you, Daniel. Without a settlement, the entirety of it became legally yours to do with as you please the instant you married me."

"Don't you see, Becky? I don't want it. My entire life I've relied on other people for support. I've never once done anything useful or anything that I or anyone else might be proud of." He shook his head. "I need to find a way to make this work on my own, and I need to do so without using your dowry, Becky. I want that money to be yours, the way it would have been if a settlement had been drawn."

Rebecca could feel her resolve weakening, and she made an effort to strengthen it once more. She still had questions that needed answering. "If your uncle cut us off, then where did you find the money to gamble?"

"He left us a hundred pounds in the safe," Daniel confessed. "Just enough to give us a chance to work something out."

"Well, you certainly found yourself an occupation worthy of the aristocracy," Rebecca muttered.

"I have no other talent," he said.

This got her attention, and she found herself dismayed by the truth that shone in his dark brown eyes. "You won," she whispered, and he nodded with a smile. "How much?"

"Just thirty pounds so far," he said, looking slightly bashful, "at vingt-et-un —my game of choice."

Rebecca just sat there, stunned. "You devil," she finally exclaimed. "You let me win!"

"Guilty," he confessed as his smile broadened to a grin.

"I have a sudden urge to throttle you, Daniel," she said, unsure of whether to laugh or cry. She frowned instead and leveled him with her most serious stare. "Were there women at this . . . venue you visited?"

"Yes, Becky, there were."

"Did you speak with any of them?"

"I did."

That surprised her. She hadn't expected him to be quite so candid. "And?"

To his credit, he didn't feign ignorance or attempt to insult her intelligence by pretending not to know what she was asking. "I saw one of my former mistresses there," he admitted, and Rebecca felt a sudden urge to be ill. "She wanted to know if I would like to invite her back into my bed, but I told her that I have no intention of slipping back into that way of life—that I'm married now and plan on remaining faithful to my wife."

Rebecca didn't move, because she feared that if she did, she might slip from the sofa and land on the Persian carpet. He'd completely disarmed her with his honesty, and she adored him for it. Still, she could not allow him to think he'd gotten away unscathed, so she kept quite still and said, "I understand your reasoning, Daniel, and I forgive you, but you should know that if you *ever* do something like this again behind my back, I will walk out the front door of this house and disappear from your life forever. Do you understand?"

A muscle twitched at his jaw as he nodded. "In that case, there's something else you ought to know."

The strain in his voice made her wary. "What is it?" she asked.

"Starkly approached me last night to warn me about Grover—says he's contemplating revenge."

"*What*?" She swallowed hard, while her heart slammed against her chest. The duke was not the honorable sort. If he wanted Daniel gone, he'd probably pay some thugs to put a bullet in his back and toss him in the Thames. She shuddered.

"Don't be too alarmed," Daniel told her. "For all I know this could be a bunch of nonsense concocted by Starkly with the sole purpose of putting me on edge. But it doesn't hurt for us to keep our guard up and to stick to more populated areas whenever we venture out."

"Well . . . thank you for telling me," Rebecca said, still stunned by this bit of information. She met his gaze. "Regardless of our reasons for getting married, I want us to work as a team, Daniel. I have no other friends, in case you weren't aware, and since you and I have to live together, I just want us to be able to trust each other. Our marriage will be unbearable otherwise."

"I agree," he said, looking sheepish and far too adorable for someone who'd just been caught with his hand in the proverbial cookie jar.

"I'm so glad you think so," Rebecca said, smiling brightly, "since you'll take no issue with me joining you this evening then."

"I beg your pardon?" Daniel asked, eyes widening with disbelief.

"Tonight when you visit that gambling hell of yours, I have every intention of coming with you."

"You can't be serious." Daniel shook his head as if to clear it. "Of course you are. You're always looking for a bit of adventure, aren't you?"

Rebecca smiled. "It keeps life interesting, don't you think?"

"I think it's madness if you must know," he said. "A place like that is completely unfit for a lady such as yourself—for my wife, to be precise. And that's without considering the potential threat from Grover."

"He won't try to do anything to either of us in public. If anything, I'd be more afraid of staying home alone than I would be of joining you at a gambling hell. Besides, if the place is all right for one of your mistresses, then it's all right for me too," Rebecca said, knowing that she was making a ridiculous point, but if Daniel was going to be in the room with such women, then so would she, no matter what Grover might be plotting.

"Former mistress," he ground out, looking not the least bit amused, "and I hope you're not attempting to compare yourself to her, Becky."

"No," Rebecca said, "but I would like to see where you spend your evenings at least once." What she hoped was that in doing so she'd prevent herself from sitting at home and imagining the worst, which, for starters, would include Daniel playing cards with a courtesan on his lap. What she might envision him doing with the imaginary woman once he'd finished gambling was not something she wished to dwell on.

"You don't trust me," he said. It wasn't a question, just a statement of fact.

She tilted her head and pondered that. He'd told her everything when she'd confronted him, and she believed he'd been truthful. She also believed that he wished to keep his word and remain faithful to her, but would he be strong enough to resist temptation? If Lady Vernon could so easily kiss him in a deserted hallway, then what might not happen after a few drinks when he was surrounded with loose women? It wasn't a concern she dared to share with him for fear that he might see the contents of her heart. "Of course I do," she said, "but as I've said before, I don't want us to have any more secrets."

"And with everything that I've just told you, there's hardly anything secret about it anymore."

"Still, I think that seeing the place for myself would give me some peace of mind."

"And I think you're just looking for an excuse to go on another adventure, unless of course your real concern is for the courtesans that are bound to be present." He stared back at her, his eyes intense, as if searching for something. "You're not jealous, are you?"

"Jealous?" Rebecca squeaked. "Why on earth would you think I might be jealous? If what you say is true, and I believe it is, then I've no cause for concern, have I?"

He frowned, his eyes not straying from hers for an instant. She started feeling queasy inside, and her hands began to tremble. He couldn't possibly know, could he?

"No," he said. "But if that ever changes, then you'll be the first to know. In fact, from this moment forth, I will be completely honest with you." And then he smiled, erasing all signs of seriousness, while Rebecca was left with a very sick feeling in her heart. "I'll allow you to accompany me this evening if that's what you want. I know that you crave the occasional exploit, and frankly I'd rather you do so in my company than on your own—as I expect you will if I don't give my consent."

Still recovering from his previous statement, Rebecca forced a smile. "You know me well already."

A knock sounded at the door, and Daniel called for whoever it was to enter.

"A letter, sir," Hawkins announced, stepping forward and presenting the missive to Daniel on a silver tray.

"Thank you, Hawkins," Daniel said as the valet left, the door closing quietly behind him.

Rebecca watched as Daniel tore open the seal on the back and unfolded the paper. "It's from Roxberry," he said. Rebecca just looked at him blankly. She'd no idea who Roxberry might be. "He writes that the person who shot you has been apprehended and that he will happily provide us with more information on the matter, but that under the circumstances, it would be best if he did so in person."

"What's that supposed to mean?" Rebecca asked, a little confused by the vagueness of the letter.

"I suppose he wants to avoid the chance of the letter falling into someone else's hands and the information becoming public," Daniel mused, looking vastly intrigued. "There is a postscript stating that the lady who was shot—that would be you—was not the target."

"That certainly is reassuring," Rebecca said.

"I couldn't agree more," Daniel said. "I wonder who the real target was then."

"You'll have to speak with Roxberry to find out. Is his estate far from here?"

"It's about an hour's drive north of Moxley," Daniel said as he set the letter aside and looked at Rebecca. "It will have to wait for now."

"Tell me, what plans do you have for today?" Rebecca asked. Following their discussion and all the revelations, she was hoping they might be able to spend the day together.

"I have to meet with my brother-in-law at two," he said, looking rather serious. "I know gambling isn't the right choice in the long run, so I'm hoping that he might be willing to advise me on how to invest some of the money I've set aside. He's been very successful himself."

"I think that's a splendid idea, Daniel," Rebecca told him. She was genuinely pleased that he was making an effort to do the right thing and that he was wise enough to seek the advice of someone with more experience.

"Perhaps once I'm done we could go to Gunther's together. It will be good for us to get out of the house, I think, and show ourselves to the *ton*—let them know we're not cowering away and that we're happy with the choice we've made. Besides, I bet you've never had an ice before, in which case it really is a treat not to be missed."

Rebecca hadn't and immediately looked forward to spending the day with her husband, laughing and joking as they usually did in each other's company. Having serious discussions like this was something she hoped they might avoid in the future. Honesty and loyalty would certainly go a long way toward achieving that, and while a part of her still warned against trusting him completely, she knew she had to at least try. The last thing she wanted was to constantly worry about what he might be doing and who he might be with, but she could not allow him to know how deep this concern ran without him discovering that she was hopelessly in love with him, a man who'd given her no reason to believe that he would ever reciprocate the feeling. It was a heartbreaking acknowledgement, really, but when she'd agreed to marry Daniel, she'd known what she was getting herself into and that love wasn't part of the bargain. She hadn't been in love with him either back then, so it wasn't something she'd worried too much about, and desperate to avoid marrying Grover, she'd accepted the condition. It would be unfair of her to voice her affection for him now and make him responsible for her heart, when this was likely the very last thing that he wanted.

So she forced her thoughts on the matter back to the furthest recesses of her mind and smiled at him enthusiastically. "I'm looking forward to it already," she said. "But first, I do believe we ought to have some breakfast."

Getting up, he grabbed her by the arm and pulled her toward him, the youthful glimmer in his eyes doing its best to melt her heart. "I'm sorry I lied to you," he said. "It was foolish of me and I . . . I regret it, Becky. I want the same as you do—for us to trust each other and for us to share the sort of camaraderie we enjoyed on our way to Scotland. I betrayed that trust because I wanted to prove myself worthy, but as a result I fear I may have done the opposite. Please forgive me."

How could she not? Hell, she already had when he'd explained himself to her the first time. "Let's start a fresh page and forget this ever happened, shall we?"

He gazed at her intently for a moment, then lowered his lips to hers and kissed her so thoroughly that she thought he might lower her onto the floor and have his way with her right there in the middle of the parlor in broad daylight. He didn't though, and she wasn't quite sure if she felt disappointed or relieved. "Thank you," he murmured, still holding her against him in a tight embrace. "I believe I must be the luckiest man alive to have been blessed with you as my wife. I'll never let you down again. You have my word."

And as she stood there, her head resting against his chest and with his strong arms around her waist, Rebecca sincerely hoped that what he said was true.

Chapter 18

Daniel's visit with Chilton went better than he had expected. He and his brother-in-law had always had a bit of a tense relationship, but once they'd begun discussing investments, the earl had become exceedingly enthusiastic. "We'll have you making a profit in no time," he'd told Daniel as he'd slid a piece of paper across the table to him. On it was a list of companies that Chilton was already investing in, along with a few that he was keeping in mind for the future. "The South Sea Company and the East India Company are good options of course," Chilton had said, "but their stock doesn't come cheap. If I were to advise you, I'd buy into newer companies that show promise. There is one particular one that I have in mind—a paint finishing company by the name of Haden Drysys. They're based in Birmingham and just started trading last year, but with the momentum they've gathered so far, I expect them to become a huge success."

An hour later, Daniel had bid Chilton a good day, thanking him for his help. He'd then returned home, happy to have found a sense of direction, though he did not fool himself into thinking that he would turn a profit from one day to the next. It would take time, and if he was to manage with what he had until then, he would have to be more careful with his spending. An ice at Gunther's was hardly going to put a dent in his pocket, however, and besides, it would be worth every penny just to watch Rebecca enjoy such a treat for the very first time.

"Are you ready to go?" he asked as he stepped into the parlor, where she was sitting, reading a book.

She looked up and smiled. "I didn't even hear you come in. How did your meeting go?" Setting the book aside, she looked at him expectantly.

"Rather well, I think," he said. "Chilton was very eager to help. I believe the information he gave me will be invaluable."

"That's wonderful news, Daniel. I'm so proud of you." Rising, she came toward him and kissed him fully on the lips before stepping away and heading for the door. "I'll just fetch my spencer and bonnet, and then we can be on our way."

The weather was pleasant, so they decided to take the phaeton, arriving at Gunther's within five minutes. The tea shop looked packed, the line of people waiting to be served ending outside on the pavement. Thankfully, another carriage pulled away just as they arrived, offering Daniel a place to park. "It appears we're not the only ones who decided to come here this afternoon," he said. "Why don't you wait here, and I'll fetch the ices. The Royal Cream is particularly delicious."

Rebecca agreed that eating in the phaeton would be much more comfortable than trying to find a table inside, but she felt a qualm at being left alone for an extended amount of time while people paraded past her, their curiosity and scrutiny visible upon their faces whenever they happened to look her way. She knew she was being silly and that she shouldn't care about their opinion, but she couldn't seem to help it. If only Daniel would soon return to keep her company, she'd feel more comfortable with him at her side. In the meantime, she decided to give her attention to the carriages that were passing by.

"Rebecca? Is that you?"

Turning her head, Rebecca spotted a petite young woman with golden hair, roughly her own age, who was looking up at her from beneath a very pretty straw bonnet that had been dressed in yellow ribbons. There was something about the woman's face that jolted a distant memory, and the manner in which she'd addressed Rebecca suggested close familiarity. "Forgive me," Rebecca said, "but I'm afraid I don't recall making your acquaintance."

The woman laughed. "It's me, Judy . . . Viscount Tromwell's daughter. We used to play together whenever you came to London as a child. Our houses were right next to each other."

"Goodness me," Rebecca exclaimed as her stomach twisted itself into a tight knot. "I didn't recognize you at all."

"Well, it has been a few years . . . twelve or thirteen, perhaps? We've both changed a great deal in that time. Had it not been for your black hair, I wouldn't have known you either."

Heart pounding in her chest, Rebecca tried to force away the memory of her last visit to Judy's house, but it was to no avail. The nickname that Judy and her friends had given her, and how ugly it had made her feel as they'd followed her about, chanting, "Gypsy" amidst mocking bursts of laughter, could not be easily forgotten. She'd cried herself to sleep that night and had never spoken to Judy since.

"No, I don't suppose you would have," Rebecca muttered.

"You know, I must confess that I'm relieved to have run into you," Judy said, her expression filled with nothing but kindness. Was she completely oblivious to the hurt she'd once caused? "The way I treated you all those years ago was unforgivable, but I was a stupid child—weak and unable to stand up against the other girls. I'm so sorry for the things we said."

Rebecca stared back at her for a long moment before eventually managing to say, "Thank you."

Regret fell across Judy's face. "It isn't always easy to understand why children do the things they do, but in your case, I do believe the other girls were jealous—you were without a doubt the prettiest one of all of us." She smiled and said, "You still are." She hesitated before adding, "Perhaps in time, you can forgive me? I should like for us to be friends again."

"Have you not heard?" Rebecca asked. "I'm a pariah, Judy. Even speaking to me like this in public could damage your reputation."

Judy raised her chin in defiance. "I abandoned you once, and I've felt rotten about it ever since. I'd like to help you this time if you will allow me."

The urge to turn her back on Judy and pretend they'd never had this conversation was there, but what would really be accomplished by harboring resentment when the woman who'd once wronged her was trying to make peace? It was unlikely they would ever be close friends again, but since Rebecca and Daniel were running low on mere acquaintances, she decided to accept Judy's offer. It would be good to know they had someone on their side. "You are welcome to try," she said.

"Wonderful! My husband and I are planning an evening out at the opera tomorrow night. You should join us," Judy said just as Daniel returned, carrying two large ices. Introductions were quickly made, then Judy said her good-byes, leaving Rebecca and Daniel to enjoy their treats in the phaeton.

"Do you know who she's married to, by the way?" Daniel asked as Rebecca savored the smooth flavor of her ice. "She's the Duke of Landborough's wife."

Rebecca stilled, her mouth falling open as she stared back at Daniel. "Are you sure?"

Grinning, he gave her a nod. "It appears you have a very important friend, Becky. With her help, we might actually stand a chance of being accepted back into Society."

"And if we're not?"

"Well, in that case, we'll have to make do with each other," he said as he put his arm around her shoulders and pulled her a little bit closer. "And frankly, that doesn't sound half bad to me."

She laughed at his playfulness. "No, I don't suppose it does, and considering that you're willing to let me accompany you tonight on your evening adventure, I daresay I've no need for anyone else."

"I wouldn't say I'm willing," he said, aiming for a bit of mischief. "Coerced by a charming wife is more like it. In fact, I think I must be completely cracked in the head to allow you to join me at a gambling hell."

"You're not having second thoughts, I hope?"

"Of course I am. You're my wife, after all, and the very thought of you entering such a disreputable place unsettles me. However, since I did agree to your request in a moment of weakness, I will not protest in the slightest; I am, after all, a man of my word." He kissed her cheek and added, "Besides, no matter how inappropriate it may be for me to take you along, I can think of no one else's company I'd rather keep, even in a gambling hell."

Chapter 19

An overwhelming smell of tobacco crammed the air, casting a foggy haze throughout the room as Rebecca followed Daniel into Riley's gambling hell later that evening, the hood of her cloak concealing her identity from anyone who happened to be passing by. She might not have been an innocent anymore, but there would still be those who would disapprove of a lady visiting such a place. Nevertheless, Daniel had assured her that once inside, none of the patrons would make a fuss, since their own reputations were more than a little bit questionable. She clasped his hand tightly as he led her past a seating arrangement where three women wearing the most outrageous gowns Rebecca had ever seen had perched themselves as if on deliberate display. Rebecca couldn't help but stare. She'd never imagined that a woman could dress more provocatively than the way Lady Trapleigh tended to do, but she'd been wrong. Why, one could actually see their nipples peeking out from beneath their scandalously low-cut bodices, and as if that weren't enough, their ankles showed!

Looking away when one of them met her gaze and

trumpeted her lips, Rebecca noticed the tables arranged all around, some with four players, and some with six. On closer inspection, not all were for cards. Hazard was being played as well.

"Stay close to me," Daniel said as he steered her toward a table where two other men were already seated. "This place . . . the clientele that frequents it is generally wealthy. Many are even peers, but Riley's affords a man who might be the very definition of a gentleman when he's out in Society an opportunity to be less so here."

"Why would you choose to come here?" she whispered.

He stopped and looked down at her. "You know I'm not accepted anywhere socially, which is why I chose not to renew my membership to my club a few years ago—no point in paying extra to drink alone when I can do so just as easily in the comfort of my home or in places like this." Straightening himself, he nodded toward the men at the table in turn. "Horton. Windham. May I present to you my wife, Lady Rebecca Neville? She wished to join me this evening. I hope you don't mind."

Horton and Windham got up from their seats and bowed toward her. "How delightful it is to make your acquaintance," Horton said, smiling in a manner that suggested he didn't consider Rebecca's presence very delightful at all. His friend seemed to share his sentiment, for he just watched her skeptically, mumbled a greeting and resumed his seat.

Rebecca tried not to take offense. She had after all unsettled the delicate balance of a very peculiar habitat, and they probably saw her as an obstacle now—a lady around whom they could not enjoy the freedom they'd come here seeking and who was likely to ruin their evening as a result. With that thought in mind, Rebecca determined to prove that she could be both fun and entertaining as well as a good sport, and that they needn't concern themselves about her presence. "I am most delighted to meet you as well," she said, claiming a seat that Daniel had pulled up alongside his own. "Now then, what are we playing this evening?"

Silence.

"Becky," Daniel whispered as he leaned toward her. "You're not suggesting that you want to participate, are you?"

"Why ever not?" she asked as she looked to each of them in turn. "It's certainly better than just sitting here and watching you."

Daniel groaned, and Horton cleared his throat. "Whist is my first choice, since there are four of us."

"Mine too," Windham agreed. "Especially after Neville beat both of us at vingt-et-un last time. What say you, Neville? Care to humor us?" With a subtle gesture, he brought over a man dressed in elegant black, who placed two unopened decks of cards on the table.

"I . . . er . . ." Daniel sounded perplexed as he looked from Horton and Windham to Rebecca.

She knew what he must have been thinking and decided not to bother herself with his concerns. She was here now, and she had every intention of having a splendid evening. "Sounds like a marvelous idea," she said, presenting each of the gentlemen with a dazzling smile. "I will partner with my husband, in which case I should probably switch seats with you, Horton, so I may sit across from him." If she wasn't mistaken,

Daniel groaned again, which in turn made her chuckle with amusement.

What the blazes had he been thinking to bring her here? He'd never been more perplexed by a decision before in his life, and now his wife was grinning happily as she prepared to gamble with two seasoned players. "I'm not entirely sure of the procedure," she was saying as she took the seat that Horton had vacated. "Should I place my bet now or after the cards have been dealt?"

Good God!

"Becky, perhaps it would be best if you sat this one out and just watched the first hand. I'm sure I can find someone else to . . ." His words trailed off at the disappointment in her eyes. Devil take it, so they'd lose a few pounds, but at least she'd be happy. He sighed and tried to look more optimistic.

"You may place your bet *after* you've taken a look at your cards, Lady Rebecca," Norton said. "I will deal the first round, if that is agreeable?"

"I have no issue with it," Daniel said as he glanced toward Rebecca, who looked undeniably cheerful. Her demeanor didn't change much when she picked up her cards and sorted them in her hand. But then she frowned, and Daniel felt doomed; she was looking at her hand as if it had been the most confusing thing she'd ever set eyes upon. Since his own hand looked fairly miserable, he decided that he might as well forget all chance of winning and just enjoy the game for the hell of it. He certainly wasn't about to gamble on their chances of winning.

The thought had just entered his head when Rebecca pulled two pounds out of her reticule and placed them on the table. Daniel stared at the money, speechless. It was a large sum for anyone to risk on one single hand. *What are you doing?* he wanted to ask, but Horton and Windham had already added their own two pounds to the pot, leaving Daniel with no choice but to follow suit. The evening was not turning out the way he'd envisioned.

Sitting at Horton's left, Daniel led the first card—the two of clubs. Rebecca stared at the card for a second, then plucked a card from her own hand and placed it on the table—the king of clubs. Windham discarded a five, and Horton took the trick with the ace.

The next card played was the three of spades. Daniel placed his only good card, the jack, on top of it, hoping that Windham wasn't sitting with the queen, king or ace. Rebecca put a low three on it, and as he'd feared, Windham took the trick with the ace. Changing colors, Windham then played the four of diamonds to his partner, who in turn played the queen. Daniel didn't even bother trying to compete with that, since he didn't have a single diamond anyway, so he played a low heart instead.

But then Rebecca leaned forward and placed the king on the table, and everything that happened from that point on was nothing short of impressive. She played the queen of clubs next, followed by the jack, the ten, the seven and the six, taking all tricks, since the rest of the clubs had already been played. She then played the king of spades, the queen of spades, the ace of hearts and eventually gave the last trick to Windham, who had the ace of diamonds.

Daniel blinked in disbelief. Raising his gaze from the table, he met Rebecca's eyes and laughed. It was impossible not to, when she looked so darn pleased with herself. "I must say you're full of surprises. After our other recent card game, I hadn't expected you to be so good."

"That's because we weren't playing whist," she said, eyes sparkling with merriment. "I'm good at whist."

"I can see that," Daniel said. He was ridiculously proud of her for doing so well and noted that they made an excellent team. They played three more rounds before Norton and Windham declared themselves so thoroughly impressed with Rebecca's card skills that they would rather try their luck elsewhere. Both of them bowed to her as they took their leave and wished both her and Daniel the best of luck with the remainder of the evening.

"What now?" Rebecca asked when she and Daniel were once again alone.

"Now, dear Becky, we find another table to play at, but this time, I'm playing vingt-et-un."

"But I'm terrible at that," Rebecca muttered. "I mean, I haven't had nearly enough practice."

"Which is why you're not playing," he said. He didn't like the look of disappointment on her face and decided he'd better explain his reasoning. "Remember why we're here, Becky. It's not to have fun but because we need an income, and as much as I've enjoyed playing with you, the stakes at whist aren't high enough. We need something with better winnings, and vingt-et-un is perfect for that, especially since I'm good at it."

"Very well," Rebecca muttered. She still didn't look too pleased about his decision, but at least she was willing to accept his reasoning.

Looking around, he spotted a table with four players

who were currently receiving their cards from a dealer, a young man with a red scar slicing across his cheek. There was a vacant chair, so Daniel hurried over and claimed it, greeting the other players as he asked if he might be allowed to join them.

"By all means," a burly-looking chap with a cigar jutting out of his mouth muttered. Whoever he was, he'd decided to get comfortable, for he'd taken off his jacket and rolled up his shirtsleeves. His cravat was no-where to be found.

"You'll have to add five pounds to the pot," another fellow added. He looked familiar, and Daniel realized that he'd actually seen this man before—yet another gentleman who favored the relaxed atmosphere that Riley's offered.

Daniel had no issue with adding the necessary blunt, and soon the game was under way. He was aware of Rebecca's presence at his right shoulder, her scent blending with the otherwise smoky air. Determined to avoid distraction, he forced his attention away from her and focused on his cards instead, claiming victory ten minutes later with a pair of aces.

He won five more rounds, but when he lost on the sixth and was forced to part with ten pounds, he fought the urge to try and win it back. *Be responsible,* he told himself. *Walk away.* He turned to tell Rebecca that he was ready to leave, only to find her gone.

What the devil?

Where could she have got to? Grabbing his win-nings, he shoved the money into his jacket pockets, then rose to his feet and scanned the room. It took him no more than a moment to spot her through the throng of onlookers gathered around the various tables, and when he finally did, his stomach lurched. She was not alone but having what appeared to be a very animated conversation with Solange.

Jesus, bloody, Christ!

His gut reaction was to turn away and try to ignore the incident. Who could blame him? He couldn't imagine any man relishing the idea of his wife making the acquaintance of his mistress, not even if he was no longer involved with said mistress. It was all most distressing, but to pretend he hadn't noticed what was going on would be cowardly. Besides, it was too late for that now—Rebecca had turned her head and seen him watching them—especially if he wanted to share a bed with her once they got home.

With a heavy sigh, he started making his way toward them, smiling as he reached Rebecca's side despite her look of displeasure. He linked his arm with hers, hoping to show where his loyalty lay. "Good evening, Solange," he then said smoothly. "I see you've met my wife."

"Indeed, I was just offering her my congratulations on her marriage," Solange said, her smile lacking any measure of kindness.

Daniel wondered what he'd ever seen in the woman, and then recalled that their relationship had been exclusively sexual and that he'd never given her character much thought. The notion that he could have been so shallow embarrassed him now, though not nearly as much as his concern for what Solange might have said to Rebecca. "Thank you," he said. It seemed like the polite thing to do.

Looking at his wife, he noted that she stood stiffly at his side, completely mute and with a look in her eyes that would have sent a demon back to hell. What the devil had Solange said to her? The woman in question leaned toward him, her lips drawn into a deliberate smile. "Should you ever reconsider the offer I gave you last night, I shall be only too happy to oblige. You know where to find me."

Hot, primal rage poured through Daniel, giving him an alarming urge to place his hands about the woman's neck and strangle her. By God, he'd never been so furious with anyone before in his life. That she would say such a thing in public, and with his wife present, was beyond the pale! It was nothing short of hateful, and he despised her for it.

With a supreme willpower he never thought he possessed, he managed to remain perfectly still as he stared back at Solange, who was still looking mighty pleased with herself. "Rest assured, madam," he said, his tone as bland as he could possibly manage under the circumstances, "that I am not a man prone to indecision. Frankly, I'm surprised you would think otherwise. But, since you have so gravely misjudged me, let me be perfectly clear; I am married now, and more than that, I am happy. You see, my wife is a very capable woman. I have no need for you."

There was a slight gasp, not from Solange, who was glaring back at him now with pure venom, but from Rebecca, who'd probably been horribly embarrassed by what he'd just said about her. He wasn't sorry he'd done it though. There was just something so utterly satisfying about telling Solange that his wife was a better bedmate than she'd ever been. Pulling himself up to his full height, he gave her his most threatening look and said, "Now, if you will please excuse us, we should like to be on our way." And with that, he led Rebecca past Solange, who looked as though she might start spewing insults after them as they left, toward the exit as quickly as he could manage.

Once in the street, he looked around for an available hackney, but all the carriages were either private or occupied. For a fleeting second he considered sending Rebecca back inside until he'd managed to procure a means of transportation for them, but then he thought better of it. They were not on a deserted street, after all. Surely she'd be safer at his side than alone in a hell full of foxed men and loose women, not to mention the unpleasant thought of what else Solange might say to her if he wasn't there to put her in her place. "Come, let's walk over to Regent Street. Hopefully we'll have better luck there." Without a word, Rebecca allowed him to lead the way. He knew he had to say something to address the situation that had just taken place inside Riley's. Deciding that an apology was probably a good beginning, he simply said, "You shouldn't have had to endure that. I'm sorry."

"I must confess I'm not accustomed to being verbally assaulted like that. It was . . . shocking."

Daniel stopped in his tracks and turned her toward him. "What exactly did she say to you?" he asked. He didn't want to know, and yet he *had* to. There was no getting around the issue.

Rebecca looked away. For a long moment she said nothing, but then she took a big gulp of air and the words suddenly poured out of her. "She told me that I'm exactly what she imagined me to be—incredibly beautiful, but young and inexperienced. She said she could see it in my face, that there was a certain element of wonder and naiveté in my eyes that would eventually vanish with age, more quickly, she reasoned, as I got to know you better and became better acquainted with your . . . needs." Rebecca's voice had softened to barely a whisper, and Daniel wanted to stop her from saying more.

Dear Lord, it was worse than he'd imagined. Solange had deliberately tried to terrify Rebecca, perhaps even poison her against him. "Whatever else she might have told you, Becky, it's—"

"She said she'd be happy to take my place in your bed if I ever grew weary of pleasing you, or if I decided that I didn't wish to comply with some of your more . . . unusual requests, whatever that might mean. Frankly, I've no desire to contemplate it, Daniel."

"She lied to you, Becky. She knows she's been tossed aside and is now lashing out in the one way that might be able to hurt me." Rebecca met his gaze, her eyes wide and soulful. "By placing doubt in the mind of the woman I replaced her with," he explained. "Becky, I would never expect you to do anything you don't feel comfortable with, and I would certainly never go to her or anyone else instead. I've told you this before—I've promised myself to you and you alone because you deserve to have a husband you can trust and because, truthfully, I've no desire for anyone else. All I want is you."

Her expression softened and her lips trembled just a little until she eventually smiled. Daniel breathed a sigh of relief. "Please don't doubt me," he said as they resumed walking, the streetlights casting a yellow glow across the pavement. "What I told her in there is true, you know—you're more than capable of attending to my needs."

He could practically feel the heat radiating off of her. He'd embarrassed her once again, but it couldn't be helped. She had to understand how much he desired her, and he would say whatever he must in order to make that happen. Besides, she'd quickly become the closest friend he'd ever had. The last thing he wanted was for someone to hurt her by filling her head with mistruths. For a split second the idea of losing her flittered through his mind, accompanied by a cold dread. It was probably the most unpleasant thought he'd had in years, if not ever, and he instinctively tightened his hold on her. Rebecca was his. He . . . cared for her and knew he'd be miserable without her company, something he'd grown very used to over the past two weeks. Heavens, was that really all it had been since he'd met her for the first time? It felt like he'd known her forever.

Daniel was still pondering the significance of this when a gruff voice interrupted his thoughts and he noticed that a large man stood blocking their path, knife in hand.

What the devil?

"Ye look like a wealthy pair, out for a lovely stroll," he said. "Now empty yer pockets and I won't have to harm ye."

Taking a moment to size the man up, Daniel contemplated his options. He could tell Rebecca to get behind him while he took his chances with the man. It wouldn't be the first time he'd gotten into a brawl, and with Starkly's warning in mind, he'd brought a weapon of his own along with him just in case—a dagger strapped to the waistband of his breeches. One thing was clear. He had to protect Rebecca. She was a liability now, and whatever happened, he couldn't risk placing her in harm's way. If the man somehow got to her and threatened her with the knife, or, worse, overpowered Daniel and kidnapped her . . . dear God, he'd never had to consider another person's safety like this before and found himself fearing not for himself but for her. He had to keep her safe at all costs, even if it meant giving up his winnings.

"You make a convincing argument," he said as he reached inside one of his pockets and pulled out a stack of bills.

The man, eyes glistening with greed, moved toward Daniel, ready to grab the prize, when Daniel heard a steady *click*. "I suggest you beat a hasty retreat, sir," Rebecca said, her hands shaky on the small pistol she was holding. Daniel stared at her and then at their assailant, who'd stopped in his tracks and was now looking very much afraid. "From what I hear," she continued, "these things have a tendency to go off without much provocation, and as you can see, I'm not very calm at the moment. I'd hate to fire upon you by accident."

Without uttering another word, their assailant took her advice and backed away slowly before turning on his heel and taking off at a run. He disappeared down the first side street. Once he was out of sight, Daniel turned to Rebecca, whose whole body was shaking, her hand still holding the pistol in an outstretched pose. Reaching for it, Daniel pried it from her fingers, placed it safely in his own pocket and hugged Rebecca fiercely against his chest, not caring who might see such a public display of affection and think it inappropriate. They could all go hang for all he cared.

"You were marvelous," he whispered against the top of her head. "Absolutely, bloody marvelous!"

He felt her breathing return to a steadier pace as she calmed herself, and then he felt her chest vibrate against his own and realized that she was laughing. Pulling away, he looked down at her and was met with a broad grin that forced a smile to his own lips. "What's so amusing?" he asked.

"I don't know," she managed between giggles. "I suppose the thought of such a large and terrifying man being so thoroughly frightened by a woman wielding a pistol. And to think that I've never been quite so scared in my life."

"That's probably what convinced him to run away," Daniel mused as he took her by the arm and started hurrying her along. He was eager to get Rebecca home, where it was safe. "A pistol in the hands of an unpredictable person can be a frightening thing indeed, and you, my dear, looked very unpredictable just then. Tell me, have you always carried a weapon in your reticule?"

Rebecca shook her head. "It was a gift from Lady Trapleigh. When I told her of my plan to escape, she warned me that the world can be a dangerous place— London in particular—and suggested I always carry the pistol on me wherever I went. It's a very handy little thing, don't you think?"

Daniel couldn't help but laugh. "It certainly is, and thank God for Lady Trapleigh and her invaluable piece of advice. She may very well have saved our lives!"

"Oh, do you really think it could have come to that?" Rebecca asked, all traces of humor vanishing from her voice.

Daniel didn't. He was confident that the villain would have run off as soon as he'd gotten some money. Risking the hangman's noose in the middle of Piccadilly was probably not on his agenda. "I don't think so, but he would have taken our money, and then where would we be? I daresay he was mistaken in assuming that we are wealthy." Speaking of their financial situation left him with a bitter taste in his mouth. He hated living like this, with the constant worry of what tomorrow would bring. Yes, he was good at gambling, and his winnings were enough to sustain them until his investments started making a profit, but what would happen if he lost, or if the companies he'd invested in didn't do as well as he was hoping they would?

Rebecca must have shared his concerns, for once they'd returned home and settled themselves in bed, she quietly said, "There has to be another way for us to get by until your investments start earning us money. I'm not comfortable with going back to Riley's again. It's too dangerous."

"A bit *too* adventurous?" he teased, attempting to calm her fears by making light of the situation. She didn't laugh this time, so he reached for her hand and gave it a gentle squeeze, saying, "I must admit that I agree, Becky. Which is why next time you'll be staying home, where it's safe."

"*What*? You can't be serious, Daniel. When I spoke of the risk, I was thinking of you as well." He heard her voice hitch a little, and then she swallowed, as if struggling to find the words. "What happened tonight . . . Dear God, if you'd been alone and . . . and . . . no, I cannot think of it. I *will* not think of what could have happened if we hadn't managed to scare that man off. Don't you see? I . . . I . . ."

Daniel found himself holding his breath as he waited for her to continue, but her words trailed off and she took a deep, shuddering breath before quietly saying, "Please don't go there again, Daniel. We'll find another way. There has to be another way for us to manage without either of us risking our safety. Please don't make me sit at home and worry for you—I don't think I could bear it."

Overwhelmed by her honesty and how deeply she seemed to care for him, Daniel hugged her against him and pressed a kiss against her temple. "I promise," he whispered, more concerned with making her happy than he was with the lack of income this would signify. They would find a way, she'd said. Hopefully she would be right.

Chapter 20

"**I**'m so pleased that you were able to join us," Judy said as she welcomed Rebecca and Daniel into the Landboroughs' private box at the Royal Opera the following evening. "May I introduce you to my husband?"

A lean gentleman with kind features stepped forward and offered Rebecca a bow. "My wife has told me a great deal about you. It is a pleasure to make your acquaintance." Turning to Daniel, he said, "From what I gather, you've caused quite the stir, Neville. Ordinarily, I probably wouldn't approve, but I also believe that every situation ought to be judged individually, as each is unique." He looked pensive for a moment. "The *ton* has been trying to flog you for years on the basis of all your alleged exploits—the majority of which lacked merit, if you ask me. In fact, I never once saw any proof of the lowly character they were trying to paint you as, which means that eloping is probably your first viable offense. Considering who you're up against, I must admit I'm on your side—can't stand Grover myself."

"It's very kind of you to say so," Daniel said, "and

a relief to find someone who's willing to keep our company."

The duke's expression turned remarkably serious. "I understand the threat of scandal all too well, but there are few who are brave enough to shoulder it as they fight for what is right and just. I admire your courage—yours too, Lady Rebecca. What you've been through cannot have been easy, and it is our hope, my wife's and mine, that by offering you our support publically like this, you will soon be granted entry to the drawing rooms and ballrooms of Mayfair."

"Thank you," Rebecca said. She looked at Judy, who was smiling back at her. Rebecca was still surprised that she had been the one to come to their rescue, proving once again that help could come from the most unlikely places.

"Come," Judy said as she took Rebecca by the arm and started toward the front of the box. "Let's have a seat over here, right in the middle, where everyone can see us."

"Are you not the least bit concerned about your own reputation?" Rebecca whispered.

"I have had the good fortune of marrying a very powerful man. There are few who would dare say a word against either of us, since doing so would mean exclusion from some of the annual events we host. But if anyone should decide, after seeing us together here this evening, that they would rather give me the cut, then that is their business. I for one mean to stick by my friends, and I will never forgive myself for not doing so sooner."

"You mustn't be too hard on yourself, Judy. Children can be cruel, not out of spite but because of their own fears and weaknesses. I cannot deny that what you and your friends did all those years ago hurt at the time, but I do believe that we can put it behind us and start a new friendship."

The music started, and they settled into a companionable silence while their husbands took their seats next to them. Almost an hour later, they were all enjoying a bit of champagne during intermission when an elegant woman whom Rebecca did not recognize entered the box. "I hope I'm not disturbing," she said, "but I thought it high time that I offer my brother and his wife my congratulations on their marriage."

"Audrey," Daniel said as he rose to greet her, "what a welcome surprise. Is Chilton here as well?"

"He was detained just outside our box by Lord Shelby, who wished to discuss something of a political nature. I decided to abandon the pair of them, so here I am."

Daniel turned to Rebecca, who had come to stand beside him. "I would like to present my sister, Lady Chilton."

"It's a pleasure to finally meet you," Rebecca said. "Thank you so much for coming over."

"Well, I had been thinking about paying you a social call at your home even though Uncle advised against it, but then I saw you here together with the Landboroughs, and I decided that anyone who disapproves of me talking to my own brother and his wife can go to the devil."

"Dear me," Daniel grinned. "Does your husband know about this rebellious streak of yours?"

"He condoned it," Lady Chilton said with a proud tilt of her chin. "In fact, he's quite impressed with the effort you're making to, as he put it, become an up-standing citizen."

Daniel laughed, and so did Rebecca. The way her ladyship had said it was just too comical. Her expression grew serious and she reached for Rebecca's hand, clasping it in her own. "I know you've been through a lot, and I should like to help in any way that I can. We are sisters now, so if you need anything—anything at all—please don't hesitate to ask."

"Thank you, my lady, I—"

"Please call me Audrey. It is only fitting now that we are family. Don't you agree?"

"Only if you will call me Rebecca in return."

"I should be delighted to," Audrey said as she made to leave. "Feel free to call on me any time. I love company, and yours will be most welcome."

It was with an immense feeling of gratitude that Rebecca said good-bye to Lady Chilton. Yesterday morning, she'd had no friends at all besides Daniel. She now had two who were willing to be seen with her publically. It was nothing short of encouraging.

"I've been thinking about our conversation last night," Daniel said after he and Rebecca arrived home and started getting ready for bed, "and I've decided that I'm going to sell the phaeton."

She turned toward him so she could meet his gaze, her own appearing troubled beneath a slight frown. "But you love the phaeton, Daniel."

"Yes, but taking care of you is my first priority now, so if selling the phaeton is what I must do, then so be it."

"I don't know. I don't want to be responsible for you having to give up on the things that you care about. Are you sure I can't convince you to use my dowry?"

He nodded. "I've taken the easy route for so long, relying on those around me for support and shirking my duties. This time I'm going to do it the hard way." When it came down to it, the phaeton meant nothing compared to Rebecca, and he'd gladly part with it if it meant that he would be able to take care of her.

There had been a time in the not-so-distant past when he'd thought of no one but himself, but this had changed dramatically since she'd come into his life, brightening his days with her cheerful disposition. It was difficult for him to imagine a life without her in it. Just thinking about it filled his heart with dread. He squeezed her hand again and placed another kiss against her cheek. For whatever reason, fate had smiled on him the night of the Kingsborough Ball, and Daniel was not about to risk ruining that. It was time he grew up and made whatever sacrifices necessary to ensure a happy future with his wife.

Chapter 21

Since Daniel had headed out with the express purpose of placing an advertisement about the phaeton in the paper, Rebecca decided to take advantage of the weather and go for a short stroll with Laura. She was still shaken from the other night's altercation, but having spent two years trapped in a room, she wasn't about to allow some low-life scoundrel to frighten her into confinement. Besides, this was Mayfair in broad daylight, with plenty of people about. It was unlikely that anything would happen, but just in case it did, she brought her pistol along with her, though she omitted telling Laura about this, just like she omitted telling her about her little adventure with Daniel the other night. Laura would only worry, and what good would that do?

Instead, Rebecca thought of Daniel and how proud she was of him for accepting to part with the phaeton. She knew the decision had not been an easy one, for he loved the vehicle. It only made his willingness to do what was best for them so much more admirable, and once they found a way in which to get back on their feet, they would buy a new one.

"You look very content," Laura said as they walked past a milliner's shop, stopping briefly to admire some of the bonnets in the window. "It appears you've settled into your new life quite nicely. I'm so very happy for you."

"Thank you, Laura," Rebecca said, aware of what Laura was describing. She was content and comfortable and happy for the first time in so very long. "I have no doubt that marrying Mr. Neville was the right decision. I find that we get along very well with each other."

"I'm sure you do," Laura murmured. "Indeed, your eyes have a tendency to sparkle whenever he is near."

"Really? How curious," Rebecca said. "I wasn't aware." In spite of how friendly she and Laura had grown with each other over the years, Rebecca had no intention of sharing her true feelings for Daniel with anyone, not even Laura. No, that was not a conversation she was prepared to have, for it would likely result in nothing but pity born from the sadness of unrequited love.

Rebecca refused to be sad when she really ought to be overjoyed. She'd escaped marrying the horrid Duke of Grover and was instead married to a man with whom she got along splendidly. He'd even allowed her to accompany him to Riley's. How many husbands would be so accommodating? And then of course there was the attraction between them. Rebecca felt her cheeks grow warm at the thought of it and decided that she had no cause for complaint at all. Daniel had turned out to be a marvelous catch for her. It was quite unexpected, really, given his past, but he showed great promise of reforming, not to mention that from what she already knew of him, he didn't seem to be nearly as bad as he claimed.

On the contrary, he'd been a perfect gentleman toward her so far. With all the talk about his tarnished reputation, she would have expected him to press his advances on her much sooner than he had. They'd had ample opportunity on their way to Scotland, but he'd waited until their wedding night instead. Clearly there had to be an inconsistency between the rumors and his actual character. Rebecca pondered it as she and Laura stopped in front of a haberdashery to admire some ribbons. He'd never ruined a woman as far as she knew, though he'd told her once that he'd taken great pleasure in flaunting a new woman on his arm each time he'd made a public appearance. They had been widows, actresses and opera singers of course, but the *ton* must have disapproved of how casual he'd been about it. Besides, he might as well have said out loud that he'd been bedding a different woman on each of these occasions, which was not something most parents wished their innocent daughters to bear witness to.

Still, Rebecca mused, deciding that she liked the red ribbons in the shop window best, it was all very ridiculous in her opinion. Daniel was such a fun and charming individual that she thought it a pity that so many had turned their backs on him. Well, perhaps once he proved to them all that he had changed, that marriage agreed with him and had encouraged him to calm down, things could be different.

"Shall we go inside?" Laura asked, looking toward the door of the haberdashery.

Rebecca thought about it a moment, then shook her head. "Not unless there's something you wish to purchase," she said. If Daniel was going to sell his prized phaeton so they could make ends meet, then she was certainly not about to spend her money on buying silly ribbons.

The door to the shop opened and a young girl no more than ten years of age stepped out. "Oh," she said, spotting Rebecca, "you're very pretty."

A lady dressed in an elegant green walking gown appeared next. "Gabrielle! What have I told you about being too forward?"

Gabrielle looked up at the woman and said, "I'm sorry, Mama."

"Please forgive my daughter," the lady in green said. "She's a very outspoken child."

"That's quite all right," Rebecca said with a chuckle, "especially since she was so complimentary." Bowing down, she looked Gabrielle in the eye as she said, "I think you're very pretty as well."

Gabrielle blushed and Rebecca straightened herself, pleased to have brought a bit of happiness to the girl's day. "Allow me to introduce myself," said the lady in green. "I am Lady Oakley—the Countess of Oakley, to be exact."

"It's a pleasure to make your acquaintance," Rebecca said, pleased with the prospect of making a new friend. "I'm Lady Rebecca Neville."

Lady Oakley's eyes narrowed marginally, and then she frowned for a second before the realization of who Rebecca was became apparent in her every feature. She grabbed Gabrielle by the hand and pulled her closer. "I wish you would have said so immediately," she said. Then, lowering her voice to a near whisper, she added, "A woman such as yourself ought to make their identity known right away so that others may choose whether or not they wish to be seen in your company. Good day."

Looking around, she stepped out into the street, pulling her daughter along by the hand as she hurried to the other side and walked away at a brisk pace.

"Is it just me, or does she look as if she's fleeing the hounds of hell?" Rebecca asked Laura in an attempt to make light of what had just happened, though the truth was that it irked her.

"I'm sorry, my lady. Apparently there are those who are not yet ready to accept you."

"So it would seem," Rebecca muttered, wondering if a day would ever come when the *ton* would realize that the true villains in all of this were not herself or Daniel but the Griftons and Grover. Determined not to allow Lady Oakley's dismissal of her to ruin her day, Rebecca forced a smile and said, "Let's go home so we can sample some of those scones Madame Renarde was baking when we left."

The two continued past the British Museum before returning home along Keppel Street. "Has my husband returned yet?" Rebecca asked Hawkins, who was there to greet them in the foyer.

"No, my lady," he replied as he took her bonnet and gloves so she could remove her spencer.

"Well, do let me know when he arrives," she said, a little disappointed that he was still absent, though in all fairness, he'd only been gone for two hours. Who knew how long it would take to place an advertisement in the paper? There might be a queue. She turned to Laura. "Now, about those scones . . ."

"Why don't you go and take a rest while I see if they're ready. You're not used to walking. I'm sure you must be tired."

Rebecca had to admit that she was a little. Her feet

ached and she was sure she felt a blister coming on, but she also craved company. Going upstairs alone wasn't something she cared to do; she'd spent enough time on her own to last her a lifetime. What she wanted now was to surround herself with conversation and laughter. "If it's all right with you, I'd like to come along," she said.

"He's been gone for quite some time," Rebecca commented an hour later when there was still no sign of Daniel.

"He probably had another errand to run," Laura said. "Gentlemen often do. I'm sure he'll be back soon."

"You're probably right," Rebecca said, determined not to worry. Daniel was used to London, after all, and as Laura had suggested, he'd probably decided to stop somewhere else on the way, since he was already out. Deciding that had to be it, yet reluctant to dine alone, Rebecca asked her staff if they would mind her joining them.

"Of course not," Laura said, breaking what could only be described as a moment of awkward silence. It was bad enough that the master and mistress of the house were helping with the chores, but to socialize to such an extent where they shared their meals with each other just wasn't done. Rebecca knew this of course and was grateful to Laura for saving her from having to sit by herself in the dining room.

The soup was eaten in complete silence, however, until Rebecca decided to take it upon herself to start a conversation. "Tell me, Madame Renarde," she began. "You've worked here a long time. What was it like when my husband's parents were living here?"

A couple of spoons clattered against the dishes, and Madame Renarde coughed quite indelicately. Reaching for her glass, she took a sip of water before saying, "If you'll please forgive me, I'm sure it's not my place to discuss such things."

"No, you're probably right," Rebecca said, "but I just . . . well, I imagine it must have been a very lively home at one time. It's perfect for hosting dinner parties and such. Whereas now . . . well, it is rather empty since we've yet to hire more staff. I suppose I was just trying to catch a glimpse of what it might be like when it's filled with people."

"Noisy," Hawkins muttered as he spooned more soup into his mouth.

"And busy, I would imagine," Molly said. "Wolvington House is like a beehive, with everyone coming and going as often as they do. It's impossible to enter a room there without finding a maid dusting or a footman polishing silver. It's quite a relief to have a bit of peace and quiet here even though it means a few more chores."

"I agree with you there," Madame Renarde said. She hesitated before setting down her spoon and dabbing her mouth with her napkin. "There has never been quite as large a staff here as there is at Wolvington House. Mind you, this house is also much smaller, so there's no need for it, but I will say this—we were all very well cared for by Lord and Lady Richard Avern, and we were happy with our situation until . . . well, I never heard anyone voice a complaint."

"I'm pleased to hear it," Rebecca said. They resumed eating until the soup was done and the pie, ham and cheese had been brought out. Rebecca accepted a slice of freshly baked bread from Molly, who'd just been to fetch it from the oven. "I think I'll take a look around the third floor later," Rebecca eventually added for the sole purpose of saying something. "I haven't been up there yet."

"I'm not so sure that's a good idea," Madame Renarde muttered. "Or rather, I believe you ought to discuss your intention to do so with your husband first."

This surprised Rebecca. Whatever did the cook mean? "But it's my home too, madame. I don't see why Mr. Neville would take issue with me looking around a bit." She paused, considering how reluctant Daniel had been to venture further upstairs, as well as the look of relief that had washed over him when Hawkins had cut his tour of the home short right after their arrival. "Unless of course you know something that I do not."

Madame Renarde stiffened, Molly started picking at her bread, Hawkins looked just about ready to flee the room and Laura was being of no use whatsoever; she sat mutely at Rebecca's side as if she wished to ignore the conversation entirely. "Oh for heaven's sake," Rebecca said, looking to each of them in turn. "Clearly you are all aware of why my husband would rather avoid the third floor of this house, and I would be much obliged if I am not the only one kept in the dark."

"It is where the nursery is," Madame Renarde said, as if this explained everything.

"*And*?" Rebecca pressed, determined to get all the information out of the stubborn woman.

"And it is where Mr. Neville found the parting note from his mother the day she left."

"Oh."

"*Exactement.*"

Rebecca considered the implication. She'd known

about the note from Daniel, of course, but she hadn't considered where he might have been when he'd found it. The thought that they were living in a place that held such painful memories for him was difficult for her to bear. He probably saw ghosts everywhere. "I know what it is to lose one's parents," she said with a knowing look to Laura, the only person present who truly understood what it had been like to watch her home go up in a blaze, knowing her parents were still inside. Rebecca had never returned there after the fire, and although this had not been by choice, she was aware that she wouldn't have gone back there regardless. Seeing the estate again would be far too painful an experience and one she'd rather avoid. She could not imagine how awful it had to be for Daniel to have to live in a place that represented so much loss for him. "But at least my childhood was a happy one."

The edge of Madame Renarde's mouth tilted upward. "Oh, I assure you that your husband's was too. His parents loved each other dearly, and they loved him even more." Rebecca opened her mouth to speak, but the cook pressed on, shaking her head and saying, "*Non,* it was not his childhood that was unhappy, for I have rarely seen a child so cherished by his mama and papa."

"But then, as if from one day to the next, his mother decided that she loved someone else more," Rebecca muttered. The devastation had to have been intense, followed swiftly by his father's departure and death. The love and devotion that his parents had showered him with from the day he'd been born had been snatched away in an instant, and as she sat there staring at the food on her plate, she felt her eyes prick with the onset of tears for the boy who'd so undeservingly been spurned by those closest to him. She suddenly had an urgent need to see him and talk to him, to tell him how she felt about him. It no longer mattered if he didn't feel capable of returning her love; she knew she could not deny him hers any longer. "If you will please excuse me," she said, pushing herself away from the table, "I think I will go and wait for him upstairs. I expect he'll return at any moment." She turned toward Madame Renarde. "The meal was lovely. Thank you."

The hours ticked by and there was still no sign of Daniel. Rebecca, who'd seated herself in the parlor with her watercolors, kept going to the window at ten-minute intervals, hoping she'd find him strolling toward the front door with that cheerful smile of his, but there was no sign of him at all. It started to grow dark, and Molly and Laura arrived to light the oil lamps and to put more wood on the fire.

"Would you like to have some tea brought in?" Molly asked. Her chirpy voice sounded forced. "Perhaps some sandwiches too?"

"Thank you, but I think I'm more inclined to have a glass of brandy," Rebecca said, her watercolors once again forgotten as she stood gazing out the window. It was more difficult to discern the faces of those passing by now, but if Daniel arrived . . . *when* Daniel arrived . . . it would probably be by hackney anyway.

"He will return, my lady," Laura said, sounding very confident indeed.

She didn't know what had happened the other night or what Starkly had said about Grover, though, and Rebecca couldn't help but worry that something terrible had occurred. In fact, she was certain that it must have, or Daniel would surely have sent her a note to inform her of his delay. The unbidden notion of him enjoying the afternoon in the company of another woman entered her mind. She tamped it down, for she knew in her heart that this wasn't what had happened. He'd promised to be faithful to her, and she knew that he had meant it. It would do her no good to allow irrational fears to gain a foothold.

"Yes, I'm sure you're right, Laura," she said. "All the same though, I do feel as if I'm in need of something a little stronger than tea."

Laura did the honors and poured a glass at the side table, while Molly took her leave of them. "I didn't realize that you liked the stuff."

Rebecca turned to look at Laura. "I can't say that I do."

Laura chuckled as she handed Rebecca the glass. Taking a small sip, Rebecca winced and set the glass on the table.

"I doubt I'll live long enough to acquire a taste for that particular stuff."

"Would you like a sherry instead?"

"No, thank you. But I would like you to take a seat and keep me company the way you used to." She could feel her agitation growing by the second, and attempting to paint had become impossible when all she could think about was Daniel and what might have happened to him. "If he's not back within the next half hour, I'm asking Hawkins to call the runners."

"Surely he will return soon," Laura said. "I can't imagine why he wouldn't."

Rebecca could, and she was now beside herself with worry because of it.

Chapter 22

Opening his eyes, Daniel squinted up at the darkened sky, or what little he could see of it from between the buildings that towered over him. Raw pain pierced his insides, and his eyes slid shut once more. Dear God, he was going to die. A groan escaped him and he grasped at the spot that pained him, only to be met with the warm wetness that saturated his shirt. He was going to die here in this alleyway with his back pressed against the ground, and not a soul would be there to bear witness.

What a spectacular ending to a perfectly unremarkable existence. He groaned again and wondered if he would be missed. Not bloody likely. On the contrary, there were probably those who would happily dance on his grave and celebrate his passing. He would no longer pose a threat to those unmarried daughters that everyone always expected him to seduce, and as far as his uncle went . . . well, he'd probably find someone more suitable of bearing the Wolvington title. Daniel winced. Nobody wanted him around, so why the devil should he even bother to try and stay alive?

Rebecca.

Her face appeared before him like a vision and his heart filled with despair. *She* would miss him, of this he was certain, and the more he considered how much his death would probably affect her, the more he realized that she was the only one who truly mattered. He thought of her smile, and then he thought of her not smiling and all dressed in black. The image greatly disturbed him. Who would care for her once he was gone? She would have her dowry, of course, as well as the freedom that came with being a widow, but her money wouldn't last forever. Perhaps she would sell the house, he thought, which would be just as well really. He ought to have sold it himself years ago.

He took a gulp of air, and his chest heaved while his wound burned. She should have had children, he thought. Rebecca would make an excellent mother. A thought struck him. What if she was already expecting? It was certainly possible, considering the number of times they'd been intimate and, in the end, all it took was one. And then a new image flickered through his head, one of Rebecca holding a dark-haired infant in her arms, and he was quite suddenly overcome with dread. How could he die and miss the chance of seeing his child? What sort of existence would such a young being have without a father? Unless of course . . . Bloody hell! What if Rebecca chose to remarry? The very idea of her in another man's arms ignited such a fury within him that he became momentarily oblivious to the pain he was in. He couldn't allow that to happen—he simply could not.

With a groan, he moved to sit up. He winced again. Christ, it hurt! But he was determined now, determined to see Rebecca again and to stop her from marrying someone else, determined to start a family with her and to laugh and play with his children. He would not abandon them the way his parents had abandoned him. No, he would love them and cherish them, and he would tell them that he did so every second of every day until they were sick of hearing it.

Staggering to his feet, he leaned against a brick wall and gasped for air, his hand clutching at his wound. Was this how bad it had been for Rebecca when she'd been shot? He shook his head with disbelief. What a remarkable woman. It wasn't the first time he'd thought so, for there were many things about her that he admired, but it was the first time he allowed himself to analyze his feelings for her, and he was stunned to discover that what he felt didn't terrify him nearly as much as the thought of never being able to tell her did.

He loved her.

Such a simple and uncomplicated thing, really. He shook his head in amazement and wondered how *long* he'd loved her. The answer surprised him more than the acknowledgement itself. It had happened quite suddenly really on their way to Scotland, when they'd sung that silly song together. Daniel blinked. He'd always had an innate fear of loving a woman who would do as his mother had done—love him back until one day she simply didn't. But perhaps he hadn't seen things for what they really had been. Perhaps his parents' marriage had not been as happy as he'd always thought it to be. They might have had problems that he, as a child, had been unaware of. One thing however was certain— his mother's departure had been extraordinarily selfish, not just because she'd left her husband for another man but because she'd left her child with no more than a simple sentence. *Forgive me.* She hadn't even had the courage to face him.

And in that instant, Daniel knew that whatever future he might be able to have with Rebecca, she would never do what his mother had done, for she possessed the characteristics his mother had lacked—bravery and selflessness. He had to see her.

Using the wall for support, he managed to make his way out into the street. He felt light-headed, but somehow he kept himself upright, his arm rising to signal an approaching hackney. The vehicle slowed to a stop and the driver stared him up and down for a second before saying, "Where to?"

"Number ten, Bedford Square," Daniel said, hoping his voice wasn't quite as weak as it sounded to his own ears. The driver nodded, so he must have heard him, and Daniel gathered what little strength he had left and climbed in.

"**A** carriage," Rebecca muttered as she stared out of the window for the hundredth time. And then, with more force behind her words, "A carriage! Laura, there's a carriage!" She flew to the parlor door and out into the hallway, where she almost ran right into Hawkins, who was presently opening the front door.

Side by side, they stood in the doorway and looked out at the hackney that stood parked in the street. "Where is he?" she asked, not caring how urgent her words sounded. "It has to be him, right? But why doesn't he alight?"

"Wait here," Hawkins said, his words firm and decisive.

Rebecca watched his back as he strode down the front steps toward the awaiting carriage. He greeted the driver, then knocked on the door. The driver said something, but Rebecca couldn't hear him. What on earth was going on? Where was Daniel? She stepped forward, intent on finding out for herself, but was stopped by a staying hand upon her shoulder.

"Let Hawkins help if help is needed," Laura said. "Whatever has happened, I suspect the last thing you'll want to do is cause a scene."

"What are you talking about?" Rebecca asked, angry that Laura would prevent her from going to greet her husband. "I hardly think my presence on the pavement in front of my own house and in my husband's company will result in a scene."

"Perhaps not ordinarily, but have you taken a look at yourself in a looking glass lately? You're hysterical. If anyone sees you in such a state, they'll think the worst, not of you but of your husband, given his reputation. You must protect him and let Hawkins deal with this until they're both inside the house."

On a quivering breath, Rebecca nodded. Laura was right. If she ran frantically into the street to greet her husband at such a late hour, people would be inclined to believe that she'd just found him guilty of adultery. She couldn't allow that to happen, not even if it might be true. It wasn't a thought she wished to entertain and it tore at her heart to even consider it after all the promises he'd made, but there was still that little piece of doubt demanding to be heard: *what if?*

But then she saw him, and whatever fears she'd had of him being with another woman flew right out the window. *Jesus, Mary and Joseph!* "We'll need supplies,

Laura," she said with a calm that belied her thumping heart and quaking nerves. "Hot water, towels, linens, brandy . . . and whatever else you can think of. Go."

Laura departed with quick efficiency and Rebecca flung the front door wide to make space for Hawkins, who was helping Daniel up the steps, his arm flung around his valet's shoulders for support. That was when she saw just how bad it was. There was blood, and it seemed to be everywhere—smeared across Daniel's left cheek, on his cravat, and most notably on his shirt and hands. Dear God! What had happened? More importantly, would he survive it? She dared not think of such an outcome and tried to ignore the tightening in her throat and the welling of tears in her eyes. He needed her help, not some useless female who was going to cry over his injuries.

"Are you able to get him upstairs?" she asked Hawkins, who was doing his best to keep Daniel upright but having a difficult time of it. Hawkins was a tall man, but so was Daniel, and right now he appeared to be dead weight as he leaned against Hawkins.

With a stiff nod, Hawkins started toward the stairs, half dragging, half carrying Daniel along with him. "I'll manage," he muttered, and to Rebecca's amazement, he did, though he looked as if he was at death's door himself by the time he hauled Daniel onto the bed.

"Thank you," Rebecca said, her hands already pulling Daniel's jacket aside so she could get a better look at the wound.

"Let's see the damage," Hawkins muttered, still breathless from the ordeal of getting Daniel up the stairs and into bed.

With trembling fingers, Rebecca reached for one of

the buttons on Daniel's shirt, but as much as she tried, she couldn't seem to push it through the buttonhole. She cursed herself for her inability to help. She was useless—utterly useless.

"Here, let me try," Hawkins said, stepping closer and nudging her gently aside so he could gain access. She allowed him his request and watched silently as he unbuttoned the shirt and pulled the fabric aside. It caught, and he slowly eased it away from a patch of congealed blood, revealing a great deal more blood at Daniel's side.

Rebecca felt ill and was relieved with the distraction of Laura's arrival. "Molly will be up in just a moment with the water and the brandy," she said, setting down a stack of towels and linens on the dresser. Rebecca noticed that she'd brought a small bottle with her as well. Laudanum. "In the meantime, let's wipe away as much of that blood as possible so we can get a proper look at the wound."

"If you can manage without me," Hawkins said, "I'll run and fetch the doctor."

"A very good idea indeed," Laura said as she grabbed one of the towels and walked across to the bed. "Thank you, Hawkins."

But the valet had already exited the room, and a moment later, Rebecca heard the front door open and close. All she could do was stand there like a trembling fool while Laura wiped away the blood from Daniel's wound. *She* should have been doing that, but she couldn't seem to bring herself to move; it was as if her shoes had been nailed to the floor. She opened her mouth to say something instead, to ask if there was something that Laura might need, but all that came out was a strangled croak. What if he died? Good God, what if he died without knowing how much she loved him? She'd been through hell, losing her parents in that tragic fire at such a young age and then having to live under her aunt and uncle's roof, yet none of that compared with what she felt as she stood there staring down at the face that had become so dear to her—a face that was meant to be filled with expressions of mischief and merriment but that now looked pale and somber. How was she to go on without him?

The door opened, admitting Molly, who was carrying a tray. Rebecca blinked, and suddenly the spell that had paralyzed her was broken. She wasn't sure how it had happened, but she knew that she couldn't just stand there and watch him die. She had to do something—she had to at least try. So she stepped forward and grabbed a fresh towel, dipped it into the hot water that Molly had brought and went across to Daniel. "Allow me," she said to Laura, who quickly moved aside without question.

Using the wet towel, Rebecca managed to wipe away the majority of the blood, revealing a round wound a little smaller than a farthing. "He's been shot," she said. "The doctor will have to extract the lead ball. Would you please dip another towel in the brandy? I need to clean this."

She wasn't sure if it was Molly or Laura who handed her the towel. All she knew was that she was thankful that she had something to do, some way in which to busy herself until the doctor arrived. What was taking them so long?

"You need to put pressure on it now," Laura said from somewhere close behind her. "Try to stop the bleeding."

Rebecca nodded and started to bunch the towel into a tight wad that she then pressed against the wound. A groan escaped Daniel's lips, and it was suddenly all too much. "Don't leave me," she whispered as the first tears started to fall. "Don't you dare leave me. I love you, Daniel. Do you hear me? I love you so terribly much."

But there was no response, just labored breathing as he lay there fighting for his life, oblivious, it would seem, to everything that was happening around him. With Laura's help, Rebecca managed to spoon a bit of the laudanum into his mouth. It was the best she could do for him for now—that, and keeping the towel pressed firmly against his side.

It seemed like an eternity passed before she heard the front door open and close again, then a quick succession of footsteps on the stairs before the door opened and Hawkins entered the room. "I've brought Doctor Fenmore along."

Rebecca looked up, bleary-eyed, to see an older gentleman striding toward her. "The lady of the house, I presume?" She nodded, and the doctor set down his bag next to the bed. "Pleased to meet you, though I do wish it had been under different circumstances. May I have a look?"

With a surge of relief, Rebecca nodded and moved aside so Fenmore could inspect Daniel more closely. He removed the towel, gently prodded the wound, waited a second and then turned to Rebecca. "As you are probably aware, your husband has been shot. He was lucky though—it appears as though the lead ball missed his organs. All in all, he should be able to make a fine recovery, but the ball will have to be removed, and that will be painful."

Rebecca knew just how painful, for it was a procedure she'd recently gone through herself. She nodded. "I've given him some laudanum, just a teaspoonful, to help him through the worst of it."

The doctor must have approved, because he didn't admonish her for her actions; he just seated himself on the edge of the bed and opened up his bag, pulling out a few different items as he rummaged through it. Once he was done, he turned to Rebecca again. "If you wish to leave, now is the time."

Leave? Not bloody likely.

"I'll stay," she said, stubborn and determined and fiercely loyal to the last.

"All right, then. I'll need some better lighting. Perhaps you could . . ." He didn't need to finish that sentence, for she'd already grabbed the closest oil lamp and was holding it over Daniel's abdomen, illuminating the area that the doctor needed to work on. And so she remained for the next half hour, biting her tongue to stop herself from berating the doctor each time Daniel groaned in agony. Hawkins and Laura both offered to take her place a few times, but she shooed them away. This was her duty, her responsibility, her husband, and she would be damned if she failed him.

"And that's it," Doctor Fenmore said at last as he tied off the thread after removing the tiny lead ball and stitching up the hole. "He'll need a fair amount of rest—a week in bed, I suspect—but I'm confident that he'll be gallivanting about again after that. He's young and strong. No need to worry. As for my fee . . ."

"Yes, yes, of course," Rebecca said, both relieved and perplexed. "How much . . . ?"

"Ten pounds should do it," he said as she reached

for her reticule. She pulled out the money and handed it to him without hesitation, thankful for his assistance.

Once he'd left, Rebecca addressed her servants. "Thank you," she said. "You were all very efficient, for which I am grateful. It's late though, and I'm sure you must be tired. Why don't you retire? I'll ring if I need anything."

None of them moved to leave, and Molly quietly said, "Cook is still in the kitchen. She'll be happy to fix a plate for you, my lady. You need some sustenance after everything that's happened, and you've had nothing since luncheon."

Was that true? Rebecca reflected on the hours that had passed since eating her meal in the kitchen. She'd been worried senseless and hadn't wanted her dinner when she'd been offered it. Aware of a growing ache in her belly, she realized she was suddenly quite ravenous. "Thank you, Molly. That would be greatly appreciated."

Bobbing a curtsy, the maid headed for the door, pausing there just long enough to say, "If you don't mind, my lady, I'd like to tell you that I think you were marvelous this evening. I would most likely have fainted had I been in your position." And with a little nod and a bit of a smile, she left to see to the food.

"Yes," Hawkins said, looking at Rebecca as if he was seeing her for the very first time. Unlike his master, he was not a man prone to smiling, and now was no exception. "You were both strong and courageous, more so than I would have expected from someone so young. Forgive me. I mean no offense. It's just . . . well, most women would have cried and swooned, but you did not, and I admire you for it." He paused, blinked and finally added, "Mr. Neville is lucky to have you."

"Why, thank you, Hawkins," Rebecca said. Her voice was unusually timid, and she decided that it was most likely because she wasn't used to being praised and was feeling rather self-conscious as a result.

The valet bid her a good night and departed, leaving Rebecca alone with Laura and Daniel. "They're right, you know," Laura said. "You really were quite splendid."

Rebecca gave a little shrug. "I only did my duty, and even then it wasn't all that much or even that difficult, for that matter. Fenmore did most of the work, and if I hadn't helped him by holding the lamp, then one of you would have done it instead."

Laura shook her head. "Perhaps, but that doesn't diminish your efforts, not to mention how calm you were. I must confess I'm quite impressed."

Calm? Laura thought she'd been calm? Was she blind?

"I was anything but calm, Laura, I can assure you."

"Well, if that is the case, then you hid your distress exceedingly well. Hawkins is right. Mr. Neville is incredibly lucky to have you."

Glancing toward the sleeping form of her husband, Rebecca quietly murmured, "It is I who is lucky to have him." She heard Laura sigh. Rebecca thought Laura might say something more, but she didn't, and when Rebecca turned back to look at her, she saw that Laura had crossed to the door.

"Good night, my lady," Laura said. "Try to rest, and please do call if you need anything."

Rebecca nodded just as Molly returned with a tray, squeezing her way past Laura in the doorway. "There's some beef with steamed carrots and gravy," she said, placing the tray on one of the nightstands, "as well as a sponge pudding which I'm sure you'll enjoy."

As soon as Laura and Molly were gone and the door had closed behind them, Rebecca expelled a deep breath. She felt drained. Never in her life had she been so scared—terrified, really. Her gaze went to Daniel and she slowly approached the bed, pleased to see a bit of color in his cheeks but concerned by how still he looked. She placed her hand on his chest and almost sagged with relief when she felt the steady beat of his heart thumping against her palm. "Don't you ever do that to me again," she murmured as she leaned over and placed a gentle kiss upon his forehead, "for I daresay I won't survive it."

Straightening, she wiped away a tear with the heel of her hand and pulled a chair closer to the nightstand so she could eat her supper, her eyes fixed on Daniel's face as she did so in case he happened to open his eyes. He did not, and as exhaustion overtook her and she finished her meal, Rebecca barely managed to lie down on the bed next to him before she fell fast asleep.

Chapter 23

When Rebecca woke the following day, she didn't open her eyes immediately, content as she was to remain snuggled up against Daniel's warm body. But then he groaned, and the memory of everything that had happened the night before came rushing back to her. She sat up, realizing to her shock and dismay that she was still fully dressed. When had she gotten into bed? She couldn't recall and decided that she must have been well and truly fatigued.

Brushing some strands of hair away from her eyes, she looked down at Daniel. His eyes were still closed but he was snoring softly, his chest rising and falling more visibly than it had last night. She wondered why he'd groaned. Was he in pain, even in his sleep? She looked toward the bottle of laudanum still on the dresser and wondered if she should give him some more. He had to be in pain after everything he'd been through. She had been when she'd been shot, and her wound hadn't been nearly as bad as his.

On the other hand, what if she woke him as she tried to administer it? He needed rest, the doctor had said. Caught with indecision, she just sat there watching him, submitting his every feature to memory and noticing the little things that she hadn't seen before, like the tiniest scar on the left side of his jaw and the fact that his hair wasn't dark brown throughout but streaked with occasional strands of auburn. She instinctively reached out to touch it but caught herself and stopped. *Leave him be,* she reminded herself. There would be plenty of time for affection later. For now, the best thing she could do for him was give him time to recover.

Two hours later, Daniel still hadn't woken, and Rebecca began to grow restless. She tried to read from a book she found in the drawer of her bedside table but was completely unable to concentrate. After rereading the same paragraph an infinite number of times, she picked a little at the remainders of last night's pudding, then crossed to the window and looked out, but since the bedroom faced a side street, there was very little going on out there, and she quickly turned away with a sigh and started to pace.

Perhaps she ought to ring for Molly and Laura to come and clear away the trays and towels that occupied all available surfaces so the room wouldn't seem so cluttered, but the disturbance might wake Daniel, so she decided against it. But when another hour passed and Daniel still showed no sign of waking up anytime soon, Rebecca knew she had to do something or she'd start clawing at the walls. So she rang for Laura, quietly nudged the bedroom door open and waited for her to appear.

"Would you please bring me my watercolors," she whispered as soon as Laura arrived, "and a cup of tea?"

Her request was met with quick efficiency, and she was soon able to sink back into one of the armchairs in the room and apply herself to her art, her model holding a perfect pose as she captured his features on paper. She'd just started on his arm, which was stretched out along the length of his side, when a movement caught the corner of her eye. Had he just blinked? She set her sketchbook aside and got up so she could take a closer look. The corner of his mouth twitched, there was a slight murmur and then . . . very slowly, Daniel opened his eyes.

Rebecca almost flung herself on top of him in her excitement, stopping herself just in time to reflect that doing so would probably not be the best idea and that Daniel would likely scold her for causing him further pain. So instead she just took his hand in hers, creating a small space next to him where she could sit. "Welcome back," she said, smiling down at him with all the love she felt in her heart, as well as a large dose of relief. "How are you feeling?"

He blinked and grimaced. "Like hell," he muttered, and then just one word. "Water."

Springing to her feet, Rebecca rushed to the bellpull and rang for someone to fetch Daniel some water, berating herself for her thoughtlessness. Of course he'd be thirsty when he came to, and yet she'd only thought of tea for herself.

When the matter had been seen to and Molly and Laura had straightened the room a bit with the promise of returning soon with some breakfast, Rebecca resumed her seat next to Daniel and quietly asked the one question that had plagued her since he'd returned home. "Who would do this to you?"

He closed his eyes and took a deep breath before opening them again. She offered him some laudanum, which he accepted. "Do you remember what happened?" she then asked, desperate for an explanation.

He swallowed, took a moment and then pierced her with his dark brown eyes. "It was Grover."

Rebecca sat back in disbelief. "Grover did this?"

Eyes closed once again, Daniel nodded. "He must have followed me—I'm not sure for how long—but when I left the *Mayfair Chronicle* I was . . . not in the best mood."

Rebecca nodded. She understood what selling the phaeton had meant for him: it was like stripping him of his pride.

"So," he continued, "I decided to take a walk. My thoughts must have been elsewhere, because before I knew it, I'd ventured almost all the way to Cheapside."

Rebecca wasn't sure how far that was exactly, but from the way Daniel said it, she gathered that it wasn't close.

"It was getting dark by then, and I decided to find a hackney to take me home." He paused, frowned. "There was nobody else about in the street I was in, and then suddenly someone called my name. I turned around and was surprised to see Grover walking toward me with great determination. With Starkly's warning in mind, I grew increasingly apprehensive about his intentions. He's an old man though, and he was alone. I didn't think he posed a threat." Daniel closed his eyes momentarily before saying, "But I was wrong. Without saying a word, he just continued toward me, and then . . . well, then he shot me."

"*What*?" Rebecca could scarecely believe that this

was how it had happened. It seemed so cold and . . . and heartless. "Just like that, without any warning?"

Daniel winced. "You should have seen the gleam in his eyes before he pulled the trigger, Becky. The man is a raving lunatic. Thankfully, he's also a dreadful shot who had no desire to linger long enough to ensure that he'd actually succeeded in killing me." He scoffed. "I suspect he might have been worried about his reputation."

Rebecca found her lips trembling with unexpected mirth. Trust Daniel to make light of such a serious situation. "But surely there are witnesses," she said. "Someone must have seen what happened, in which case Grover ought to face charges for attempted murder. Surely London must have constables who can investigate and—"

"It will be my word against his, Becky. It was dark in a deserted alleyway. There was no one else around, and he is a duke, while I . . . well, I'm sure there are many who have wondered why I haven't gotten myself shot any sooner than I did."

"Daniel! That's a terrible thing to say."

"It's the truth," he muttered, his eyes meeting hers. "What Grover and the Griftons did or tried to do to you was wrong, but to steal you away at your engagement ball, to humiliate a duke like that and to marry you in haste the way I did was to ask for trouble. I believe it put Grover over the edge."

"I don't—"

He silenced her by pressing a finger to her lips. For a long moment he just lay there, staring back at her in silence, and she couldn't help but notice how his eyes brightened as he looked back at her. When he spoke again, his voice was quiet and filled, she realized, with wonder. "I want you to know that I would do it all again," he said, "just to be with you."

Rebecca's stomach tightened, and her heart thumped wildly in her chest. "Even getting shot?" she whispered.

"Even that."

Her palms grew clammy and her breath was a little bit shaky when she exhaled. She dared not ask him why he felt that way because it would only sound as if she was trying to get him to say something he might not be ready to say. Perhaps it was more than he felt even, though he surely cared for her if he was willing to go through so much trouble for her. But love? She knew she loved him and she wanted to say so, but if she did so now, then wouldn't it seem as if she expected him to say it in return? No, she had to tell him—she'd resolved to do so, and she wouldn't allow another moment to pass without sharing what was in her heart.

"I love you," she said, and then she blinked, realizing that he'd spoken at the exact same time as her, his words mirroring her own. "Did you just say . . . I mean, it sounded like you—"

"I love you, Becky," he repeated, and reaching for her hand, he clasped it with his own before bringing it to his lips for a kiss.

Rebecca was speechless. Was it true? Did he really love her? She felt her body flood with warmth as she stared back into his eyes, eyes that were usually filled with laughter and mischief but were now filled with something else entirely—an honest vulnerability that spoke to her heart. "I . . ." she began, not sure of what she would say or of what she *could* say to express how much his declaration meant to her.

"I know," he murmured, nuzzling her hand with his cheek. "You don't have to say anything else. I know exactly how you feel." And then he smiled that wonderful smile she'd come to adore, and the only thing she could think to do was kiss him, so she did. She kissed him with all the love and passion she felt for him until they were both breathless.

"I'm sorry," she whispered, pulling away just enough to look him in the eye. "You must be in pain."

"Just a little," he said. Rebecca looked at him dubiously, at which he sighed. "Very well, it hurts like blazes, but that doesn't mean I can't enjoy you taking advantage of my immobile state." His smile widened to a cheeky grin. "As you can see, I'm still in working order."

Rebecca followed his line of vision until, "Oh! I say . . . er . . . well then."

Her befuddled state just made him laugh even more until he groaned and winced in pain. Closing his eyes, he took a deep breath, then exhaled slowly. "I think it might be best if I refrain from laughing, though I must say that you should have seen your face just now. It was precious."

Rebecca's cheeks still felt hot. Trust Daniel to make her blush even when he'd been shot and confined to his bed. He was incorrigible, really. "May I take a look at the wound?" she asked. "I'd like to ensure that the stitches are holding and that there's no sign of infection."

Giving her a nod of approval, Daniel allowed Rebecca to tend to him. With gentle fingers she removed the linen strips that the doctor had wrapped around his abdomen to keep the compress in place. Peeling away the wad of cotton, she breathed a sigh of relief. His flesh looked a little pink around the wound, but other than that, it looked healthy and clean. She replaced the used wad of cotton with a clean one, then bound him back up. "I'll call Hawkins so he can help you tend to your toilette," she said, placing a tender kiss against his forehead, "and then we'll have something to eat. I'm sure Molly will be up any moment with that tray."

"**I** still don't think that we should allow Grover to get away with this," Rebecca said a short while later after finishing off a slice of buttered toast. "There has to be a way to make him pay."

"I assure you I can think of several," Daniel muttered. He'd barely touched his food, but he'd already drained two cups of tea.

Rebecca offered him a third. "I was thinking of something legal, Daniel."

"Ah, well in that case I'm not sure a solution will present itself. As I said, there were no witnesses."

"Hmm . . . it's just . . ." Rebecca set the teapot down and returned to her seat. She hesitated for a second, not wishing to alarm him, but eventually decided to share her concern. "Sooner or later he will discover that he didn't finish you off, and once that happens, he might come after you again."

Daniel nodded. "The thought has crossed my mind."

Rebecca sighed. Lord, she was tired. "Then we must be prepared," she said, "or better yet, we must preempt his next move by making one of our own."

"Well, you're the creative one, Becky. If anyone can think of a way to trap Grover, then I believe it's you."

He yawned, placed his teacup on the table and slid down beneath the covers. "Let me know if you think of something we can use, and please . . . don't do anything without talking to me first."

"You have my word on it," she promised.

"Good, because I'm telling you, the man's unpredictable. If he shot me just like that on a street in the middle of London, then we can't be sure that he won't try to harm you as well. We must be"—he yawned again, and his eyes slid shut on the word—"careful."

Rebecca nodded. Daniel was right. Grover had clearly gone mad if he thought he could murder the Marquess of Wolvington's nephew in cold blood. She wondered if her aunt and uncle were aware of what he'd done. After everything they'd put her through, there was no telling what they might be capable of, though she wasn't sure they'd go quite this far. One thing was for certain though, and that was that she detested Grover with every fiber of her being. As deep as her love for Daniel ran, so too did her hate for the duke. To think that he'd almost succeeded in taking Daniel away from her made her tremble with rage. She had to think of something— something clever—because she couldn't possibly allow Grover to get away with what he'd done.

Chapter 24

"**I** believe I've just figured out how to trap Grover," Rebecca told Daniel when he woke the following morning. "Don't ask me how inspiration strikes, for I cannot possibly answer that," she said, "but for now, we have two things working in our favor. First, Grover thinks you dead. I suggest we keep it that way. And second, we know that he has a sick obsession with me; we can use that to our advantage."

Daniel couldn't see how they were going to do that, but then again, he had lost a great deal of blood. "Go on," he said simply.

"The other night at the opera, Landborough wasn't the least bit subtle about his dislike of Grover. His hatred of the man was palpable, leading me to suspect that he might welcome the opportunity to exact his own revenge. If that is true, then he will prove a powerful ally for us."

"You mean to pay a visit to Judy, I take it?"

"I do, and I also intend to call on your aunt and uncle, as well as your sister. They will need to be informed of the truth as well as of my plan, since I shall also be requiring their assistance."

"I doubt my uncle will want to listen to anything regarding me," Daniel muttered.

"Nevertheless, I must try." She sighed as she patted his arm, a distant look in her eyes suggestive of rapid creative imaginings. She was plotting. "And then I shall go into mourning. As a widow with no enduring fortune, I have no doubt that Grover will be knocking at the door soon enough, offering his support."

"You will *not* be entertaining Grover," Daniel snapped. "If that is your plan, forget about it. It's too dangerous and too . . . disturbing to even contemplate. There has to be another way, and if not, then we'll simply have to accept that he got away with it."

Her eyes ignited with passionate anger. "And give him the opportunity to make another attempt on your life? The man could have killed you, Daniel!" And then, in a softer tone, she added, "He almost did." A lonely tear trickled down her check and she hastily brushed it away in a very businesslike manner. "No, I will not allow him to get away with what he did to you. It's time for me to play another part, my love—that of the poor widow in need of a husband. Grover will rise to the bait, I have no doubt about that, and once he does, I shall lure him back to the scene of the crime."

"And how on earth will that prove his guilt, Becky? It's a public street that he could have any number of reasons for walking on." Whatever she was thinking, he wasn't seeing it.

"I assure you that he will have only one reason to go back there," Becky said, smiling like the cat that got the cream.

"And what reason will that be?"

"Why, he shall be looking for something, of course."

Of course?

"Something belonging to me, to be precise . . . something that was on your person when you were shot and has since gone missing—something that he will want to have because of how obsessed he is." She paused for emphasis before adding, "My miniature."

"He would have no way of knowing where to look for it unless he was aware of where the shooting took place, and the only way he would know that is if he was there," Daniel muttered as the idea began to take root. It was brilliant if it worked, but the idea of Rebecca being near that man again made his skin crawl. "I don't know . . ." he murmured, feeling tired once again. He needed to sleep.

"It's the only thing I can think of that won't require an outright confession from him, and since he's not a fool, I doubt he'll ever give us one willingly."

"Very well then," Daniel said. "But you will not be alone with him at any time, Becky. Promise me that you will keep other people close to you when you meet with him. He's unpredictable and clearly willing to do whatever it takes to have you for himself. You mustn't take any chances."

"I promise," she said, bending to kiss him lightly on the forehead. "You look tired. Why don't you get some rest while I pay a visit to your aunt and uncle. I won't be long."

He nodded, his eyes already beginning to close. "I love you," he whispered as he slipped lower beneath the covers.

There was a rustle of skirts as she moved across the room. He heard the door open, a pause, and then, very softly and with so much warmth, "I love you too."

Half an hour later, Rebecca was comfortably seated in one of the drawing rooms at Wolvington House. "I can certainly see what he sees in you," Lord Wolvington said. His tone was gruff but not unfriendly.

"Thank you," Rebecca said, deciding to take that as a compliment. She turned toward Lady Wolvington. "And thank you so much for inviting me to stay for tea. I must admit I was worried you'd turn me away."

"Yes . . . well . . ." Lord Wolvington grumbled, not giving his wife a chance to respond. "You must forgive us for not calling on you to congratulate you on your marriage, but the thing of it is that—"

"We caused quite the scandal and you wished to distance yourself from us so it wouldn't affect your own good standing?" Rebecca asked, looking to each of her hosts in turn. Both nodded with some surprise, no doubt because of her bluntness. "I completely understand. After all, you, my lord, are a marquess. I'm sure you must hold a very important seat in Parliament that you would not wish your unruly nephew to affect with his thoughtless escapades. And then of course there is his sister to consider, and her family. By cutting Daniel off you effectively told Society that you thoroughly disapproved of his actions, thus saving yourself, your wife, your niece and her son from being tainted by his scandalous behavior. You washed your hands of him, so to speak, and I am sure that the *ton* approves of your decision."

The Wolvingtons were now gaping at her as if she'd been a complete lunatic who'd recently escaped from Bedlam. Well, time was of the essence—no sense in beating about the bush, as it were. "However, whatever your opinion of Daniel may be, I would like to inform you both that he saved me when he helped me flee from Grover. Had it been possible to do things differently and without journeying all the way to Scotland, we would have done it, but I was under my aunt and uncle's guardianship and they were determined that I should marry the duke. They had a lot to gain from that union."

"It doesn't change the fact that you left your fiancé to elope with another man," Lord Wolvington said. "An act which is viewed as most dishonorable, to say nothing of the embarrassment you have caused Grover as a result."

"I know that this is how it appears, but surely you must realize that things are not always as black and white as all that. In this instance, Daniel is the one who did the honorable thing by helping me escape marrying a beast of a man."

Lord Wolvington's eyes widened and Lady Wolvington gasped. "You are speaking of a duke," Lord Wolvington told Rebecca sharply. "He may not be the most likeable sort, but he is a million miles above you on the social ladder even if you are the daughter of an earl. I will not allow you to speak of him with so much disrespect."

"And what if I were to tell you that he tried to kill Daniel?" She gave Lord Wolvington the hardest stare she could manage, hoping it might help melt his stern exterior and force to the surface some of the affection he surely felt for his nephew. If the Wolvingtons didn't care for Daniel, they never would have demanded that he abandon the rakehell lifestyle he'd embraced since losing his parents, of this she was certain.

"Wh-what are you saying?" Lady Wolvington asked, the pain in her eyes a confession of the deep love she felt for Daniel.

Rebecca smiled with gentle reassurance. "The doctor says that he will be fine, but he is in a great deal of pain. He was shot by Grover and left for dead in an alley."

"Bloody hell," Lord Wolvington said, eyes flashing with the onset of rage. "I'll kill the bastard myself, and I daresay it won't take much to snap that neck of his. Why, I . . ." His words trailed off as he looked at his wife and Rebecca. "Please forgive me, ladies, but even if Grover's feathers have been ruffled, it does *not* give him the right to murder my heir."

"I am in full agreement with you, my lord," Rebecca said, "though I do believe I have a better solution to the problem—if you'll allow me to explain."

When Rebecca left Wolvington House again, it was in the company of the marquess and marchioness, who had both decided to escort her on her visit to Daniel's sister, after which they made another stop at the Landborough residency. "So what you're saying is that Grover tried to kill your husband and you'd like my assistance in making him pay?" the Duke of Landborough asked.

"That is correct," Rebecca said as she met Judy's gaze.

"Well count me in," Landborough said. "I've been waiting years for such an opportunity, and now that it's here, I find that I'm rather looking forward to it."

After thanking the Landboroughs for their support and departing their home, the Wolvingtons then ac-

companied Rebecca to a modiste shop so she could be
fitted for a mourning gown. Conveniently, the dress-
maker had three black gowns set aside in various sizes
in the event that one would be needed, so all that was
required were a few minor adjustments before one of
the gowns fit Rebecca perfectly.

Seated in the Wolvington carriage on their way back
to Avern House, Lady Wolvington surprised Rebecca
by assuring her that extra servants would be sent to
her home later in the day. "The house is understaffed,
and now that you have a bedridden husband to care for
you'll need all the help you can get." Rebecca didn't
argue, knowing that things had not been easy for any of
the servants even before the shooting, when Daniel had
been able to help. She was grateful to Lady Wolvington
for the consideration.

"And I will make a deposit to Daniel's account,"
Lord Wolvington said. To clarify, he added, "It is clear
that he did the right thing, even if it does go against the
rules of Society. He did save you, and the fact that he is
willing to do whatever is necessary in order to support
you shows a level of maturity in him that he did not
possess before he met you."

"Thank you, my lord," Rebecca said, happy that
Lord Wolvington was willing to forgive what Daniel
had done and was finally able to see what a wonderful man he truly was. But she was reluctant to accept
his offer of financial support, knowing that Daniel had
wanted to try and manage on his own—to prove himself capable of supporting his family without relying on
help from anyone. So she said, "That is most generous
of you, but I would advise that you discuss doing so
with Daniel first."

"You think he might refuse?" Lord Wolvington asked, sitting back and looking moderately surprised.

"I do," she said. "Not because he holds a grudge toward you but because he's quite determined to prove himself capable of more than what everyone expects of him."

There was an unmistakable look of admiration in the eyes of the Wolvingtons as they gazed back at Rebecca. "Whatever you've done . . . thank you," Lady Wolvington said, her eyes glistening with emotion. "We've been so worried about him and his future for so long, but it is clear that you have had a positive effect on him."

Lord Wolvington cleared his throat. He looked slightly uncomfortable with the direction in which the conversation was heading. "When he's feeling better I should like to speak with him," he said. The carriage rolled to a stop in front of Rebecca's home. "Until then, however, I trust that you will keep us informed of any further developments?"

"You have my word on it, my lord."

He nodded, but there was no mistaking the concern he felt, for his face was grave and his voice quite serious when he said, "Please be careful, Lady Rebecca. We know what Grover is capable of now, and if he wanted Daniel dead so he could have you for himself . . . I would hate to see you harmed in any way."

Lady Wolvington nodded in agreement, and Rebecca promised them both that she would take care. The door to the carriage opened, and Hawkins was there to help her alight and to carry her parcel into the house. An obituary would appear in the paper the following morning— Daniel's brother-in-law had promised to see to that—and once that happened, Rebecca was certain that Grover would come calling.

"How did it go?" Daniel asked when she returned. "You were gone for some time, so I imagine you were successful?"

"Yes. I spent a lovely afternoon with your family, and I also have a new gown." She placed her box on the bed next to Daniel's legs and pulled back the lid to reveal the black twill. "So from this moment forth, you will not move from this room. We must be as convincing as possible—the slightest suspicion and our plan will fail. And to that effect, I should like to change into my new dress if you would be so good as to unbutton the back for me." She came around to his side of the bed and sat down on the edge of it, close enough for Daniel to offer his assistance, his fingers making quick work of the long row of buttons. When he was done, she felt his breath against her back, followed by a quick succession of kisses along her spine. She felt her breath catch and her skin grow hot, but she pushed the temptation aside and stood up. "Forgive me, but I really must get ready, my love. Your aunt is sending servants over, and I should like to be there to greet them when they arrive."

"Servants?"

"The Wolvingtons forgave our decision to elope after realizing what Grover is truly like. Your uncle was particularly incensed at discovering Grover tried to murder you." She slipped out of her gown and picked up her widow's weeds, stepping into the black dress while Daniel watched with delicious appreciation in his eyes. She had to try and focus on the issue at hand. "He wants to make amends and even offered to make a deposit in your account. I asked that he speak with you first."

Daniel nodded and she turned her back on him, resuming her seat on the edge of the bed so he could button up her new gown. "You did the right thing," he said, "for I should like to make an attempt at making a living on my own. If I fail, we can turn to my uncle, but I should like to at least try and manage without him first."

Chapter 25

"The Griftons are here to see you, my lady," Laura announced the following morning. Her dislike for the visitors was clear in every part of her being, including her voice, which dripped with distaste, as if she'd just bitten into a bad apple.

Rebecca looked up and smiled. "Thank you. If you would please ask Molly to arrange for some tea, I'll be right down."

When she stepped out of the bedroom, Laura was still there, waiting for her. "I didn't want to say anything in front of the master, but I was wondering if you would like me to join you in the parlor so you don't have to be alone with them."

"Now that you mention it, Laura, I do believe I'd appreciate that. Do you have some embroidery with which to pass the time?"

Laura nodded. "I'll take the seat in the corner, but I'll be there should you need me."

Rebecca felt awash with relief. She hadn't realized how much she'd been dreading this encounter, for her last meeting with her aunt had not gone well. The woman was simply incapable of saying anything pleasant. On a deep breath, Rebecca descended the stairs and entered the parlor, where she greeted her aunt and uncle, who were already comfortably seated side by side on the sofa. "What a pleasant surprise," she said, hating the good manners and proper upbringing that forced her to be polite and wishing she'd had the audacity to ask them to leave and stay away from her instead.

"Well, we just had to come right over after seeing the announcement in the paper this morning," her aunt said. There was a beat of silence, and then she asked, "Is it true? Well, I suppose it is, considering the way you're dressed. Such a pity, really. Black never was your color, and especially not with that raven-colored hair—why, you look positively ghoulish! Never mind though. I'm sure you'll marry again soon enough and then we can put this disaster of a marriage behind us. Why, it didn't even last two weeks, but then again, I doubt anyone is surprised by that, considering Mr. Neville's history. In fact, I'm surprised it took this long for someone to off him." She heaved a big sigh that made her entire body shake. "If only you'd listened to us in the first place, this never would have happened. Thank goodness the duke is the forgiving sort though; a missive from him arrived just as we were heading out, informing us of his intentions to resume his courtship of you now that you are no longer attached. I hope that you will show him the gratitude he deserves this time."

Rebecca stood openmouthed, staring back at her aunt, who had finally come to a stop in her diatribe. Rebecca's husband was supposed to be dead and her aunt was sitting there on a sofa that *he* or his parents had once purchased, cheerfully saying what a fortunate occurrence his sudden demise had been. It was abhorrent. And then, without stopping for breath, she'd gone on to push Rebecca back in the arms of Grover. It didn't matter that this was exactly in line with Rebecca's plan; her aunt's attitude still disgusted her. Rebecca sat down in one of the armchairs and stared back at her relatives, wondering how the woman before her could possibly have been her father's sister. Rebecca's father had been nothing like this. He'd been kind and gentle. "I think it in poor taste to speak ill of the dead, Aunt, especially since I chose Mr. Neville for myself," she said, proud of how steady her voice sounded.

"And what a foolish thing that was," her uncle said. "You jeopardized your chance with Grover when you ran off with that good for nothing. Your aunt is right— your husband meeting such an early end was the best thing that could happen to you. It will give you a chance of righting your mistake, of that I have no doubt."

What was going on? Did they think her an imbecilic child to imagine they could speak to her about Daniel in that way? The fact that he was still alive and well upstairs was inconsequential when it came to the anger that rushed through her. She clasped her hands in her lap and prayed for strength, but all that came to her was a vision of strangling both of the people in front of her. She smiled and was relieved from having to respond when Molly arrived with the tea. The butler, a man whom the Wolvingtons had sent over the day before, no doubt with the intent that he would double as body-guard, given his massive size, arrived on Molly's heels to announce the arrival of the Duke of Grover.

"You see," Rebecca's aunt crooned. "I told you he'd come for you."

Rebecca hadn't doubted it for a second, imagining that he'd probably consider her a trophy. And then the man in question arrived, strolling into the room and smiling happily when he set eyes on Rebecca. "Lady Rebecca," he said, "you're looking radiant as always, even under such strained circumstances. My sincerest condolences on the passing of your husband. How tragic that he should die so young."

"Thank you," she said, laying her hand obediently in his outstretched one so he could bend over it and place a kiss upon her knuckles. She felt a subtle movement of air as he lingered for a brief second, and then realized to her horror that he was sniffing her. He looked up, their eyes met and she instinctively drew back, away from the greediness that lurched beneath the surface of his stare.

Grover straightened, and when offered to take a seat, he claimed the one directly next to Rebecca's, moving the chair closer to the table so his knee touched hers whenever he leaned forward to pick up his teacup or take a biscuit. He turned to Rebecca with an edge of determination about him that made the fine hairs at the back of her neck stand on edge. "It cannot be easy for you," he said, his voice low and smooth, "to find yourself so suddenly alone and without protection."

"I'm not sure I follow," Rebecca said, hedging. She had a part to play, but she was finding it incredibly difficult to do so: to be amicable in the company of such distasteful people required her to suppress her emotions and look otherwise pleasant. "The Wolvingtons—"

"It is no secret that they didn't support your husband's behavior. Rumor has it that they turned their back on him and that he was forced to earn his own income, which I hear he did by gambling . . . little surprise there." Grover smiled at her, his lips stretched wide and his eyes glistening the way a pirate's might upon spotting a bounty of treasure.

"Rebecca, it is quite clear that you cannot go on alone," her aunt said very matter-of-factly. "This house is not a simple country cottage. There are expenses to be paid—excessive expenses, since it is in London— and then there's the staff, of course. Eventually your dowry will be depleted and you will require the security of another marriage."

"I would be most happy to oblige," Grover said as he turned in his seat, his knee touching hers as he leaned toward her and added, "you'll want for nothing as my duchess, of that I can assure you."

The way he said *my duchess* made her skin crawl. She felt sick. It wasn't the first time she'd sensed that he was talking of so much more than marriage. He wanted to own her.

She swallowed the nausea that threatened to overwhelm her at his closeness and said, "How kind you are after everything I did to you." Would he notice that she hadn't once apologized? She wasn't about to begin now.

Grover waved his hand, and the tips of his fingers brushed fleetingly against her shoulder. "Of no consequence, my dear. I do not blame you, for it is clear that you were influenced in your judgment, and since I have admired you for so many years now . . . well, I must confess that I am willing to do a great deal in order to win your hand."

No doubt about that!

"Can't you see that he adores you?" Rebecca's aunt pressed. "His devotion to you is quite apparent."

"My dear, I am sure the duke is capable of making his own suit," Lord Grifton told his wife as he bit into a biscuit and started to chew while crumbs sprinkled onto his lap.

"Perhaps an outing would heighten your spirits," Grover suggested. "We could go for a ride in the park together."

"Thank you, Your Grace, but we haven't even had the funeral yet." Rebecca turned her most imploring gaze on him, hoping it would do the trick. "I know that my situation is desperate and that I am in need of help. Please know that I am most grateful for your offer and that I should like to accept, but I was hoping that you would allow me to mourn my husband for at least a week before resuming your courtship."

Grover frowned as he considered Rebecca's request. Her aunt started to say something, but Grover stopped her with a staying hand. "I think a week will be acceptable," he said, his eyes trained on Rebecca's, "but no more. And as for a courtship, it shall be brief, for I find myself quite eager to be wed."

A shiver traced the length of Rebecca's spine, and when Grover took her hand and clasped it between his own, there was something so possessive about it that Rebecca had to struggle not to flinch or pull away. And then her aunt and uncle were scrambling to their feet and rushing to the door as they made their farewells, saying something to the effect that they ought to allow Rebecca and the duke a bit of privacy, thank you for the tea and they would see Rebecca soon enough to make the necessary arrangements for the wedding. The door closed behind them with a thud and Rebecca felt her skin prickle. Her hand was still being clutched by Grover, who appeared to have moved closer. Clenching her jaw, she looked toward Laura, who'd abandoned her embroidery and whose posture was suggestive of a cat preparing to pounce.

"I must tell you," Grover said, his voice a low whisper that only Rebecca would be able to hear, "that I'm a little disappointed knowing that you shan't be coming to my bed an innocent."

His thumb stroked along her hand, the feel of a lizard caressing her skin, and she held still with every ounce of restraint she possessed and thought of her plan. She could not fail now, though her heart pounded wildly in her chest and she could feel herself begin to tremble with disgust.

"I had hoped to rob you of that myself, but no matter. I'm sure there's pleasure to be had in a woman with more experience." His words were scandalous and they repelled her, but just when she thought it couldn't get much worse than this—they were in her parlor, after all, and with a maid nearby as chaperone—Grover placed one hand against her knee and squeezed. Rebecca almost shot out of her chair, or would have done had he not held her firmly in place. "Yes, we shall do very well together, you and I. The way you react to my touch is most promising, and now that you have seen what a man looks like *en déshabillé,* you will be less shocked by what I have to offer." He leaned closer still, so close that she could feel his breath against the side of her neck. It was sickening. "I have needs, Rebecca. Needs that I cannot wait for you to—"

"If you will pardon my interference, Your Grace," Laura said. She had come to stand next to Rebecca with a very disapproving glare trained on the duke. "My mistress has an appointment with the priest that she must keep."

"Thank you for reminding me," Rebecca said, pulling away from Grover and rising to her feet with a slowness that belied her desire to race out of the room. Placing an entire continent between them would not be enough as long as she knew that they still inhabited the same planet. "And thank you for calling on me, Your Grace. I will look forward to seeing you again in a week's time."

With a scowl at Laura, Grover bid Rebecca farewell and departed Avern House while Rebecca stood by the window and watched him go. When he was finally out of sight, she allowed herself a sigh of relief, then turned to Laura and said, "I believe I am in desperate need of a bath."

With the Wolvingtons', Chiltons' and Landboroughs' help, Rebecca managed to make the necessary arrangements for a fake funeral. Three days later, they all watched solemnly and with tears in their eyes as an empty coffin was lowered into the ground at St. James's. She invited them back to Avern House for tea afterward, remaining in the parlor with her guests while Lord Wolvington was shown upstairs to visit with Daniel.

"You love him very much, don't you?" Lady Wolvington asked Rebecca quietly as she sat down next to her.

Rebecca nodded. "It's impossible not to," she said. Pouring each of them a cup of tea, she considered her next words carefully, wondering how much she ought to say and deciding that since Lady Wolvington obviously cared for Daniel, she needed to say *something*. "I know that he hasn't exactly behaved the way you might have wanted in the past, my lady, but that doesn't mean that you failed him in any way. It was very difficult for him to lose his parents the way he did. He felt abandoned and betrayed, and the hurt made him lash out the only way he knew how."

"Until he met you," Lady Wolvington said. She was watching Rebecca with a measure of wisdom in her aging eyes. "You made him want to do better."

Rebecca gave a little shrug and smiled. "I don't believe anyone could *make* Daniel do anything, but because he liked me and because that like turned to love, he decided that he wanted to make me happy and proud."

"And are you?" Lady Wolvington asked. "Happy and proud?"

"Immensely, my lady, though I believe I'll be more happy once this business with Grover has been settled."

Lady Wolvington nodded, took a sip of her tea and said, "I just hope that the plan works."

"It will," Rebecca said, not so much for Lady Wolvington's benefit but to reassure herself. Failure wasn't an option. The plan *had* to work. Four more days—that was all they had before Grover returned.

"How are you feeling?" she asked Daniel later that day when they were once again alone in their bedroom.

"Much better, thank you," he said, and he sounded it. The color had returned to his face and he was sitting up in bed more.

"Did you have a nice chat with your uncle earlier?" He'd given no indication of how his conversation with Lord Wolvington had gone, but he didn't appear angry or worried, which was a good sign.

He regarded her thoughtfully and with a distant look in his eyes, eventually saying, "He says he's proud of me."

Rebecca could feel her lips stretching wide in a foolish smile. What a relief. "And he has every reason to be."

"I refused his offer to renew my allowance, and I think he was quite impressed with the sacrifices I was willing to make in order to support you. I told him that they weren't really sacrifices at all and that when given the choice between you and the phaeton and my love of gambling, the decision was easy. I pick you above all else, Rebecca, and I always will." The smile that graced his lips was different than usual. More shy and self-conscious, perhaps? Whatever the case, Rebecca found it utterly charming. She went to him, seated herself on the edge of the bed and kissed him with everything she had in her, robbing them both of breath. "Did I have a nice funeral?" he asked as she nuzzled her cheek against his.

She chuckled. How typical of him to ask such a question. "Yes," she said. "It was quite lovely."

"Did you cry a lot?"

"We all did," she said.

"But you especially?"

"Yes."

She heard him take a deep breath and then exhale it. "Good," he said.

Good?

She leaned back and stared down at him in dismay. "If I didn't know any better, I'd think my account of the tears I shed as I watched an empty coffin sink into the ground just made you really happy."

He gave her a cheeky smile. "I confess that I'm rather pleased to know that my wife would be sad to see me depart this earth."

"You're a beast," she said as she swatted him playfully with her hand.

"I know," he grinned, pulling her back for another kiss, a longer one that left no doubt in her mind about the love he felt for her. It was overwhelming.

"Do you think you will be ready to get back on your feet in four days?" she asked a while later as they ate the supper that Laura and Molly had brought up to their room.

"And if I'm not? What will you do then?" he asked, pinning her with his dark brown eyes.

"I don't know . . . manage without you somehow." It would lessen their chance of success, but she also didn't want Daniel staggering about London if he didn't feel as though he could manage it. He'd been through a lot, but she'd only been able to buy him a week in which to recover, unless of course she wished to prolong Grover's advances. They had both agreed that doing so was out of the question.

"No. I will be fine. We will proceed as we have discussed."

She nodded, but she sensed that he was pulling himself together for her sake and worried if it wasn't a mistake for him to venture out of bed so soon after sustaining his injuries. "I just don't want you to be worse off because of this."

"I won't be. I promise, Becky." He took her hand in his and looked at her more seriously than ever before as he said, "But we must put an end to this so he cannot harm us again. We've a better chance of seeing him charged with attempted murder if I do my part to help."

Chapter 26

The days passed and Daniel began to feel better. He was still sore, but at least the sharp pain he'd experienced at first was no longer more than an ache. He still couldn't fathom how happy he was in light of everything that had happened, but since Rebecca had declared her love for him, he'd had a perpetual smile on his face. It was a magical feeling really, and one that he hadn't expected. Thinking back on the time they'd spent together and the bond that had gradually grown between them, it probably should have occurred to him that she cared for him. But to actually hear the words whispered across her lips was the sweetest pleasure and a most welcome surprise.

Love.

He'd been loved by his parents once, and then he hadn't been. It was strange to discover how quickly something that should have been infinite could come to such an abrupt end. He'd turned to a life of recklessness instead, burying the pain of his loss by seeking comfort in the arms of meaningless women and distracting himself with parties and gambling. It had been such fun at the time, so much so that he'd barely had time to spare his missing parents a second thought, but it had also been dreadfully empty and, truth be told, utterly pointless. What had he achieved? Nothing but to distance himself from anyone who might have cared. He hadn't wanted to face the pity in their eyes or their words of reassurance, so he'd spurned them all and gone his own way.

But then his uncle had come up with his ultimatum. Daniel made a mental note to thank him for that because he'd done him a huge favor. He'd forced Daniel to take control of his life, and while Daniel confessed that he'd done so on his own terms and in a very rakehell sort of way, he'd married Rebecca, and nothing in the world would ever make him regret doing so. She was quite simply wonderful, and she made him want to get his life back together so he could be the sort of man she would be proud of. Would he have sold his phaeton if it hadn't been for her? It was unlikely. The phaeton had been his pride and joy since he'd bought it two years earlier, but he would happily chop it to kindling himself if it meant offering Rebecca the sort of life she deserved.

And she deserved a lot. Christ, his parents might have abandoned him, but Rebecca had lost hers in a fire and then been forced to live with hateful relations who'd wanted to force her into marriage so they could line their own pockets. The thought of it still disgusted him. But she was his now, and he loved her. He still wasn't sure how on earth he would manage to support her in the long run now that he'd promised he'd quit his gambling. The phaeton would probably bring in a handsome sum, but that money wouldn't last forever, and what then? He would have to find a job, he supposed, until he was able to benefit from his investments. Then, of course, he could sell the house and get a smaller apartment. The thought of living so measly didn't appeal in the least, mostly because he wanted more for Rebecca. She was an earl's daughter, and as such she ought to have a proper home with a decent number of servants to tend to her needs.

He sighed and briefly considered her dowry. No, he told himself firmly. He wouldn't touch it. There had to be a way—something he'd yet to discover—by which to earn a proper income. Since he was sitting about all day anyway until he was fully recovered, he might as well put his time to good use and take a look at the advertisements in the newspaper Rebecca had left on the chair by the door. She'd read him a couple of columns from it earlier before stepping out to discuss the evening meal with Madame Renarde.

Throwing back the covers, Daniel eased himself up and out of bed, taking a moment to adjust to being fully upright and without support. He felt slightly lightheaded, so he remained perfectly still until it passed. Then he began taking slow steps toward the chair and the newspaper lying on it. "Got you," he said, grabbing the paper and feeling pretty triumphant with his achievement. But then his gaze settled on what was beneath the paper and he paused, his eyes taking in the sketch that graced the paper. It was drawn in a sure hand, with confident brushstrokes coloring the image that filled not even half the page.

Bending over it, he looked at it more closely and discovered that it was him. The likeness was impeccable, and he reached out to pick up the sketchbook, then paused. Rebecca had mentioned that she liked to paint, but she'd never shown him any of her work. What if she didn't want him to see it? The thought that she wouldn't gave him pause, and he pulled back. He would have to ask for her permission, he decided, and he became quite impatient for her to return so he could do so. She might protest, but he would convince her. He smiled as he made his way back across the carpet to the bed. Convincing her would probably be a great deal of fun.

"I brought you some mint tea and a sandwich," Rebecca announced as she stepped back into the room a short while later. She was carrying a tray, her smile bright and cheerful as always.

It struck Daniel that he'd always adored that smile, for it was so warm and inviting, and yet it was different now. She loved him, and it showed in her smile, or was he just being fanciful? He smiled back, happy that she'd finally returned even though she'd been gone for barely half an hour. "Could you hear my stomach growling all the way to the kitchen?"

Closing the door, she chuckled as she waited for him to sit up properly. He put the newspaper aside, and she placed the tray upon his lap. "Oh yes. It almost sounded as if a lion had taken up residency." She nodded toward the newspaper. "I see you've had a little out of bed adventure. Did you manage all right?"

Daniel nodded as he chewed on the bite he'd just taken. "I felt a bit dizzy at first," he admitted, "and it did ache a fair bit, but I made it to the chair and back without too much difficulty."

"Well, you should probably still take it slow, though I'm glad to see that things are moving in the right direction and that you're recovering." Turning, she went to take a seat in the chair, then paused as her eyes fell on the sketchbook. "I . . . er . . ."

"Yes, I was rather wondering when you were going to show me that," Daniel said, following his comment with a sip of tea as he watched her closely. Her face was turned away, so he couldn't see her expression, but her posture appeared to have grown a little tense. Was she upset over what he'd seen? Well, she should have closed the book and put it away if she wanted to be certain he wouldn't look, but then again she probably hadn't thought he'd go roaming around the room.

"It's nothing really," she muttered, picking up the sketchbook and snapping it shut, "just a bit of scribbling really—something with which to pass the time."

Daniel stared at her. *Scribbling?* How could she possibly pass such a wonderful sketch off as nothing but scribbling? And then it hit him. She had no idea how talented she was, which would also explain why she'd never shown him her drawings. In all likelihood it was something she very much enjoyed but didn't think worthy of volunteering for someone else's perusal. "Becky," he said, his voice soft and with an edge of surprise to it that could only signify deep admiration, "I think your drawing . . . painting . . . of me is quite marvelous."

She looked over her shoulder at him with a little frown creasing the bridge of her nose and the edge of her mouth tilting up in a half smile. "Really?" There was something so vulnerable and hopeful in her eyes as she said it, as if she feared he might not have been sincere in his compliment or, heaven forbid, said it because he loved her and didn't want to hurt her feelings.

"Absolutely," he said with a confidence that would brook no doubt, or so he hoped. He added, "Of course

I've only seen the one painting, so I've no way of knowing if the rest of your work is rubbish or not." She scowled at him, but there was laughter in her eyes. His attempt at humor had paid off, and she was relaxing. Putting all the reverence he felt for her into his voice, he finally said, "I would be honored if you would allow me to see your sketchbook, Becky."

Standing perfectly still, she looked back at him, considering his words, and Daniel could scarcely breathe from the anticipation of what she might say. If she denied him the request, it would mean that she didn't trust him with something that clearly meant a great deal to her. The thought of that troubled him, and he knew he had to do whatever he could to prevent such an outcome. After all, wasn't she the great advocate for honesty and full disclosure? That they would be closer if they shared everything with one another? No secrets. And yet he didn't want to force her hand either, so he decided to make her an offer instead. "Oh, and if you agree, then I shall give you a reward for each of the pictures I see."

"A reward?"

Ah, now he had her attention. He looked at her as if she'd been standing naked before him. Waiting for realization to dawn on her features, he nodded with satisfaction when she squeaked a little "Oh!"

"Yes, Becky . . . a *reward*."

She turned to face him fully, hands on hips and looking quite adorably flustered, though she was clearly attempting a more composed demeanor. "Why, Mr. Neville, I do believe you have a rather wicked streak."

Daniel almost sputtered his tea across the bedcovers with laughter. Her declaration spoken in such a prim manner was just too much. "Surely you haven't just found this out now," he said when he was once again capable of speech.

"Perhaps not," she admitted, "but it seemed like the proper thing to say."

Pushing the tray from his lap, he scooted away from the edge and patted the spot he'd just vacated. "Come sit. Bring your sketchbook, and I'll show you precisely how wicked I can be."

Shaking her head in surrender and smiling as if it was she who'd just gotten the better of him and not the other way around, Rebecca picked up her sketchbook and did as Daniel asked, perching herself on the edge of the bed as she handed him the book. He eyed her for a second. She looked nervous again, as if his opinion was of the utmost importance. The notion made his heart swell, and he reached out his hand to gently stroke her cheek. "Don't worry," he said. "I know I'm going to love your pictures, Becky." And then he opened the sketchbook and was quite literally rendered breathless.

This was not what he had envisioned at all, not still life studies of vases filled with flowers or boring fruit bowels. This . . . this was fantasy—a group of fairies dancing, their whispery gowns twirling about their legs while huge blooms of wildflowers dwarfed them from overhead. They were all barefoot, he noticed, and with lovely translucent butterfly wings. "I don't know what to say," he muttered as his eyes fell on a small ladybird nestled between the straws of grass.

"I know it must seem unusual and well . . . unfinished with all the pencil strokes still visible beneath the paint, but like I said, they're just a bit of scribbling really and—"

"It's brilliant," Daniel said, raising his gaze to meet hers. "It's absolutely magical, Becky, and with a sense of movement that I don't believe would be there at all if the pencil strokes weren't visible."

She blinked, her lips parting slightly with undeniable astonishment, and Daniel couldn't help himself. Reaching out, he pulled her closer until their lips finally met, gently at first and then with growing urgency, their tongues toying eagerly in the confines of their hot mouths. Daniel suppressed a groan, not from pain but from a different kind of torture altogether. Dear God, he wanted her. Clearly the act of being shot had not dampened his virility in the least. On the contrary, abstaining for several days had heightened it. He sucked in a breath. One painting, one reward; he would make this better for both of them if he drew it out as long as possible. So he pulled back, relishing the sigh that left her lips at their parting, and boldly turned the page of her sketchbook.

Three fairies were having a race in this one, each of them riding a beetle with ribbons tied on as reins. "You really do have quite the imagination," he said as he traced a slow line along the edge of Rebecca's bodice, dipping a finger between her breasts. She sucked in a breath and he smiled as he noted the flush in her cheeks. "I wonder what your reward shall be this time . . . perhaps something like this?" And easing his finger along, he found her pebbling nipple.

"Yes," she sighed, her back arching to offer him more. With a greedy chuckle, he tugged and pinched her gently until she was groaning with pleasure—a pleasure that hardened him to frustration.

Flipping another page, he glanced down at the next

painting, scarcely registering what it was in his need for more of her. More fairies . . . more magic. He tugged at her bodice, freeing her to his gaze, then placed his mouth upon her, his tongue working her nipple as he suckled her.

"Daniel," she gasped, her hands thrusting through his hair and holding him tightly against her. "Daniel, please . . ."

He withdrew and gave her a wolfish grin. "Would you like another reward?"

She nodded and he turned the page, discovering a picture that caught his attention. "It's us," he said, incredulous at the detail and level of skill the picture portrayed. "This was when we danced at the Kingsborough Ball . . . right before . . ." An image further down the page showed her lying on the ground with blood oozing from her shoulder.

"I've no memory of this of course, so it's entirely based on my own imagination," she said.

Daniel swallowed hard at the memory of what had happened. He ought to meet with Roxberry so he could discover the culprit behind the shooting and, more to the point, wring the blighter's neck. Caught up in the story the pictures seemed to convey, he quickly turned the page to find Rebecca greeting him through her bedroom window.

His gaze fell on a picture of himself and Rebecca side by side in her wardrobe, and as he recalled how wonderful that first kiss had been, he reflected on everything they'd been through since—a winding path that had led them to this moment.

"You've forgotten your promise," she said.

The reward.

"Guilty, I admit, but these are just so incredible that I couldn't help myself. It's as if you've catalogued every key moment of our acquaintance. Look, even Grover's ball and the carriage ride to Scotland are here . . . our wedding too . . ." His words trailed off as a daring image of their wedding night caught his eye. "I believe I've just found your true reluctance for showing me these. This is quite risqué."

He liked it though, the way she'd captured the passion between them as they'd tangled between the sheets. Not even a breast was visible, yet that only seemed to make it so much more erotic. "You're right. I must reward you now, and for more than one picture." He closed the sketchbook and set it on the bedside table. "However will I manage?"

Rebecca was quite convinced he'd think of something—something utterly indecent. Her breasts grew heavy at the very thought of it. She hadn't realized how much she'd missed their coupling these past few days, but now, with his eyes hot upon hers, it was all she could do not to clamber all over him until they both screamed with pleasure.

He was injured though, and she had no desire to cause him further harm, so she held still instead and waited for him to make his move.

"Stand up and face the bed," he said.

She complied, the skirts of her gown falling loosely around her legs and her bodice still disarranged and baring her breasts to Daniel's wanting gaze. He fingered the fabric of her skirt with an air of pensiveness, then began to pull at it, hoisting it up over her knees, thighs and hips. He held it like that for a moment while he stared at her, a greedy hunger reflecting her own growing desire. She knew what he was seeing, for she was naked beneath, and somehow, the idea that he might pleasure her like this, still fully garbed, aroused her beyond all measure. When he did nothing, however, she spread her legs wider apart in invitation, thrilling at the groan that came from somewhere deep inside him.

"My God" was all he said before she felt the wet tip of his tongue upon her, one slow stroke that sent a pulse of heat shooting straight through her. She felt her knees grow weak and her whole body begin to sag until she had no choice but to reach out and steady herself on the bedside table.

"Like that, did you?" Daniel was sitting back again and looking up at her with a very wicked gleam in his eyes.

"More," was all she could manage, and even that was barely audible.

But Daniel must have heard her, for he grinned, adding a flash of white teeth—the primal look of a man intent on ravishing her. Looking up at her, his eyes darker than before, two fingers found her center, parted her flesh and slipped inside. Heaven above she was lucky to still be upright. His fingers moved and she gasped. "Daniel . . . I . . ."

"Yes?" The wicked man was teasing her. To prove it, he moved his fingers again—in and out they went until she felt herself grow taught. She couldn't speak, could barely form a coherent thought as a wave of heat rose up her legs to meet the swirling flush of tingling warmth that fanned out from her core. And then she shattered on the sound of his name, torn from deep inside her chest. It had not taken long, two minutes at most, but it had felt incredible.

With a sigh of sated satisfaction, Rebecca savored the feeling of her limp body returning to a more grounded state of being. She knew she shouldn't feel embarrassed by what had just transpired between them, but she couldn't seem to stop her cheeks from flooding with warmth, and even less so when she noticed the peak in the sheets. Her desires had been expertly quenched, but Daniel's had not. "I . . . er . . ." she began hesitantly.

He raised an eyebrow.

Oh bother.

She wasn't usually the shy sort. In fact, she was generally quite outspoken, but this was new territory for her, and finding the right words was not as easy as she'd thought it would be when she'd opened her mouth to speak. *Pull yourself together, Rebecca. You're a married woman and not nearly as innocent as you were two weeks ago.* She gazed back at Daniel, who was watching her most expectantly. There was no reason for her to feel embarrassed. He was her husband, her friend, her ally, and more than that, he loved her. She straightened her back a little with new resolve and said, "If you would like, I would very much enjoy returning the favor." His eyes widened and his jaw dropped. She hastily added, "Unless of course you think it would be too painful for you, in which case we can just sit for a bit and look at the paintings if you like or . . . oh . . . I don't know, play a game of cards or something." She was babbling now, she realized.

Idiot.

"Cards?" Daniel sounded as if he'd been choking.

Rebecca frowned. "Are you all right?"

He groaned. Poor man, his wound was clearly pain-ing him. "I'm sorry," she said. "We never should have done what we just did. You obviously need rest."

"Stop," he muttered, the words sounding like a croak. "Please, Becky, stop talking."

She said nothing further and just watched as he sank back against his pillows, closed his eyes and heaved a great big sigh. There was still a peak in the sheets. *Oh dear.* Biting her lip, she tried not to stare at it.

"May I be perfectly frank with you?" Daniel asked.

"Of course."

"Very well then. As you may have noticed, I have a bit of a situation." He waved one hand in the general direction of his groin. "So there is some discomfort, not from my wound but from my overwhelming lust for you." He paused, the edge of his mouth kicking up a bit until his signature smile of mischief returned. "I cannot be very active, given my current condition, but if you were serious before when you asked if you could return the favor, then yes, by all means, you may— indeed, I would relish it."

A warm, fuzzy feeling swept through Rebecca at his words. There was nothing crass about it, and he was making no attempt to seduce her back into a state of wantonness. All he'd done was explain his current state of being and what might be done to alleviate it. She felt humbled really that he would talk so plainly to her about his needs, and thrilled that he trusted her not to shy away from him. "I would do anything for you," she told him reverently as she pulled the bed sheet away from him.

"Anything?" he murmured, his eyes opening into two narrow slits. She nodded, and a deep rumble shook his chest. "I'll have to remember that for later."

"For now, however," she purred as her fingers curled around him, "I shall take great pleasure in doing this." And then she bent forward and covered him with her mouth.

Dear merciful God in heaven.

It took every ounce of willpower within him to remain perfectly still while his wife did what no proper lady of breeding would ever do—or so he'd heard. Even his mistresses had seemed reluctant, never offering such pleasure of their own free will but only if he asked.

Yet Rebecca . . . his hand fisted through her hair as her tongue worked magic along the hard length of him, her lips pulling and sucking as if . . . dear God, she *was* taking pleasure in this. The notion stunned him, and he thanked his lucky stars for whatever deity had brought her his way. What a lucky devil he'd turned out to be.

Her hand stroked up his thigh and he felt a light tremble in his groin—the knowledge of what she would do . . . hoping for it . . . and then she did it, the one thing nobody had ever done before. She cupped him, fondled him gently and then . . . She lifted her head with a frown, a few strands of hair trailing lightly against her cheek. "Is this all right?" she asked. She looked truly unsure and concerned. "I mean, is this . . . do you like it?"

Like it?

He wanted to raise her to bloody sainthood for her efforts. "Yes," he rasped. "Yes, Becky, it's . . . very . . . very good . . . the best . . . ever." Good Lord, he could barely get the words out, he was breathing so hard. The smile she offered in response was not in the least bit innocent—it was tantalizing and greedy, like that of a siren who'd just spotted a lonely sailor. She bent her head again and he closed his eyes, giving himself up to the pleasure of her ministrations until he began to feel his inner thigh muscles starting to strain. He pulled at her hair, tugging her away from him and asking her to use her hand instead as tingles started to spread across his skin. The pressure intensified with each stroke she made until he felt himself burst, heart bouncing in his chest, his breath coming in heavy gusts as he spent himself on his belly and her hand.

He felt both exhausted and immensely gratified. "Thank you," he said as he opened his eyes to gaze up at her wondrous face. "I don't know what I did to deserve you."

She stepped away from the bed, righting the bodice of her gown as she went to the dresser and pulled out a couple of handkerchiefs so they could clean themselves. "You were just you, Daniel," she said, "and you were . . . you *are* . . . everything I've ever dreamed of."

"Except for my inability to support you," he said, the depression he felt whenever he considered their financial state taking hold of him once more.

She scoffed at that, the little minx. "I think you're doing just brilliantly under the circumstances. After all, you lost the financial backing your uncle had assured you of if you married, upon which you used your skill at gambling to help us get by for a bit, and when that turned out to be too dangerous you sold your beloved phaeton. On top of that, you've invested in some promising companies, which only proves your dedication to doing what is right and best for us. I'm proud of you, and I have no doubt that we'll get through this somehow."

How could she be so relaxed about it? "I've considered selling the house as well," he told her.

She paused, then seated herself on the edge of the bed and took his hand in hers. "I understand that it has some unpleasant memories which I assume must be linked to your parents. Madame Renarde mentioned that the upstairs remains locked, and I have noticed that there are some rooms that you choose to avoid."

He didn't wish to talk about this now, but since she was asking and he did not wish to brush her aside, he steeled himself. "You know that my mother left quite suddenly. We were here when it happened, enjoying the London Season. It was just as splendid as it had been the previous years, with picnics in the park, trips to Gunther's and outings to toy shops. My parents had a lot of friends whom they would invite for daily visits. Many of them had children that I could play with. We were a happy family and a very loving one.

"But then it all changed. One second my mother was there, joking and laughing with my father and me . . . and then she was gone." He shook his head, still unable after all these years to fathom how she could have done it. He hated her for abandoning him like that, hated thinking of her laughing happily with a new family . . . new children that she loved more than she did him. And he hated her for pushing his father to the limit, for taking his father away from him as well. He wondered if she even knew that he had died somewhere in France. "How can a mother's love for her child fade like that?" he asked.

"I cannot answer that," Rebecca said, her voice filled with pain and regret, "for I do not know."

Damn, how he hated the melancholy that had settled upon them. He made an attempt to brush it aside.

"Anyway, I found that note she left me in the nursery and have never returned there since. I try to avoid some of the other rooms as well, like the study, where I'll always see my father seated behind his desk, and the music room. My mother loved to play the piano."

"Is that why this room is so much smaller than the guest bedroom?"

He nodded. "I switched the two when I realized that I'd soon be returning with a wife. It was the only thing I could think of in order to preserve my own sanity."

She gazed back at him with big round eyes, and then she leaned toward him, not to kiss him but to embrace him, her slim arms coming around him in a tight hug. "I'm so sorry," she whispered. "No child should have to go through something like that."

He said nothing, just taking comfort in the warmth of her closeness and the love she imparted to him with every breath she took. What he needed—what they both needed—was a fresh start. He pulled away and looked at her with renewed determination and with a clear vision of what he wanted for his future. "We'll sell the house and find something else—a place where we can make our own happy memories without any of the unhappy ones lurching in the shadows. And if you will permit," he said as he reached for her sketchbook, "I think these fairy pictures of yours would work brilliantly for a children's storybook."

Rebecca's lips parted in surprise. "A storybook?"

He nodded. "Yes. I mean, they practically tell a story on their own, but if we add some words I'm sure it would become immensely popular. Kingsborough's brother runs a small publishing house, you know, so I could speak to him."

"I don't know what to say." She glanced hesitantly at the sketchbook. "Do you really suppose it might be a success?"

"I am confident of it." He smiled reassuringly. "Why don't you fetch some paper so we can get started, and I'll ask Hawkins to send a note over to Lord Winston requesting an interview. Surely he must be back in town by now."

Three hours later, they had the basics for their story and had cut out the pictures and pasted them on separate sheets of paper with the text below each one, creating a sample of what they envisioned for the final book. "I think it looks great," Daniel said as he leafed through the pages, "and I cannot wait to show it to Lord Winston. I have every confidence that he'll agree to publish it for us." And if he didn't, Daniel would take the book elsewhere. Somehow he'd ensure that it made its way into shops all over the country, because the pictures were just too incredible to be hidden away—they deserved to be seen by everyone.

Chapter 27

"**T**he Duke of Grover to see you, my lady," Hawkins announced the following day. Rebecca had expected his visit and had seated herself in the parlor, still dressed in her widow's weeds and with Laura in attendance.

The duke entered with a smug expression upon his face and executed an elegant bow. "Your beauty always astounds me," he said as he reached for her hand and kissed it. He was carrying a bouquet of flowers, which he thrust in Laura's direction. "Perhaps you'd be good enough to put these in some water while I keep your mistress company. There is a matter that she and I must discuss in private."

A queasy sensation settled upon Rebecca, and she looked to Laura with concern.

"I'll ring for Molly to take care of it, Your Grace," Laura dutifully said. "After all, it would be the height of impropriety for me to leave you completely alone with my mistress. Why, you—"

"She is not an innocent and has no virtue to protect," the duke ground out, his warm gaze from a moment earlier transformed into a deadly glare. "Besides, I've no desire for an audience when I propose. I wish to do so *privately.*"

"But I—"

"You are nothing more than a servant, and I suggest you remember your place," he said, cutting Laura off. "Now be off with you and be sure that you close the door behind you so Lady Rebecca and I can be alone."

"Your Grace," Rebecca said, desperate to prevent a disastrous situation, "my maid is merely concerned about my welfare. I've been terribly distressed lately after everything that has happened, particularly after discovering that the miniature of me that my parents acquisitioned for my thirteenth birthday has gone missing." She threw her hands up in the air and dropped onto the sofa, hiding her face in her hands as she started to sob.

There was a beat of silence before the duke slowly asked, "Have you no idea of where it might be?"

Raising her head, Rebecca looked back at him, bleary-eyed, and sniffled. He pulled a handkerchief from his pocket and handed it to her as she replied, "I gave it to my husband as a wedding gift and he carried it with him wherever he went, but it was not on his person when he was brought to the morgue at the hospital. I asked the coroner myself." She sobbed again and drew a quivering breath, hoping that she looked convincing in her grief.

"Perhaps it fell from Mr. Neville's pocket when he got shot," Grover muttered.

"The thought of it falling into a stranger's hands is so distressing, Your Grace, but I suppose it is an outcome that I must accept."

"You've no idea of where to look for it?" Grover asked, looking pensive.

"None at all," Rebecca said, praying that Grover would believe her. "I was informed of my husband's death when the coroner discovered his calling card in his pocket, confirming his identity, but when I asked where the shooting had taken place, no one could give me an answer. Apparently the men who brought his body to the morgue disappeared again before they could be questioned."

Grover stared back at her for a second and then addressed Laura. "The flowers will wilt if you don't put them in water quickly. Don't argue. Just do it." He licked his lips and looked at Rebecca. "I will comfort your mistress until you return."

Looking hesitantly at her mistress, Laura waited for a nod of approval from Rebecca before hurrying to do the duke's bidding, leaving the door to the parlor wide open as she left. Grover frowned, but he didn't try to close it, seating himself at Rebecca's side instead. He took her hand in his and turned to face her, piercing her with his stare. "It is a great pity that your miniature has gone missing, my dear, but perhaps it will surface again soon. I certainly hope so, for I would love nothing better than to carry it with me the way Neville did."

Rebecca held her breath. It appeared her plan was working.

"I trust you've had no second thoughts about becoming my wife?" the duke asked bluntly.

Swallowing hard, Rebecca tried to ignore her dislike for the man and slowly shook her head. "No, Your Grace."

A smile of pleasure slid across the duke's lips, and

he leaned toward her as he lowered his gaze to her bosom. "We will marry tomorrow then," he murmured as he trailed his finger along the length of her arm. "I still have the special license, if you recall."

Every fiber of her being was rebelling against his touch, yet she somehow managed to force a smile and say, "How very convenient."

"I will inform your aunt and uncle of the development then and will ensure that your bedchamber at Grover House is made ready to receive you." The chuckle that followed was perverse.

Rebecca stiffened at the unwelcome implication and was thinking of an excuse to distance herself from the duke when he surprised her by pressing her against the corner of the sofa and licking the side of her neck. "Your Grace!" she squealed, struggling to escape him but finding it difficult to do so. He was stronger than he appeared, and his determination to press his advances on her made him impossible for her to budge. This was exactly the sort of thing that Daniel had warned her about, but it was not an outcome she would have expected with the parlor door wide open as it was. If only Hawkins or Laura would see what was happening so they could interrupt the duke's amorous efforts.

"I can hardly wait to undress you," the duke was saying.

"Please release me, Your Grace. What you're doing is unseemly," she said as she squirmed against his embrace.

He laughed with menace and placed his palm against her breast. "I find it amusing that you're always trying to play the part of a proper young lady who has no need for a man's touch. You needn't keep up the pretense for my benefit however, for I am more than happy to accommodate your every desire—indeed, I've fantasized about doing so since seeing you for the very first time three years ago."

Rebecca gasped at the outrageousness of what he was saying and the troubling thought of what this awful man might have imagined doing with her. Dear God, she had to get away from him quick, but without causing suspicion. Where on earth was Laura? "Your Grace, you are being too forward. Someone might see. If you would please wait until tomorrow night when we are alone, then I will be happy to accommodate your every need."

He leaned back and smiled with approval just as Laura returned with a look of alarm on her face. Her breath was coming fast, suggesting that she'd hurried back as quickly as possible. "I can scarcely wait," Grover said as he rose to his feet and went to the door. "Now, if you'll excuse me, there is a matter that I must attend to. I will return tomorrow morning to escort you to the church."

As soon as he was out the door, Rebecca collapsed against the sofa, her whole body trembling with disgust. She looked at Laura, who appeared overwrought by the state her mistress was in. "I'm so sorry that you had to endure his presence alone," Laura said. "I never should have left you with him."

"I will survive it," Rebecca muttered, "though I daresay another bath would be most welcome." Rising, she crossed to the door and headed numbly toward the stairs. As much as she dreaded telling Daniel about everything that had transpired, she determined to do so as soon as he returned home. She would not keep secrets from her husband, no matter what. Hopefully by the time she told him about the duke's advances, Grover would no longer pose a threat to either of them and the anger that Daniel was likely to feel would be alleviated a little as a result.

Hidden away in a dark doorway, Daniel leaned against his walking stick and listened for the click of footsteps that were sure to arrive at any moment. In anticipation of Grover's arrival at Avern House, he'd snuck out through the kitchen earlier in the day and had been keeping watch on the alley ever since. He was getting tired of standing up, but he couldn't risk moving and being seen. So he bit back the ache in his midsection and the exhaustion he felt in his bones, and remained perfectly still . . . watching and waiting.

Dusk began to fall, deepening the shadows, and a chill set in. Pulling the collar of his greatcoat up around his neck, Daniel leaned back against the door and briefly closed his eyes. He *had* to get through this, if not for his own sake, then for Rebecca's, so they could have a chance at a happy future together. He drew a deep breath and exhaled it slowly, stiffening at the sound of a soft thud. A cane or a heavy footstep? He opened his eyes and peered out into the murky darkness, noticing nothing out of the ordinary. A foot scraping against the paving stones said otherwise, and Daniel straightened himself, careful not to make a sound that might give him away.

Leaning forward just a little, he peered around the edge of the doorway and went still as he spotted the silhouette of a slim man. He was hunched over and obviously searching for something. Daniel squinted. He had to be sure of the man's identity before he revealed himself to him, so he waited, not even realizing until his chest began to ache that he'd been holding his breath. He exhaled and the man straightened, then turned, as if trying to work out where to look next. For the briefest second, Daniel caught a glimpse of his eyes as they glistened through the darkness.

Supporting his weight on his walking stick, Daniel stepped out of the doorway and pulled a small, oval-shaped object from his coat pocket. "Looking for this?" he asked, his voice resonating against the brick walls of the alley.

There was a beat, and then the silent sound of a man attempting to work out how to evade capture. "Who goes there?" Grover asked. The tremor in his voice betrayed the composed sense of calm he was aiming for.

"A ghost perhaps?" Daniel offered as he moved slowly toward him, step by step. "After all, I was shot *and* buried. For all intents and purposes, I am dead."

"Not dead enough," Grover bit out, his previous tone of uncertainty turning to anger.

Daniel chuckled. "No, I suppose you must be somewhat disappointed with that."

They were close now, so close that Daniel could make out the features on Grover's face, from the hawk-like nose to the drawn cheeks and thin lips. "My wife was right about you, wasn't she?" he asked, noticing how Grover's eyes turned to slits at the mention of Rebecca. "You are dangerously obsessed with her and will stop at nothing until you make her your own. Am I right?"

"She belongs to me, Neville. I paid good money for

the right to bed her. If anyone is in the wrong, it is you—you stole her from me!"

"I saved her from an existence that she had no desire to endure," Daniel said, his own anger rising at the thought of Rebecca having to lay with this man. "And if you must know, it was she who devised this brilliant plan to have you proven guilty of attempted murder."

"Ha! And how will you do that, Neville? I am a duke and you're a careless, womanizing scamp. Nobody will take your word over mine."

"Are you sure about that?" Daniel asked, enjoying the fleeting look of fear in Grover's eyes. He held up the small, oval-shaped object again, affording Grover a good look at it. It was the miniature of Rebecca. "She told you I had this on me when I 'died' and that it had been lost, but she didn't tell you where in London I was shot. You knew though, because you were the one who shot me. You knew where to look for the miniature, such a personal item belonging to the woman who haunts your every thought . . . we were certain you'd want to have it for yourself, just as much as you want to have her."

Cold fury flashed in Grover's eyes. "I will see you in your grave, Neville." Moving surprisingly fast for his age, Grover made a grab for the miniature, his long fingers curling around it and snatching it out of Daniel's grasp with a mad laugh of victory. "You won't leave here alive, you good-for-nothing scoundrel," he said as he stepped back and pulled a pistol from his pocket. "Not this time."

"You're wrong about that, Your Grace," a deep voice said as a broad-shouldered man rounded a corner and stepped into the alley behind Grover. It was the magistrate, accompanied by a constable and two runners. "I suggest you put your weapon down and step away from Mr. Neville, or the constable here will have no choice but to fire."

"You have two options, Your Grace," came a voice from behind Daniel. It was Landborough, who'd closed off the other end of the alley together with Lord Wolvington, making any attempt at escape impossible. "You can either be tried by your peers, or you can flee this country, never to return. From what I hear, America is lovely this time of year. If you choose the first option however, I advise you to consider that I shall be one of the men deciding your fate."

A crazed look came over Grover's eyes, and Daniel took an involuntary step back as he realized the duke's intent. He had no plan of surrendering but would take his shot and suffer the consequences, even if it meant death. *Holy hell!* Daniel had considered this outcome of course, but as he watched Grover raise his pistol with a menacing snarl on his lips, he was beginning to think that the plan might not have been as great as he'd initially thought.

He was just beginning to ready himself for the blazing pain about to tear through him once more when a loud crack ripped through the air, followed closely by a second. If he'd been shot, he felt remarkably well. Daniel blinked, the sound of gunfire still ringing in his ears as he stared back at Grover, whose snarl had now twisted into an awful grimace. Dropping his pistol so it clattered against the ground, the duke clutched at his arm. "You bloody bastards," he said as the constable and runners came up behind him, intent on taking him away. He struggled against them only briefly before giving up, the pain in his arm where the constable had shot him an obvious ailment. "Your sister was lucky that I bothered with her at all, Landborough—willful chit that she is."

Landborough stepped forward, his eyes dark with rage. "Whatever punishment you receive, I will never think it sufficient. You ought to hang for your transgressions."

"And I probably would have had you not wished to avoid scandal. But if there was one thing that I knew I could count on, it was that you wouldn't want anyone to discover what really happened at your home that day."

"Be silent, Grover," the magistrate warned, "or I might be tempted to leave you here alone for a few minutes with only Landborough and Neville to keep you company."

Daniel glanced toward Landborough, impressed by the man's ability to restrain himself. Daniel didn't know exactly what had happened to the duke's sister, but from what little Grover had said, it was clearly worse than what he'd done to Rebecca. Jaw clenched, Daniel watched as the constable and runners led Grover away. "Thank you," he told the magistrate. "I trust you'll see to it that he never troubles us again?"

"You can count on it," the magistrate said. He then bid everyone a good night and disappeared after the others.

"I owe you a debt of gratitude as well," Daniel told Landborough.

"Likewise," the duke said. "I can finally rest easy knowing that he will not go unpunished. You're a good man, Neville. The *ton* is wrong about you, and I for one am proud to call you a friend."

"You do me great honor, Your Grace. Perhaps you and your wife would like to dine at Avern House tomorrow evening?"

"Only if you promise to call me Landborough instead of Your Grace."

Daniel grinned. "I believe I can manage that," he said.

"You did well, Daniel," his uncle said as he slapped him on the shoulder a few minutes later, "and by this time next week, word will have it that you're a hero for uncovering a cold-blooded killer in our midst. Just leave it to me, and I'll make sure of it."

"Thank you," Daniel said, not so much for his own sake but for Rebecca's. He wanted her to be welcomed into Society, and with a little help from those around them, he believed that this would happen sooner than he or Rebecca had expected a week ago.

"No need," his uncle said. "You deserve everyone's respect for what you've achieved. The way in which you've managed to reform in so little time is truly remarkable."

"As far as I recall, you gave me little choice."

His uncle grinned. "No, I suppose not, though I must admit that I wasn't convinced you'd manage to prove yourself worthy of the Wolvington title. I have never been happier to have been proven wrong."

It was a simple declaration, but it was one that went straight to Daniel's heart. "Rebecca and I are going to try to publish a book together," he said as they strolled back to the awaiting Wolvington carriage. "Lord Winston—Kingsborough's brother—owns a publishing house. I plan to speak with him to see if we can work something out."

His uncle met his gaze and smiled. "Sounds like a marvelous idea, Daniel. She's been good for you, and she's done what no one else was capable of—she's made a respectable man out of you. I daresay she's quite remarkable and a fine addition to our family."

"I couldn't agree more," Daniel said as he thought of the woman who was waiting for him at home. He was suddenly quite desperate to see her again. "She's a splendid painter, by the way."

"Is she now?"

Daniel nodded. "And a brilliant actress. She knows several of Shakespeare's plays by heart, and while she can't really carry a tune, her wit and kindness are in such ample supply that a man will never find himself in ill humor whenever she is near." Good God, he couldn't seem to stop himself from singing her praises now that he'd begun.

He was just about to start on her show of bravery outside Riley's and how well she'd cared for him after he'd been shot, but he stopped himself, noticing that his uncle was finding it difficult to hide his mirth. "Heaven above," Wolvington said, "if you're not completely and utterly in love with her."

"Of course I am," Daniel said. "It's impossible not to be."

His uncle's smile fell away, and he leveled his nephew with a serious stare. "Even more reason for me to be happy for you, Daniel. I can't wait to tell your aunt. She'll be ever so pleased as well." His smile returned and he nodded toward the carriage. "Now, how about if we get you back to Avern House as quickly as we can so you can be with your wife? I'm sure she's eagerly awaiting an account of everything that's happened."

Daniel was sure of it, and as he leaned back against the swabs of the Wolvington carriage, grateful for a chance to sit down and rest his legs, all he could think of was that the carriage wasn't moving nearly fast enough. He was suddenly rather impatient to be with his wife.

Chapter 28

"**Y**ou could have died," Rebecca said when Daniel finished telling her about what had happened. After seeing how tired he'd looked upon returning home, she'd insisted that he get into bed right away, which he'd done without argument. Laura and Molly had brought them some food, and as they'd eaten, Daniel had answered all of Rebecca's questions. She felt sick knowing how close they'd come to disaster, her eyes burning at the possibility of her husband's body lying lifeless in the street if Grover had managed to take better aim. "It was a foolish plan, one that could have gotten you killed."

"But it didn't," Daniel said. "Yes, there was risk involved—more so than I realized, I'll admit. I didn't think that he would actually try and kill me with witnesses present, but I was wrong." He shook his head. "You should have seen the look in his eyes, Becky. It was inhuman."

Rebecca nodded. "I'm just thankful that it's over now so we can go on with our lives in peace." Heart beating in her chest, she said, "But first, I must tell you of my own encounter with Grover." Distancing herself emotionally from the unpleasant experience she'd had with the duke earlier in the day, she recounted every detail of their conversation and the way in which Grover had forced his advances upon her. "I'm so sorry," she finally said, her eyes burning with the onset of tears. Somehow, she'd managed to maintain a measure of calm until now, but telling Daniel about the experience was forcing her to confront the depravity of it.

Daniel clenched his jaw. His eyes had grown dark with fury. "I'm sorry that you had to endure his company for even a second, but at least he no longer poses a threat." Finished with her food and relieved that her husband didn't blame her for having been alone with Grover even though he'd specifically insisted she not be, Rebecca put her tray aside and climbed up onto the bed next to Daniel, putting her head against his shoulder. "We've been through a lot together these past few weeks," she said.

He took her hand in his and gave it a gentle squeeze, then kissed the top of her head and whispered, "That we have, Becky, but I do believe we're stronger because of it."

"Lord Winston to see you," Hawkins announced two days later as he stepped into the parlor where Rebecca and Daniel were sitting.

It was getting easier for Daniel to move about. He no longer required assistance when going up and down the stairs, for which he was grateful. He rose now to greet Winston. "I hope you'll forgive me for not coming to see you at your place of business," he said as he stuck out his hand, "but I'm afraid I'm still having a bit of trouble getting around."

Winston shook his hand and frowned. "From what I read in the paper, I understand that Grover shot you."

"That's right," Daniel said. "Hurt like the devil."

"I can only imagine," Winston said with a shake of his head. "Hopefully it's not becoming a family habit." He looked to Rebecca, who was standing beside Daniel, and bowed. "Congratulations on your recent marriage, Lady Rebecca. You are looking much better than when I last saw you."

Rebecca looked puzzled, so Daniel clarified. "Lord Winston was there when you were shot. He offered his assistance."

"Thank you, Lord Winston. It is a pleasure to make your acquaintance," Rebecca said as she beamed at the man before her.

He smiled in return. "Likewise."

"If you would please have a seat," Daniel said, gesturing toward an armchair.

"A maid will be in shortly with some tea," Rebecca added, "unless of course you would prefer a glass of claret, or perhaps some brandy?"

"Tea will be fine, thank you," Lord Winston replied as he sank back into his chair and crossed his legs. He looked at Rebecca and Daniel in turn and then finally said, "I must say that I think it very fitting that the two of you should end up together. You seem to be extraordinarily well suited for each other."

Rebecca blinked. Well, that was unexpected. She tried to think of an appropriate response, but Daniel beat her to it, saying simply, "Allowing her to marry the Duke of Grover just wouldn't do."

Lord Winston looked suddenly grim. "No, I daresay he would have been the death of her. If any man can kill a woman's spirit, it is surely he."

"Thank you for your support, Lord Winston," Rebecca finally managed. "It is reassuring to know that we have your support."

The corner of Lord Winston's mouth edged upward. "I can assure you that my wife agrees with me. There is no question that it would have been a pity to see you married to Grover." He tilted his head. "The *ton* can be very judgmental. Especially against those who veer away from what is expected, and let's be honest, you did embarrass the duke quite thoroughly, no question about that."

"And we eloped," Daniel said with a hint of mischief in his voice.

"Yes, you did," Lord Winston said, "though I suppose one might say that you rescued the lady from a fate worse than that of marrying a rake."

"That is precisely what he did," Rebecca said. She'd grown tired of everyone thinking the worst of them—of Daniel in particular. What a relief it had been to have his name cleared in the *Mayfair Chronicle* the day after Grover had been arrested. "My aunt and uncle practically put me up for bid."

Lord Winston frowned. "I must confess that I never liked Grover or the Griftons, if you'll excuse my saying so." His eyes met Rebecca's.

"No need for that, my lord. I can assure you that I was never very fond of them myself," she said.

There was a measure of sadness in Lord Winston's eyes as he nodded in understanding. "Nevertheless, I didn't think them capable of such cruelty—of forcing you to marry a man like Grover for their own selfish gain."

There was a soft knock at the door and Molly entered, carrying a tray, which she set down on the table before placing a cup and saucer in front of each of them. She left with her usual cheerful smile and a bob, after which Rebecca took it upon herself to serve the gentlemen their tea.

"It hasn't been easy for her, I can assure you," Daniel said with an edge of protectiveness that wrapped itself around Rebecca's heart. "But it has given her the opportunity to explore her creative talents. I think that you will be quite impressed."

Rebecca felt her stomach quake in much the same way it had when Daniel had asked to see the rest of her paintings. She'd never shown them to anyone, not even Laura, though Rebecca suspected that her maid must have caught the occasional glimpse; if Laura had, however, she'd kept quiet about it. Painting was a common pastime activity for ladies to engage in, but most of them favored landscapes and still life, certainly not the otherworldly creatures Rebecca had conjured, for as she'd later revealed to Daniel, she hadn't painted only fairies but goblins and giants as well. Sharing these with others and making herself susceptible to judgment made her so nervous that for once she was completely unable to utter a word or to smile. So she just sat there quietly clutching her hands together in her lap while Daniel passed the draft of their book over to Winston.

Hoping to calm herself, Rebecca took a sip of her tea and watched as Lord Winston leafed through the pages. She tried to judge his opinion by studying his

face, but his expression was inscrutable—not a smile
or a frown, just intense professional perusal.

He eventually looked up and stared across at Rebecca with the utmost seriousness.

Oh dear.

He didn't like it. Her pictures were too sketchlike—
scribbles, just as she'd told Daniel. Her stomach quiv-
ered, and she feared for a fleeting moment that she
might be ill. This was why she didn't want anyone else
to see her cherished pictures. She couldn't stand the
idea of anyone scrutinizing them and was suddenly
quite annoyed with Daniel for talking her into this foolish endeavor. "Not quite what you expected, is it?" she
said dryly as she reached out to snatch the pages back
from Lord Winston so she could tuck them away somewhere safe.

"Not in the least," Lord Winston said, removing
the pages from her reach. He was looking at her as if
she'd been mad. The man had only just met her, and
he probably thought her a half-wit for painting such
silly things. Well, they were her silly things, and she
would be damned if anyone was going to say otherwise. "These are exceptional."

What?

Rebecca froze. She turned her head to look at Daniel,
who was now grinning quite happily where he sat, annoying man that he was. She returned her gaze to Lord
Winston, still not trusting her ears. "I beg your pardon?"

Lord Winston's expression relaxed. "I hope you
don't take offense at this, but for a woman who fooled
the entire *ton* into thinking her mad for two years—
whatever your reasons might have been—you have surprisingly little faith in your own creative talents."

She pulled back and dropped onto her seat. "What exactly are you saying?"

Lord Winston blinked. "I thought I just made myself perfectly clear." He shook his head and chuckled. "I've never seen anything as marvelous as this, and I would love nothing better than to publish it."

Rebecca fought for an appropriate response, but the words seemed to cram together in her throat, all eager to get out, then Daniel was hugging her and telling her how proud he was of her and asking if she now realized how skilled she truly was.

"The story is quite fun too," Lord Winston added when Rebecca and Daniel were once again sitting still, "though I would like to have one of my editors review it."

"Yes, of course," Daniel said as he took Rebecca's hand in his and gave it a gentle squeeze. "The story was just something we quickly threw together so we'd have something to go with the pictures—they are the real gems, don't you think?"

"Not only that," Lord Winston said as he raised his cup to his lips and took a long sip, "they are quite unique." He must have noticed the uncertainty Rebecca felt, for he quickly added, "And I mean that in the most complimentary way possible. You must not doubt yourself but be proud of your work. I'm sure your husband can assist in that regard, for he is clearly impressed with what you've accomplished, as am I."

It took a second for Rebecca to recover from the flattery enough to manage a response, for she was quite overwhelmed by Lord Winston's kind words. "Thank you," she said, then, with a bit more strength behind the words and the beginnings of a smile, she added, "thank you very much indeed."

Lord Winston grinned. "Well, first of all, I have with me a contract that I think you ought to take a look at before we decide to go any further." He opened the portmanteau he'd brought along and pulled out some papers, which he placed on the table directly between Daniel and Rebecca. "In addition to the royalty payments outlined therein, I would, on the basis of what you have just now shown me, like to offer you an advance of one hundred pounds."

Rebecca's mouth dropped. It had all become suddenly real. Somebody actually liked her work enough to pay good money for it—very good money. "That's a generous offer, Lord Winston. I believe that if Daniel agrees, I should like to—"

Lord Winston stopped her with a raised hand. "I understand your enthusiasm, but this offer isn't going anywhere, and I would not feel comfortable with allowing you to sign a document you haven't thoroughly read, even in good faith. Take your time, Lady Rebecca, and look it over with your husband. If you are willing to agree with all the terms, then you know where to find me." He got to his feet, ready to take his leave and bowing to Rebecca as she and Daniel stood to see him out. "Once again, it was an absolute pleasure."

The door closed behind him, and Rebecca turned to Daniel. "Thank you for everything you've done for me."

"I would do it all again if it would make you happy and keep you safe," he said as he kissed her temple. "When I think of what my life was like without you in it . . . so empty and meaningless . . . I thank my lucky stars I met you that night at the Kingsborough Ball."

"Me too," she whispered as she rose up on her toes, leaned toward him and pressed a slow, lingering kiss upon his lips, a simple caress that spoke of her love and admiration for this wonderful man who'd battled his demons and won. "And I will be thanking *my* lucky stars for the rest of my life that you climbed through my window—my very own hero, disguised as a rake."

Epilogue

Nuit House, Portman Square
One year later

"**T**he guests will be arriving soon," Rebecca said as she stood in front of the full-length mirror and attempted to straighten her gown—a task that was proving difficult, since Daniel kept kissing the side of her neck and her shoulders.

His arms came about her waist. "Five minutes is all I need," he whispered on an inhale of jasmine. He would never tire of her scent.

She laughed, the ring in her voice filling the room. "You are incorrigible."

"I am a rake, if you'll recall," he said as he playfully ran his tongue along her warm skin, loving the way in which she sucked in her breath in response.

"A reformed rake, I believe," she said. He could tell that she was trying to be firm with him but was failing miserably, for there was a sparkle in the eyes of her reflection.

"*Mostly* reformed."

"Mostly?" Her voice sounded faint.

"There is one area in which my rakish nature will never be tamped down, and that is the area involving you." To prove his point, he spun her around in his arms and lowered his mouth over hers, kissing her with thorough determination and with a wicked promise of what he had planned for them once the guests had once again left their home. After selling Avern House eight months earlier, they'd relocated to a new address, where Daniel wouldn't feel haunted by the constant memory of his parents. When deciding on a name for their new home, he'd suggested Nuit House, both in honor of Rebecca and as a private tribute to the night they'd first met. Since moving in, they'd been quite busy filling the place with happy memories, so much so that it had become difficult for Daniel to enter a room without thinking of ravishing his wife. "You, on the other hand . . . you deserve more than five minutes." He offered her his arm, accompanied by a cheeky smile. "So I will try to be patient and wait until later."

He adored the flush that filled her cheeks at the implication and how much fuller her lips looked after their kiss. How on earth he would manage to get through the next few hours without hauling her back upstairs and showing her precisely how much he loved her was beyond him. It had been a year—one full year—and he still couldn't keep his hands off her. More than that, he still had no desire to see other women. Rebecca was the only woman he would ever need, as a friend, wife and lover. She was perfect in every way.

"Congratulations on your latest release," Winston said, greeting his host and hostess upon his arrival.

"Thank you, my lord," Rebecca said. "We were

both surprised by how well the first book did, so we're eager to see if this new one will be just as popular." She turned to the woman beside him. "I'm so happy that you were able to join us this evening, Sarah. It's been far too long since you and I had a proper chat."

"I actually wanted to tell you both that our boys loved your first book, though they did ask me to request that your next one be about pirates."

Rebecca laughed. "What a brilliant idea. Perhaps we could even add a few sea monsters."

"Creative as always, I see," Daniel said, taking her hand in his and placing an adoring kiss upon the knuckles.

"As far as this new release goes," Winston said, "I have no doubt that every parent will want to own a copy. In fact, my mother has already put in an order, intending to gift it to my brother and sister-in-law when their baby arrives in another month's time."

"May I say that I absolutely love the cover?"

Turning his head in the direction of the voice that had spoken, Daniel smiled as he spotted Landborough. He was holding one of the advance copies that Rebecca and Daniel had put on display for their guests. "Lord Winston is to thank for that," Daniel said. "It was his idea to put one of my wife's colorful pictures on the front."

"Very eye-catching, I must say," Landborough said as he greeted Winston and bowed toward Sarah. The duke and his wife had become good friends of Daniel and Rebecca's and were often invited over for dinner, along with Daniel's sister, Audrey, and her husband, the Earl of Chilton, who'd gifted Daniel with a beautiful notebook the day he'd made his first revenue.

"And I shall look forward to reading it to my grand-niece or -nephew in the not-so-distant future," Lady Wolvington said, approaching the group with her husband at her side.

Daniel smiled at his aunt, who'd been doting on Rebecca since the moment her pregnancy had been announced, going so far as to have the occasional word with Madame Renarde to ensure that Rebecca was receiving the best food possible. "Our child will be lucky to have you in their life," he said as he stepped forward and pressed a kiss against his aunt's cheek, not caring one way or another if it was appropriate to do so. He loved his aunt and uncle, and it was about time he showed it after everything they'd done for him.

"May I say that you are looking radiant this evening," Lord Wolvington said as he took Rebecca's hand in his and placed a kiss upon her knuckles. The old man was just as fussy about Rebecca's welfare as his wife was, always inquiring if she was warm enough or in need of sitting down. "Would you like something to drink? Some lemonade perhaps?"

It was damn near impossible for Daniel not to smile at the way in which his aunt and uncle had welcomed Rebecca into the family. They obviously cared for her and she for them, as was evidenced by her eagerness to join them for tea or to go for walks with them in the park.

"Thank you," she said, "that's most kind of you, but I just had some not so long ago."

"Something to eat then?" Lord Wolvington pressed. "I saw a very tempting bowl of fruit on the refreshment table. I'd be happy to arrange a plate for you."

Leaning toward Rebecca, Daniel whispered, "If you want to make him happy, then you'd better agree."

She chuckled and nodded toward Wolvington, who returned a smile of great appreciation. "I'll be back before you know it," he said as he walked away from them.

"Winston mentioned that you will be removing yourself to the family estate near Winchester for your confinement," Sarah said.

"Yes, the Wolvingtons have graciously offered me their home," Rebecca said with a smile directed at Lady Wolvington.

"It is your home as well now, my dear," the marchioness declared. "Besides, we can't have you rusticating in London when you're expecting. The fresh air will do you good, and there's plenty of that at Pondsly."

"Not to mention that it will be nice to get away from it all and spend some time together, just you and I, before the baby arrives," Daniel said as he wrapped his arm around Rebecca's waist and pulled her against him for a gentle squeeze. "I'm already looking forward to taking my aunt and uncle's curricle out on country drives and going on picnics. There's a lake, too, with willow trees flanking the edge of it—it's lovely for boating."

A memory of him doing just that with his parents flashed in his mind, but rather than feeling angered or pained by it, he felt excited at the prospect of sharing the place with Rebecca. She was right. They would make their own memories, and in time, they would outshine the old ones. Lowering his mouth to the curve of her ear, he whispered, "You're the best thing that's ever happened to me, and I love you with every beat of my heart."

She turned her head to gaze up at him, her eyes brimming with happiness, and then she smiled, that brilliant smile that always made him catch his breath. "As I love you, Daniel, forever and always."

It didn't matter that they were surrounded by guests and that kissing one's wife publically simply wasn't done. After all, there had to be some perks to being a former rake, and Daniel was about to take full advantage. So before one and all, he lowered his mouth to Rebecca's and kissed her with every ounce of his being, loving her and thanking her for the light she'd brought into his life, until everyone else slipped away and it was just the two of them caught in the moment—proof that a happily ever after can be had by even the most forsaken scoundrel, as long as the right woman comes along and saves him.

Don't miss how the ball began!

Keep reading for an excerpt from
THE TROUBLE WITH BEING A DUKE
At the Kingsborough Ball

Available now from Avon Books

"I really must commend you on the pie, Mrs. Chilcott," Mr. Roberts said as he picked up his napkin, folded it until it formed a perfect square and dabbed it across his lips with the utmost care and precision. "It is undoubtedly the best one yet—just the right amount of tart and sweet." The slightest tug of his lips suggested a smile, but since he wasn't a man prone to exaggeration, it never quite turned into one.

Isabella stared. Was she really doomed to live out the remainder of her days with such a dandy? Mr. Roberts was unquestionably the most meticulous gentleman she'd ever encountered, not to mention the most polite and the most eloquent. In addition, he never, ever, did anything that might have been considered rash or unexpected, and while there were probably many who would think these attributes highly commendable, Isabella couldn't help but consider him the most mundane person of her acquaintance. She sighed. Was it really too much to ask that the gentleman who planned to make her his wife might look at her with just a hint of interest? Yet the only thing that Mr. Roberts had ever looked at with even the remotest bit of interest was the slice of apple pie upon his plate.

Isabella wasn't sure which was more frustrating—that he lacked any sense of humor or that he valued pie more than he did her. The sense of humor was something she'd only just noticed recently. Unable to imagine that anyone might be lacking in such regard and taking his inscrutable demeanor into account, she had always assumed that he favored sarcasm. This, it turned out, was not the case. Mr. Roberts simply didn't find anything funny, nor did he see a point in trying to make other people laugh. This was definitely something that Isabella found herself worrying about.

"You are too kind, Mr. Roberts," her mother replied in response to his praise. "Perhaps you would care for another piece?"

Mr. Roberts's eyes widened, but rather than accept the offer as he clearly wished to do, he said instead, "Thank you for your generosity, but one must never overindulge in such things, Mrs. Chilcott, especially not if one desires to keep a lean figure."

Isabella squeaked.

"Are you quite all right, Miss Chilcott?" Mr. Roberts asked.

"Forgive me," Isabella said. "It was the tea—I fear it didn't agree with me."

Mr. Roberts frowned. "Do be careful, Miss Chilcott—it could have resulted in a most indelicate cough, not to mention a rather unpleasant experience for the rest of us."

Isabella allowed herself an inward groan. The truth of the matter was that she'd been forcing back a laugh. Really, what sort of man would admit to declining a piece of pie because he feared ruining his figure? It was absurd, and yet her mother had nodded as if nothing had ever made more sense to her. As for the threat of a cough . . . Isabella couldn't help but wonder how Mr. Roberts would fare in regards to their future children. He'd likely barricade himself in his study for the duration of their illnesses—all that sneezing and casting up of accounts would probably give him hives otherwise.

Her father suddenly said, "Have you heard the news?"

"That would certainly depend on which news you're referring to," Mr. Roberts remarked as he raised his teacup, stared into it for a moment and then returned it to its saucer.

"More tea, Mr. Roberts?" Isabella's mother asked, her hand already reaching for the teapot.

"Thank you—that would be most welcome."

Isabella waited patiently while Mr. Roberts told her mother that he would be very much obliged if she would ensure that this time, the cup be filled precisely halfway up in order to allow for the exact amount of milk that he required. She allowed herself another inward groan. He'd just begun explaining why two teaspoons of sugar constituted just the right quantity when Isabella decided that she'd had enough. "What news, Papa?" she blurted out, earning a smile from her father, a look of horror from her mother and a frown of disapproval from Mr. Roberts. A transformation Isabella found strangely welcome.

"Apparently," her father began, taking a careful sip of his tea while his wife served him another generous slice of apple pie, "the Duke of Kingsborough has decided to host the annual ball again."

"Good heavens," Isabella's mother breathed as she sank back against her chair. "It's been forever since they kept that tradition."

"Five years, to be exact," Isabella muttered. Everyone turned to stare at her with puzzled expressions. She decided not to explain but shrugged instead, then spooned a piece of pie into her mouth in order to avoid having to say anything further.

The truth of it was that the annual ball at Kingsborough Hall had always been an event she'd hoped one day to attend—ever since she was a little girl and had caught her first glimpse of the fireworks from her bedroom window. She hazarded a glance in Mr. Roberts's direction, knowing full well that a life with him would include nothing as spectacular as the Kingsborough Ball. In fact, she'd be lucky if it would even include a dance at the local assembly room from time to time. Probably not, for although the life she would share with Mr. Roberts promised to be one of comfort, he had made it abundantly clear that he did not enjoy social functions or dancing in the least.

Perhaps this was one of the reasons why he'd decided to attach himself to *her*—an act that she'd always found most curious. Surely he must have realized by now that they had very little in common, and given his current station in life, he could have formed a favorable connection to a far more prosperous family. Of course he would probably have had to attend a Season in London in order to make the acquaintance of such families, and his reluctance to do so certainly explained why he was presently sitting down to tea in her parlor instead of sending flowers to a proper lady of breeding.

Isabella had on more than one occasion brought the

issue regarding Mr. Roberts's displeasure for social-izing to her mother's attention, complaining that her future would consist of few diversions if she were to marry him, but her mother had simply pointed out that the only reason young ladies attended such events was with the direct purpose of drawing the attention of the gentlemen present. Once married, there would be little reason for Isabella to do so and consequently no point in engaging in anything other than the occasional tea party. And as if this had not been enough, her mother had added a long list of reasons why Isabella should be thankful that a man as respectable and affluent as Mr. Roberts had bothered to show her any consideration at all. It had been rather demeaning.

"Well, it's nice to see that they seem to be recover-ing from the death of the duke's father," Isabella heard her mother say.

"I couldn't agree more," Isabella's father said. "It must have been very difficult for them, given the long duration of his illness and all."

"Indeed," Mr. Roberts muttered without the slight-est alteration of his facial expression.

A moment of silence followed until Isabella's mother finally broke it by saying, "Now then, Mr. Roberts, tell us about that horse you were planning to buy the last time we saw you."

And that was the end of the conversation regarding the Kingsborough Ball—but it was far from the end of Isabella's dreams of attending. In fact, she didn't spare a single thought for anything else during the remainder of her tea, though she must have managed to nod and shake her head at all the right times, for nobody appeared to have noticed that her mind had exited the room.

"Was afternoon tea as delightful as always?" Jamie, Isabella's younger sister, asked when they settled into bed that evening. At thirteen years of age, she was a complete hoyden and just as mischievous as any boy her age might have been, getting into every scrape imaginable. After deliberately sneaking a frog into Mr. Roberts's jacket pocket three months earlier, she'd been barred from attending Sunday tea. Her punishment for the offense had included two weeks of confinement to her bedroom, as well as some choice words from Mr. Roberts himself. Needless to say, Jamie's approval of the man had long since dwindled.

"It was better, considering I was hardly aware of Mr. Roberts's presence at all."

Jamie scrunched her nose. "Honestly, Izzie, I don't know why you suffer the fellow. He has no sense of humor to speak of, is much too reserved to suit your vibrant character, not to mention that there's something really queer about him in general. I don't think you should marry him if he offers."

Isabella attempted a smile as she settled herself into bed, scooting down beneath the covers until she was lying on her side, facing her sister. They each had their own bedroom, but with the nights still cold, Jamie often snuck into Isabella's room so they could snuggle up together, talking about this and that until sleep eventually claimed them. "I have to think rationally about this, Jamie. Mama and Papa are struggling to keep food on the table, and there's also you to consider. I want a better life for you than this, with more choices than I've been afforded."

Jamie shook her head as well as she could, considering she was lying down. "I don't want you to sacrifice yourself for me. I'll never be able to forgive myself for being the cause of your unhappiness."

There were tears in her young eyes now that made Isabella's heart ache. Isabella loved her sister so dearly and knew that her sister loved her equally. "It's not just you, Jamie, but Mama and Papa as well. Mr. Roberts will ensure that they want for nothing."

"And in return, you will probably have to kiss him." Jamie made a face.

Isabella's hand flew up to whack her naughty sister playfully across the head. "What on earth do you know of such things?" Was there anything more appalling than talking with one's kid sister about kissing?

"Enough to assure you that you might want to think twice before giving that particular right to a man like him."

With a sigh, Isabella rolled back against her pillow and stared up at the ceiling. Jamie was right, of course, but what was Isabella to do? Her family's future depended on her seeing this through to the end. Really, what choice did she have?

"So, what did you daydream about this time?" Jamie asked, changing the subject entirely.

"What do you mean?"

"You said before that you barely noticed Mr. Roberts's presence during tea. I assume your thoughts must have been elsewhere."

"Oh!" Isabella sat up, turning herself so she could meet her sister's eyes. "The Kingsborough Ball. Papa says they're hosting a new one. Oh, Jamie, isn't it exciting!"

Jamie jumped up. "You have to attend."

"What?" It was preposterous—absurd—the most

wonderful idea ever. Isabella shook her head. She would not allow herself to entertain the notion. It would only lead to disappointment. "That's impossible," she said.

"Why?" The firm look in her sister's eyes dared her to list her reasons.

"Very well," Isabella said, humoring her. "I have not been invited, nor will I be."

"We'll sneak you in through the servant's entrance. Cousin Simon can help with that, since he works there."

Isabella rolled her eyes. Trust Jamie to have that problem already worked out. "I'm not an aristocrat—they will notice I don't belong," she countered.

Jamie shrugged. "From what you've told me, the Kingsborough Ball is always masked, is it not?"

"Well, yes, I suppose—"

"Then no one will notice." Jamie waved her hand and smiled smugly. "Do go on."

"I . . . I have no gown that I could possibly wear to such a function, and that is the deciding factor. No gown, no ball."

"Ah, but you are wrong about that," her sister said, meeting her gaze with such cheeky resolve that Isabella couldn't help but feel a growing sense of apprehension. "There's always the one in the attic to consider, and I'll wager—"

"Absolutely not," Isabella said. She knew exactly which gown her sister was referring to, for it was quite possibly the most exquisite thing Isabella had ever seen. It had also given rise to a string of questions that would probably never be answered, like how such a gown had found its way into the Chilcott home in the first place. Fearful of the answer and of the punishment they'd likely have received if their parents had discovered they'd been playing in a part of the house that had been off limits, they'd made a pact to keep their knowledge of the gown a secret.

"But Izzie—"

"Jamie, I know that you mean well, but it's time I faced my responsibilities as an adult. The Kingsborough Ball is but a dream that will never amount to anything more."

"A lifelong dream, Izzie," her sister protested. Jamie took Isabella's hand and held it in her own. "Wouldn't you like to see what it's like living it?"

It was tempting of course, but still, wearing a gown that had in all likelihood been acquired under dubious circumstances, as it was one her parents couldn't possibly afford, would be harebrained. Wouldn't it? After all, it had probably been hidden away for a reason. Her mother had never mentioned that it existed, which was also strange considering it would make an excellent wedding gown for Isabella when she married Mr. Roberts. No, there was something about that gown and its history. Isabella was certain of it, for the more she considered it, the more wary she grew of what she might discover if her questions were one day answered.

In any event, she couldn't possibly wear it to the Kingsborough Ball. Could she? She would be betraying her parents' trust by doing so. It would certainly be the most daring thing she'd ever done. And yet . . . this would be her last chance for a fairy-tale experience. Closing her eyes, she made her decision. She would do it. Isabella would seize a moment for herself—one night of adventure that would have to last a lifetime. She only hoped that she wouldn't one day look back on it with longing and regret.

Next month, don't miss these exciting new love stories only from Avon Books

Romancing the Duke by Tessa Dare
When her godfather leaves her a rundown, reportedly haunted castle, Izzy Goodnight is shocked to learn the place is already inhabited—by a recluse claiming to be the Duke of Rothbury. Ransom Vane intends to find the castle's rumored treasure—all he has to do is resist Izzy's charms, a task that proves impossible once she becomes the prize he craves the most.

The Cowboy of Valentine Valley by Emma Cane
Ever since the heated late-night kiss she shared with cowboy Josh Thalberg, former Hollywood bad girl Whitney Winslow hasn't been able to get him out of her head. When she decides to use his leatherwork in her upscale lingerie shop, Whitney's determined to keep things strictly professional. But Josh has never met a challenge he isn't up for . . . and he'll try anything to convince her that some rules are worth breaking.

Wulfe Untamed by Pamela Palmer
The most enigmatic and tortured of the Feral Warriors, Wulfe is haunted by the beauty of a woman who no longer remembers him. He took Natalie Cash's memories and sent her safely back to her human life. But now the Mage are threatening Natalie and he will risk anything to protect her. In order to survive in a world of intrigue and danger, Natalie and Wulfe must trust one another . . . and surrender to a wild, untamed love.